Ben Da— 4/27

W9-ACY-334

Praise for Kelley Armstrong

Bitten

"Frisky . . . Tells a rather sweet love story, and suggests that being a wolf may be more comfortable for a strong, smart young woman than being human." —*New York Times Book Review*

"Modernizes and humanizes an age-old tale."
—*New York Daily News*

"Graphic and sensual, an exciting page turner . . . [Does] much the same thing for werewolves that Anne Rice did for vampires in her *Interview with the Vampire*."
—*Rocky Mountain News*

"Armstrong is up with the big girls of the genre like Laurell K. Hamilton." —*Kansas City Star*

"For readers who like a twist of the supernatural, Kelley Armstrong's *Bitten* may just be the right trick and treat . . . It's enough fun to make you howl for the sequel."
—*New Orleans Times-Picayune*

"Sometimes there's nothing more fun than an excellent debut novel, and Kelley Armstrong's *Bitten* fits the bill. It's witty, suspenseful, and a well-paced tale. [Armstrong] spins an intricate but comprehensible plot around compelling characters and produces a book that will both thrill and absorb you. Bring on the sequel, we're ready for more."
—*Houston Chronicle*

"It's terrific. The heroine is the most appealing I have come across in ages. It's clever, quirky, hip and funny, skating between genres with style and grace. More please!"
—Joanne Harris, author of *Chocolat*

"[T]his debut novel from a Canadian writer proves that solid storytelling and confident craftsmanship can rejuvenate one of the hoariest of all horror clichés . . . Armstrong's true achievement is her depiction of werewolf nature in believably human context . . . the sensuality of Elena's transformations and the viciousness of her kills mesh perfectly with her tough personality . . . Filled with romance and supernatural intrigue, this book will surely remind readers of Anne Rice's sophisticated refurbishings of the vampire story." —*Publishers Weekly*

"With a howl, Kelley Armstrong's *Bitten* plunges headlong into a murderous plot rife with violence, lust and intrigue. . . . Armstrong has created a breathless, sexy story . . . gorgeous and grotesque in the best sense of the word. Rumors of a sequel have never been better news."
—*Boulder Weekly*

"Kelley Armstrong's debut novel, *Bitten*, combines hints of the strong decadent sexuality and cool-outsider mystique of *Interview with the Vampire* with the creepy hominess of Stephen King. . . . Realistic details . . . complement a convincing portrait of werewolf society and its intricate codes of behavior. . . . *Bitten* will satisfy genre fans and those who like their thrills served up with literary savvy."
—*Quill and Quire*

"It's as smooth as cream all the way, sure to gain fans."
—*Kirkus Reviews*

"There's nothing overtly gothic about this fast-paced, sexy thriller and its model contemporary heroine—it's just that she's a werewolf who is trying to make a go of things among humans. When her pack is threatened by a new group of violent psychotic werewolves, she is drawn back into the old ways." —*Bookseller*

4/24 $1

"Brings a new brand of ferocity to horror literature . . . *Bitten* is a lightning-paced, violent and completely readable entertainment that entertains loudly and abundantly."
—*Hamilton Spectator*

"Wicked writing gets noticed, and first-time novelist Kelley Armstrong has written a deliciously wicked book. . . . This is no ordinary werewolf tale, but a werewolf mystery with a huge dollop of romance thrown in." —*Toronto Star*

"The plot of *Bitten* has echoes of the best crime thrillers . . . the story is fast and entertaining. But what makes the novel so gripping is Armstrong's talent for vivid description and her interest in both the sensuality and psychology of werewolfhood, a fascination that greatly enhances the world she creates while never slowing down the breakneck plot. At every turn, her depiction of physical sensation is precise and compelling. . . . Surely one of the sexiest, most energetic novels published in a long time . . . [A] Canadian mother of three who hails from rural southwestern Ontario has created a smart, original thriller, destined to keep people reading on into the night." —*The Gazette*

"Armstrong has a definate talent for sensual descriptions. The wolf creatures are vividly created in gestures and behaviour, and most of the sexual encounters would knock one's socks off (not to mention other things)." —*National Post*

"*Bitten* is hip and postmodern. . . . Those who enjoy the vampire books of Anne Rice, or Canadian vampire writer Nancy Kilpatrick, will love it." —*Globe and Mail*

"An impressive debut thriller . . . Kelley Armstrong is very good on the sheer exhilaration of shape-changing, of running on four feet through forests, suburban greenery and urban back alleys." —Roz Kaveney, Amazon.com

"A very contemporary, funky supernatural thriller with a particularly provocative heroine." —*Hello*

"A hair-raising story for the she-wolf in us all."
—Shannon Olson, author of *Welcome to my Planet*

"Entertaining new take on an old thriller story form. Makes Buffy look fluffy." —*Daily Express*

"A tasty confection of werewolves, sex and vendettas . . . after the first nibble it's quite hard to stop . . . Elena and her acid repartee successfully steal the show throughout, she has bags of charm. Gory, sexy fun." —*SFX*

"A thrilling adventure . . . who'd want to be human? Great fun." —*Big Issue*

"Good slick fun; expect the television series soon." —*Guardian*

Stolen

"[A] fast paced story." —*Orlando Sentinel*

"Demonstrates a sharpening of Armstrong's narrative skills."
—*Rocky Mountain News*

"A sure-footed follow-up to *Bitten*." —*Publishers Weekly*

"Richly done." —*Kirkus Reviews*

"In *Stolen*, Kelley Armstrong delivers a taut, sensual thriller that grips from the first page. Elena Michaels is at once sublime and sympathetic, a modern heroine who shows that real women bite back."
—Karin Slaughter, *New York Times* best selling author of *Indelible*

"Like *Bitten*, *Stolen* paints a perfectly convincing portrait of a woman who quite literally runs with the wolves. . . . Armstrong has created a persuasive, finely detailed otherworldly cosmology—featuring sorcery, astral projection, spells, telepathy and teleportation—that meshes perfectly with the more humdrum world of interstate highways and cable news bulletins. . . . More than just a thriller with extra teeth, *Stolen* is for anyone who has ever longed to leap over an SUV in a single bound, or to rip an evil security force to shreds, or even just to growl convincingly." —*Quill & Quire*

"The narrative veers between clever, scholarly distinctions among different sorts of magical powers, and a lot of action-movie-style sex and violence. . . . What's interesting are the twists and turns along the way, boosted by bits of philosophy and arcane knowledge Armstrong adds to her strange brew. . . . We meet enough truly entertaining creatures along the way to make us wish that this will not be the last romp for Elena and her pack." —*Toronto Star*

"Armstrong is a clever writer. . . . [and *Stolen*] grabs you at the outset." —*Winnipeg Free Press*

"*Stolen* is a delicious cocktail of testosterone and wicked humour. . . . too earnest to attempt parody, [Armstrong's] take on the well-travelled world of supernatural beings is witty and original. She's at her best when examining the all-too-human dilemmas of being superhuman . . . [*Stolen*] bubbles with the kind of dramatic invention that bodes well for a long and engrossing series. . . . This can only be good news for the growing Michaels fan club." —*Globe and Mail*

"Mesmerizing . . . the 'other-worldly' atmosphere conjured up by Armstrong begins to seem strangely real. Armstrong is a talented and original writer whose inventiveness and sense of the bizarre is arresting." —*London Free Press*

"Elena Michaels, the only known female werewolf, cavorts on a more fully cultivated supernatural playing field in this sure-footed sequel to *Bitten* . . . [*Stolen* is] a prison-break story spiffed up with magic . . . Armstrong leavens the narrative with brisk action and intriguing dollops of werewolf culture that suggest a complex and richly imagined anthropologic back story. The sassy, pumped-up Elena makes a perfect hardboiled horror heroine . . . This novel will please not only horror fans but also mainstream readers who like strong female characters." —*Publishers Weekly*

Dime Store Magic

"[A] sexy supernatural romance [whose] special strength lies in its seamless incorporation of the supernatural into the real world. A convincing small-town setting, clever contemporary dialogue, compelling characterizations and a touch of cool humor make the tale's occasional vivid violence palatable and its fantasy elements both gripping and believable." —*Publishers Weekly*

"Kelley Armstrong is one of my favorite writers."
—Karin Slaughter, author of *Indelible*

"From the first page, *Dime Store Magic* captures the attention and never lets go. Magic, mayhem and romance all combine to create a novel that pleases on every level. The pace is fast, the dialogue witty, and the characters totally unique and enjoyable. From the villains to the good guys, each is fully developed, entertaining and believable . . . A tale that will have you reading long into the night and keep the adrenaline flowing, *Dime Store Magic* is the perfect read. . . . First-rate suspense, action packed, and an all round terrific read, I highly recommend *Dime Store Magic* and proudly award it RRT's Perfect 10!"
—Romance Reviews Today

"There are so few authors out there who can write this well and it makes the perfect read for a few hours of escapism. If you enjoyed the first two books, *Dime Store Magic* is a refreshing change of direction that looks set to keep the series going for a good few books yet." —SFCrow's Nest

"After only three books, Kelley Armstrong has proven her talent in creating a truly imaginative and trendy realm. If you're into supernatural stories with a fresh twist, *Dime Store Magic* is just what you're looking for." —BookLoons

"Kelley Armstrong continues to dazzle readers with *Dime Store Magic*, her latest addition to the 'Women of the Otherworld' series. Plenty of characters populate this novel, new ones and old, and there's conflict between and within these powerful magical beings. Armstrong's portrayal of her characters, especially Paige and Savannah and their troubled relationship, is utterly lifelike, passionate and captivating. By setting the story and characters in a current context, Armstrong makes the magical happenings look and feel natural and plausible. Paige's growing dissatisfaction with the increasingly narrow-minded Coven and her struggles to master the grimoires and keep Savannah safe are depicted with sensitivity and an intense depth of feeling. Savannah is a typical teenager with fantastic magical powers, and this combination of immaturity and massive potential proves to be deadly. The book abounds in exciting moments, such as when a necromancer brings the dead to life or when the protagonists are involved in a midnight chase through the graveyard pursued by police and spirits alike. With such crisp, stylish writing and a tautly suspenseful, well-crafted plot, this new installment in the 'Otherworld' series showcases Kelley Armstrong at her best." —CurledUp.com

"*Dime Store Magic* is the best book in this series that has been excellent since Book I. Light humor makes the dramatic ending stand out in sharp contrast. Most laudable is the fact that each book in this series stands alone and complete, so that you can enter it at any point; and though eager for the next book, readers are not left dangling in mid air."
—*Huntress Reviews*

"A terrific contemporary fantasy that makes sorcery and witchcraft seem genuine . . . The action-packed storyline is fast-paced and provides strong characterization."
—*Midwest Book Reviews*

Industrial Magic

"Set in a supernatural but credible underworld of industrial baron sorcerers and psychologically crippled witches . . . breakneck action is tempered by deep psychological insights, intense sensuality and considerable humor."
—*Publishers Weekly*

"Dark, snappy and consistently entertaining . . . Armstrong never loses the balance between Paige's sardonic narration, the wonderfully absurd supporting characters and the nicely girlie touches that add a little lightness to the murder and mayhem . . . Armstrong knows how to keep the reader constantly engaged. There's never anything that could be described as a dull moment or filler and for nearly 600 pages, that's quite an achievement. The series, in general, is developing into something more interesting and less predictable with every installment." —*SF Crow's Nest*

"Armstrong's world is dangerous and fun, her voice crisp and funny . . . a solidly engaging novel."
—*Contra Costa Times*

"Not to be missed. The action is fantastic and the drama is very intense." —*Huntress Reviews*

"I found a lot to like in the humor and diversity of Armstrong's world." —*Denver Post*

"*Industrial Magic* is a book not to be missed. The action is fantastic and drama is very intense. Kelley Armstrong creates such fun characters that really jump off the pages. The book is fast paced with lots of unexpected turns. Like the other books in the series, I wanted more after finishing *Industrial Magic*." —*SFSite.com*

"One of Armstrong's strengths is the creation of plausible characters, which is a real bonus in a series based on the premise that there are supernatural creatures walking and working beside us in our contemporary world. Her werewolves, witches, sorcerers, et al. are convincing as people, not just as monsters or super-humans; despite their powers, they have relationship problems, personal insecurities, and family conflicts. Yet there is nothing maudlin about these books. A dry sense of humor runs through all of them and is particularly pronounced in *Industrial Magic*. The female characters are refreshingly strong without becoming bitchy caricatures, and while some of the male characters are stereotypically testosterone-driven (as seen through Paige's eyes, at least), most are more balanced than that. Armstrong includes a healthy dose of sex and romance as well, without going overboard à la Laurell K. Hamilton. There is a recurring motif of gender conflict in the series, but it is muted in this novel, taking a back seat to the theme of family relationships. None of the supernaturals, it seems, has anything like a normal family life, and those that came closest at one point—Paige and Savannah—are now orphans. *Industial Magic* is a page-turner and is very hard to put down." —*Booksluts.com*

Also by Kelley Armstrong

BITTEN
STOLEN
DIME STORE MAGIC
INDUSTRIAL MAGIC

HAUNTED

KELLEY ARMSTRONG

SEAL BOOKS

COPYRIGHT © 2005 BY KLA FRICKE, INC.

All rights reserved. No part of this publication may be reproduced
or transmitted in any form or by any means, electronic or mechanical,
including photocopying, recording, or by any information storage and
retrieval system, without permission in writing from the publisher.

Seal Books and colophon are trademarks of
Random House of Canada Limited.

HAUNTED
Seal Books/published by arrangement with
Random House Canada
Seal Books edition published May 2005

ISBN 0-7704-2978-5

Cover illustration © 2005 by Franco Accornero
Cover design by Jamie S. Warren Youll

Seal Books are published by Random House of Canada Limited.
"Seal Books" and the portrayal of a seal are the property of
Random House of Canada Limited.

Visit Random House of Canada Limited's website:
www.randomhouse.ca

PRINTED AND BOUND IN THE USA

OPM   10 9 8 7 6 5 4 3 2

To my daughter, Julia.
Like Eve, I know I'll have to start letting go soon . . .
but I'm not quite ready yet.

Acknowledgments

As always, I'm deeply indebted to everyone who helped get my book from that first spark of an idea to a complete novel. Heaps of thanks to my agent, Helen Heller, and my editors: Anne Groell at Bantam US, Anne Collins at Random House Canada, and Antonia Hodgson at Time Warner UK.

A special thanks this time around to my Web site moderators, who've really helped ease the workload on my burgeoning discussion board. To Ian, John, Julia, Katrina, Laura, Raina, Sonny, Taylor, and Tina. Thanks so much— without you guys, I'd never have time to actually *write*.

France / 1666

MARIE-MADELINE LIT THE FLAME UNDER THE BOWL. A draft through the empty fireplace blew it out. She adjusted the metal screen in front of the hearth, then moved the bowl and tried again. As the flame took hold, smoke swirled through the room, filling it with the acrid stink of burning hair and the sweet smell of rosemary.

"*Entstehen, mein* Nix," she said, tongue tripping over the foreign words. She recited the rest of the incantation. The air rippled.

"You have failed . . . again," a woman's voice whispered.

Marie-Madeline's fingers trembled around the bowl. A few red-hot cinders tumbled out, and scorched her hand. "It isn't my fault. You aren't giving me enough. This—it isn't easy. I need more."

"More?" the voice hissed, circling her head. "This is not one of your potions, witch. You cannot drink until you've had your fill. What I give you is the power of will, a finite quantity of that which you so sorely lack. Whether you choose to use it is your own decision."

"But I *want* to use it. Gaudin must have his revenge, and I must have my freedom."

The Nix's voice sounded at her ear, words blasting on a

stream of hot air. "You are a fool, Marquise. A mewling little worm of a woman who stumbled upon that spell to summon me, then lied to me and wasted my time. You do not want resolve. You want deliverance. You want me to do this thing for you, to absolve you of the responsibility and guilt of patricide."

"N-no. I'd never ask—"

"I will grant it."

Marie-Madeline went still. "You will . . . grant it?"

"You are not the only one to dabble in arcane magics, witch. I have a spell that I have been waiting to use, waiting for the right vessel—a worthy vessel. With it, you can allow me to possess your body, carry out this deed, and have my reward. Then you may claim the credit to your lover."

"What is the spell? Tell me now. Please. Gaudin grows impatient."

The Nix's chuckle wafted through the air. "As do I. Listen carefully, my Marquise, and we will be done with this thing before daybreak."

The Nix opened her eyes. She was lying on the floor. Candles blazed all around her, their light so harsh it made her blink. The smoke filled her nostrils. She coughed instinctively, then jumped, startled by the sensation.

She lifted her hands. Human hands, soft and bejeweled. The Marquise's hands. She flexed, then clenched them. The long nails drove into her palms and she gasped. So that was pain. How . . . intriguing. She dug her nails in deeper, letting the pain course down her arms. Blood dripped onto her gown. She reached down and touched it, lifted her finger to her nose, inhaled the scent, then stuck out her tongue and tasted it.

The Nix pushed to her feet, wobbled, caught her balance. She'd taken on human form before, but never like this, inhabiting a living being. It was very different. Awkward . . . and yet interesting.

She lifted her head and sniffed the air. Dawn was coming. Time to get to work.

She carried the soup to the Marquise's father, bearing it before her like an offering, luxuriating in the heat that radiated through the bowl. It was so cold here, the stone walls leaching drafts at every turn. She'd commanded the staff to light more fires, but they'd only mumbled something vaguely obeisant, then shuffled off and done nothing. Such insolence. If she were their master—but this was only a temporary inhabitation, to test the spell.

As she stepped into the room, she looked at the old man, seated with his back to her. Then she glanced down at the bowl of poisoned soup. The dose had better be right this time. Marie-Madeline had tested it on her maid, Françoise, but the girl hadn't died, so her lover, Gaudin Sainte-Croix, had adjusted the dosage. But rather than try again on a fresh subject, they'd declared the mixture sufficient.

Lazy, imperfect humans, and their lazy, imperfect half-measures. Like the servants who didn't wish to venture outside the castle walls and chop more wood for the fire. What lessons she could teach them! Perhaps she would. As she crossed the floor, looking down at the bowl of soup, she realized, with a jolt of surprise, that the next move was hers. She could give the poison to Marie-Madeline's father or she could feed it to the lazy servants who had ignored her command. For once, she was the actor, not the spectator.

For three hundred years she'd had to sit by and hope humans used the resolve she gave them. Her reward was pain and suffering and chaos. But if they failed, she was left hungry—as helpless as a starving street urchin, begging for a crust of bread. That was what the humans had called the offspring of the Nixen—urchins—as if they knew and laughed at the power they wielded over these demi-demons. And yet, here she was, bearing in her hands the power of death, to deliver as she saw fit. She smiled. Perhaps she would stay a little longer than Marie-Madeline intended.

Hearing her footsteps, Marie-Madeline's father turned. "You didn't need to bring that yourself."

She curtseyed. "It is a daughter's duty, and privilege, to serve her father."

He beamed. "And it is a father's joy to have such a dutiful daughter. You see now that I was right about Gaudin Sainte-Croix. You belong with your husband, and with your father."

She bowed her head. "It was a passing fancy, one that shames me all the more for the shame it brought on my family."

"We will speak no more of it," he said, patting her arm. "Let us enjoy our holiday together."

"First, you should enjoy your soup, Father. Before it grows cold."

For the next four days, d'Aubrey suffered the agonies of a slow death. She stayed at his side, genuinely doing all she could for him, knowing it wouldn't save him, using the excuse to linger and drink in his suffering. At last, he lay in her arms, a hairsbreadth from death, and he used his last words to thank her for everything she'd done.

"It was my pleasure," she said, smiling as she closed his eyes.

It took six years for the Nix to grow bored of Marie-Madeline, and exhaust the possibilities of her silly little life. Time to move on, to find fresh opportunities . . . but not before she had wrung the last bit of merriment from this one.

First, she'd killed Sainte-Croix. Nothing personal in that. He'd been a fine lover and a useful partner, but she had no more need of him, except to let him play his part in the last act of the drama. He'd died in his laboratory, an apparent victim of his own poison, his glass mask having slipped off at an inopportune moment.

After anonymously alerting the police about Sainte-Croix's death, she'd rushed to the commissary and demanded the return of a box from the sealed laboratory. The box was hers, and must be returned unopened. Naturally, that only guaranteed that the police would open it. Inside, they found the bond she'd given Sainte-Croix for the poison used to kill the Marquise's father, plus Sainte-Croix's legacy to her—an assortment of poisons the likes of which the French authorities had never seen. She'd fled Paris, and taken refuge in a convent. The trial came and Marie-Madeline, having not appeared to defend herself, was sentenced to death.

And so it was done.

The Nix returned to Paris, where she knew Marie-Madeline would be swiftly apprehended. Taking a quiet room in an inn, she lay down on the bed, closed her eyes, and recited the incantation for ending the possession. After a few minutes, she opened her eyes and lifted her hand. Still human.

With a grunt, she closed her eyes and repeated the spell. Nothing happened. She snarled, gathered her spirit form into a ball, and flung herself upward, saying the words again, voice rising, filling with fury as her soul stayed lashed to this human form. For two hours, she battered herself against the flesh walls of her prison.

Then she began to scream.

Nicolette peered out across the crowd amassed in the courtyard, praying she'd see no one she recognized. If her mother found out she was here—she shuddered, feeling the sting of her mother's tongue. Death is not a spectacle, she'd say. Nicolette should know that better than anyone. Yet she wasn't here to see the Marquise de Brinvilliers die . . . not really. It was the spectacle surrounding the spectacle that drew her, the chance to be part of something that would be the talk of Paris for years.

A young man pushed through the crowd, hawking pamphlets describing the torture of the Marquise. When he saw Nicolette, he grinned as his eyes traveled over her.

"A pamphlet, my lady," he said, thrusting one at her. "With my compliments."

Nicolette glanced down at the paper he held out. Across the front was a crudely drawn sketch of a naked woman, her body arching as if to a lover, limbs bound to the table, a funnel stuffed into her mouth, face contorted with agony. Nicolette shuddered and looked away. To her left, an old woman cackled. The pamphleteer pressed closer to her, mouth opening, but a man cut him short, and sent him off with a few gruff words.

"You should not be out here, my lady," the man rumbled near her ear when the pamphleteer was gone. "This is no place for you."

No, her place was up in the balconies, where she could watch with an unobstructed view, dining on cakes and wine. Nicolette had tried to disguise herself, to blend in with the common folk, but they always knew.

She was about to move on, when the prison doors opened. A small entourage emerged. At its center was a tiny woman, no more than five feet tall, her dirty face still showing signs of the beauty she must have possessed. Dressed in a plain shift and barefooted, she stumbled forward, tripping and straining at the ropes that bound her, one around her hands, one around her waist, and a third around her neck.

As the guard yanked the Marquise back, her head rose and, for the first time, she saw the crowd. Her lips curled, face contorting in a snarl so awful that the old woman beside Nicolette fell back, hands clawing for her rosary. As the Marquise snarled, her face seemed to ripple, as if her very spirit was trying to break free. Nicolette had seen ghosts before, had been seeing them since she was a child—as did her mother and great-uncle. Yet, when the Marquise's spirit showed itself, everyone around her fell back with a collective gasp.

Nicolette snuck a glance around. They'd seen it, too?

The guard prodded the Marquise into a tumbril. No horse-drawn gilt carriage for this voyage. Her conveyance was a dirty cart, barely big enough to hold her, filthy straw lining the bottom. She had to crouch in the cart like an animal, snarling and cursing as the cart disappeared.

Around Nicolette, the crowd began to move, heading for the Notre Dame Cathedral. She hesitated, quite certain she didn't want to see the final part of the Marquise's journey, but the mob buoyed her along and, after a few weak struggles, she surrendered.

They'd erected the platform before Notre Dame. Nicolette watched as they dragged the Marquise up the steps, forced her down, and began cutting her long hair.

Nicolette had a better vantage point than she liked, but the crowd behind her was so thick she had no chance of escaping. As she tried to divert her attention from the platform, a man stepped from the crowd. A foreigner, with olive skin and dark wavy hair. That alone might have been enough to grab her attention, but what held it was his beauty. Nicolette, who considered herself above such things, found herself staring like a convent schoolgirl.

He looked like a soldier—not his clothing, which was everyday, but his bearing. A man who commanded attention . . . yet not one eye turned his way. To Nicolette, that could only mean one thing. He was a ghost.

The ghost climbed the platform. At the top, he stopped and stood at attention as the guard continued to hack at the Marquise's hair. Clearly the ghost wanted a front-row seat. Had he been one of the Marquise's victims?

Finally, as the executioner withdrew his saber from the folds of his robe, the ghost held out his hands, palms up. An odd gesture, as if checking for rain. His lips moved. Something shimmered in his hands, then took form. A sword. A huge, glowing sword. As he slid his hand down to the hilt, Nicolette realized what he was, and dropped to her knees, crossing herself.

As dense as the crowd was, the angel noticed her gesture, his eyes meeting hers. In that moment, every misdeed she'd ever committed flashed through her head, and her gut went cold, certain she was being judged . . . and found wanting. But the angel's lips curved in the barest smile, and he tipped his head, as casual as a passing neighbor. Then his gaze returned to the Marquise, and his expression hardened.

The executioner's saber sliced down. A sigh rose from the crowd as the Marquise's head thumped onto the platform. Nicolette didn't see it fall. Instead, she stared, transfixed, as a yellow fog rose from the Marquise's body. The fog twisted and grew dense, taking on the form of a young woman.

The angel lifted his sword, and his voice rang out, as clear and melodious as the bells of Notre Dame. "Marie-Madeline d'Aubrey de Brinvilliers, for your crimes, you have been judged."

As he swung that huge sword, the spirit flowing from the Marquise's body threw back its head and laughed.

"I am not the Marquise, fool," it spat.

The angel's brows knitted in a look of confusion as human as the nod he'd given Nicolette. But the sword was already in flight, cleaving toward the ghost.

The spirit's lips twisted. "You have no jurisdiction over—"

As the sword struck the spirit, it let out a scream that made Nicolette double over, hands to her ears. All around her, people jostled and pushed, trying to get a closer look at the Marquise's body as they set it afire, oblivious to the screams.

Nicolette raised her head. There, on the platform, stood the angel, with the spirit skewered on his sword. The thing twisted and shrieked and cursed, but the angel only smiled. Then they were gone.

1

"COME ON," SAVANNAH WHISPERED, TUGGING THE young man's hand.

She climbed a wooden fence into the backyard of a narrow two-story house.

"Watch out for the roses," she said as his feet threatened to land in the border. "We gotta come this way or the old bugger next door will bitch about me having friends over when no one's home."

"Yeah," the boy said. "I get shit from my folks about that, too."

"Oh, Paige and Lucas don't care, as long as I clean up and don't have any monster parties. Well, they might care if they found out I was bringing a guy over. But if that old man sees me having friends over? He starts telling people that Paige and Lucas are crappy guardians, shit like that. Makes me want to—" She swallowed her next words and shrugged. "Tell him off or something."

I was less than a half-dozen paces behind, but they never turned around, never even peered over their shoulders. Sometimes that really pisses me off. Sure, all teenagers ignore their mothers. And, sure, Savannah had a good excuse, since I'd been dead for three years. Still, you'd think we'd have a deeper connection, that she'd somehow hear me, if only as a voice in her head that said "Don't listen to that girl" or "That boy's not worth the trouble." Never happened, though. In life, I'd been one of the most powerful women in the supernatural world, an Aspicio half-demon and witch master of the black arts. Now I was a third-rate ghost who couldn't even contact her own daughter. My afterlife sucked.

Savannah took the boy through the lean-to, dragged him away from Lucas's latest motorcycle restoration project and into the house. The back door swung shut in my face. I walked through it.

They shed their shoes, then climbed the small set of stairs from the landing to the kitchen. Savannah headed straight for the fridge and started grabbing sandwich fixings. I walked past them, through the dining room, into the living room, and settled into my favorite spot, a butter yellow leather armchair.

I'd done the right thing, sending Savannah to Paige. Quite possibly the smartest thing I'd ever done. Of course, if I'd been really smart, Savannah wouldn't have needed anyone to take her in. I wouldn't have been in such a hellfire rush to escape that compound, wouldn't have gotten myself killed, wouldn't have endangered my little girl—

Yes, I'd screwed up, but I was going to fix that now. I'd promised to look after my daughter, and I would . . . just as soon as I figured out how.

Savannah and her friend took their sandwiches into the dining room. I leaned forward to peer around the corner, just a quick check in case . . . In case what, Eve? In case she chokes on a pickle? I silenced the too-familiar inner voice and started to settle back into my chair when I noticed a third person in the dining room. In a chair pulled up to the front window sat a gray-haired woman, her head bent, shoulders racked with silent sobs.

Savannah brushed past the woman, and took a seat on the opposite side of the table. "Did you hear Ms. Lenke might not be back before the city finals? She'd better be. Callahan doesn't know the difference between a dead ball and a free ball."

The boy snorted. "I'd be surprised if that moron could tell a basketball from a football. At last week's practice . . ."

I tuned them out and focused on the woman. As I drew near, I could hear her muted sobs. I sighed and leaned against the dining room doorway.

"Look," I said. "Whatever happened to you, I'm sure it was bad, but you have to move on. Go into the light or click your heels three times or whatever. Get thee to the other side, ghost."

The woman didn't even look up. Only thing worse than a stubborn spirit is a rude one. I'd seen her here at least a dozen times since the kids had moved in, and not once had she so much as acknowledged my presence. Never spoke. Never left that chair. Never stopped crying. And I thought I had a lousy afterlife.

I softened my tone. "You have to get over it. You're wasting your time—"

She faded, and was gone. Really. Some people.

"Where's that new stereo you got?" the boy asked through a mouthful of multigrain bread.

"In my room." Savannah hesitated. "You wanna go up and see it?"

The boy jumped to his feet so fast his chair tumbled over backward. Savannah laughed and helped him right it. Then she grabbed his hand and led him to the stairs.

I stayed at the bottom.

A moment later, music rocked the rafters. Nothing I recognized. Dead three years, and I was already a pop-culture has-been. No, wait. I did recognize the song. "(Don't Fear) the Reaper" . . . but with a techno beat. Who the hell was this? Not Blue Oyster Cult, that's for sure. What kind of crap—? Oh God, I was turning into my mother. I'd avoided it all my life and now—

A man walked through the wall. Two inches taller than me. A decade older. Broad shoulders. Thickening middle. Thinning blond hair. Gorgeous bright blue eyes, which followed my gaze to the stairs.

"And what does our daughter desperately need your help with today?" he asked.

Kristof Nast's contribution to "our daughter" had been purely biological, having not entered her life until just days before the end of his. My choice, not his. After I'd become pregnant, I'd skedaddled. Took him thirteen years and a mortal blow to the head, but he'd finally caught up with me.

He cocked his head, listened to the music, and pulled a face. "Well, at least she's out of the boy-band stage. And it could be worse. Bryce went through heavy metal, then rap, then hip-hop, and at each phase I swore the next one couldn't be any worse, but he always found something—" Kristof stopped and waved a hand in front of my eyes.

"Come on, Eve," he said. "Savannah's taste may be questionable, but she doesn't require musical supervision."

"Shhh. Can you hear anything?"

He arched his brows. "Besides a badly tuned bass guitar and vocals worthy of a castrated stray cat?"

"She has a boy up there."

Another frown, deeper this time. "What kind of boy?"

"Human."

"I meant what 'sort' of boy. This isn't the same one—"
He closed his mouth with an audible click of his teeth,
then launched into a voice I knew only too well, one I
heard in my head when he wasn't around. "All right. Savannah has a boy in her room. She's fifteen. We both
know they aren't up there on a study date. As for exactly
what they're doing . . . is that really any of your business?"

"I'm not worried about sex, Kris. She's a smart girl. If
she's ready—and I don't think she is—she'll take precau-
tions. But what if *he's* ready? I barely know this guy. He
could—"

"Force her to do something she doesn't want?" His
laugh boomed through the foyer. "When's the last time
anyone forced *you* to do something against your will? She's
your daughter, Eve. First guy who puts a hand where she
doesn't want it will be lucky if he doesn't lose it."

"I know, but—"

"What if they *do* turn that music down? Do you really
want to hear what's going on?"

"Of course not. That's why I'm staying down here. I'm
just making sure—"

"You can't make sure of anything. You're dead. That boy
could pull a gun on her and there's not a damn thing you
could do about it."

"I'm working on that!"

He sighed. "You've been working on it for three years.
And you're no better off than when you started." He hesitated, then plowed forward. "You need to step back from
it for a while. Take a break."

"And do what?"

"Well, funny you should ask. That's what I wanted to

talk to you about. I happen to have a temp job lined up for you. Full of adventure, mystery, maybe even a little danger . . ."

"Just a little?"

He grinned. "Depends on how you play it."

I paused, then glanced up the stairs. "We'll talk about it later."

Kristof threw up his hands and disappeared into the wall. I plunked down onto the step. Savannah and I had a special bond he couldn't possibly understand . . . I only wish that were true. Kris had single-parented both his sons after his wife had left them while his youngest was still in diapers. Soon after we'd met, his secretary had paged him because Sean had been hit in the head during a baseball game. For barely more than a bump, he'd blown off an important dinner meeting to catch the next plane home. And that's when my opinion of him had begun the slow but steady shift that led to Savannah.

It had ended there, though. Once I'd realized I was a black witch carrying the bastard child of a Cabal sorcerer heir, I hadn't been dumb enough to stick around and see what his family thought. As for what Kristof thought of me taking our daughter away . . . well, I'd spent twelve years trying not to think about that. I knew I'd made a mistake, an error in judgment overshadowed only by that final error in judgment I'd made in the compound.

Yet for twelve years I'd been able to coast on my guilt trip, telling myself maybe Kristof hadn't really cared that I'd taken Savannah. Bullshit, of course. But not having him there to say otherwise had made it easier . . . until six months after my death, when I'd seen him fight for custody of her, and die trying to protect her.

Upstairs, the music ended. Savannah popped in another CD . . . or switched MP3s . . . or whatever music came on these days. The next song began, something slow, and definitely soft enough for me to hear giggles and murmurs.

Damn it, Kris was right. Following my daughter to the mall was one thing. Listening to her make out with a boy was wrong. And creepy. But now I was stuck here. If Kristof found out I'd left right after him, he'd know I'd seen his point, and I wasn't ready to admit that. Maybe—

A sharp oath burst from the living room. I took a cautious step toward the corner. In life, I would have strode over there, defensive spell at the ready. But here? Well, here things were different.

Kristof stepped from behind the sofa, picking what looked like cobwebs from his rumpled shirt. The back of his hair stuck straight up, as if someone had run a static-charged hand through it. His tie was shredded.

He gave a fierce wet-dog shake. When he finished, he was immaculate again . . . except for his tie, which was tucked into his shirt. I plucked it out and straightened it.

"Let me guess," I said. "Wrong turn . . . again?"

He gave a helpless shrug. "You know how I am with spells."

"Uh-huh."

I glanced back at the stairs. A sigh floated down.

I turned back to Kris. "Want a lift?"

"Please."

2

TRANSPORTATION IS MY AFTERLIFE SPECIALTY—MY quest to help Savannah meant I spent a lot of time tracking down sources. In other areas of ghost activity, I'm not so good, though I didn't think the Fates needed to send me through that damned orientation course three times.

My afterlife world was a version of earth, with some weird subdimensions that we really tried to avoid. Everyone here was a supernatural, but not every supernatural was here. When I'd died, my first thought on waking had been "Great, now I finally find out what comes next." Well, actually that had been my *second* thought, after "Hmmm, I thought it would have been hotter." Yes, I'd escaped the fiery hell my mother and many others had prophesied for me, but in dying, I hadn't found out what comes next, only what came next for *me*. Was there fire and brimstone somewhere else? Were there halos and heavenly harps? I have no idea. I only know that where I am is better than where I expected to be, so I'm not complaining.

I dropped Kristof off on the courthouse steps. Yes, we have courts here. The Fates take care of all major disciplinary issues, but they let us handle disputes between ghosts. Hence the courts, where Kristof worked. Not that he'd practiced law in real life. The day he'd passed the bar exam, he'd gone into business with his family. But here he was, playing lawyer in the afterlife. Even Kris admitted this wasn't his first choice for a new career, but until they started a ghost world NHL franchise, he was stuck with it.

Speaking of jobs . . . Kristof was right. I needed a break. I'd known that for a while now, but couldn't bring myself to admit it. I knew Kris's "temp job" wouldn't be the kind of employment the Fates would approve of, but that was more incentive than obstacle.

That thought had no sooner left my mind than a bluish fog blew in and swirled around my leg.

"Hey, I was just—"

The fog sucked me into the ground.

The Searchers deposited me in the Fates' throne room, a white marble cavern with moving mosaics on the walls. The Fates are the guardians of the supernatural layers of the ghost world, and just about the only time they call us in is when we've screwed up. So as the floor began to turn, I braced myself. When it didn't turn fast enough, I twisted around to face the Fates myself. A pretty girl threaded yarn onto a spinning wheel. She looked no more than five or six years old, with bright violet eyes that matched her dress.

"Okay," I said. "What did I do?"

The girl smiled. "Isn't the question: What did I do *now*?"

I sighed, and in less time than it takes to blink, the girl morphed into a middle-aged version of herself, with long graying dark hair, and light-brown skin showing the first wrinkles and roughness of time.

"We have a problem, Eve."

"Look, I promised I wouldn't use the codes for *excessive* unauthorized travel. I never said—"

"This isn't about unauthorized travel."

I thought for a moment. "Visiting Adena Milan for spell-swapping? Hey, that was an honest mistake. No one told me she was on the blacklist."

The middle-aged Fate shook her head. "Admittedly, there might be some amusement to be had in making you recite the whole list of your infractions, but I'm afraid we don't have that much time. Eighteen months ago, you made a deal with us. If we returned Paige and Lucas to the living world, you'd owe us a favor."

"Oh . . . that."

Damn. When they hadn't mentioned it again, I'd hoped they'd forgotten. Like that's going to happen. The Fates can remember what Noah ate for breakfast on the morning of the flood.

My first instinct was to weasel out of it. Hell, what's the worst thing that could happen? Well, for starters, they could undo their end of the bargain and bring Paige and Lucas back to the ghost world. So no weaseling out of this one. Besides, I *had* been looking for a distraction. Which made this all seem very coincidental.

"Did Kristof put you up to this? Finding me something to do?"

The Fate morphed into her oldest sister, a hunch-backed crone with a wizened face set in a scowl.

"Kristof Nast does not 'put us up to' anything."

"I didn't mean—"

"Nor are we going to be doing favors for the likes of him. We thought that lawyer job would keep him busy." She snorted. "And it does. Keeps him busy getting into trouble."

"If you mean the Agito case, that wasn't Kris's fault. The plaintiff started lying, so he had to do something. It wasn't *really* witness tampering . . ."

"Just a means to an end," she said, fixing me with that glare. "That's how you two think. Doesn't matter how you get there, as long as you do."

The middle sister took over. "An interesting philosophy. Not one we share, but in some cases . . . useful. This particular job we need done may require some of those unique skills."

I perked up. "Oh?"

"We have a spirit who's escaped from the lower realms. We need you to bring her in."

The lower realms are where they keep the ghosts who can't be allowed to mingle with the rest of us—the seriously nasty criminals. Hmmm, interesting.

"So who is—"

"First, you need to do some research." The middle-aged Fate reached into the air and pulled out a sheet of paper. "This is a list of books—"

"Books? Look, I'm sure you guys are in a hurry for me to get this job done, so why don't we skip this part? I'm really more a hands-on kind of gal."

The girl appeared, grinning mischievously. "Oh? Well, in that case, let's do it the hands-on way."

She waved a hand, and a ball of light whipped out and blinded me.

"What the—" I began.

"Shhhhhh."

The light fell in a shower of sparks. I blinked, then saw only darkness. The same voice continued to shush me, a long-drawn-out monotone of a breath that, after a moment, I realized wasn't a voice at all, but the rush of air past my ears.

I squeezed my eyes shut and shook my head, willing my night-vision to kick in. Like all my visual abilities, this one came supercharged, the legacy of having the Lord Demon Balam, Master of Sight, as a father.

A sharp wind whipped through my clothes. Something tickled my fingers. I grabbed it, and with a tug, the thin strand broke free. I lifted it to my nose. Grass.

My sight began to clear. The first thing I saw was waves, the rhythmic rise and fall of waves rippling toward shore. But I didn't smell water. Didn't feel the spray of it or the weight of it in the air. Instead, the wind was dry and smelled of . . . grass. I blinked again and saw waves of grass, rising and falling on hilly soil, bowing in the wind. An ocean of grass.

Once upon a time, this would have surprised me, but after three years of traveling around the ghost world, I've seen some pretty strange geography. In the unoccupied areas, plains are common, vast empty stretches of rock or sand or grass. I'd even popped into a plain of lava once. Not pleasant . . . especially when I realized it wasn't as empty as it appeared. At that thought, I peered into the long grass. It didn't look like there was anything down there, but you could never be sure.

I looked up. Sky. A night sky, overcast.

"Okay," I called to the Fates. "You can skip the detention. I'll do my homework."

A high-pitched laugh answered me. Now, I'm sure the child Fate would get a giggle out of their trick, but the voice sounded too old to be hers, and neither of her sisters was the giggling type.

When no one answered, I headed in the direction of the laugh. If there was someone else in this ghost-world wasteland, it probably wasn't someone I wanted to meet, but a little danger would at least liven things up.

The wind picked up to a whine that cut right through my thin shirt. I thought of willing myself a jacket, but didn't. In the ghost world, you could pass weeks, months, even years without ever feeling temperatures that went beyond pleasantly warm or pleasantly cool. Once in a while, discomfort wasn't so bad.

I walked into a deep dip that sheltered me from the wind. I rubbed my ears. As they thawed, my hearing improved. Not that there was much more to hear, just the whistle of the wind overhead. No, wait, something else. I cocked my head to listen. A thump, then a swish. Silence. *Thump, swish.* Silence. *Thump, swish.*

I readied an energy-bolt spell.

The thumping sound could be slow footsteps. But the swish? I didn't really want to think about that. The next thump brought a nails-down-a-chalkboard screech. A muttered oath. An exchange of words, one voice male, one female. A grunt. A thud. Then it resumed. *Thump, swish. Thump, swish.*

I cast a blur spell—if it worked in this dimension, it should distort my shape enough to let me sneak past anyone who wasn't looking for me. Then I climbed to the top of the knoll. Less than twenty feet away stood a young woman holding a flashlight. I quickstepped back down the hill, then sharpened my sight.

I peered over the hill. The woman was shining the

flashlight on a man digging a hole. That was the noise—the thump of the shovel digging in and the swish of the dirt as he tossed it aside.

The couple were both in their twenties. The man was small and skinny with a greasy mop of hair. The woman was blond, with her hair piled high in a god-ugly outdated do. Her clothing was equally out-of-date—miniskirt, high boots, and a car coat. That wasn't surprising. In the ghost world you get used to seeing a historical fashion show. Most ghosts stick with whatever style they enjoyed in life. Well, unless that style included corsets or other instruments of torture.

Here we had two ghosts, circa the sixties . . . or the seventies. Being my "growing-up years," the two decades merged into a shapeless whole of miniskirts, tie-dyed tees, go-go boots, and disco.

"Deep enough?" the man said, rubbing his hands together. "Bloody cold out here tonight."

The woman leaned over to peer into the hole, then nodded. She laid the flashlight on the ground and the couple walked into the darkness beyond. They returned carrying a long, wrapped bundle between them.

"It's not big enough," the woman said. "He's taller than I thought."

The man nodded, lifted his shovel, and resumed digging. As the woman watched, she wrapped her arms around herself and shivered. Given the cold, and the task at hand, a shiver was not out of place. But the look on her face was, her eyes gleaming, tongue darting out.

"It was good," she said. "Better this time. We shouldn't wait so long next time."

"We need to be careful," the man said without looking up.

"Why? No one can catch us. We're invincible. This . . ." She shivered again and waved at the body. "It makes us invincible. It makes us special."

The man looked up at her with a small smile. He nodded, then reached out of the hole and grabbed the wrapped body. As he dragged it, the other end flapped open in the breeze. A young boy's dead eyes stared up at the night sky.

The scene disintegrated into darkness.

I've seen dead bodies before. Sent many into the ghost world myself. You screw with dark forces, you have to accept that an early grave may be your reward. But by "early grave" I mean dying before you're old and gray. The murder of anyone too young to defend himself is the only act that is unforgivable under any circumstances.

So this woman was the murderous spirit the Fates wanted me to find? Consider it done. The only reward I wanted was to be there when they cast her back into her hell dimension. The darkness lightened, and I looked up, expecting to see the throne room. Instead, I stood in front of a frost-covered window. I touched my fingers to the glass. Cold and slick, but my fingers left no marks on the pane. When I peered through a clear corner, I could see sunlight shimmering through falling snow. Strange. Like seeing sunbeams through the rain.

A woman's laugh made me jump and my mind jumped with it, right back to the grassy plain and the laugh I'd first heard out there.

"Oh, wait!" a woman said. "This is the best part. Slow it down."

I turned from the window. On the other side of the

room, a young couple was curled up on the couch, watching television. The man had a remote in his hand, pointed at the VCR.

Did they have VCRs in the sixties? No, wait. It was a different man. So I was someplace else. Or was I? My gaze snagged on the young woman. A blonde, early twenties, round face, marginally pretty. Same woman. Or was it? The hairstyle was still overdone, but in a style I remembered from high school. And her skirt was still mini but, again, a modern mini. I tried to zoom in on her face, but it was turned to the television, giving me only a quarter-profile.

"Okay, here it comes."

The woman leaned toward the television. Her eyes glowed. Another jolt as I recognized the same rapturous expression I'd seen on the woman at the grave-site.

"Come on, turn it up," she said, socking the man in the arm.

He laughed and raised the volume. From where I stood, I couldn't see the screen, but I could hear the tape. The voices on it were distorted. Home-movie quality.

I cast a blur spell and crept across the carpet until I could see the screen. It was blocked by a light green shirt. Someone with his back to the camera. Typical. The shirt moved aside. A shot of flesh. A naked female leg. Oh, yeah. A very typical home movie, the kind video recorders were made for. This I did not need to see.

I started to turn away when the camera pulled back and I saw the full image. A girl, no older than Savannah, naked and bound to a bed. Bloodstained bedding.

"Here it comes." The woman's voice rose a few

notches, and she imitated the girl's sobs. "I want my mommy!"

With a roar, I launched myself at the woman on the sofa. My hands flew for her throat, nails out. I hit her, passed right through, and tumbled into darkness.

3

I LANDED HARD ON THE MARBLE FLOOR OF THE throne room. It didn't hurt. I wished it did. I even slammed my fist into the floor, hoping for a jolt of pain to knock the rage from my brain, but my hand only bounced off as if I'd socked a pillow.

I scrambled to my feet. The middle Fate stood there, watching me.

"Send me back," I said.

"Eve, you—"

"Send me back now! You can't show me that and then rip me out of there before I can do anything about it."

"You can't do anything about it," she said softly. "It's over. Long over. What you saw was a memory."

I rubbed my face. A memory. A glimpse into the past. I stared at the white wall, let it clear my mind. I didn't have a clue who the people had been. Obviously serial killers and probably infamous, but I'd never been one to follow crime. In my world, the killers I had to worry about were the ones in my little black book, not the ones on the eleven o'clock news.

When I glanced up, the elderly Fate was at the spinning wheel, and I braced myself, sure she'd jump on me for an answer. Yet she didn't even look up. Just clipped off the length of yarn the middle Fate had measured out for her, then handed it to a wraith-clerk. Then the child Fate took over and threaded the spinning wheel. She lifted her eyes to mine, then quickly looked back down.

So what was the connection between the two sets of murders? Or were they two sets? There was only one spirit missing from the nether regions. Two women, similar in appearance, both killing teens. So they had to be the same person. To a human, such a thing would be impossible, but supernatural minds are more open to other possibilities.

I knew I should think through those possibilities, and come up with the most likely one, to impress the Fates with my astounding capacity for logical reasoning. I knew that . . . and I blurted out the first thing that came to mind.

"Vampire," I said.

The youngest of the Fates glanced around the spinning wheel, her face screwed up in a look every mother recognizes as "Huh?"

"Two sets of murders, both committed by the same woman, who doesn't age between the time of big hair and miniskirts and, well, big hair and miniskirts. Similar fashion styles, but definitely a twenty-five, thirty-year gap without so much as a wrinkle. She must be a vampire. Most vamps stick to their necessary kill quotas but there are always those who get a taste for it and—"

The crone took over. "It's not a vampire, Eve. We have our own ways of dealing with vampire spirits, which you would know if you took any interest at all in the world around you. Try again."

The old Fate's bright eyes pinned me like a butterfly to

a mat. In school, I'd had very little respect for my teachers, and for grown-ups in general. Only one teacher had ever been able to make me squirm. Grade six. Mrs. Appleton, the kind of sour old woman whose very gaze is acid to your self-confidence, who always looks as if she expects very little from you, and is never disappointed. The old Fate had that look down pat.

"Uh, I, well . . ." I straightened. "Okay, well, I don't know a lot about time-travel"—I caught her look—"but I do know that's not what's going on here. So the explanation must be . . ."

I studied her gaze. No clues there. Forge ahead.

"Reincarnation," I said.

The crone morphed into the middle-aged woman. "How much do you know about reincarnation, Eve?"

A lightning-bolt switch and the old woman cut in. "Not nearly enough, considering she's been here three years." She fixed me with one eye, squeezing the other shut. "Well? Let's hear it. Everything you know about reincarnation. Should take a good five, ten seconds."

"I know it's possible," I said. "Rare, but possible."

"Three seconds? I overestimated you again."

The middle Fate appeared. "Yes, it's rare, Eve. Very rare. It's allowed only under special circumstances, when a spirit meets certain criteria that lead the Creator to decide that the soul should be allowed another chance at life."

The old Fate cut back in. "And murdering children doesn't qualify."

Again, the middle Fate pushed her sister aside. "What we want you to find is called a Nix. Do you know what that is?"

I expected the hag to pop back and needle me again, but she didn't.

"Demi-demons," I said slowly, as my memory banks creaked open. "In German folklore a Nix is a mischievous temptress spirit. A cross between a siren, an imp, and Mae West."

"That's the mythical version," she said. "And the reality?"

"I—I'm not sure. I've never run into one, or anyone who has." I thought harder, then shook my head. "I don't remember reading any references to a real version."

"Probably because it's very obscure knowledge. In folklore, as you said, they are considered mischievous spirits, water pixies, actually . . ."

The Fate continued, giving me the condensed version of Nixen mythology. Some humans believe a Nix is a siren who lures humans to watery graves. In other words, an excuse for idiots who dove into deep water and discovered they couldn't swim. Mythological Nixen were both male and female, but the females were more successful at capturing their victims, maybe because guys are more likely to stand on a riverbank and yell, "Hey, watch this dive!"

The truth is, Nixen have nothing to do with water. When early folklorists learned that Nixen were temptresses, they'd probably jumped to the conclusion that they were a form of siren. Nixen are also all female . . . or that's the form they manifest in, as full demons manifest as male. It's probably more an aesthetic choice than a gender difference. Finally, Nixen aren't truly temptresses at all. Instead, they are sought out by those who already *are* tempted—by wealth, power, or sex—and looking for a delivery shortcut. What a Nix provides is the resolve they need to carry out an act they lack the courage to perform, murder being most common.

"Okay," I said when she finished. "Nixen help people kill, and those scenes you showed me were obviously murders, but where's the connection? Those women were humans. How would they have conjured up a Nix? Even if they did, you sure as hell can't want me to chase down a Nix. They're demi-demons, not ghosts, so they wouldn't be in one of your hells."

The youngest Fate cut in. "Don't worry. We didn't expect you to see the connection. It's all very strange." She leaned around the wheel, her eyes aglitter. "See, what happened was—"

Her middle sister took over. "This particular Nix is quite different from her brethren. In the seventeenth century, she made a deal with a witch who wanted her father dead."

"And gave her the guts she needed to do it."

"That's the usual process. However, in this case, it didn't work. A Nix's power has one significant limitation—she cannot compel a person to kill. The will and the intent must still be there. Conscious will and conscious intent. This witch was conflicted over her wish. Yet Nixen thrive on chaos, and they don't appreciate being summoned without that end reward, so the Nix made a suggestion. She told the witch where to find a spell that would allow the Nix to take over the witch's body, temporarily, and commit the act herself. The witch agreed, and the Nix—"

The girl leapt in, bubbling with the enthusiasm of a child who simply must tell the rest of the story. "—takes her over, and kills the woman's father. And then she's supposed to give the body back. Only she doesn't. She uses the body to cause all kinds of trouble."

The middle sister cut in. "And many people died . . . including the Nix herself, eventually. Trapped in a corporeal body, she died the death of a corporeal being. Having been in a witch's form, she was brought here, to the supernatural realms. Although we aren't equipped to handle a demi-demon, we managed to trap her in a hell dimension. For a while."

"She escaped."

"And that is a serious problem because this Nix isn't flitting about the living world as a spirit. Having moved into a human body once, she is now able to do it at will."

"So that's the connection. It's not the same woman. It's the same Nix in different women. She takes them over—"

"Not exactly. Being a dead spirit, she can no longer fully take over a living body. Instead, she must cohabit, giving them resolve to carry out their desires."

"So she doesn't jump into innocent women and turn them into rampaging killers. Are the hosts always women?"

The Fate nodded. "Having first leapt into a host of that gender, she is now restricted to it."

I paused. "If you ladies know so much about how she operates, I'm guessing she's been out there for a while."

"A little over a hundred years."

"Uh-huh. I suppose that means I'm not the first person you've sent after her."

"There have been three who've gone before you. We took three different approaches with varying degrees of success. All three . . . ended badly."

"What did she do to them?"

The child Fate appeared, laughing. "Her first question, and it's the one none of the others even thought to ask.

When we told them that the others had failed, they only asked how the Nix got away. That's what they figured she'd do—give them the slip and run. But you know better."

"Common sense. The best way to stop being chased is to stop the person doing the chasing. But that's a problem here, isn't it? Can't kill a ghost. Can't even hurt one. So how the hell do you force one to stop chasing you?"

The middle Fate returned. "There are worse things than physical torture."

"Not if it's done right."

The eldest one popped in, glower already in place. "You have an answer for everything, don't you?"

"No, I was just pointing out—"

"You want to know what she did to one of your predecessors, Eve? Let me show you."

4

THE TRAPPINGS OF THE THRONE ROOM VANISHED.
Even the floor evaporated, and I tensed, waiting to drop
into some hell dimension. Instead, I found myself floating, naked, in gray nothingness.

Was I really floating? Beneath my bare feet a sheet of
gray, as smooth as glass, stretched to meet the gray sky. I
could see my feet planted on the floor, yet I felt nothing
beneath them. I closed my eyes and lowered my hand.
My hand stopped at floor level. I leaned forward, but still
couldn't feel pressure against my palm.

Okay, that was creepy. Still, there were a thousand
worse places that the Nix could have sent her last hunter,
and if this unsettling illusion was the best she could
manage, I was laughing.

I closed my eyes and wished for clothing. When I
looked again, I was still naked. Hmmm. I guess naked-
ness was part of the torture. And for some people, maybe
it was, but I'm not the type to be plagued by nightmares
of walking through the shopping mall starkers, so it was
really no big deal, especially considering there was no
one else here to see me.

No one to see me, and nothing for me to see. Nothing
to hear, either. Reminded me of the first hour I'd spent

alone as a ghost. The most shocking thing about that hour was the silence. When we're alive, quiet is a relative term. Even if you manage to drown out all the background noise—the clacks and grunts and hums of water pipes and furnaces and refrigerators—you can always hear something, even if it's only the sound of yourself breathing. But when you're dead, all the sources of those noises, internal and external, are gone. Still, there's usually something, if you listen hard enough—the footsteps of someone walking by, a laugh from a neighbor, a bird chirping. Here, in this empty dimension, the silence was absolute.

I could see how this could become annoying after a while. Sensory deprivation, isn't that what they call it? I remembered reading that this kind of thing could serve as a form of torture. Pretty clever, actually. Didn't leave any marks, and you couldn't be accused of doing anything to your prisoner because you weren't doing a damn thing. Interesting, in a theoretical kind of way.

Right now, all that mattered was that I got the point. The Nix could send me someplace where I wouldn't want to spend a whole lot of time.

"Okay—" I stopped. I'd felt myself say the word, but hadn't heard anything. "Okay, ladies!"

The silence sucked up my words before they left my lips.

"Hello?" I tried to say. "Hello, hello, hello!"

Creepy, but not like it mattered. The Fates seemed to hear me whether I spoke aloud or not. When they were ready, they'd bring me back. I settled onto the ground to wait.

* * *

Still waiting.

At least a couple of hours had passed. Obviously the Fates wanted to give me a real taste of this wasteland. Like I had time for this. Well, if they weren't going to bring me back, I'd look after it myself.

I said the words of a travel incantation. I still couldn't hear myself, but I was speaking and, in magic, there's no bonus for blaring. I finished the incantation. Nothing happened. I tried a few more, but stayed where I was. Fine. I could wait.

Okay, now I was getting mad. I'd been here at least a few hours, tried every damned spell I knew, even ones that had nothing to do with transportation, and not one of them had worked. What the hell were the Fates doing? They had a murderous demi-demon on the rampage, probably planning her next atrocity against humankind at this very moment, but that didn't stop them from sparing a few hours to piss me off.

The old Fate was behind this. She hated me. Like my teacher, Mrs. Appleton. I'd never known what I'd done to earn Mrs. Appleton's hate, but I hadn't been able to shake the feeling that she'd seen something in me, something bad, something waiting to emerge. When the old Fate looked at me, I felt the same thing.

I pulled my knees up to my chest, rested my chin on them, and tried to chase these thoughts from my brain. They clung like burrs, rubbing raw spots in my confidence. I needed to clear my head, needed to do something. But there was nothing here to do. Except think.

* * *

"Hello! Goddamn it, answer me! I get the point! Now open the fucking door!" It was nighttime. Here the light never changed, just a dull glow that came from nowhere, illuminating the emptiness, reminding you that there was no one here, nothing to see. My gut told me it was night, though. Kristof would be at my house, waiting to talk about that "temp job" he'd mentioned.

I closed my eyes and concentrated on a communication spell.

Hey, Kris? Think you can help me out?

Nothing.

My internal clock told me that night had come and gone. Hadn't slept. We could sleep, but I'd never been able to just curl up anywhere and drift off, not unless I was very, very tired. A ghost never tires. So, unless I was in my bed, I didn't sleep.

I'd been here for over twenty-four hours. I was sure of that. Okay, enough waiting around for fate to intervene. Time to take matters into my own hands . . . or onto my own feet. Maybe I couldn't teleport out of here, but I could still walk.

So I picked a direction, and started out.

Still walking. When I looked around, I saw the same damn thing I'd seen when I'd started, as if I were on a treadmill. But I was moving. I knew it. The lack of landmarks just made it seem as if I wasn't going anywhere. Every dimension I'd ever been in had come to an end. This one would, too, if only I walked far enough.

* * *

It was night again, and I hadn't reached the end. Hadn't reached anything. My legs didn't hurt, though. No pain means endless energy. I could walk forever, and I damned well would if that's what it took to get out—

The throne room appeared, just as I'd left it, with the elderly crone still at the wheel.

"Happy?" I snarled, voice cracking from disuse. "I bet you got a good chuckle out of that. Were you watching? Seeing how long I'd take to snap? Sorry to disappoint."

She looked up from her wheel. Her gaze met mine, face expressionless.

"I can't believe you did that," I said. "This Nix is out there, killing people, and you left me there for two days!"

"It was two minutes, Eve."

"Bullshit! Days passed there."

"Yes. Nearly three. But here it was only minutes. The Nix sent our first seeker there, and it took us five years to find her. That's what I wanted you to see. That is what this Nix can do."

Five years in our time? That had to be lifetimes in that place. Alone, with nothing to see, hear, feel, smell . . .

The middle Fate appeared. "She went mad, Eve. We've done our best, but she's been back with us for over sixty years, and she's no saner than the day we found her."

"And the others?" I said slowly. "You said there were two others."

"The second one failed us. The third one the Nix cast into a different dimensional plane."

"Where?"

"We don't know."

My head shot up. "You haven't found him yet? Excuse me if the job suddenly doesn't sound so attractive, but—"

"We have safeguards in place now. We've figured out her tricks."

"So she can't toss me into an alternate dimension?"

"Not for long."

"Uh-huh."

The old Fate took over, eyes sparkling. "Job too tough for you, Eve?"

"Don't bother challenging me," I said. "I'll do this because I made a promise, and I always keep my promises. You've shown me the worst, so I'm forewarned and ready to start."

"Good, then the first thing we want you to do is—"

"The first thing you need to do is tell me how this Nix got out of her hell, and why she isn't going to do the same thing as soon as you toss her back in."

"She won't."

"Details?"

"I'm not about to explain our security arrangements to—"

The middle Fate interceded. "We initially put her in a place protected against dimensional travel and teleportation, but, after two centuries of trying, she managed to open a portal into the kind of dimension we never dreamed she'd use as an escape route. You've heard of animals that will gnaw off a limb to escape a trap? The Nix knowingly leapt into a dimension that made her hell look like paradise, and did so with only the faintest hope of ever leaving it."

"And that surprises you?" I shook my head. "Never mind. Just tell me that she won't have that choice to make the next time."

"She won't."

"Good. On to step one, then. I want—"

"We've already arranged a plan for you, Eve."

"Great, and if it's better than mine, let me know. Now, first, I want to talk to one of these 'seekers' you sent after her. Under the circumstances, it isn't tough to figure out which one I'll have to choose: the bounty hunter behind door number two, the guy you pink-slipped."

The child Fate took over. "Can't do it. Where he is, you can't go. And, believe me, you don't want to. You thought that last place was bad? Paradise compared to where he is."

"But you said the Nix didn't catch him. You fired him."

"Yep, we did. Fired him right down to—"

Her middle sister cut in. "You can't speak to him."

"Hold on. Is this the incentive program? If I fail, you send me someplace worse than the Nix would send me? No wonder you can't find any volunteers."

"We didn't punish—" She sighed and shook her head. "The details aren't important."

"To you, maybe—"

"There is no punishment for failure," she said. "Even if you could talk to this man, he wouldn't tell you anything. You need to pick one of the others."

"The hopelessly insane one or the hopelessly misplaced one. Hmm, tough choice."

"It's unlikely you could find Zadkiel—"

"No kidding! If you guys have been searching—"

"So I'd recommend Janah. The ascended angel."

"Angel?"

"The first seeker. The one who went mad."

"Uh-huh."

"First, though, we have to prepare her. In the meantime, you can—"

"In the meantime, then, I want to talk to someone who worked with one of these seekers. A supervisor, a partner, anyone who might be able to give me some insight into how your hunters worked, because I strongly suspect Janah isn't going to be my most reliable source of intel."

"Your partner has experience with the Nix."

"Partner? What—?"

"You'll meet him when you speak to Janah. It may take a day or two to prepare her, so we'd suggest you rest—"

"Then I need a necromancer." Before she could argue, I hurried on. "If I'm tracking a spirit who can enter the living, then I need access to the living world—something you ladies have been denying me since I got here."

"For very good reason—"

"So I don't contact Savannah. Fine. But now I need that access."

The Fate nodded. "You do, and we recognize that. We've already arranged—"

"I want Jaime Vegas."

"I see," the Fate said slowly. "And that choice would have nothing to do with the fact that she is acquainted with your daughter, and now serves on the supernatural council with Paige?"

"It has everything to do with that. Jaime knows Paige, who can vouch for me. Try finding another necro, outside the black market, who'll want to work with Eve Levine. Of course, I could just go to the black market, call up one of my old friends . . ."

"Which you know we wouldn't allow." She paused, lips pursing, then shook her head. "Don't think we fail to see this for what it is, Eve—a not terribly discreet attempt to pursue your favorite—your only—pastime here. But I will allow it, for the duration of this quest, and on the understanding that you will devote your time with Jaime to that quest, and not ask her to break necromantic law by contacting Savannah for you."

I sifted through her words for a loophole. I didn't see it right off, but I'd find one eventually. Before I could ask where to find Jaime, the Fate lifted her hands, and transported me away.

5

I OPENED MY EYES AND FOUND MYSELF STARING INTO the über-bright glare of the sun. Blinded, I stumbled, and landed on my ass. A roar of laughter boomed from all sides, and I jumped up so fast my vision jolted back into focus. In front of me was a packed auditorium.

"Well, that's what happens when you deal with the dead," said a woman's voice. "Some of them just aren't too bright."

I turned a glare on the speaker, but saw only the back of a redhead sitting at center stage. As she continued talking, I realized I was on a television set. The redhead and another woman sat in a pair of comfy armchairs in a set designed to look like someone's living room.

I walked onto the stage, but every gaze stayed riveted to the two women. Wherever I was, I was still a ghost. I peered over for a closer look at the host, and mentally groaned. I'd seen her show once, when I'd been bedridden with morning sickness, too queasy to change the channel. I forgot the exact topic, but it had been the kind of "every life has meaning" psycho-crap gobbled up by people whose existence proved the credo wrong. The uplifting message did make me feel better, though. Uplifted my stomach right into the toilet, and after that, I'd felt much better.

I circled closer to the stage. I had a good idea who the redhead was, and another step confirmed it. She was a few years older than me, but didn't look it. Long legs, bee-stung lips, and green eyes made Jaime Vegas the kind of woman for whom the phrase "sultry redhead" was invented. She packaged that sex appeal with her mediocre necromancy talents, and sold it to the grief-stricken. Some might call it a reprehensible way to make a living. I called it survival.

"But seriously," Jaime said, as the latest round of laugh-ter died down. "What I do can be lots of fun, and I love that side of it, but what I love more is what it brings to other people's lives: the closure, the peace."

The talk show host nodded. "And that's really what spiritualism is all about, isn't it? Healing the spirit. Not the spirits of the dead, but those of the living."

Oh, God, someone pass the barf bag. The audience only beamed and echoed a chorus of yeses and Amens, like an army of zombies before a Vodoun priestess.

"Is it just me?" I said. "Or is that seriously creepy?"

Jaime jumped like a scalded cat. As she twisted, she saw me and her face went white. I'd say she looked as if she'd seen a ghost, but for a necromancer, that's pretty much a daily occurrence. You'd think she'd have grown used to it by now.

"Nice gig," I said. "Is it almost over? I need to talk to you."

"Jaime?" the host said, leaning forward. "What is it? Do you see something?"

"Seems you have a resident ghost," Jaime said. "Nor-mally I need to open myself up to see them, but some-times they shove their way right through. Impatient as children." A razor-sharp glare my way. "Rude children."

"Rude? You're a necro. I sure as hell don't expect you to jump every time a ghost—"

"Can you see him?" the host whispered.

"Her. It's a woman." Jaime paused for effect. "A witch."

A murmured gasp from the audience.

"Not a real witch, of course," Jaime said, her voice taking the soft singsong tone of a storyteller. "Though she thought she was. Thought she was all-powerful, but she wasn't."

"*Excuse* me?"

"She lived by violence, and died by it. And now she's a tormented, lonely spirit, caught between the worlds, looking for redemption."

I snorted.

"And if she's not"—Jaime aimed another glare my way—"she should be, because she has a lot to atone for."

I rolled my eyes and walked off the stage.

In the wings, I prepared a second plan of attack. When Jaime stepped off the stage ten minutes later, I fell into step beside her.

"Okay, now that you have that off your chest, let's talk. Obviously you know who I am."

She kept walking.

"You want a formal introduction?" I said. "Fine. I'm Eve Levine, ghost. You're Jaime Vegas, necromancer. Now, what I need is—"

She had veered around a corner before I noticed. I had to backtrack and jog to catch up.

"I know you can hear me," I said. "And see me. So let's cut the crap and—"

She turned into an open dressing room and slammed the door.

I followed. "Maybe I can walk through doors, but that doesn't give you any right to slam them on me. It's still rude."

"Rude?" she said, spinning on me so fast I took an involuntary step back. "Rude? You just—the most important spot of my career, the chance of a lifetime and you—"

Her hand flew to her mouth. She dove into the bathroom and leaned over the toilet, gagging.

"If it makes you feel any better, she has the same effect on me."

Jaime wheeled, eyes flashing. She pulled herself to her full height . . . at least five inches below my six feet. Very intimidating.

"Find yourself another necro, Eve. One who's stupid enough to let you speak to Savannah. And my advice? When you find one, at least make some effort to follow proper protocol. That shit you pulled out there may have worked in life, but it doesn't work now."

There was a proper protocol? Damn.

Jaime stalked past me into the dressing room. When I followed, I found her rooting through an oversize makeup bag. She took out a bowl and a few pouches of herbs.

"A banishing mixture?" I said. "Look, Jaime, I know you don't do a lot of real necromancy, so I'll let you in on a little secret. That mixture only works on human ghosts. For it to work on a supernatural, you have to be a damned good necromancer and, no offense, but—"

Someone jostled me from behind. A physical jostle that, considering I was in the living world, should have been impossible . . . which meant that whoever hit me had to be another ghost.

"Watch where you're going there, sweetheart."

I looked over my shoulder to see a guy about a half foot shorter than me, dressed in spats and a straw hat, with a machine gun slung over one shoulder. He grinned, tipped his hat, and slid past.

I was on a sidewalk, across from a soot-crusted brick building with boarded-up windows and a sheet of paper plastered on the door. I sharpened my vision to read the paper on the door across the road. A notice of closure, in accordance with the Prohibition Act of 1920.

Ghost-world Chicago. Like most major cities in the afterlife, the landscape of Chicago was frozen in its heyday, and many of the residents, like the portly gangster, played along with the period. But if I was here, that meant Jaime really had banished me. Damn.

There were ways to avoid banishing. A few months before, Kristof had needed a necro's help, and went to one who owed him major favors. Guy made the mistake of thinking Kristof's death canceled out those IOUs, then made the even bigger mistake of trying to banish Kristof when he came to collect. Kris had done something that rendered the necro's banishing powers impotent for the next few months, a reminder that you didn't screw with a Nast—even a dead one.

So all I had to do was track down Kristof and ask for his help. Sounds easy enough . . . except for the part about asking Kristof for help. Oh, he'd give it to me—without a moment's hesitation and with no expectation of anything in return. That was the problem. When I took something, I always gave something back—no favors owed, no debt remaining. While I counted Kris as a friend—the best I had in the ghost world—I hated asking him for anything. I'd taken enough from him already.

Better to try again on my own.

Jaime's dressing room was empty.

"Damn," I muttered.

There were ways to track a necro, but I hadn't bothered to learn them. We were in Chicago, in late March. If she'd left the building, she'd have taken her coat, which was gone, as was her purse. But the suitcase with her outfit for the show was still here. I remembered her bout of dry heaves earlier, and guessed she'd gone onstage with an empty stomach. Now she'd likely slipped out for chow.

I considered dropping in on Savannah, giving Jaime time to eat and return. It'd only been a few hours since my last check-in, but a lot can happen to a teenage girl in a few hours. And yet . . . well, I had Jaime in my sights, and I hated to veer off track, even for Savannah. I'd almost certainly have time for a check-in after dealing with Jaime, as I waited for the Fates to prepare Janah. Better to stay on the trail for now.

I found Jaime a few doors down, sitting at a café window, pushing salad around her plate.

"Doesn't look very appetizing to me, either," I said.

This time she didn't jump, just turned and glared.

"You know what I don't get?" I said, taking the seat across from her. "How they can serve weeds like dandelion greens and expect people to pay triple what they would for regular lettuce."

"Leave me alone," she said, without moving her lips.

"I just want to talk to you."

"And this seems like a good place to do it?" she whispered. "Do you know what I'm doing right now? I'm talking to myself."

Her gaze cut to the table beside her, where an elderly woman stared, brow furrowed, at the poor woman carrying on a conversation with an empty chair.

"Damn. That *is* a problem."

"Which is why you aren't supposed to contact me in public," she said, again trying to talk without moving her lips.

"You want to go outside?"

"I'm eating."

"Doesn't look like it."

Another glare. She forked a few weeds into her mouth.

"Tell you what, then," I said. "You eat, I'll talk."

She opened her mouth to snap something back, then stopped and rubbed a hand over her eyes. Her shoulders sagged, and when she pulled her hand away, there was an exhaustion in her face that no makeup could hide.

"Go ahead," she murmured.

She listened, without comment, to an edited version of my story. Then she stifled a snort of laughter.

"Eve Levine, on a mission from God. I really must be wearing my stupid face today."

"Trust me, if I were making this up, I'd have come up with something more believable. Remember a couple of years ago when Paige and Lucas ended up in the ghost world? Ever wonder how they got back? I cut a deal. Paige was there. Call her up and ask. She's not supposed to talk about it, but she'll confirm it."

"Oh, don't worry, I *will* make that call. As soon as I'm near a phone."

"Good. Please do that."

Some of her unease evaporated, but there was still a healthy dose of caution behind her shuttered gaze. Nothing new for me. I'd spent my life trying to build a reputation as a fair dealer, but when you've also built a rep in the black arts, no one ever gives a shit about how fair you are. Blast a person's eyes from their sockets, and you can be sure that story will blow through the grapevine faster than an energy bolt, but somehow, the part about the "victim" siccing a demon on you gets lost in the transmission.

I opened my mouth to say more, when something across the café caught my attention. I'm not easily distracted, but this was a sight to divert even the most focused mind. A man, in his early thirties, weaving between tables, with his head in his hands—literally, his severed head in his hands. Gore trickled from his neck stump, congealing on the collar of his dress shirt. Intestine poked through a small hole in his shirt. All around him people continued to eat and talk and laugh. Which could only mean one thing.

"Ghost at ten o'clock," I murmured to Jaime. "And it's a ripe one."

She turned and gave a tiny groan, then sank into her chair.

"Not a first-time visitor, I'm guessing," I said.

The man strode up to the table. His gaze cut to me.

"What are you looking at, spook?" he snarled.

"Exactly what you want me to be looking at," I said. "Kill the theatricals. The necro is not impressed, and neither am I."

"Oh, does the horror of my death offend you? Well, excuse me. Next time, I'll make sure I die all neat and tidy." He slammed his head onto Jaime's salad plate. "There. Better?"

Jaime's cheeks paled. I swung my gaze up to glare at the ghost . . . only his eyes weren't there, which made the move slightly less effective. I glowered down at him.

"She's not talking to you until you put your head back on," I said.

"Fuck y—"

"Put your goddamned head back on now."

He crossed his arms. "Make me."

I slammed my open palm into his ear. His head flew off the table, rolled across the floor, and settled in front of a seeing-eye dog. The dog lifted its muzzle, and its nostrils flared as it picked up the whiff of decay.

"Yum," I said. "Go on, boy. Take a bite."

The ghost's body flew across the restaurant, plowing through tables and diners. Beside me, Jaime made muffled snorting noises, stifling laughter. She mouthed, "Thank you."

The decapitated ghost stomped back to the table. Only he was decapitated no more, having apparently decided his head was safer attached to his shoulders. He'd also freshened up his wardrobe. This would be his normal ghost self. The headless accountant look was a glamour, a trick some ghosts used to revert to their death body—the condition they'd been in when they'd died—either to play on a necromancer's sympathy or to scare the bejesus out of humans with a little necro blood.

"Now, doesn't that feel better?" I said.

"Oh, you thought that was funny, did you?" he said, advancing on me. "It's always funny to pick on those less fortunate than yourself. Maybe when you're done here, you can go back to paradise, and have a good laugh, tell them how you abused the earth-spook."

"Earth-spook?"

"I'm a spirit in torment," the man said, his voice rising like a preacher at the pulpit. "Condemned to tread the earthly realm until my soul finds peace. For five years— five unimaginably long years—I've been trapped here, unable to move into the light, seeking only a few minutes of a necromancer's time—"

Jaime thudded face-first onto the table and groaned. The elderly woman at the next table inched her chair in the other direction.

"See how she treats me?" the man said to me. "She could set me free, but no, she's too busy going on talk shows, telling people how she helps tormented spirits find peace. When it comes to an actual spirit, though? In actual torment? Who only wants to avenge himself on the driver who ended his life, left his wife a widow, his children orphans—"

"You don't have any children," Jaime said through her teeth.

"Because I died before I could!"

I leaned toward Jaime and lowered my voice. "Look, the guy's a jerk, but if you helped him, you could get him off your back—"

She swung to her feet and strode toward the door. When I jogged up beside her, she said in a low voice, "Ask him how he died."

The ghost was right behind me, and answered before I could ask. "I remember it well. The last day of my life. I was happy, at peace with the world—"

"There's no Oscar for death scenes," I said. "The facts."

"I was driving home after a business meeting," he began.

"A meeting held in a bar," Jaime added as she turned into an alley.

"It was after office hours," he said. "Nothing wrong with a drink or two."

"Or five or six." She stopped, out of earshot of the sidewalk now, and turned to me. "Coroner reported a blood-alcohol level of at least point two five."

"Sure, okay, I was drunk," the man said. "But that wasn't the problem. The problem was a seventeen-year-old kid joyriding in my lane!"

"You were in *her* lane," Jaime said. "Got a police report to prove it. Who killed you? The idiot who got behind the wheel of his convertible, so pissed he couldn't even fasten his seat belt. That kid you hit will spend the rest of her life wearing leg braces. And you want me to help you exact revenge on *her*?"

I turned on the man, eyes narrowing. He met my gaze and took a slow step back, then wheeled and stalked away.

"Don't think this is done!" he called over his shoulder. "I'm coming back. And next time you won't have your ghost-bitch bodyguard to protect you."

"You want my help, Eve?" Jaime said. "Make sure he *doesn't* come back. Ever."

I smiled. "Be glad to."

Massachusetts / 1892

THE NIX SNIFFED THE AIR. IT REEKED OF HORSE AND human, the sweat and shit of both. That hadn't changed. She stood in the intersection of a street wide enough for four or five buggies to pass. Metal rails were embedded in the road, and a strange horseless carriage glided along them. Wooden poles lined the street, with wires strung from pole to pole, crisscrossing over the rows of brick buildings three, four, even five stories high.

Gone were the bustling markets, the narrow cobbled streets, the pretty little shops she remembered. The last time she'd walked the earth, this New World had been nothing more than a few bleak settlements on a wild continent, a place to send murderers and thieves.

The Nix rolled her shoulders, twisting her neck, trying to get used to the feel of this new form. In all the years she'd inhabited Marie-Madeline, she'd never quite grown accustomed to the stink of it, the pain and tedium of a mortal existence. Still, there had been a freedom there that she'd never known in her natural form—the freedom to act in the living world and wreak her own chaos. But now she was in another shape, somewhere between human and demon, a ghost.

A horse and coach veered toward her. She reached out,

fingers curving into claws, ready to rip a handful of horse-flesh as the beast ran past. The horse raced through her hand without so much as a panicked roll of its eyes. She hissed as it continued down the road. Even a human ghost should be able to spook a horse. Once, her very presence would have put such fear into the beast that it would have trampled anyone who came near. She closed her eyes, and imagined the chaos she could have created. And now what? After two hundred years of damnation, had she escaped only to moan and lament what she had lost? No, there had to be a way—there was always a way.

The Nix took a few steps down the road, sampling the passing humans, tasting the thoughts of each. The men's minds were now closed to her. She'd learned that soon after her escape. Having died in the form of a woman, her powers were now restricted to that gender.

Her gaze slid from face to face, looking for the signs, searching the eyes first, then the mind. Sometimes humans hit on a moment of profundity more complete than their dim minds could comprehend, and they took that nugget of truth and dumped it in the refuse for the bards and the poets to find, and mangle into yodeling paeans to love. The eyes were indeed the windows to the soul. Clear eyes, and she passed by without pause. A few wisps of cloud behind a gaze, and she might hesitate, but likely not. Storms were what she wanted—the roiling, dark storms of a tempest-tossed psyche.

She made it halfway down the street, finding nothing more than a thundercloud or two. Then she had to pause before a woman with downcast eyes. In her late twenties with a plain, broad face, the woman waited on the side-walk outside a store. A man exited the store, swarthy and rough-skinned, dressed in the clothes of a working man. As he saw the woman, a smile lit his face.

"Miz Borden," he said, tipping his hat. "How are you?"

The woman looked up with a shy smile. "Fine, thank you. And how are you?"

Before he could answer, a tall man with white whiskers strode from the store, his eyes blazing. He grabbed the woman by the arm and propelled her to the street without so much as a glance at the other man.

"What were you doing?" he hissed.

"Saying hello, Father. Mr. O'Neil greeted me, so I—"

"I don't care what he did. He's a farmhand. Not good enough for the likes of you."

What man is good enough for me, Father? None, if it means you and she would have to hire a second servant to replace me. The thought ran through the woman's mind, spat out on a wave of fury, but only the barest tightening of her lips betrayed it.

Her gaze lifted enough for the Nix to see eyes so clouded with hate they were almost black. The Nix chortled to herself. So she wished her father dead . . . just like Marie-Madeline. What an appropriate start to this new life.

The Nix reached out and stroked her fingers across the woman's pale cheek. *Would you like me to set you free, dear one? With pleasure.*

6

AN EARTH-SPOOK. THOUGH I'D NEVER HEARD THE term, I understood the concept. When we die, most of us go on to an afterlife, but a few stay behind. Some are what the headless accountant purported to be—spirits trapped by unfinished business. Only they aren't really trapped. Like the crying woman in Savannah's house, they're stalled, thinking they have unfinished business.

This could have been the headless accountant's problem, but I'd lay even money that he fell into category two of these "earth-spooks," those who were sentenced to this limbo for a period after death. If so, he wasn't going anywhere until the almighty powers decided he'd learned his lesson. At this rate, he'd be pestering necromancers into the next millennium. But I was about to strike one off his calling list.

Since my quarry was trapped in this plane and couldn't teleport out, following him was easy enough. Although I followed less than fifty feet behind, he never noticed me. I'd changed into a baggy windbreaker and blue jeans, put my hair in a ponytail, and slapped on a ball cap. I kept a cover spell readied, with my blinding power as a backup, though I wasn't sure how well either worked in this plane. I had a lot to learn.

I gumshoed him halfway across the Windy City, taking two city buses plus the el train. Then he marched across the lawn of the ugliest building I had ever seen. It looked like my high school, which—to me—had always looked like a jail. Part of that was my own feelings about formal education, but I swear the architect of that school had a real grudge against students. Probably spent his teen years stuffed inside a locker, and vowed revenge on every generation to follow. This building was that same shit brown brick, that same looming bland facade, those same tiny windows. It was even surrounded by a similar ten-foot fence.

My first guess was, of course: jail. Seemed like a good place to keep Mr. DUI. But when I passed the ancient sign out front, I read: DALEWOOD PSYCHIATRIC HOSPITAL. So the headless accountant was hanging out in a psych hospital? Didn't seem to be helping.

In the parking lot, I waited behind a minivan until my ghost went in through a side door, where a half-dozen staff members stood getting a quick nicotine fix, huddled against the bitter chill as the sun dropped below the horizon. I crossed the grass-free strip of lawn, skirting past the smokers. Two steps from the door, a beefy bulldog-ugly orderly stepped into my path. I didn't slow, expecting to pass right through. Instead, I hit a solid wall of fat and muscle. Another ghost. Damn.

"Where you think you're going, boy?" he rumbled.

As I lifted my head, he blinked, realizing his gender blunder. "Look, lady, this is private property. You wanna join, you gotta talk to Ted."

I looked him full in the eyes, and switched on my blinding power.

"You deaf or something, hon?" he said. "I know I'm good-looking, but you ain't my type. Stop staring and start walking or I'm going to introduce my boot to your pretty butt."

As quick as I am to correct an insult, I'm just as quick to recognize an obstacle when I see one. Sure, I could probably just kick his ass the old-fashioned way, but that might tip off my quarry. So I murmured an insincere apology and trekked back down to the end of the laneway.

As a kid, when my mother had harangued me to get involved in extracurricular activities, I'd signed up for track-and-field. Was pretty damned good at it, too. Got to the city finals. I can still remember that moment, poised at the starting gate, before a crowd that had included my mother and all the Coven Elders. I crouched, waiting for the starter pistol, then leapt forward . . . and snagged my shoelace in the gate. Fell flat on my face. And that was pretty much how I felt now. My first job in the ghost world, and I was sucking dust at the starting line.

The worst of it was that, like forgetting to tie my shoe, my mistake was inexcusable. That earth-spook bouncer had clearly known I was a ghost—that's why he'd stepped into my path. How had he known? I'd been careful not to walk through anything. And why hadn't *I* recognized what *he* was? Basic afterlife skills. Time to admit I needed help.

*   *   *

My house was in Savannah's historic district. Before my daughter had been born, I'd scoured the supernatural world for greater sources of power, and a few of those stops had been in Savannah. I'd loved the place. I don't know why. Savannah was the epitome of genteel Southern charm, and there wasn't an ounce of gentility or charm in my body, nor did I want there to be. Yet something about the city struck a chord in me, so much so that I'd named my daughter after it. After I died, and had my pick of places to live, I'd chosen Savannah.

My house was a two-story antebellum manor, both levels decked out with verandahs and thin columns looped with ivy. A squat wrought-iron fence fronted the tiny yard, which was filled with so many palms, ferns, and rhododendrons that I had yet to see a blade of grass.

Kristof calls this my "Southern Belle" house, and laughs each time he says it. When he teases me, I remind him of where he's ended up. This is a man who has spent his life in ten-thousand-square-foot penthouses, with every possible modern convenience at his fingertips and a full staff ready to operate those conveniences for him, should he not wish to strain said fingertips. And where had he chosen to live in the afterlife? On a boat. Not a hundred-foot luxury yacht, but a tiny houseboat that creaks as if it's about to crack in half.

Kris wouldn't be at his houseboat now. He'd be in the same place he'd spent almost every evening for the past two and a half years. At my house. He'd started coming by as soon as he'd realized we shared the same ghost dimension. Less than a week after his death, he'd showed up at my door, walked in, and made himself comfortable, just as he used to do in my apartment thirteen years before.

At first, I hadn't known what to make of it, chalked it up to death shock, and told him, very nicely, that I didn't think this was a good idea. He ignored me. Kept ignoring me, even when I moved on to less polite forms of rejection. After a year, I couldn't be bothered objecting with anything stronger than a deep sigh, and he knew he'd won. Now I expected to see him there, even looked forward to it.

So when I peered through the front window, for a second, I saw exactly what I expected to see: Kristof sitting in his usual armchair before a crackling fire, enjoying a single-malt Scotch and his evening reading material—a comic book or a back issue of *Mad* magazine. Then the image vanished and, instead, I saw an empty fireplace, an empty chair, and a stoppered decanter.

I blinked back a dart of panic. Kristof was always here, as reliable as the tides. Well, except on Thursdays, but that's because on Thursdays we—Shit! It *was* Thursday, wasn't it?

I raced through a travel incantation, and my house disappeared.

A blast of cold air hit me. The bone-chilling cold of the cement floors seeped through the soles of my sneakers. In front of me was a scarred slab of Plexiglas, so crisscrossed with scratches I'd need my Aspicio powers to see what lay on the other side. To my right rose a wave of bleachers, wooden planks so worn that I couldn't guess what their original color had been.

I moved past the Plexiglas to an open section of the boards. Two teams of ghosts ripped around the ice, skates flying, their shouts and laughter mingling with those from the stands. I scanned the ice for Kris's blond head. The first place I looked, I found him: the penalty box.

Hockey had always been Kris's secret passion. Secret because it wasn't a proper hobby for a Nast, especially a Nast heir. There were two sports a Cabal son was expected to play. Golf, because so many deals were brokered on the greens, and racquetball, because there was nothing like a kick-ass game to show your VPs why they should never cross you in the boardroom. Baseball and basketball were good spectator sports for impressing prospective partners with skybox and courtside seats. But hockey? That was little better than all-star wrestling. Nasts did not attend hockey games, and they sure as hell didn't play them.

As a child, Kristof had never so much as strapped on a pair of skates. Not surprising for a native Californian. At Harvard, he'd had a roommate on the hockey team. Get Kristof close to anything that sounds like fun, and he has to give it a shot. Once back in L.A., he'd joined a league, using a false name so his father wouldn't find out.

When we'd been together, I'd gone to all of his games. Yet I'd waffled about it every week, telling him maybe I'd show up, if I had the time, but don't count on it. Of course, I'd never missed a game. I couldn't resist watching him play, beaming behind his face mask as he whipped around the ice, grinning whether he scored, missed, or got knocked flat on his ass. Even sitting in the penalty box, he could barely manage to keep a straight face. How could I miss out on that?

He'd joined this ghost-world team about six months ago, and by then, we'd been close enough that I'd made sure I was always in the stands to watch.

I checked the scoreboard and wondered whether I

should wait for the period break or head back to the hospital and try to muddle through on my own. I was about to teleport back to the return marker I'd laid, when Kristof hit the boards beside me, hard enough to make me jump.

"Hello, gorgeous," he said.

He pulled up to the side and grinned, his smile so wide it made my heart do a double-flip. Impossible for a ghost, I know, but I swear I still felt it flip, as it had since the first time I'd seen that grin; the gateway to "my" Kris, the one he kept hidden from everyone else.

As he planted his forearms on the boards and leaned over, a shock of hair flipped up from the back, mussed out of place by his slam into the boards. I resisted the urge to reach out and smooth it down, but let myself move a step closer, within touching distance.

"I thought you were in the box," I said.

"They let me out every once in a while."

"Silly them."

Our eyes met and his grin stretched another quarter-inch. Another schoolgirl flip—followed by a very un-schoolgirl wave of heat. He leaned even farther over the boards, lips parting to say something.

"Hey, Kris!" someone yelled behind him. "If you want to flirt with Eve, tell her to meet you in the penalty box. You'll be back there soon enough."

Kristof flashed him a gloved middle finger.

"He's right," I said, shaking it off as I stepped back. "Time to play, not talk. I just wanted to say I'm sorry for being late. I was busy and completely forgot."

A soft sigh as the grin fell away. "What did Savannah need now?"

"Sav . . . ?"

Having spent days in the time-delayed throne room

and that wasteland dimension, I'd forgotten that only hours had really passed since I'd last seen Kristof.

"No, it wasn't Savannah," I said. "The Fates have been keeping me busy. Seems you're not the only one who thinks I need a job."

"The Fates? What—?"

A shout from a teammate cut him short. He waved to say he'd be right there.

"Go on," I said. "I can talk to you later."

"Uh-uh. You aren't tossing out that teaser and running off. Stay right there."

He skated back to talk to his teammates, and within minutes was off the ice, back in street clothes, and escorting me outside to talk.

"Bounty-hunting for the Fates, hmm?" he said, settling onto a swing-set outside the arena. "Well, if it keeps you from obsessing—" He bit the sentence short. "If you need to know how to deal with haunters, you've come to the right place."

"You've haunted?"

"Surprised?"

I laughed. "Not really."

"I tried it. Didn't see the attraction. A hobby for cowards and bullies. But I learned enough to help you take care of this guy. First, we need to teach you how to get past the earth-spooks without being made as a ghost." He leapt off the swing, landing awkwardly, but righting himself before he toppled. "Ghost lesson number one, coming up."

"You don't need to—"

"I know."

His fingers closed around mine and we disappeared.

Back inside the arena, we switched dimensions, slipping into the living world. On the other side of the Plexiglas barrier, a troop of preschoolers lurched past on tiny skates. Decked out in snowsuits that made them as wide as they were tall, they bobbed and swayed like a flock of drunken penguins, struggling to cross the few yards of ice between themselves and the instructor. One near the middle stumbled, and knocked over a few of her fellows. A cry went up and a gaggle of parents swooped down. A few kids on the edges of the pack decided to topple, too, so they wouldn't be left out of the sympathy rush.

"You must have taught Sean and Bryce how to—" I stopped, noticing I was alone. "Kris?"

"Eve!"

Kristof slid onto center ice, arms up as he pirouetted in his street shoes. I bit back a laugh.

"Test number one," he yelled. "How can you tell I'm a ghost?"

" 'Cause you're standing in the middle of a frigging ice rink wearing loafers and a golf shirt, and no one's yelling, 'Hey, get that crazy bastard off the ice!' "

He grinned and shoe-skated over to the boards. When he reached the gate, he grabbed the edge with both hands and jumped. Fifteen years ago, he could sail right over it, even in full hockey gear. Today, well . . .

"Hey, at least you cleared it," I said as he got up off the floor.

"You know, I hate to complain," he said, brushing invisible dirt from his pants. "The Fates take away all those twinges and aches of middle age, and that's great, but would it kill them to give us back a little flexibility?"

I kicked one leg up onto the top of the boards. "Seems fine to me."

A mock glower. "No one likes a show-off, Eve. And, I could point out, if I'd died at thirty-seven, instead of forty-seven, I'd have been able to do that, too."

"A good excuse."

"And I'm sticking with it. On to test number two."

Before I could object, he jogged into a group of parents hovering around the boards.

"How can you tell I'm a ghost now?" he called.

"Because you're walking through things. I know all this, Kris. It's common sense. If I want a ghost to mistake me for a corporeal being, then I have to act corporeal. When I passed by that group of people outside the hospital, I moved *around* them."

"Ah, but you missed something. Last demo. Professional level now."

He bounded up a half-dozen steps, then walked into a bleacher aisle. As he slipped past people, he was careful to make it look as if he were squeezing around their knees, even murmuring the odd "Excuse me." Halfway down he turned and lifted his hands expectantly.

I shook my head. "You would've fooled me."

"Only because *you've* never gone haunting. Haunters have to be extremely careful. Bump into the wrong ghost, and you'll be reported in a heartbeat. Now I'm going to try it again, and this time don't watch me. Watch them."

He came back my way, still skirting knees and whispering apologies. I watched the faces of those he passed, but saw nothing. They just kept doing what they were doing, acting—

"Acting as if you aren't there," I said. "That's it. They don't react to you."

"Correct," he said, jogging down the steps. "At that hospital, you walked past a group of people, and not one even glanced your way. That isn't natural. Especially if any of them were male."

A wink and an appreciative once-over. Had I been alive, I'm sure I would have blushed. But Kris just smiled and launched into a quick list of tips, the compliment tossed out as casually as a comment on the weather. Typical. Kris knew all the tricks, all the ways to say "I want you back" without ever speaking the words. An offhand compliment, a lingering look, a casual touch—silly little things that somehow sent my brain spinning.

I wanted him back. No question about that. I'd never stopped wanting him, and there were times when I'd look at him, feel that ache of longing, and wonder why the hell I *was* holding out. I wouldn't be going anywhere I hadn't been before. And that's exactly why I wouldn't take that next step. Because I *had* been there before.

I wasn't cut out for relationships. I've never felt the need to share my life, never sought out others for more than casual friendship and professional contacts. When someone did worm their way in—Ruth Winterbourne, then Kristof, then Savannah—I let them down, making choices that always seemed so right at the time. As much as I wanted to say I now resisted Kristof to avoid hurting him, I knew I was, at least in equal part, protecting myself.

Kris finished his list of tips. "That's all I can think of, for now. Time to put the theory into practice."

"Practice? You mean with the haunters? Thanks for the offer, but—"

"It isn't an offer; it's a demand. You owe me."

"Owe you?" I sputtered.

"I tried to give you some work at the courthouse—work that would have given me an excuse to pursue adventures otherwise unsuitable for an esteemed member of the judicial system. You turned me down. Robbed me of the first chance for hell-raising I've had in—"

"Hours. Maybe days."

He shot a grin my way. "Much too long. Now you've brought me a replacement opportunity, and I'm not about to let it slip past."

"So I'm stuck with you?"

His grin widened. "For now and forever."

I muttered under my breath, grabbed his hand, and teleported us back to my marker.

Before we were close enough to the hospital for the phantom bouncer to recognize me, we skipped around to the back. Once inside, we went in search of our haunters. Didn't take long to find them. Just had to follow the screams.

1

WE WERE IN A DARKENED THERAPY ROOM. THE SHOUTS
came from the adjoining room. Using my Aspicio powers,
I cleared a peephole in the wall and looked through.
Kristof slid onto the desktop to wait, knowing only I
could see through the holes I created.

Three people sat in the next room. The oldest was a
woman in her late fifties, seated behind a steel desk. She
wore a multicolored caftan, enormous loop earrings, and
a necklace with an ugly wooden elephant slipping trunk-
first between her breasts. The elephant looked scared. I
didn't blame him.

The woman was leaning back in her chair, writing in a
small notepad. Over her head, a huge poster screamed,
YOU ARE THE CAPTAIN OF YOUR OWN SHIP. The photo was
the famous *Titanic* shot of Leo and Kate with their arms
spread on the bow. Stick me in front of that poster for an
hour a week and *I'd* be ready to commit myself.

A man and a woman, both in their late twenties, both
dressed in jeans and sweatshirts, sat across from the
therapist. The woman had one foot pulled under her, just
as comfy as could be. Her neighbor was so tense he
seemed to be hovering above the chair, poised to leap up
at any provocation.

"No, she's right here!" the young man said. "Why can't you see her?"

"Tell me what *you* see," the therapist intoned.

"I've told you!" the man said. "I've told you and I've told you and I've—"

"Barton," the woman said. "Remember what we say? Anger has no place in our house. Like trash, we must take it to the curb."

"God, what a bunch of horse crap," the younger woman said, yawning as she stretched her legs. "Tell her she's a bitch. A stupid, blind old cow."

"You're blind," he said to the therapist. "If you can't see her sitting right here—"

"For God's sake, Bart. Stop being such a pussy. She's a bitch. Say it to her face."

"No!"

"What, Barton?" the therapist asked. "What's she saying to you?"

Barton clamped his mouth shut and shook his head. The younger woman leaned over and whispered into his ear. He tried to brush her off, like a buzzing fly, but his hand passed right through her face.

"Go on, tell her," the ghost urged Barton. "Better yet, take a swing. Smash her smug face in. Now, *that'd* be real therapy."

Barton leapt to his feet and took a swing . . . at the ghost. When his fist passed through her, he threw up his hands and howled. Then he stopped and slowly turned to the therapist, who scribbled furiously. The ghost convulsed with laughter.

I clenched my fists and turned to Kristof.

"Can I smack her? Just one good smack—"

"Oh, we'll do better than that," he said. "But first we have to find the others."

Again, the ghosts gave themselves away, this time not by making patients scream, but by sitting around chatting about it. No one knows why some mental patients can see ghosts. Maybe mental illness breaks down the boundary between possible and impossible, so, like small children and animals, the brains of the mentally ill weren't always jumping in to edit their perceptions. Or it could be that these people have necro blood, but their families have strayed from the supernatural community. When they began hearing voices and seeing apparitions, everyone around them would assume the problem was psychological.

So when we came across a group of four people, laughing about how they'd made a patient piss his pants, we knew we'd found our haunters. Either that or we'd found the world's first psych hospital staffed by the National Sadists Institute.

"No, no, no!" said an elderly man with a snow-white Van Dyke beard. "We had one better than that. Ted, re-member Bruce? The one you convinced he could fly?"

"Oh, yeah," chortled a ghost with his back to my wall.

"What happened?" asked a plump teenage girl.

Ted shifted to better face his audience and I recognized my headless accountant. I backed up and motioned to Kristof that I'd found our ghost. He nodded, and I returned to my peephole.

". . . sailed clean off the roof." Ted was laughing so hard he could barely get the words out. "Like Superman. Only, as he soon discovered, he couldn't fly. Landed right on Peterman's Jag. Hit so hard his fucking teeth popped out like Chiclets. Peterman was picking them out of his seats for weeks. That's what he gets for leaving his sun-roof open."

The haunters roared with laughter.

The old man waved his arms again, like a bird attempting takeoff. "The best part was when the dumb fuck hits the roof. For a second, he just lies there, dying. Then his spirit starts to separate. He looks around, gives the biggest grin you've ever seen, then jumps up and dances a little jig on the top of the Jag, yelling, 'I did it! I did it! I can fly!' Then—"

Ted stepped in front of the old man. "Then he just happens to look down, and there, under his feet, is this body. *His* body. He stops—freezes on the spot—stares down, and goes, 'Oh.' "

"Just like that," the old man chortled. " 'Oh.' "

I looked at Kristof.

"More smacking in order?" he murmured.

"Smacking's too good. Think I can rip out their intestines and use them for harp strings?"

"You could try. Or . . ."

He tilted his head toward the paper-thin wall.

". . . are the best," someone said, then sighed. "We haven't had a decent new one in weeks."

I glanced at Kristof. We smiled at each other.

We found an empty room farther down the hall, where we could talk without being overheard by the haunters.

I perched on the bed. "So one of us will play patient and the other should be a nurse or—"

"First, I need you in a nurse's uniform."

"I don't think I saw any nurses on the way in. I should go see what kind of outfits—"

As I slid off the bed, he put out a hand to stop me.

"I think I can handle this," he said. "May I?"

Being able to change women out of their clothing may be most adolescent boys' idea of heaven, but ghosts can't do it unless they're given tacit permission by the other party. I closed my eyes and concentrated on letting Kris change my clothes.

"There," he said.

I looked down and saw my boobs looking back at me. Well, the tops of them anyway, stuffed into a white shirt with cleavage so low I was bound to pop out if I so much as sighed. I wore a skintight white nurse's dress that barely covered my rear. Speaking of adolescent fantasies . . .

I glared at Kris, who was grinning like a thirteen-year-old.

"Hey, it's a nurse's uniform," he said.

"Yeah . . . from a porn movie."

A wide grin. "Works for me."

As I sighed, he stepped closer, finger sliding along the hem of my dress, rippling the fabric so it tickled against my thighs.

"Remember the last time you played nurse for me?" he murmured. "I was working at the New York office, and you came up for the weekend. We were supposed to get together for dinner, but you called—"

"I remember," I said, quickstepping away. "Now, we need a plan—"

"Oh, you had a plan." He stepped as close to me as he could get without touching. "I was on my way to a meeting and you called and said, 'I can't wait for tonight, Kris.'"

I opened my mouth to say something—anything—but his gaze met mine, and the words dried up, leaving me standing there, lips parted, face tilted up to his.

He continued, "You said I didn't sound very good, and suggested I come by the hotel room so you could play nurse for me. Which you did. Most effectively. Ordered me into bed . . . and, by the time you were done, I couldn't have got out of it if I wanted to." A slow grin. "Of course, neither could you."

Thank God for ghost-hood sometimes. No need to worry about pounding hearts or sweaty palms or heavy breathing. All I had to do was keep my gaze down, and he wouldn't know how badly I wanted to say "To hell with it" and cross that last quarter-inch between us.

His lips moved closer to my ear. "I remember every second of that afternoon, Eve. I've replayed it so many times . . . in bed, in the shower, even in the car, once during a traffic jam—I was sitting there and I saw a billboard for the hotel we'd stayed in and next thing you know . . ." A deep chuckle. "I found a way to make the delay a whole lot more bearable."

I backpedaled so fast I fell right through the wall. Kristof grabbed my arm to steady me, but I moved out of his way.

I righted myself and glowered at him. "God, you are—"

A quick grin. "Incorrigible?"

"Oh, that wasn't the word I had in mind."

"I like incorrigible. Much better than desperate. Or horny. Or desperately horny."

"Arghh!" With a blink, I changed back into my jeans. "There, better?"

He took my hand and pressed it to his crotch. "Nope, no change. Have I ever mentioned how great your ass looks in those—"

"If you do, you're going to find yourself on the wrong end of a shock-bolt spell."

"Hmmm."

"Don't even try it."

"Not going to. I'm just wondering whether I should risk unzipping or just let you continue like this."

"Like what?" I followed his gaze down to see my hand still pressed against his crotch. "Damn you!"

"I take it that's a no on the unzipping?"

I bit back a retort and settled for striding across the room, giving my brain time to find its way out of the lust-fog. "I need a real nurse's uniform."

"No, you're going to be the patient."

"But you said—"

"I said *I* needed to put you in a nurse's uniform. I didn't say it was part of the plan."

I rolled my eyes and fought the urge to laugh. "Okay, tell me what you have in mind."

I was going to play patient—a more thorough disguise, since two of the haunters had already seen me. Stained, baggy sweats, my hair snarled and oily, eyes red and sunken—the look of someone for whom personal hygiene has been a low priority for a while. After I finished the glamour, Kristof conjured a wheelchair for me, and we headed back to the haunters.

8

"YOU SHOULD HAVE SEEN BART'S FACE." THE YOUNG woman who'd been taunting Barton to violence had returned to the other haunters. "Franco couldn't write her report fast enough. She was on the phone to Peterson before Chang even came to collect ol' Bart."

Kristof wheeled me into the room, and silence fell as every eye turned our way. Outfitted in a generic orderly's uniform, he grumbled under his breath about the nurses being too busy to help settle me in. He steered carefully, making sure not to run through anything that should be solid. He left me in the middle of the room, and grabbed the folded bedding from the foot of the bed. With a quick conjure, he duplicated it into a ghost-world set, then began unfolding the top sheet. I sat motionless, chin on my chest, gaze downcast.

"Well, looky-looky," chortled Ted, my headless accountant.

I lifted my head and scanned the room. I frowned over at Kristof.

"We got audio," the teenage girl said. "But I think the video's on the fritz."

"Damn," the other woman said.

"I prefer the listeners," Ted said as he sauntered

toward me. "Much more unsettling, isn't it, honey? You can hear us, but you can't see a damned thing."

"Who—who's there?" I said.

Ted leaned down to my ear. "I'm right here. Can't you see me?"

"N—no."

"Well, maybe that's because you're crazy."

The others laughed.

"Only crazy people hear voices," Ted whispered. "Are you crazy, honey? Lost your marbles? Not playing with a full deck? Loony as a . . . loony as a . . . "

"Jaybird," Kris said.

They all looked over at Kristof. He shook out another sheet, and let it drift onto the bed.

"Did he . . . ?" Ted said.

"I don't think so," the old man said. "Maybe he was just—"

"Jaybird," Kris said, his back still to them. "The word you want to finish your insult is 'jaybird.' There are others, but that is most correct. Loony as a jaybird."

He pivoted slowly. His eyes glowed neon blue. It was a simple glamour, but the teen girl gasped and backpedaled.

Kristof lifted his hands over his head, a rain of sparks falling from his fingertips. The ghosts stared like cavemen seeing their first eclipse. As Kris's hands fell, the orderly's uniform morphed into a high-collared black shirt and black pants. A final flourish, and bolts of energy leapt from his palms, rebounding off the far wall and ping-ponging through the room.

The old man ran for the door. Kris lifted one finger in a fast circle—the gesture for a barrier spell. He let me cast the actual incantation under my breath. Barrier spells were sorcerer magic, but Kris's was less than reliable, and he knew it.

When the old man smacked into the barrier, he tottered back. The woman bolted for the nearest wall, only to hit the barrier there.

"Who are you?" Ted demanded.

"Who am I?" Kris's voice took on a tone that had cowed many an insubordinate junior exec. "You dare to ask? You *need* to ask?"

"See, dearest?" I said as I rose from my wheelchair. "I told you he didn't recognize me earlier."

The teen girl stared at me—the new me, cleaned up and dressed in a short black dress with a mandarin collar to match Kris's. Ted turned and blinked hard.

"You," he said. "You're that bitch from—"

I slammed a shock bolt into his gut. Didn't hurt him, but he felt the jolt, especially when he hit the floor. I strolled over, and cast a binding spell that froze him bowed over, half-standing.

"There," I said. "That is the proper position to take before me. Leave it, and I'll give you something to make that shock feel like a love tap."

I broke the spell. Still crouched, he glanced around at his fellow haunters, but they all looked away.

Ted's gaze lifted to mine. "I don't know what kind of ghosts you guys are—"

"Ghosts!" Kris thundered, striding over to him. "First you trespass on our territory, then you mistake us for ghosts?"

"Your territory?" the old man said. "Is this yours? We didn't know—"

"Then your ignorance adds insult to injury. You have trespassed, and you shall pay."

"P—pay?" the teenage girl said. "But I didn't—I've only been here a week. They told me it was okay. They said no one would bother us—"

I caught her in a binding spell and she went silent.

"Thank you," Kris said. "Now, as for the rest of you . . ."

"May I have them?" I said. "Please? Something new to play with."

"Wait," the old man said. "We didn't know. It was an honest mistake. No one told us—"

"No one should need to tell you."

I glided over to Kristof. "I don't need quite so many pets. Perhaps we should show them that the gods aren't the only ones who can be merciful." I smiled. "I'm sure they would be indebted to us for our mercy."

"Yes," the old man said quickly. "Very indebted. Let us go, and you'll never have to worry about us coming here again."

Kris looked him in the eye, making his own blaze with the glamour. "We'd better not."

"Or you'll wish you'd stayed with me," I said.

I undid the barrier spell as Kris waved it away.

"Now go," he said.

They bolted for the nearest wall. I grabbed Ted as he leapt to his feet.

"I'm not giving up all my toys," I said. "You, I'll keep." I smiled, showing my teeth. "First, I'll teach you how to play hide-and-seek . . . with your head."

Ted's gaze shot to Kristof, eyes widening. "But you—you said—"

Kris only shrugged.

"Show me your guts again," I said. "I want to see how far I can pull out your intestines, maybe wrap them around your neck and use them as a leash."

Ted opened his mouth, but only a squeak came out.

"He'll make a fine pet, my dear," Kristof said as he stepped behind me. "I can't wait to hear him scream."

I smiled. "You won't have to wait long."

Kristof slid a hand across my bare thigh. As his fingers crept up to my rear, I leaned back into him, twisted to his ear, and whispered, "Keep going, and I'll play with *your* intestines."

A throaty chuckle, as if I'd said something wickedly sexy. His hand slid to the back of my leg . . . and stayed there. At a warning look from me, he withdrew, but not before tickling his fingers over my inner thigh and sending a shiver through me.

"Let's hurry," he murmured, loud enough for Ted to hear. "We'll take him down and show him his new home . . . see how fast you can make him scream."

He started a phony incantation, then stopped. I shot a questioning look over my shoulder.

"Perhaps we should have kept another," Kris said. "A guard might have proved useful, to ensure none of them returns, and no others take their place."

"Guard," Ted squeaked. "I'd make a great guard." He sidled toward Kris. "I'll watch the place for you, and keep out trespassers and anything else you—"

Kris flung him away with a knock-back spell.

I leaned back against Kristof. "You take him. I'll find another."

"*I'll* find you another."

I smiled. "Even better. And if this one doesn't do his job—"

"I will," Ted said. "I'll stay right in this hospital—"

"No, you'll stay right outside it," Kris said. "And you

won't bother any of the patients. They're ours, under our protection."

"Speaking of ours," I said. "What about Jaime?"

"Is she yours, too?" Ted said. "No problem. I'll stay away from her."

"Of course you will," Kris said. "Because you'll be here, on the grounds, and you will not leave until we return and tell you to go."

"Got it."

Kris made Ted swear a soul-binding oath. It was magical mumbo-jumbo, but Ted bought it . . . and the rain of sparks and ending clap of thunder were nice cinematic touches. Then Kris waved his hands, and a swirl of fog rose from the floor. When it enveloped us, we transported back to the ghost world, and found ourselves in an open field.

I poked Kristof in the chest. "*You* were amazing."

"The thunderclap was a bit much. And maybe the lightning bolts."

"Never. You were perfect."

As his eyes lit up, my laugh floated through the field.

"You miss that?" I said. "Not having flunkies telling you how wonderful you are?"

His gaze met mine, and his voice softened. "Never mattered. You're the only one who ever said it like it might be true."

I dropped my gaze and stepped back. "I should go and tell Jaime her problem's been solved. Thanks for—"

"Anytime. You know that."

I nodded. "I'm off, then. Check in with you later?"

"Please. Oh, one last thing. When you're talking to Jaime, I'm sure my name won't come up . . . but you might want to make sure that it doesn't."

I sighed. "What'd you do to her?"

"It wasn't me—"

"Let me rephrase that. What did your employees do to her on your orders? Or, on second thought, don't tell me." I rolled my eyes. "Guess I should have known—if I'd never done anything to her, you would have. I swear, between the two of us we've pissed off ninety-five percent of the supernatural world."

"And killed the other five."

"We gotta work on our people skills, Kris."

"And what would be the fun in that?"

I smiled, shook my head, then transported to Jaime's apartment.

9

IF I SUCCEEDED IN GETTING RID OF JAIME'S STALKER-spook, I was supposed to go to her apartment and wait for her there. When I found her apartment, I did indeed wait for her . . . waited at least a good ten minutes. Then I started hunting for clues to tell me where she'd gone. I found the answer on the calendar—she'd been invited to an event at some city councillor's place. That didn't give me much to go on, but I struck it lucky a second time by finding a small stack of invitations on her desk.

Of course, tonight's wasn't on the top of the pile. That would be too easy. So I had to drill down through them using my Aspicio powers. That took some work—I could easily have cleared a peephole right through the stack and the desk, but going down layer by layer was much tougher. After about thirty minutes of working at it, I got down to the right invitation. That provided me with an address. Then I had to pop back to my house in Savannah, grab my book of city maps, and find out where that address led. I only knew three travel codes for Chicago, so the closest I could get was six miles away. Could be worse, I guess, but it was still quite a hike.

When I finally arrived at the house, it was past midnight. The street was lined with cars, people spilling from the house, eager enough for fresh air that they were willing to brave the cold—or too drunk to notice it.

I found Jaime in the dining room, talking to an immaculately dressed and coifed woman in her fifties. Now, I'd learned my lesson back at the TV studio. Or, I should say, I admitted that Jaime had a point about ghosts shanghaiing her when she was in the middle of a conversation with a living person. So I hung back out of her line of vision, and waited. Waited some more. Waited another thirty seconds, then decided to slip closer and see if I could politely divert her attention.

As I drew near, I got a better look at Jaime's companion. Even from the back, she screamed upper-class professional, with perfect posture, a designer suit, and short hair artfully laced with silver, allowing the appearance of a graceful descent into maturity. An executive or a lawyer, maybe even the councillor hosting the party. Her posture and gestures oozed the confidence of a woman who's found her place in life and settled happily into it. But when I circled around enough to see her face, it told a different story. Deep-etched lines made me add another decade to my age estimate. Her eyes were rimmed with red but dry, her face taut, as if fighting to maintain composure.

"No, I completely understand," Jaime said. "Believe me, it's not a question of—"

"Is it money? Money is not an issue, Jaime. I've said that and I mean—"

"Money isn't the problem."

The woman's hands clenched around a food-stained napkin. "I'm sorry. I didn't mean to insult—"

"You didn't. But I can't help you. Honestly. If I could find your daughter—"

"I don't need you to find her. Just tell me if she's there. On the other side. I just need . . . it's been so long. I need to know."

Jaime snapped her gaze from the other woman's, her eyes shuttering. "You need resolution. I understand that. But it doesn't work that way."

"We could try. There's no harm in trying, is there?"

"There is, if it gets your hopes up. I—I'm sorry. I have to . . ."

She mumbled something, and darted away. I followed her through the next room and out the back door. She hurried past those gathered on the deck, and walked into the empty yard, pausing only when she reached the back fence and could go no farther, then leaned against it, shivering.

"That must be a shitty thing to have to do," I said.

Her head jerked up, then she saw me. I walked over.

"You know you can't help her. *I* know you can't help her. But nothing you say is going to convince her of that. You did your best."

Jaime wrapped her arms around her chest and said nothing.

"Got rid of your headless stalker," I said. "If he ever comes around again, give me a shout, but I don't think he will."

She nodded, still shivering so hard I could hear her teeth chatter.

"You want to go someplace warmer?" I asked.

"Not cold. Just . . ." She shook her head, then gave herself a full-bodied shake, and straightened. "Thanks for the help. With the stalker. I owe you."

"And I'm sure you'll get the chance to repay me soon. I don't know exactly what I'll need or when I'll need it, but we should set up something, so I can find you when I need to."

She agreed. The Fates gave me just long enough to make arrangements for contacting Jaime again, then sent the Searchers to retrieve me.

The Searchers dropped me off in a foyer the size of a school gymnasium. It was white marble, like the throne room, but without any decoration or furnishing—a room for passing through on your way someplace else.

Lots of people were passing through it at that very moment. Wraith-clerks, those who kept our world running smoothly. Wraiths are pure spirits, beings that have never inhabited the world of the living, and they look more like classic ghosts than we do. Everything about them is white. Even their irises are a blue so pale that if it weren't set against the whites of their eyes, you'd miss the color altogether. Their clothing and skin are almost translucent. If they cross in front of something, you can see the dark shape pass behind them.

Wraith-clerks can't speak. Can't or don't—no one is sure. They can communicate telepathically, but never telegraph so much as a syllable if a gesture will suffice.

As I walked through the foyer, wraith-clerks flitted past, pale feet skimming above the floor. They smiled or nodded at me, but didn't slow, intent on their tasks.

From the center of the room, I surveyed my directional choices. Too damned many, that was for sure. At least a dozen doorways off the foyer, as well as a grand arching staircase in each corner. No helpful building map to show the way. Not even discreet signs above the doors.

"Okay," I muttered, "what am I doing here and where am I supposed to be going?"

Without so much as a hitch in their gait, the four wraiths closest to me lifted their translucent arms and pointed at the northwest staircase.

"And what's up there?" I asked.

An image popped into my head. A winged angel. Whether the wraiths had put it there or I'd made the mental jump on my own, I don't know, but I nodded thanks and headed for the staircase.

The staircase ended at a landing with three doors and another, narrower set of stairs spiraling up. As I stepped toward the nearest door, a passing wraith-clerk pointed up.

"Thanks," I said.

I climbed the next staircase, found three more doors and another, still narrower staircase. Again, a wraith showed me the way. Again, the way was up. Two more landings. Two more sets of doors and a staircase. Two more helpful wraiths. I knew I'd reached the angel's aerie when I had only a single choice: a white door.

Beyond that door was an angel. A real angel. I'd never met one before. In the ghost world, angels were rarely discussed, and then only in tones half-derisive, half-reverent, as if we supernaturals wanted to mock them, but weren't sure we dared.

Angels are the earthly messengers of the Fates and their ilk. Every now and then we'd hear of an angel being dispatched to fix some problem on earth. Never knew what the problem was—probably some tear-jerking misfortune straight out of a *Touched by an Angel* episode. The angels went down and flitted about, spreading peace, joy, and goodwill like fairy dust, realigned the cosmos before commercial break, and winged back up to their clouds to await the next quasi-catastrophe.

Why the Fates would dispatch an angel to catch that murdering bitch of a demi-demon was beyond me. Like sending a butterfly after a hawk. The Nix had done exactly what I'd have expected, chewed the angel up and spit her out in pieces. But, as the Fates admitted, they'd had no idea how to handle the Nix. When she'd escaped, their first reaction, understandably, had been to send their divine messengers after her.

As I reached out to knock on the door, a jolt of energy zapped through me. When I caught my balance, I looked down at my hand and flexed it. No pain . . . just surprise. A mental shock.

I cautiously extended my fingers toward the door again, braced for the jolt. Instead, a wave of some indefinable emotion filled me, amorphous but distinctly negative. A magical boundary. Instead of physically repelling me, it triggered a subconscious voice that said, "You don't want to go in there."

But I *did* want to. I had to.

So, pushing past the sensation, I knocked. For a split second, all went dark. Before I could even think "Oh shit," the darkness evaporated. The door was gone. The foyer was gone. Instead I stood in yet another white room. This one, though, appeared to have been built of brick, then plastered and whitewashed, the pattern of the brick just barely showing through. The floor also looked brick, but darker and patterned. In the middle was a large reed mat surrounded by several high-backed wooden chairs, a few tables, and a carved sofa piled with embroidered pillows.

A window covered the far wall. Beyond it was a desert dotted with boxy pyramids. An illusion, I assumed, but a nice one nonetheless. If the people who ran that psych hospital had given such thought to their patients' surroundings, I doubt the haunters would have found them such easy pickings.

"Hello?" I called.

No one answered.

As I turned to look for a door, something moved at the base of the window. I peered around the divan. On the other side, huddled by the window, sat a woman, her back to me. A flowing, silvery robe swallowed her tiny form. She couldn't have been more than five feet tall. Bird-thin wrists poked out of the loose sleeves. Dark hair tumbled over her back, the ends kissing the floor. No wings that I could see, but that billowing gown could have hidden wings and a set of carry-on luggage. One thing was for certain—I sure wouldn't have sent this fragile little thing after a Nix.

"Janah?" I said softly.

She didn't move. I slid across the room, moving slowly so I didn't startle her.

"Janah?"

She lifted her head and turned. Huge brown eyes locked on mine. Those eyes were so devoid of thought or emotion that I instinctively yanked my gaze away, as if they could suck what they lacked from me.

I crouched to her level, staying a few yards away.

"Janah, my name is Eve. I won't hurt you. I only came to ask—"

She sprang. A mountain-lion screech ripped through the room. Before I could move—before I could even *think* to move—she was on me. I pitched back, head whacking against the floor. Janah wrapped both hands in my long hair, vaulted to her feet, and swung me against a grouping of urns. Pottery shattered and I sailed clear over the divan.

"Div farzand," Janah snarled.

She charged. I lunged to my feet and spun out of her reach. When I cast a binding spell, it didn't even slow her down. I leapt onto the divan and bounded across the cushions, then jumped onto the table. As she charged me, I tried to blind her. Either that didn't work on angels or she was indeed blinded . . . and didn't give a damn.

I swung around for a sidekick, but a mental barricade stopped my foot in mid-flight. Kicking a mad angel? My moral code may be a little thin, but that broke it on two counts.

I jumped across to an end table and looked around for a door. There wasn't one. The only way out of this gilded cage was the window, and I knew that was an illusion. Here, walls were walls. Even ghosts can't walk through them.

As I leapfrogged back onto the coffee table, I recited the incantation to take me home. It didn't work. Tried another one. Didn't work, either. Whatever mojo the Fates had going in this angel's cell, it was obviously designed to keep her in. All things considered, that didn't seem like such a bad idea. If only I weren't in here with her.

"Yâflan dâdvari!" she spat at me.

"Yeah? Right back at you, you crazy bitch."

She stopped and went completely still. Then she stepped back, lifted her arms and face to the ceiling in supplication, and began an incantation.

"Hey, I didn't mean it," I said, stepping to the edge of

the table. "If you're calling the Fates, that's fine. They sent me."

Something shimmered in Janah's raised hands, slowly materializing from the ether. It looked like a piece of metal at least four feet long and so shiny it seemed to glow. Etched along the side were inscriptions in an alphabet that looked vaguely familiar.

As the object solidified, a burnished handle appeared on one end. Janah gripped it, fingers closing around the handle, eyes shutting, lips parting, as if sliding into a glove of the softest leather. She raised the object over her head—the pointed shaft of the biggest goddamned sword I'd ever seen.

"Holy shit!"

The words were still whooshing from my lips as that sword cleaved through the table legs like they were sticks of warm butter. As my perch crumbled, I managed to scamper onto a chair. When I dove over the back of it, the sword sheered toward my knees. I hit the floor. The tip of the blade jabbed through the upholstery, within an inch of my shoulder.

Janah leapt onto the chair and plunged the sword down at me. Ghost or no ghost, I got the hell out of the way. Doesn't matter how invulnerable you think you are, facing off against a psychotic angel with a four-foot samurai sword is not the time to test that theory.

I scampered across the room, casting spells as I ran. None of them worked.

"Demon-spawn!" Janah shouted.

Couldn't argue with that.

"Infidel!"

Debatable, but sure, I'll give you that one, too.

"Satan's whore!"

Okay, now *that* was uncalled for. I spun and kicked. This time, my conscience stood down and let my foot fly. I caught Janah in the wrist. She gasped. The sword flew from her hand and clattered to the floor. We both dove after it. As Janah's fingers touched the handle, I smacked it out of her reach, then twisted and grabbed the blade.

White-hot pain ripped through my arm. I screamed, as much in shock as pain. In three years I hadn't suffered so much as the pang of a stubbed toe, and never expected to again, so when the blade lit my arm afire, I let out a scream to rock the rafters. But I didn't let go. I lifted the sword by the blade, pain still throbbing down my arm.

Then all went dark.

"I think you were supposed to wait for me."

The voice was male and so rich it sent chills down my spine. I looked around. I was sitting on the floor in Janah's front hall, outside the white door.

In front of me stood a pair of legs, clad in tan trousers with an edge sharper than Janah's blade. I followed the legs up to a green shirt, then up higher, to a pair of eyes the same emerald shade as the shirt. Those eyes were set in an olive-skinned face with a strong nose and full lips quivering with barely concealed mirth. Tousled black hair fell over his forehead.

The man reached down to pull me up. His grip was firm and warm, almost hot.

"Thanks for the rescue," I said, "but I think I had things under control."

The grin broke through. "So I saw." He jerked his chin at the door. "Not what you expected, I suppose."

"No kidding." I glanced down at my hand. It looked fine, and the pain had stopped the moment I'd let go of the blade. "So that's an angel?"

"By occupation, not by blood. She's a ghost, like you. A witch as well . . . which is probably why she went easy on you." He extended his hand. "Trsiel."

I assumed that was an introduction, but it didn't sound like any name—or word—I'd ever heard. Though I refrained from a rude "Huh?" my face must have said it for me.

"Tris-eye-el," he said.

His phonetic pronunciation didn't quite sound like what he'd said the first time, but it was as near to it as my tongue was getting.

"Bet you got asked to spell that one a lot," I said.

He laughed. "I'm sure I would have . . . if I'd ever needed to. I'm not a ghost."

"Oh?" I looked him over, trying to be discreet about it.

"Angel," he said. "A full-blood."

"Angel? No wings, huh?"

Another rich laugh. "Sorry to disappoint. But putting wings on an angel would be like hitching a horse to a motor car. Teleportation works much faster than fluttering."

"True." I glanced toward Janah's door. "But teleportation doesn't work for her, does it? Or is that because of the anti-magic barrier?"

"A bit of both. It doesn't always work for full-bloods, either. There are places—" His faced darkened, but he shrugged it off. "Even full-bloods can be trapped. Like Zadkiel."

I nodded. "The last one who went after the Nix."

"Normally, he'd be here, helping you. That's his job, to assist on the inaugural quests. But obviously he can't, so I've been asked to step in. I'll be helping you with anything that might be difficult for a non-angel, like talking to Janah."

"So that's her problem. Now that she's an angel, she doesn't like talking to us mere ghosts?"

"It's not that. She picked up the demon blood in you. Her brain, it misfires, gets its connections crossed, especially when it comes to anything that reminds her of the Nix."

"She sensed demon, and saw the enemy."

He nodded. "She even does it to me now and then."

I frowned.

"Because of the demon blood," he said.

"I thought you said you were—"

"Demon, angel, all the same thing if you go back far enough, or cut deep enough. I wouldn't advise saying that too loudly, though. Some don't appreciate the reminder. When Janah sees you or me, she sees demon, which to her means the one demon she can't forget: the Nix who put her in there. I can usually get through to her, though. Ready for a rematch?"

"Bring it on."

San Francisco / 1927

THE NIX ROUSED HERSELF INSIDE JOLYNN'S CON-
sciousness, struggling to stay alert as the woman droned
on about her life. The subject, as dull as it was, wasn't the
only cause of the Nix's lethargy. She was growing weak—
a concept so repugnant that she fairly spit each time she
thought of it. Once she'd sipped chaos like fine wine;
now it was like water. Too long without it, and she weakened.

She was too particular in her choice of partners. Yet
she still refused to lower her standards. Selecting the
wrong partner was like quenching her thirst with sewer
water.

This time she'd waited longer than usual, probably because her last partner had been such a disappointment.
That's why she'd taken a chance with Jolynn. No smarter
than her last partner—perhaps even stupider—with the
vacuous self-absorption that sometimes afflicted young
women with not enough going on behind their pretty
faces. Yet Jolynn lacked more than common intelli-
gence—she had an empty head, and an empty soul to
match. The Creator, perhaps realizing the defect, had
given her to a minister and his wife, as if hoping they'd
supply what she lacked.

Jolynn's missing soul had proved to be a moral blank slate. Her parents inscribed goodness on it, and she became good. She married a good man, a doctor many years her senior, and followed him into the wilds of Africa, bringing medicine to the afflicted. But when she contracted malaria, her husband sent her home to recuperate, not with her aging parents, but in a California sanitarium. Freed from the watchful eyes of parents and husbands, the truth about Jolynn's soul became clear. It was indeed a slate, and could be erased just as easily as it had been written.

Jolynn had never returned to Africa. She found a job, took a lover, and fell into a crowd that valued a good martini over a good deed. But, after five years, she was growing bored. When the Nix had been looking for potential partners, she'd stumbled on Jolynn and, seeing what the woman was contemplating doing to ease her boredom, the Nix had offered her help.

Now Jolynn sat on the porch behind her apartment, mentally prattling on about what she was going to wear to the party that weekend, who she hoped would be there, and so on, the trivialities streaming from her empty head like bubbles. The Nix felt herself drifting with those bubbles, becoming weightless with weakness and tedium, fluttering—

"Can we do it after the party?" Jolynn asked. She didn't speak the question, just thought it, directing it at the Nix, who'd taken up residence inside her.

The Nix roused herself with a shake. "Yes, that should give us time to plan. How do you want to kill them?"

A pout. "I thought you were going to tell me that."

"I could . . . and I will, if you'd like, but you'll derive

more satisfaction from it if the method has some meaning to you."

From the mental silence, the Nix knew she was talking
over Jolynn's head . . . again. She bit back a snarl of frustration. *Patience,* she told herself. *Take her hand and show
her the way, and she will reward you for it.*

"We'll work on an idea together," the Nix said. "It might
help me plan if I knew why you want to kill them.
They've been your friends for years. Why now?"

Jolynn brightened. "Because now you're here to help me."

"No, I mean why *them.* What have they done to you?"

"Done to me?"

"Never mind," the Nix said. "Let's just—"

"No, I should have a reason. It's only right." She
squinted up at the bright sky. "Ummm, they've been
sleeping with my man, and I'm jealous."

"Of course you are. That must have come as a horrible
shock."

"Oh no, I've known about it for years. I don't mind—
heck, I introduced him to them." She paused. "But it's a
good *excuse,* don't you think?"

Jolynn sat in her friends' tiny kitchenette, sipping hot
milk and chatting about the party. Earlier that evening,
Jolynn had introduced her lover to a pretty blond nurse,
and Nellie and Dot hadn't been pleased about it. Jolynn
didn't understand the fuss. There was more than enough
of Bradley and his money to go around. When Jolynn introduced him to a little tomato that he liked, more of that
largesse came her way.

Maybe that's what Nellie and Dot were in a snit
about—that they hadn't found someone for him first.

Whatever the reason, they were mad. Not mad enough to argue, but, as the Nix whispered, the situation might be useful, if things came to that. As Jolynn sipped hot milk and listened to Dot and Nellie chatter about the party, the Nix whispered ideas in her ear.

". . . not just jealousy," the Nix said. "It has to be more than that. They're angry because . . . because of something about the nurse. She has . . . syphilis. That's it. They heard a rumor that she has syphilis."

"They did?" Jolynn nearly sloshed milk onto her lap. "Why didn't they tell me? That's horrible. If she has syphilis, she could give it to Bradley—"

"She doesn't have syphilis. But that's what we'll say, if things go wrong. Naturally, they'd be furious with you for exposing them. You tried to tell them it was just a rumor, but they accused you of being careless, thoughtless. You tried to leave, but they wouldn't let you."

The Nix continued to plot. Such an imagination. She was so clever. Jolynn shivered, counting her lucky stars that the Nix had chosen her. As a child, Jolynn had always wanted an imaginary friend, but she'd never been lucky enough to find one. She'd always thought, if she did, she'd name her Victoria.

"I'm going to call you Victoria," she announced.

The Nix stopped whispering. "What?"

"I'm going to call you Victoria." She paused. "Unless you'd prefer Vicky, but I don't really like Vicky."

"Victoria is fine," the Nix said. "Now, we— Wait, they're talking to you."

Jolynn popped out of her reverie and smiled at her friends.

"Hmmm?" she said.

"That dress Rachel was wearing," Dot said. "That's the same one you wore to Buzz's party last month, wasn't it?"

"Probably the *exact* same dress I wore. I did donate it to charity."

Dot snickered.

"Oh, and speaking of cast-offs," Nellie said. "Did you notice Millie's handbag?"

Dot arched her brows. "Was that a handbag? I thought she was carrying . . ."

Jolynn tuned out again and stifled a yawn.

"Can I kill them yet?" she asked the Nix. "I'm getting awful sleepy."

"Yes. That's the perfect excuse," the Nix—Victoria— said. "Yawn again, but don't hide it. When they notice, tell them you should be leaving, and get up."

"What? Leave? But I haven't killed them!"

A sigh fluttered through Jolynn's mind. Victoria explained the plan again. She was so clever. They were going to be best friends. Yes, siree, friends for life. Jolynn shivered, barely able to suppress her grin.

"Good," Victoria said. "Now follow that with a yawn."

Jolynn yawned, and lifted her hand to cover it, but missed.

"Oh, my," she said, wide-eyed. "Excuse me."

"I think someone's getting sleepy," Dot said with a smile. "Do you want to stay here tonight, hon?"

"Oh, please, if I could."

Jolynn lifted her handbag from the chair. She peeked inside. The shiny metal of the gun winked. She winked back.

* * *

"Oh, wasn't that fun," Jolynn said as she rummaged through the kitchen cupboards. "Did you see the look in their eyes?" She pouted. "Too bad we couldn't let them scream."

"Not with people sleeping in the apartment overhead. The gunshot was loud enough, even through the pillow."

"You're right. And Nellie did kind of shriek. That was nice." She lifted two knives from the drawer. "The boning knife or the cleaver?"

"You'll probably need both."

"Good idea. Oh, and what about a saw? I think Dot keeps a saw in the closet. One of those little ones, for cutting metal and stuff?"

"A hacksaw."

"That's it. Should I get that, too?"

"If you can find it."

Jolynn found the hacksaw right where she remembered seeing it, in the closet with some other tools. With the hacksaw and boning knife in one hand, and the cleaver in the other, she headed for the bathroom, where Dot was waiting in the tub.

This was going to be *such* fun.

Two trunks. That was all that remained of the luggage from that morning's train from San Francisco. Two black trunks with silver handles. They looked brand-new, not the sort of thing you'd expect someone to abandon at the train station . . . unless they had a good reason.

The moment Samuel saw those big trunks, he knew someone was up to no good. Damn things were big enough to fit two, maybe three, crates of bootleg hooch. The owner probably saw a few uniforms milling about, got cold feet, and ran. The Southern Pacific railway didn't hold with bootleggers. As a baggage-checker it was Samuel's job to, well, check the baggage. And if there were as many bottles in these trunks as he suspected, no one would miss one.

He marched over to the trunks. The minute he got within a foot of them, he reeled back, hand shooting up to cover his nose. Goddamn! If that was hooch, he didn't want even a sip of it. Smelled like something curled up and died in there. He was surprised the baggage-handlers in San Francisco hadn't noticed. Maybe it hadn't smelled that bad before spending a half-day in a baggage car, baking in the August heat.

As Samuel reached for the latch, a pickup truck backed up to the receiving dock. A young man stepped out from the driver's side, but Samuel barely got a look at him before his attention was snagged by the passenger. A brunette. A real doll. Swanky, like some kind of movie star.

The young couple walked toward him, the woman holding out a baggage-claim slip.

"These your trunks, ma'am?" Samuel asked.

She smiled. "They are. Sorry we're late. I got off the train, then realized I had to get my brother to bring the truck around for the trunks. They're quite heavy."

"May I ask what's in them?"

"Oh just . . . personal items." She smiled. "You know how women pack."

Her brother snorted. "Got that right. Two trunks for a weekend visit. You'd think she was moving back home."

The young man moved toward the trunks, but Samuel lifted a hand.

"There's a . . . funny smell coming from them, ma'am."

The woman's blue eyes widened. "There is?"

"There sure is," her brother said, nose wrinkling. "And there's something oozing out the bottom. Jeepers, Jo, what you got in here?"

Before she could answer, Samuel stepped up to the first trunk. He reached for the latch, but saw that it was locked.

"Ma'am? I'm going to need to ask you to open these."

Jolynn stared at the baggage-handler, as if not under-standing his request.

Victoria? What do I do now?

She waited, but her friend didn't answer. She must have been thinking up a plan. As the baggage-handler and Ricky waited, Jolynn rummaged through her purse, pretending to look for the keys.

Victoria?

"Ma'am, I need those—"

"Wait," she snapped. "I'm looking for them."

Victoria? Please, please, please. We're in trouble.

Nothing.

Victoria!

The name echoed through the silence of her brain.

10

TRSIEL TOOK US BACK INTO JANAH'S ROOM, WHERE I waited as they went at it. No, I don't mean an angel-on-angel sword-slamming duel, though that would have been kind of fun. This was a fight of the verbal variety . . . and not much of a fight at that.

Trsiel talked to Janah in what I assumed was her native tongue, and she eventually calmed down, though I suspect it had more to do with his tone than his words. Trsiel had two voice settings. One, probably his natural voice, could have stopped traffic. The moment you heard it, you'd stop whatever you were doing, just to sit and listen. If he kept talking, you'd keep listening, but probably not hear a word he said, too intent on the voice to comprehend the message.

That's the voice he'd first used to get my attention, and it was the one he now used to calm Janah. But when he switched to conversation mode, he adopted a more "normal" tone, one that would be a DJ's dream, but not so spellbinding that you'd ignore what he was saying.

Finally, he changed to English for my benefit. He explained my mission, and with each word, Janah's gaze unclouded, as her mind cleared and focused. Then she turned to me, eyes narrowing.

"They send this one after her?" She snorted. "And they call me mad."

I started to retort, but Trsiel cut me off.

"The Fates know what they're doing," he said.

"No, they do not. She will fail."

"Perhaps, but—"

"She *will* fail. No 'perhaps.' This is a job for an angel, and she is not an angel."

"Not yet."

"Not yet *what*?" I said.

"This is her inaugural quest?" Janah leapt to her feet. "This is not—it cannot be— Fools!"

Trsiel tried to quiet her, but she lunged at him so fast I saw only a blur. Trsiel didn't move. She stopped, with only an inch between them, and pulled herself up straight. She barely reached his chest, but that didn't keep her from rattling off a tirade of invective—or what I assumed from her tone was invective, though she'd reverted to her own language. Trsiel put his hands on her arms, but she flung him off and stalked to her window.

"Without the gift, she will fail," Janah said. "Do not ask me to lead her to her destruction. I will not."

Janah dropped to the floor with a thud, pulled her knees to her chest, and turned to stare out her window. Even from across the room, I could see that stare go empty as her mind retreated.

Trsiel laid his hand on my forearm, and we zapped out of Janah's room.

Trsiel didn't take me back to the foyer, but to some kind of waiting area, empty except for two white armchairs.

"She's right," he said, dropping into one of the chairs. "You can't do this without the gift."

"What gift?"

He waved me to the other chair, but I shook my head.

"What gift?" I repeated.

"An angel's power. Full-bloods always have it. The others get it when they ascend. The Fates must know you need it for this, so what could they be . . ." His voice trailed off, his brow furrowed.

"Is it the sword? I wouldn't mind the sword."

A tiny smile. "No, the sword is a tool. You'll get that, too, when you ascend—"

"Ascend?"

"Yes. But the gift is a skill, an ability. Not essential in most of an angel's tasks, but obviously Janah thinks you need it for this one, and she's not talking until you have it. But you won't get it until you ascend and you won't ascend until you complete your inaugural quest."

" 'Complete'? You think I'm auditioning for angel-hood?"

"It isn't something you can audition for. You must be chosen, and if you're chosen, then you have to complete an inaugural quest. Finding the Nix is yours."

"I'm fulfilling a promise here, not completing an entrance exam. The Fates did me a favor a couple of years ago, a very big favor, and this is how they want it repaid."

"Perhaps I was mistaken, then."

His tone said he didn't believe it for a second, but I fought the urge to argue. The Fates would set him straight eventually. Maybe the misdirection was intentional—assuming Trsiel would be more apt to help a future fellow angel rather than a mere contract bounty-hunter.

"So this gift," I said. "What is it? Maybe we can see whether—"

"See!" He shot up straight in his seat. "That's it. Your father is Balam, right?"

"So they tell me."

"That explains how the Fates expect us to get around the problem." A slight frown. "Or so I think." The frown deepened, then he sprang to his feet. "We'll need to test it."

He grasped my forearm, and the room disappeared.

We emerged in a long gray hall that stank of ammonia and sweat. A young man in an orange jumpsuit mopped the floor, swishing the water around haphazardly, coating the floor in a layer of dirty soap, with no apparent interest in cleaning the surface beneath. At the end of the hall, a door swung open and two armed guards strode through. Their shoes slapped against the wet concrete. The young man gripped the mop handle tighter, putting a little elbow grease into it, even whistling for good measure.

"Exactly what kind of 'gift' is this?" I asked Trsiel.

"You'll see . . . or so I hope."

He led me through the door the guards had used. On the other side was a huge industrial space flanked with two layers of prison cells.

"Uh, any hints?" I asked.

Trsiel kept walking. "If I tell you what to expect, then you'll expect it."

"Uh-huh."

He continued walking, without a glance either way. We passed through two sets of armored doors, and came out in a long hallway. The moment we moved through those doors, a preternatural hush fell, and the temperature dropped, like stepping into an air-conditioned library. But even in a library, you can always hear sounds, the steady undercurrent of stifled coughs, whispering pages, and scraping chairs. Here, there was nothing. Life seemed suspended, waiting with bated breath.

As we drew closer to the end of the corridor, we heard faint noises—the clatter of a dish, a mumbled oath, the shuffle of feet on concrete. Then a softer sound, a voice. A supplication carried on a sob. Prayer.

We stepped into a single-level cell block unlike the earlier ones. At the ice rink, I'd reveled in the sensation of cold. Here, the chill went right to your bones, and had little to do with air-conditioning.

Each cell here had only one bed, and we passed two vacant ones before reaching an occupant, a man in his late twenties, head bent, face hidden as he prayed. The words tumbled forth, barely coherent, voice raw as if he'd been praying for days, and no longer expected a response, but wasn't ready to give up hope, praying like he had so much to say and so little time to say it in.

"Death row," I murmured.

Trsiel nodded and stopped before the man's cell. He went very still, then shook his head sharply and moved on. "We need someone to test this on. Someone who's guilty."

"Guilt—you mean he's innocent?"

My gaze slid back to the praying inmate. I'd never been what you call a religious person. I've even been known to be somewhat disparaging of faith, and those who throw themselves into it. Too many people spend their lives focused on insuring a good place in their next one, instead of embracing the one they have. That smacks of laziness. If your life sucks, you fix it, you don't fall on your knees and pray for someone to make it better the next time.

But here, watching this man pray so hard, with so

much passion, desperation, and blind hope, I couldn't help feeling a twinge of indignation.

"Isn't this what you guys are supposed to do?" I called after Trsiel. "Right wrongs? See justice done?"

He slowed, but didn't turn.

"This justice belongs to the living," he said softly. "We can only right it after they've exacted it. He'll see his freedom soon enough, on the other side."

Trsiel moved between two cells. There was a man in each, one about fifty, but looking twenty years older, shoulders stooped, hair gray, skin hanging off his frame as if he'd lost a lot of weight, fast. The other man was maybe thirty, hunched over a pad of paper, writing as furiously as the first man had been praying.

Trsiel considered them both, then nodded at the writer. "He'll do. I'll be acting as a conduit. Through me, you'll see what I see, by tapping into a higher level of Aspicio sight powers. Give me your hand."

I reached out and grasped his fingers.

"I'm not sure whether this will work, or how well," he said. "So be patient . . . and be ready." He turned his gaze on the man. "Now . . ."

A wave of emotion hit me, so strong it was like a physical blow. I fought to free myself, but the undertow sucked me into a roiling whirlpool, then spit me out into a nursery. A giant's nursery, with soaring walls, stuffed bears the size of grizzlies, and a rocking chair so high I could barely have climbed into it. Across the room, a huge woman stood beside a crib.

"Momma!"

The shrill plea screeched from my throat. It wasn't my voice, but that of a child, a preschooler's, still at the age where it's difficult to tell boy from girl.

"Momma!"

"Shhh," the woman said softly, smiling over her shoulder at me. "Let me feed the baby. Then I'll read to you."

"No! Read now!"

She waved me off and leaned over the crib.

"No, Momma! Me. Me, me, me!"

The baby screamed. I screamed louder, but he drowned me out. I gnashed my teeth and howled, stamped my feet and roared. Still she heard only him. Saw only him. Always him. Hated him. Hated, hated, hated! Wanted to pick him up and smash him, smash him like a doll, smash him until he broke and—

The nursery vanished.

A cat yowled, the sound piercing to the core of my brain. I laughed. A boy's laugh now, nearing puberty. Buildings loomed on either side, pitching day into night. An alley. I stalked along it, chuckling to myself. The cat yowled again, a shriek of terror, like a baby's . . . like a woman's. The cat had reached the end of the alley and was trying to climb the wall, claws scrabbling against the brick. The stink of charred fur filled the narrow alley. The cat's tail was burned to the bone, but it no longer seemed to feel the pain, no longer cared, only wanted to escape, to survive. It screamed again. I closed my eyes, and absorbed the scream. My groin tingled. A new sensation, strange but not unpleasant. Definitely not unpleasant.

I looked at the cat. Then I flicked open the switchblade. The cat continued to screech, darting back and forth along the bottom of the wall. It saw the knife, but it didn't react, didn't know what the knife meant. As I took a slow step toward the cat, I thought how much better it would be if it understood what was coming.

"No!"

The part that was still me tried to block the vision. For a split second, the scene did go black. But then a fresh wave of hate hit me. Hate and rage and jealousy intertwined, inseparable, one feeding the other, growing like a snowball rocketing down a hill.

"Bitch! Whore!"

I slammed the knife down. Saw blood splatter. Heard screams. A woman's scream, hoarse and ragged with animal panic, as confused and terrified as the screams of that cat in the alley. She pleaded for mercy, but her words only fed the hate.

I slammed the knife down again and again, watching flesh become meat, waiting for release, and, when it didn't come, growing all the more frenzied, stabbing and tearing, then biting, ripping mouthfuls of flesh—

Arms closed around me. I threw them off, seeing only the knife and the blood, feeling the hate, wanting it out of my brain, kicking and punching against whatever held me there—

I ricocheted back to reality so fast my knees gave way.

Trsiel's arms tightened around me. "Eve, I am so—"

"Goddamn you!" I wrenched free. "How dare—you could have said—goddamn you!"

I staggered across the room, legs unsteady, as if still unsure they were mine. The visions were gone, but I could feel them there, burying into the crevices of my brain. I shuddered and tried to concentrate on something else, something good. But the moment Savannah's image popped into my head, I felt *him* there, as if he was watching her through me. I shoved Savannah aside, someplace safe. When I looked up, I expected to see the killer in his cell. But we were back in the white waiting room.

"I'm sorry," Trsiel whispered behind me. "I didn't—it's

not normally like that. I thought I could filter it, guide you, but you tapped in directly."

He laid a hand between my shoulder blades. I shrugged it off and stepped away. The images and emotions were fading, but my brain kept plucking them back, like picking at a scab to see whether it still hurt. I pressed my palms to my eyelids and let out a shuddering sigh.

"So that's it, then," I said. "Your 'gift.' You see evil. See it, feel it . . ."

"We learn to control it," Trsiel said. "Focus, so we see only what we need. When you—" He stopped, audibly swallowing his words. "I'm—this isn't—Zadkiel does this—handles the inaugural quests and the new recruits, guides them, teaches them how to use the gift. It's not . . ."

He sighed and I heard him sink into a chair. When I turned, he was slouched in the white armchair, head resting on the top, gaze fixed on the ceiling.

Surely, if you're as old as Trsiel had to be, you'd have enough experience and enough confidence in yourself to act, if not with perfect results, then at least with perfect resolve. Yet he looked as frustrated as any human thrust into a job he's not qualified for.

I walked to the other chair, and perched on the armrest. "What do you normally do, then? Angels, I mean. This—that 'gift'—somehow, I doubt you guys use it to flit about spreading messages of peace and hope."

A slow shake of his head. "That's for the living. Angels aren't evangelists. We're warriors. Instruments of justice."

"Hence the really big swords."

His lips twitched and he rolled his head to the side, his eyes meeting mine. "Yes. Hence the really big swords."

"You see evil because that's what you fight."

"Some of us—only the ascended ones these days. The

full-bloods—" He bit the last words off and gave a sharp shake of his head. "Things have changed, and—"

Another sharp shake. He looked away for a moment. Before I could say anything, he continued, "The traditional job of angels, full-blood or ascended, is to enforce certain codes on an individual level. Clearly, as you just said, we don't—can't—stamp out evil in every form. We are given quests, not unlike the one you're on, to bring certain souls to justice."

"Celestial bounty-hunters."

His gaze met mine, eyes sparking in a tiny smile. "Exactly."

Again, an image of Savannah sprang to mind, but this time I left it there. "So . . . you can affect the living world? Protect people in it?"

"Within limits."

"What limits?"

He shrugged and pushed to his feet. "It's complicated, but you'll get to that when it's time. For now, since we know you can access the gift through me, let's get back to Janah."

11

TRSIEL DID ALL THE TALKING AGAIN. HE TRIED CARRY-
ing on the conversation in English, but it was obvious
Janah was more coherent, and comfortable, in her native
tongue, so with a quiet apology to me, he switched lan-
guages. When they'd finished, he took me back to the
white room. He grabbed the second chair and swung it
around to face the one he'd been using earlier, then sat
on the edge of his and motioned me into the other one.

"You need to find the Nix's last partner," he said.

"Okay. So we talk to the Fates and find out who—"

"While the partner is alive, the Fates don't know who
she is."

I sighed. "Of course not. That would be too easy. So somehow I find this latest partner, hope the Nix is still in her—"

"Our chances of finding the Nix while she's still cohab-
iting are next to nil—by the time the police solve the
crime, the Nix is long gone. Yet when she leaves a partner, part of her stays behind, a thread of consciousness.
Completely one-way, and completely passive. Her partners can't communicate with her nor she with them. Instead they catch glimpses through her eyes, in sporadic
visions."

"So that's why we need this angel gift. Hook up with

her last partner and we'll see what the Nix is up to now. This is where my necromancer will come in handy. With her help, I can dig through recent cases of female murderers . . ." I looked over at Trsiel. "The Fates showed me two past partners. Both serial killers. Both with male partners. Is that the Nix's MO?"

Trsiel frowned.

"Her usual method," I said.

He shook his head and stretched his legs. "Coincidence. But you're on the right track. Two partners, two sets of sensational murders—"

"Headline-grabbers. Nixen, like most demons, get off on chaos. The more chaos, the more payoff. The crimes will be front-page news. So I should look for women accused—" I stopped. "But if they've been accused, they've probably been caught, and this Nix must have learned a thing or two about hiding her crimes by now."

"She may, but she doesn't bother. For her—"

"The more chaos, the more payoff. Right. Commit a few nasty murders, cover your tracks and move on, and people will forget. Let the killer get caught—or make *sure* she does—and you double your fun."

He arched his brows. "You have an innate sense of—"

"Let's just say the Fates didn't pick me for my charm."

How much *did* he know about me? Dumb question, I suppose, considering what that "gift" of his did. But if it bothered him, he hid it well.

"So I'll find the partner, then you move in and do your thing."

"That's probably what the Fates had in mind. But that doesn't mean I couldn't help—"

"Thanks, but this I can handle."

He hesitated, as if this wasn't the answer he'd wanted.

"Yes, well, don't worry about whittling the list down too much. I can help with that. I've dealt with this Nix."

When I looked up in surprise, he shrugged, and continued. "A couple of times ... briefly. First when I brought her in—"

"You're the one who captured her?"

"It was more a delivery than a capture. I was sent to retrieve the witch she first inhabited."

"And the second time?"

"Hmmm?"

"You said you met her a couple of times."

He hesitated. "Right. Well, there's not much to tell about that one. No capture or delivery involved, unfortunately." He got to his feet. "I'll leave you to your investigating, then. If you want anything, just whistle."

"You know how to whistle, don't you?" I said, in my best Lauren Bacall voice.

As the words left my mouth, I mentally slapped myself in the forehead, expecting Trsiel to turn to me with that confused frown he'd given when I'd said "MO." Instead, he smiled.

"Bogie and Bacall," he said. *"To Have and Have Not."*

"Very good. When he died, she buried a gold whistle with him, inscribed 'If you want anything ... just whistle.' "

A corner of his mouth twitched, twisting his smile into a crooked grin. "I didn't know that."

"Well, now you do," I said. "So when I need you ..." I grinned. "I'll just put my lips together ... and blow."

I did just that. Put my lips together, and blew. Then disappeared. Let's see Bacall top that.

12

IT WAS NOW NEARLY TWO IN THE MORNING, WELL PAST necro office hours. Time for a much-delayed Savannah checkup. I popped over to Portland, and found her asleep. I could hear Paige and Lucas downstairs, discussing a new case, some wrong that needed righting. And if anyone had ever told me that I'd be doing the same thing, I'd have pissed myself laughing.

I lingered for another minute, sitting beside my daughter and catching snatches of the impassioned debate downstairs. Then I kissed Savannah's forehead and left.

My first urge was to hunt down Kristof and get his take on everything that had happened. Yet if I was going to use him, even just as a sounding board, I had to do something for him in return . . . even if it wasn't a favor I could tell him about. I'd checked in on one of his children. Now, time for the other two . . .

Kristof limited himself to one parental checkup a month. He thought it was better that way. I disagreed, of course, but I tried to see his point and, in the meantime, did more frequent checkups for him.

*   *   *

Kris's younger son, Bryce, was in California, asleep in his grandfather's villa. He should have been in college, but he'd dropped out last term. Kristof's death . . . well, naturally it affected both his boys, but in different ways; maybe the opposite of what anyone would have expected. Bryce had always been the difficult child, the one who'd started pushing Kris away even before the Great Divide of adolescence. Kris had respected Bryce's rebellion, stepping back, yet staying close, always there to catch him when he stumbled.

When Kris died, Bryce had been in his first year of college, a music major, having declared that he had no intention of following his father into Cabal corporate life. After Kris's death, Bryce had dropped out of school and decided to work for the Cabal part-time. Now he was a company AVP, living with his grandfather—the CEO—and planning to return to college in the fall, not to music at Berkeley, but political science at Harvard, with law school to follow—the same path Kristof had taken.

Next I headed to New York, where Sean was finishing his MBA. He shared an apartment with his cousin Austin, but only Austin was there, sitting up watching CNN. I was about to leave when the doorknob turned, so slow I thought I was imagining it. The door eased open and Sean peered around the edge of it.

The sight of Sean always made me smile. He reminded me so much of Kris when we'd first met, tall, lean, and broad-shouldered, with thick blond hair and gorgeous big blue eyes. Kris had lost that lean build, and about half the hair, but there was still no mistaking the resemblance. In personality, Sean and his father couldn't be more different, but Sean did share his father's values. He was the only Nast who'd made any effort to contact Savannah—and had not only contacted her, but had become a part of her life, despite his grandfather's disapproval. That made Kristof prouder than Sean could ever imagine.

As Sean opened the door, he saw the light on in the living room and winced. He was tiptoeing past the living room entrance when Austin turned.

"Hey, Casanova," Austin called. "I thought you were studying tonight. Library closes at eleven."

"I went out for a couple of drinks."

Austin leaned over the back of the sofa, grinning. "A couple, huh? What are their names?"

Sean mumbled something and slid toward the bathroom. Austin zipped through the kitchen and cut off his cousin.

"Oh, come on. You used to tell me everything. What's happened? Meet someone special? That's what Granddad thinks. He called tonight and when I told him you were out, he said to tell you to bring her home next month."

Panic shot through Sean's eyes, but he dowsed it fast and shrugged as he slipped past Austin.

Sean had indeed met someone . . . and he would never take that someone home to meet his family. For a Cabal son, there was only one thing worse than bringing home a witch—bringing home a lover who was never going to produce that all-important heir.

Even as a teen, Sean had unabashedly looked up to his father as a role model, did whatever he thought Kris wanted, not because Kris demanded it, or even requested it, but because Sean was that kind of kid, good-natured and eager to please. He'd been ready to follow Kris's example, marry for duty and produce the essential "heir and a spare." But now Kris was gone, and so was Sean's reason for fighting his nature. Yet he still hid it, not yet ready to make that commitment and risk being ostracized by his remaining family.

The time would come, though, when he would take that step, and when he did, he'd need help. His father's help. One more reason I needed to figure out a way for us to break through to the living world. I owed Kris that much.

Now, finally, I'd earned myself some Kristof time.

I found Kris on his houseboat. He was reading in his narrow cabin bed. From the glasses perched halfway down his nose, I knew he was engrossed in something more serious than comic books. Of course, Kris didn't need glasses; all of our physical infirmities are cured in death. But he'd been wearing reading glasses for about ten years before his death, so putting them on had become part of his study habits. Like eating, sleeping, even sex, there are things we continue to do as ghosts long after the need disappears.

I stood in the doorway a moment, watching him stretched out on the bed, pants gone, shirt unbuttoned, socks still on, as if he'd started getting undressed, then become distracted by his studies and forgotten to finish.

I cast a blur spell to sneak up on him. When I got to the end of the bed, I saw the title of the book he was reading. *Traditional German Folklore*. I hesitated just a moment, then leapt. Kris rolled to the side. I slammed onto the bed and got a mouthful of pillow.

"Saw me, huh?" I said as I lifted my head.

"The moment you stepped in the door."

"Damn." I pulled myself up and sat on the edge of the bed. "Reading up on Nixen?"

"I thought I'd fill in my own blanks, and maybe give you a hand at the same time."

"You didn't need to—"

He lifted a hand to stop my protest, but I beat him to it, pressing my fingers to his lips.

"I was going to say 'You didn't need to . . . but thank you.' So what have you learned?"

He confirmed that Nixen, like all forms of cacodemon, thrived on chaos. "Thrived" might be the wrong word, implying that they needed it for survival. For cacodemons, chaos is like drugs or alcohol. They get a rush from it, and they'll seek it out whenever they can. Some are addicted, but for most it's a luxury, something to be indulged in sparingly.

He also discovered that Nixen share a couple of common demonic powers. One, they can teleport. Second, like most demons, Nixen possess superhuman strength. Given what the Fates had said, I was certain the Nix could still teleport. As for superhuman strength . . . I was definitely adding that to my list of things to ask them about.

"Great stuff." I leaned over him. "I owe you."

"And you can repay me by satisfying my curiosity. What happened after the hospital?"

I didn't get past the part about my epic battle with Janah before he laughed.

"Pummeled by an Angel?" he said.

"Glad you're amused. Next time, you can handle sword-ducking duty."

He smiled. "Next time I suspect it'll be Janah doing the ducking. I'll admit, I'm envious. I've always been curious about the angels."

"Well, keep helping me and you'll probably meet one yourself. Might not be what you expect, though."

I told him about Trsiel. His brows arched.

"From what I've heard, they're usually more . . . otherworldly," he said.

"Maybe he's playing up the human side for my benefit."

I peered across the room. While I'd been telling him about the case, dawn had erupted into daybreak. I finished my story, then promised to return for another update when I could.

I found Jaime in her condo, awake earlier than I would have expected. She sat on the living-room floor, in front of the TV, following along with a Pilates tape. She was balancing on her rear, legs up and crossed at the ankles.

"Christ," I said. "I'm dead three years and that crap's still alive?"

Jaime thumped over backward, legs still entwined in a position that looked damned uncomfortable. She peered up at me, eyes narrowing.

"That reminds me," I said. "Something I forgot to ask you yesterday."

"How to approach a necro without scaring the shit out of her?"

"Uh, right." I took a seat on the sofa arm as she untangled her limbs. "Might seem obvious, but it isn't. I can't phone first. Can't knock. Can't even walk loudly. I could sing . . . no, that's pretty scary, too. How about one of those discreet, throat-clearing coughs? Read about them all the time, but never tried it myself."

"Just make noise. Any noise. Preferably not right at my ear."

"I've always preferred the element of surprise, but I'll give it a shot." I walked to the TV and made a face at the screen. "I can't believe this crap is still around. Doesn't it put you to sleep?"

"It relaxes me. Gets the tension out."

"So does kickboxing. More useful, too. What do you get from this . . . besides bored?"

Her eyes narrowed to slits, like she was trying to figure out whether I was making fun of her. When she decided I wasn't, she relaxed and shrugged.

"It keeps me toned."

"So does kickboxing. And it's a damned sight more practical, too. Some guy jumps you in an alley, what are you going to do? Assume the lotus position?"

"The lotus position isn't Pilates. It's—" She shook her head, then flicked off the tape, and grabbed her water bottle. "And what do you need, Eve? I assume you aren't here playing personal trainer."

"Looking for intel, for the next part of my quest. I need to find the Nix's last partner."

Jaime gave a slow nod. "Okay. So she's dead?"

"Probably not. This time I need your hands, not your necro know-how. There's a serious lack of Internet service providers in the ghost world."

"So you need me to search and find a suspect—"

I shook my head. "Just search and print, based on some criteria I'll give you. That should square us for yesterday's haunter extermination job. After that, we'll work out payment as we go along."

"You don't need to repay me for something like this. Consider it my karmic payback."

"Uh-uh. Pay as you go, that's my way."

Jaime studied me for a moment, then nodded. "Okay. So what will you do with this last partner? Get her to tell you about the Nix?"

I slid onto the seat cushions. "Bit more mystical than that. The hosts are still linked to the Nix. They see images of her, what's she's doing, stuff like that. Those images can then be passed to me through an angel."

She stopped drinking her water, mid-chug, and frowned. "A what?"

"Yeah, that's what I said, too. Demons I understand. But angels?"

"You're breaking up," Jaime said, her frown deepening. "Damned cosmic editing."

I twisted to look at her as she recapped her bottle.

"That's what I call it," she said. "There are things ghosts aren't supposed to talk about, so I just catch words here and there, like a CB transmission breaking up."

"Oh, that's right. Necros can't ask about the afterlife. I guess angels cross the same boundary."

"You're cutting out again."

She stripped off her tank top and streaked on deodorant.

"What if I spell it?" I said.

She pulled on her shirt. "Never tried that. Could get you in trouble, though."

"No place I haven't been before."

She smiled. "Go for it, then."

"A-n-g-e-l."

"Nope. Not even a letter."

"Charades, anyone?"

I stood and pantomimed a wings and halo.

"Oh, weird," Jaime said. "You blinked right out. Disappeared."

"Damn, they're good."

She chuckled. "If only my e-mail spam filter worked so well."

"Ah well, it isn't important. Speaking of e-mail, we'll need a computer." I looked around the room. "I'm assuming you have one."

"I do. Only one problem." She checked her watch. "I have a show in Milwaukee tonight, and I need to check out the theater before noon, which is why I'm up bright and early. But my afternoon is free, so if you can tag along, or meet me there . . ."

"Better tag along. Less chance to lose you." And less chance for Jaime to change her mind. "We can find an Internet café. Libraries usually have free access, but this isn't something you want to be seen researching in a library."

She pulled on her jeans. "Internationally—well, okay, nationally renowned spiritualists can get away with stuff like that. Catch me researching murders, and people just assume I'm on the job." She raked her fingers through her hair. "Trouble is, they also assume it might be newsworthy. Wrong person catches me looking up murders, and it'll be splashed across next week's tabloid headlines. Then my phone will start ringing off the hook, people wanting me to start looking for their loved one's killer."

"And you get enough of that."

She fussed with the button on her jeans, gaze downcast, answering with an abrupt nod. "I think we can manage part of the search without the Internet." She rooted around in her purse and pulled out her cell phone. "Direct link to a discreet journalist."

I gave Jaime my list of criteria. She wrote it down, then made her call. I waited on the sofa. Though I was too far to hear someone answer on the other end, I knew the moment someone did, by the look that crossed Jaime's face—half delight, half abject terror.

"Uh, oh, Jer—Jeremy," she stammered. "It's me—it's Jaime. Jaime Vegas, from the, uh—" A short, embarrassed laugh. "Right. Well, just thought I'd make sure, in case you didn't recognize my voice—er, not that I'd *expect* you to recognize it, but you might know other Jaimes . . . or you might have forgotten who I was since the council meeting, uh . . . oh, I guess that was just last month, wasn't it?"

The moment Jaime said "council" combined with "Jeremy" I knew who she was talking to. Jeremy Danvers, Alpha of the werewolf Pack. Never met the guy. Never even heard of him until after I was dead. Now Savannah spent an increasing chunk of her summer vacations hanging out with the werewolf Pack, so I'd come to know all the players. Jeremy was as far from the stereotypical werewolf-thug as one could get. He not only tolerated my kid running around underfoot, but paid attention to her, always listening to her problems and helping her with her art. Savannah adored him. And judging by the cringe-inducing display I was witnessing right now, she wasn't the only one.

"So, uh, oh, right, I was calling for Elena," Jaime finally managed to get out. "Is she there?"

Slight pause.

"Oh, umm, yes, I have her cell number, and I could call, but, uh—" Nervous laugh. "Well, if she's out with

Clayton, it can wait. Or it had *better* wait. Not that he's—well, you know—"

A pause, and a high-pitched laugh. Jaime closed her eyes and mouthed an obscenity. The only thing worse than acting like a fool is hearing yourself do it and not being able to stop.

"So I'd better not disturb them if I want to stay on his good side—well, assuming I am on his good side, which, of course, I can never tell, but I figure as long as he's not paying much attention to me one way or the other, that's probably not a bad thing." She took a deep breath and squeezed her eyes shut, wincing. "Anyway, I'll let you go and I'll call Elena later. I just wanted her to check the newswire for me—"

Pause.

"No, past stuff. Well, recent past. Murders. Not the kind of thing you'd read, of course—"

Another pause. Another spine-grating laugh.

"Oh, right. That's exactly the kind of thing you read. Gotta keep your eye out for those brutal wolfy slayings—er, not that all werewolves are brutal or, uh, well—" Deep breath. "Let me run it by you."

Within ten minutes, she had a page filled with cases, a few complete with names, but most with just locations or details that would make further searching a snap.

"Wow," she said. "You're amazing—I mean, your memory is amazing. Not that you aren't— Oh, someone's at the door. Thanks so much. I appreciate it. Really appreciate—"

She winced and I could see her literally chomp down on her tongue. She signed off quickly, then slumped forward, muttering under her breath.

"You should ask him out," I said.

She shook her head sharply. "No way."

"Please don't tell me you think guys should make the first move. That is so—"

"Trust me, I have no problem taking the initiative. It's just—he—Jeremy—is not the kind of guy you walk up to and say, 'Hey, let's go grab a beer.'"

"You could try."

She must have considered it, judging by the look of terror that passed behind her eyes. She reached up, tugged out her hair clip, and wound her hair around her hand, walking to the mirror as she did. Nothing more painful than a crush. I remember my last one. Greg Madison. Deep dimples and a laugh that made my heart flutter. Damn, that had been painful. Of course, I'd been fourteen at the time, not forty. But I suppose infatuation is infatuation at any age, and maybe even worse when you're old enough to recognize the symptoms, be mortified by your reaction, and still not be able to do anything about it.

13

JAIME'S DRIVER WAS DOWNSTAIRS WAITING TO PICK HER up. My first thought was "Wow, she has a chauffeur," but once we were behind the soundproof tinted glass in the backseat, she assured me that the driver was a rental, hired for the trip by her production company. Jaime didn't own a car—she was rarely home, so a car would have sat in the parking garage. Milwaukee was less than a two-hour drive from Chicago, so there was no sense flying. The driver was just a bonus, the kind of luxury that comes with being semifamous.

We spent the afternoon in the hotel business lounge. Other people came and went, popping in just long enough to check their e-mail or send a fax. One stuck around, a guy in his early thirties, still young enough to be impressed by the posh hotel his company had put him up in, and to expect others to be equally impressed. When that and his pricey suit didn't win him coy glances from Jaime, he switched to that modern-day equivalent of dragging in a freshly killed hunk of meat—attempting to wow her with his computer skills.

She assured him that she could handle it, but he still

hovered at the next terminal, pretending to work, stopping every few minutes to make sure Jaime was "still doing okay," hoping she'd become hopelessly snarled in the Web, and he would swoop to her rescue, maybe win an invitation back to her room and hours of acrobatic sex with a gorgeous flame-haired stranger. Hey, it happens in the *Penthouse* letters column all the time, and they don't put stuff in there that isn't true.

When Jaime finished, she escaped with the old "just running to the ladies' room" line. Now, if it'd been me . . . but it wasn't me, so I kept my mouth shut.

Once back in the hotel room, Jaime grabbed a roll of hotel-supplied Scotch tape from the desk, and plastered the walls with the printouts so I could read them. There were over a hundred pages, detailing twenty-three cases, some obvious suspects, some your garden-variety domestic murders but with something extra that had warranted national attention. When she ran out of wall space, she laid pages on the bed and sofa. Then she checked her watch.

"I'm supposed to be in makeup in twenty minutes."

"Go on." I looked around. "This is fine."

"So long as housekeeping doesn't decide to slip in and turn down the sheets." She glanced around the room and shuddered. "Even the showbiz spiritualist gig wouldn't explain this."

"I'll cast a lock spell on the door."

My spell wouldn't work on a door in the living world, but there was no harm in trying, if it made her feel better.

"Good luck," I said. "Or is it 'break a leg'?"

She gave a wan smile. "Sometimes I think a preshow broken limb wouldn't be such a bad thing." Her eyes clouded, but the look evaporated with a blink. "I should be wishing you luck, too. If you need anything, just pop by the theater." She hesitated. "But if you do pop in—"

"Don't really *pop* in. Got it."

She murmured a good-bye, grabbed her purse, and left.

I spent the next hour reading through the first wall of printouts. I made two mental lists, one for likely suspects and one for possible. Some were obvious noncandidates. Like the hooker who accidentally killed a john, robbed him, then decided murder was more lucrative than turning tricks. Or the teen who'd set a bomb in the girls' changing room during cheerleading practice and later told reporters "the bitches got what they deserved." Women like that didn't need the Nix's booster shot for resolve. Likewise, I could exclude the women who'd committed their crimes under the influence of drugs or alcohol. The Nix needed very clear criteria for her partners, those on the verge of murder, needing only her extra push.

A low whistle sounded behind me. "You *are* busy." Kristof stepped up to me and scanned the wall filled with articles. "I thought maybe you could use some research help, so I put on my bloodhound nose."

I smiled. "You're very good at that, you know. Scary good."

"If I want something, I find it." Kristof turned to the wall. "Where can I start?"

I hesitated, then pointed to the pages strewn over the bed and told him my criteria.

"I'll cull the ones that fit," he said. "Then you can read them, make your own decision."

*   *   *

The more I read, the more I wanted this part of my mission to be over. I don't have any hang-ups about violence. For a witch in the supernatural world, being powerful meant mastering the dark arts. Paige was trying to change that, and all the power to her. But when I was her age, I saw only two choices: become a black witch or accept that my powers were good for little more than spell-locking my door and cowering on the other side.

So I'd followed the path of dozens of young witches before me: I'd left the Coven. Left or was kicked out, depending on who you ask. Once gone, I'd devoted myself to learning stronger magic, which meant sorcerer magic, plus the odd black-market witch spell I managed to master. To become more powerful, I had to dig deep into the underbelly of the supernatural world and gain the respect of people who don't respect anything but violence. It became a tool, one I learned to wield with little more concern than I would wield a machete to chop my way out of a jungle.

But the violence I saw in these pages wasn't chopping down your enemies or fighting for survival. This was hate and jealousy and cowardice and all the things I'd felt inside the skull of that sick bastard on death row. The more I read, the more I remembered what it had been like to be in his head, and the more I wanted to be done with this chore.

Kristof saw or sensed my discomfort. But he said nothing, not an "Are you okay?" or, worse yet, a "Here, let me do that for you." He just glanced my way now and then, knowing if I wanted to talk about it, or if I wanted to stop, I'd say so.

Finally, on the final wall, I hit *my* wall, the article that made my brain scream that it'd had enough. The headline read: MODERN-DAY MEDEA MASSACRES TOTS. The jaunty, off-the-cuff alliteration enraged me almost as much as the article itself. I could imagine the reporter, sitting at her news desk, completely oblivious to the details of the crime, the unthinkable horror of it, as she struggled to find the right headline. *Gotta keep it short and catchy. Hey, look, I even tossed in a classical reference—guess that college education paid off after all.*

My own education didn't include a college degree, but I knew who the mythological Medea was, and what she'd done. As I'd suspected, the article was about a woman who'd killed her children to punish her husband. Three children, all under five, drowned in the tub, then laid in their beds. When her husband came home, he'd gone in to kiss them, as he always did, and found them cold and dead. His crime: philandering. Theirs? Absolutely none. Victims of a revenge that no crime imaginable could warrant.

Kristof slid over and read the headline over my shoulder. He put his hand on my hip and I let myself lean into him and rest there a moment before I pulled away.

"Gotta hope there's a special place in hell, I guess," I said.

"I'm sure there is."

I'd have been just as happy to stick this crime on my "no" list, and never have to think about it again, yet something near the bottom made that impossible. A quote from a friend of the family. The kind of thing ordinary folks say when a microphone is thrust into their face, their opinions sought, wanted, important. The kind of thing they'd hear played on newscasts for days and sink a little with each iteration, wanting to scream "I didn't mean it like that!" The perfect sound bite. The friend had admitted that Sullivan had threatened revenge against her unfaithful husband, horrible, violent revenge. So why had no one reported it? "Because we didn't think she had the guts to pull it off."

I glanced over my shoulder at Kristof, and saw his mouth tighten as he read the same line.

"Guess I should move her to the top of my short list," I said.

"Definitely. I've found one or two other possibilities over here."

We finished the last few cases. When we were done, I had a list of six possibilities plus three very good candidates.

"I think I'll get Medea out of the way first," I said. "All three are in jail, and I have transportation codes for those cities. So it's just a matter of getting to the prisons from there."

"Do you want me to come along?" he asked.

I shook my head.

"Then why don't you get Jaime to help you locate the first one, and while you're gone, I'll dig up directions for the other two."

"Thanks."

We agreed to meet up back at my house, and I left in search of Jaime.

14

I MET JAIME IN THE LOBBY AS SHE WAS RETURNING from her show. The business lounge was open around the clock, so she found directions for the prison easily. I took them and left.

To get to Amanda Sullivan's prison, I had to walk fifteen miles beyond the city drop-off point. Most of the way, I jogged. I needed to stretch my muscles and shuck the faint sense of claustrophobia that settles in me after spending too long in any one place. After reading those articles, inactivity wasn't the only thing that got my legs moving. The Fates said the Nix struck every few years, and that left the illusion that I had plenty of time. Maybe they'd done that intentionally, so I wouldn't feel pressured into rushing, but those articles had made me painfully aware that just because the Nix struck on average every two years didn't mean she wasn't out there right now, lining up her next partner.

By the time I reached the prison, it was morning. I entered through the visitors' door. Got to skip the security check, though. Good thing, too, because there was quite a lineup.

I slid through the metal detector, past the two women at the front of the line. Both were older than me, one maybe in her late forties, the other fiftyish. Mothers of inmates; I could tell that by looking at them.

The older one held her chin high, defiant, certain someone had made a terrible mistake, that her child was innocent, and someone would pay for this travesty. The younger one kept her chin down, meeting the guard's questions with a polite murmur and sad smile but not meeting anyone's gaze. The guilt of a mother who sees her child in prison and sees herself to blame, not quite sure what she's done, but certain she's done something— maybe it was that glass of wine in her first trimester or that parent-teacher meeting she missed in fifth grade, some minuscule parenting oversight that had led to this.

I walked past them and into the waiting room—a windowless gray blob of a room that said "We'd really rather you didn't come at all, but if you must, don't expect the damned Hilton." Shabby red-vinyl chairs dotted the room like an outbreak of chicken pox. Goodwill rejects, by the looks of them. Yes, there are things even Goodwill won't touch. From the way the visitors milled around the chairs, giving them wide berth, they weren't touching them, either.

As I crossed the room I passed spouses, lovers, parents, and friends, all waiting impatiently . . . eager to see their loved ones or eager to get this duty visit over with. In the far corner, nearest the guard station, stood a huddle of college-age kids, mostly male. Their badges proclaimed them to be visitors from the state police college. Not one of those badges was flipped over or tucked under a jacket, but all were displayed prominently, lest someone mistake them for a real visitor, someone who actually knew one of the lowlifes in this place. An attitude that would serve them well in law enforcement.

I walked past the cop wannabes, past the guard station, crossed to the prisoners' side of the Plexiglas partition, then headed through the door they'd enter. I came out in a single-level cell block. The first couple of cells I passed were empty, though they showed signs of habitation—a shirt draped over a chair here, a paperback open on a bed there. The inmates must have been out doing something. Work detail maybe, or occupational therapy, exercise, whatever. The particulars of prison life were a mystery to me, though some might say it was a life experience I'd earned many times over.

I only hoped Sullivan was here someplace, both because it would make my job easier and because, after what she'd done, I didn't want her experiencing the pleasure of life beyond bars ever again—not even to break rocks under a hot Texas sun.

I continued down the row of cells. The odd one was occupied, the inmate maybe awaiting visitors or maybe held back as punishment, like a kid forced to stay at school during a field trip. I'd almost reached the far end when a giggle exploded behind me. I turned to see a small figure squeeze through the bars of a cell. It looked like a little boy.

The child scampered the other way, his back to me. Then he paused and looked into the cell on either side. He clutched his hands in front of him, cupping something. Dark-haired and dark-skinned, he wore clothing that had been mended and remended in a way rarely seen since the advent of garment factories and cheap ready-made goods. His shirt, blue faded into gray from washing, was several sizes too large, the elbows patched, as were the knees of his too-small pants, the frayed cuffs riding midway up his calves. His feet were bare.

I quietly walked up behind him, pausing a few yards away so I didn't startle him. And startle him I could—I was almost certain of that. He had to be a ghost. And yet . . . well, it didn't make sense. The boy's clothing was a century out of fashion, but the divine powers weren't so cruel as to make a soul spend eternity in a child's form. Young ghosts matured to young adulthood before the physical aging process ended. And when the Fates picked parents for child ghosts, they chose only the best, those who'd longed for children in life and never been blessed, or those who'd longed for more after Mother Nature closed their reproductive window. Child ghosts were, thank God, rare enough that the Fates could afford to be picky, and they would never select someone who let their child run around a prison.

I gave one of those "throat-clearing" coughs I'd promised Jaime. The boy didn't notice. Instead, he walked to the next cell, looked inside, and smiled. Then he turned sideways and squeezed through the bars, acting as if the metal was a physical barrier, and yet when his toe struck one, it passed through like any ghost's. I crept close enough to see inside the cell. In the bed lay a young woman, no older than twenty, her eyes blazing with fever.

The boy walked to the bedside and opened his hands. On his palm lay a tiny blue feather. He held it out to the sick woman, but she only moaned. A frown crossed his thin face, but lasted only a second before the sun-bright smile returned. He reached over and laid the feather on her pillow, touched her cheek, then tiptoed to the bars and squeezed through.

As he came out, I crouched, bringing myself down to his height. He saw me and tilted his head, faintly quizzical.

"Hello, there," I said. "That was a very pretty feather. Where did you find it?"

He grinned, motioned for me to follow, then tore off.

"Wait," I called. "I didn't mean—"

He disappeared down a side hall. I followed. Medea could wait.

When I rounded the corner, the boy was standing in front of a door, dancing from foot to foot with impatience. Before I could call to him, he grabbed at the door handle and pantomimed opening it. It didn't budge, but he acted as if it had, scooting through the imaginary opening.

The door led into a short hall lined with shelves and cleaning supplies. At the end, a hatch in the floor had been boarded over. Again, the boy went through the motions of opening it.

"I don't think you should—"

He darted through. I walked to the hatch door, lowered myself to all fours, then pushed my legs through. Stuff like this was tricky—mentally disorienting. Like walking on floors or sitting on furniture in the living world. Seems simple enough, until you consider that those floors and that furniture don't exist in my dimension. So what keeps ghosts from dropping through? Voluntary delusion. If you believe the floor exists or the chair exists, you can treat it as a physical object, at least in the sense that you won't fall through it. So when passing through this trapdoor, I grabbed the floor and lowered myself down, even though I couldn't feel anything under my fingers.

As my feet went through the boarded-up door, I cast a light-ball spell. My stronger magic might be hit-and-miss in this world, but I could still count on the simple stuff. Beneath the trapdoor was a ladder, a rickety half-rotted thing that promised to collapse under the slightest weight. Luckily, I was weight-free these days. So I set my foot onto the first rung, and climbed down.

I landed in a tiny, dark room. Concrete walls sweated rivulets of water that stank of sewage. I cast my light around. Nothing to see. Just bare walls and a bare dirt floor. I turned. On the wall behind me was a wooden door crisscrossed with boards. As I stepped toward it, something jabbed the bottom of my foot and I jumped in surprise.

I moved my light down to see a small green globe, half-buried in the dirt. Bending over, I picked it up. A marble. Jade green, its glassy surface clouded with scratches. I turned it over in my hand and smiled. A ghost marble, like the ghost wheelchair Kristof had conjured in the psych hospital. I tucked the marble into my pocket, then walked through the door.

I came out in a long hall. Doors lined one side, thick wooden doors reinforced with steel bands, solid except for a slit about two-thirds of the way up, covered with a metal plate.

When I reached the third door, I heard crying. I stopped and listened. It came from behind the door. I stepped through into a small room, less than five by five. On the wooden floor lay a moldering pallet, half-covered with a moth-eaten, coarse blanket. The room was empty, yet I could still hear crying. It came from all sides, as if the very walls were sobbing.

"Didn't mean it, didn't mean it," whispered a voice.

"Who's there?" I said, twisting, trying to pinpoint the source. "Is that you, hon? You didn't do anything—"

"Sorry, so sorry, so sorry."

The words came louder now, the voice distinctly female. Wrenching sobs punctuated the babble of apologies. I stepped into the empty rooms on either side. From both, I could still hear the voice, yet it obviously came from the middle cell.

"Hail Mary, full of grace, hail—" A sob. "I don't—don't remember. Hail Mary . . ."

"Hello?" I walked back into the middle cell. "It's okay. I'm not going to hurt you."

The only answer was a soft clacking. I thought of the marble in my pocket.

"Hail Mary," the voice whispered. "Hail Mary, full of grace."

Rosary beads. The click of someone counting off rosary beads. A distant door banged. The voice gasped, choking back her prayer mid-word. Footsteps sounded in the hall—the thud of heavy, booted feet. I stepped through the door. No one was there. Yet I could still hear the footsteps, growing louder as they came down the hall toward me.

From inside the room came a muffled whimper. As I looked around, a new sound filled the air, a steady thumping, softer than the footsteps, growing faster as they drew nearer. The tripping of a frightened heart.

"Holy Mary, mother of God."

The prayer came out no louder than a breath, whispering all around me, barely audible over the patter of her heart. The footsteps stopped outside the door. A jangle of keys followed. A whimper, sounding as if it came from right beneath me. A key screeched in the lock.

"No, no, no, no."

The door hinges squealed, and I heard it open, yet the door stayed shut. The woman gave a sudden cry that nearly sent me to the rafters. I whirled around, but I was still alone. From beneath me came the frantic scuffle of someone scrambling across the wooden floor.

"Hail Mary, full of—"

A laugh drowned out her prayer. The door slammed shut. The woman screamed. Then a slap resounded through the room, so loud I reeled as if I'd felt it. Another scream, a bloodcurdling scream of fury and fear.

And all went silent.

I looked around, tensed, waiting for the next spectral sound. But I heard only the faintest scratch of tiny claws from a distant rat.

Slowly, I stepped from the cell. The boy was right there. I jumped, letting out an oath. He waggled a finger at me, then motioned with the same finger, and took off.

I hesitated, getting my bearings, then went after him.

15

THE BOY LED ME THROUGH YET ANOTHER BOARDED-UP door, into another room that stank of rot and stale air. There, wedged between two towers of rotting wooden crates, he'd hidden his stash of treasures—a handful of marbles, some colored stones, feathers, a tin cup painted sky blue, and a hand-sewn animal that was either a dog or an elephant.

"I think you're missing something," I said as I crouched beside the pile.

I pulled the green marble from my pocket. The boy gave a wordless chirp, then threw his arms around me. I hesitated, surprised, then hugged him back.

"What's your name?" I asked.

He only looked at me, smiled, and nodded.

I pointed at myself. "Eve. I'm Eve. And you are . . . ?"

The smile brightened another few watts but, again, he answered only with a nod.

"I'm going to help you get out of here. Take you some-place nice. Would you like that?"

He nodded, still smiling. I suspected that if I asked whether he wanted me to take him dogsledding in Siberia, he'd have given the same nod and smile, having no clue what I meant, but perfectly amenable to anything I suggested.

"We'll leave soon, hon," I said. "I just have to do one thing first. Find someone. Someone here." I paused. "Maybe you could help."

His head bobbed frantically, and I knew that this time he understood me. So I described Amanda Sullivan. But as I did, his eyes clouded with disappointment, and he gave a slow shake of his head. Finding someone was a concept he understood—applying a verbal description to that person was beyond him.

I concentrated on the news article I'd read, the one with Sullivan's photo, and tried to make it materialize. Nothing happened. No problem. My skills on this side might be weak, but I could do it easily enough in my own dimension, so after promising to be right back, I popped into the ghost world, conjured up the photo, and returned to the other side.

"This is a picture of the woman I'm looking for."

He let out a tiny shriek and dove behind me, clutching my leg, face buried against my thigh. I dropped to my knees. He pressed his face into my shoulder. His thin body quaked against mine and I cursed myself. He knew—or sensed—what Sullivan had done. For a few minutes I held him, patting his back and murmuring words of comfort. When he stopped shaking, I shoved the photo into my pocket.

"Forget about her," I said. "Let's get you—"

He grabbed my hand and tugged, his tear-streaked face determined. When I didn't move, he sighed in exasperation, released my hand, and took off. I raced after him.

*   *   *

I followed the boy back through the underground row of cells, up through the hatch door, through the cell block, through a few more rooms, through another guard station and even more heavily armored doors, into a second, smaller cell block. All of these cells were full. The maximum-security ward. He led me to the last one. Inside, reading *Ladies' Home Journal,* was Amanda Sullivan.

I turned to the boy. He'd ducked back behind the cell wall, so Sullivan couldn't see him.

"It's okay," I said. "She can't hurt you. I promise."

A slow smile, and a nod. He darted out, arms going around me in a tight, fleeting embrace. Then he raced off back down the hall.

"No," I shouted, lunging after him. "Come—"

A hand grabbed my arm. I turned to see Trsiel.

"The boy," I said. "He's a ghost."

"George."

"You know him?"

"His mother was an inmate. He was born here, and died here five years later. Smallpox."

"He lived *here*?"

"When George was born, the prison doctor was at home. Apparently, he decided not to lose any sleep by coming in. George was born with his umbilical cord wrapped around his neck. His mother's cellmate revived him but the damage to his brain was done."

"So no one wanted him," I murmured.

Trsiel nodded. "He was allowed to stay here, with his mother."

"Why's he still here? Shouldn't someone—"

"Rescue him? In the beginning, we tried, but he always found his way back here, like a homing pigeon."

"Because this is all he knows. And he's happy here." I

thought of the boy pretending to open doors before walking through them. "He doesn't realize he's dead."

"Is there any reason to enlighten him?"

I gave a slow shake of my head. "I guess not."

"This"—Trsiel gestured at the building around us—"won't last forever. When they tear it down, or abandon it, we'll take the child, probably reincarnate him. In such a case, that's the most humane thing."

"In the meantime, leaving him here is the most humane thing." I shook off thoughts of the boy and turned toward Amanda Sullivan. "That is candidate number one."

As Trsiel looked over at her, his eyes blazed. His right hand clenched, as if gripping something . . . like the hilt of his sword.

"Good choice," he said.

"You can see already?"

"Enough to know she's a good choice. More than that requires concentration." He glanced at me. "I could do this for you."

"It's my job." I held out my hand. "Let's get it over with."

A montage of images flipped past at hyperspeed, so fast I saw nothing but a blur of color. Then the reel slowed . . . on darkness. I waited, with growing impatience, like a theatergoer wondering when the curtain is going to rise.

A voice floated past. "I want to hurt him. Hurt him like he hurt me."

There are many ways to say this line, many shades of emotion to color and twist the words, most of them angry, the flash fire of passion, later repented, or the cold determination of hate. Yet in this recital, there was only the petulant whine of a spoiled child who'd grown into a spoiled adult, never learning that the world didn't owe her a perfect life.

Another voice answered, a whisper that rose and fell with the cadence of a rowboat rocking on a gentle current. "How would you do that?"

"I—I don't know." The pout came through loud and clear, then the demand. "Tell me."

"No . . . you tell me."

"I want to hurt him. Make him pay." A pause. "He doesn't love me anymore. He said so."

"And what do you want to do about it?"

"Take away what he *does* love." A trill of smug satisfaction, as if she'd surprised herself with her insight.

"What would that be?"

"The kids."

"So why don't you do it?"

I waited, tensed, expecting the obvious reason—the natural reason, mingled with a stab of horror for having thought of such a thing in the first place.

"I'm afraid," she said.

"Afraid of what?" the voice asked.

"Of getting caught."

I snarled and threw myself against the confines of the darkness that surrounded me.

The voices vanished, and I found myself in a small room. I was humming, rubbing my hands together. I looked down at my hands. A bar of soap in one, a washcloth in the other. A splash and a shriek of delight. I looked up, still humming, to see three small children in the bathtub.

I tried to wrench my consciousness free from Sullivan's,

my mental self kicking and screaming. The scene went mercifully dark.

Hate washed through me. Not my hate for her, but hers for another. I was back inside Amanda Sullivan, in another dark place. Dark and empty. The Nix was gone.

Gone! The bitch! She abandoned me, left me here alone. She promised I wouldn't get caught. Promised, promised, promised!

The world around me cleared, like a fog lifting. The endless litany of hate and blame and self-pity still looped through my brain. Before me sat a pleasant-looking man in a suit.

"This voice . . ." the man said, his voice an even baritone. "Tell me more about the voice."

"She told me to do it. She made me."

The man's eyes pierced Sullivan's, probing, not buying this line of bullshit for one second. "Are you sure?"

"Of course I'm sure. She told me to do it."

"But when you spoke to the police, you said she *encouraged* you. That's not the same as telling you."

"My children were dead. Dead! And I used the wrong word, so fucking sue me, you son of a bitch. I was devastated." A practiced sob. "My world . . . ripped apart."

"By your own hands."

"No! She did it. She . . . she took me over. It was her idea—"

"You said it was your idea. You thought of it—"

"No!" Sullivan flew to her feet, spittle flying. "I didn't! I didn't think of it! It was her idea! Hers! All hers!"

Again, the scene went dark. A few others passed by . . . the arraignment, the hearing where she'd been denied bail, the failed insanity bid, two attacks by fellow inmates who wanted her punished as much as I did. Then it ended.

Trsiel released my hand.

"Nothing," he said. "The Nix has crossed back."

"Huh?"

"She's returned to the ghost world, probably right after the crime. So long as she's there, the link between her and this partner is severed until she returns to this dimension."

"What if we kill her?"

Now it was Trsiel's turn to go "Huh," though he did it only with a frown.

I continued, "We kill Sullivan, she goes to the ghost world, and hooks into the Nix there."

He continued to frown.

"What?" I said. "You don't think it'll work?"

"Well, yes, I'm not sure it'll work, but I'm still stuck on the first part of the solution."

"Killing her? Oh, please. Don't give me some cock-and-bull about letting human justice run its course. Screw that. She killed her kids. She deserves to die. That's what that big sword is for, right? Administering justice. Doesn't get any more just than that."

"Yes, well, uh—"

"You don't want to do it? Here, let me. Be a pleasure."

For a moment, he just stared at me. Then he gave a sharp shake of his head. "We can't do it. Even if she were dead, I might not be able to contact the Nix through her."

"So? No harm in trying. Worst thing that happens, she dies, goes to her hell and, whoops, it didn't work after all. What a shame."

"No, Eve. We can't."

I strode over to the bars and glared through at Sullivan,

then turned that glare on Trsiel. "So her life is worth more than those of the Nix's next victims? Oh, geez, no, we can't kill this murdering bitch because that would be *wrong*. Fuck this! Tell you what, you've warned me, right? You've done your job. So how about you just pop back over to cloud nine, or wherever it is you guys hang out, and let me do *my* job."

"You can't."

"Can't read her mind? I know that. I can't follow her into her ghost-world dimension, either. That's your job. I'll just deliver her."

"How? You can't influence anything in the living world, so you cannot kill her. That's my point. I understand that you want to stop the Nix before she takes more victims, but she won't. Not right now. While she's in the ghost world, she can't harm anyone. We just need to wait for her to resurface—"

"So we just sit around and do nothing?"

His gaze met mine. "This has happened before and it will happen again. Both of the angels who pursued her faced the same problem. The Nix crosses back to your ghost-world dimension and they can't find her until she resurfaces in the living world. All we need to do is keep an eye on this one." He gestured at Sullivan. "When the Nix comes back, she'll feel it."

"What's she doing?"

He looked at Sullivan, frowning.

"No, not *her*. The Nix. You said she crosses back all the time. And does what?"

He shrugged. "We don't know."

"Well, shouldn't you? 'Cause she sure as hell ain't sunning herself in the Bahamas, enjoying a well-earned vacation. She's doing *something*."

"It doesn't matter. She can't kill anyone—"

"Yeah, yeah. Heard that part. Listen, you want to twiddle your thumbs, waiting for her to reappear, you do that. You said she was in *my* ghost-world dimension, right?"

He nodded. "Having died in a witch's form, she's considered a supernatural shade, so—"

"Good. Then I'll go look for her. If I need you, I'll call."

His mouth set in a hard line. Before he could pry those lips open to argue, I left to find a partner more to my liking.

Cleveland / 1938

AGNES MILLER WAS A ZEALOT. SHE WAS ALSO MAD. THE latter, the Nix reflected, often seemed a prerequisite for the former. Or perhaps it was simply an unavoidable result of the former.

Waxing philosophical. Not something the Nix was accustomed to. She blamed it on good eating. When the belly is full, and there's no need to worry about where your next meal is coming from, the mind can turn to the indulgence of philosophizing.

"I need you," Agnes said.

The Nix roused herself from her thoughts and peered out through Agnes's eyes. They stood behind a crumbling wall, looking down at a man sleeping at its foot, a ragged blanket pulled up under his chin.

"Good choice," the Nix said.

Agnes didn't acknowledge her. In Agnes's eyes, the Nix was a tool, not a partner—the only flaw in an otherwise perfect relationship. As flaws went, though, it was a large one, and becoming more frustrating—

"I'm ready," Agnes said.

She stood over the sleeping vagrant, cleaver raised like a guillotine. Not a bad way to go, really. The Nix knew that firsthand, which is why she'd tried to cajole Agnes from the start to change her method, but—

"I'm ready," Agnes repeated.

"Yes, yes."

The Nix concentrated on pouring her demonic strength into Agnes's arms. That was all the woman required from her. When it came to resolve, she was already overflowing with it.

The blade swung down, and the vagrant's head rolled to the side, eyes still closed. Hadn't even woken up. What was the fun in that? But that was one reason Agnes insisted on beheading—it was quick and merciful.

Agnes set about working on the body.

"This time they will pay attention," Agnes whispered aloud.

"As I've said before, if you want them to pay attention, you have to kill more than petty criminals and vagrants, Agnes. Now, if you took a nice girl from a wealthy family . . . maybe the daughter of the mayor or the head of—"

"That is not the point," Agnes snarled. "The point is this . . ."

Her hand swept across the festering wound that was the landscape surrounding the Cuyahoga River. Blast furnaces and mills squatted like ogres, belching black smoke. The stink of sulfur was so strong the Nix knew she'd be smelling it on Agnes for days, long after she'd returned to her little house and scrubbed the filth of Kingsbury Run from her skin.

"It's a disgrace," Agnes said, as she gestured toward the rusted shacks of Hobotown. "A *national* disgrace. They come here from everywhere, lured by the promise of work. They leave their homes, their families, because they want a job, to work hard, make a living, and contribute to society. And how does society treat them? Tells them there are no jobs. Grinds their self-worth into the dust. And then, when they're too humiliated by failure to return home, it gives them this—this *hell* to live in."

The Nix started to respond, but Agnes was on a roll, her audience forgotten.

"They leave them here, in conditions not fit for dogs, in the very shadow of that." She pointed to a skyscraper that rose above the squalor, sparkling in the moonlight. "The Terminal Tower. One of the tallest buildings in the world. *Such* an accomplishment." Her lip curled. "A monument indeed—to the greed of America, lording it over these poor souls, forever taunting them with what they will never have."

The Nix waited another moment to make sure Agnes was done. "But still, *killing* them doesn't seem to be helping."

"It will. Mark my words. Soon the blind shall see. Even that arrogant boy shall see."

The Nix didn't need to ask who the "arrogant boy" was . . . she didn't want to sit through another diatribe on the ineptitude and inexperience of Eliot Ness. The year before, Mayor Burton had appointed the young man as Cleveland's safety director, head of the police and fire departments. As good as Ness was at cleaning up mobsters and gambling dens, he—and the rest of his force—were clueless when it came to the serial killer in their midst.

"Six victims, all decapitated," Agnes stormed. "Do you know how rare that is?"

"Um-hmm," the Nix said, stifling a yawn.

"But do they see the connection? Oh, dear me, we seem to have an unrelated rash of beheadings in the city. Fancy that."

"They're starting to pay attention," the Nix said. "Articles in every major paper after that last one. The fear is spreading."

"And spread it shall. Like wildfire, purifying the city."

The Nix smiled. This was more like it. "A veritable feast of fear."

"And well they should fear. The wrath of God is upon them—"

"Um, Agnes? It's getting late. It'll be dawn soon."

"Oh?" Agnes looked into the sky. "So it will. Thank you."

The Nix gave Agnes the strength to cut the vagrant's torso in two.

"Are you taking this one back to Kingsbury Run?"

Agnes nodded and kept cutting.

"May I make a suggestion?"

Another abrupt nod as Agnes began to saw off the legs.

"Throw the pieces in the creek. Someone's bound to see one of them floating along. But hide the head." She paused. "And maybe the hands. Yes, hide the head and the hands. They'll need to call in help to dredge the creek, and that's bound to draw attention."

Agnes rocked back on her heels and stared out into the night, then nodded. "Yes, I think I shall. Thank you."

"I'm here to help."

The Mad Butcher of Kingsbury Run. Agnes hated the name the press had given her. The Nix agreed it was rather harsh. Mad? Yes. But "butcher" was uncalled for. Agnes was a qualified surgeon, and the expert dissection should have made that clear.

Several people had speculated that the killer was indeed a surgeon, maybe even a crusader, but the public preferred the image of a raging maniac with a meat cleaver and bloodstained apron. If that scared them more, well, the Nix wasn't about to argue.

Some had even whispered that the killer could be a woman, because the first two victims had been emasculated, but this idea was quickly shot down. No woman would ever do such a thing—to suggest it was to taint the very notion of womanhood. That had made the Nix laugh so hard she'd nearly popped right out of Agnes's body. Clearly these people didn't run in the same circles she did.

As they moved through Agnes's clinic, the Nix basked in the fear that swirled about, thick as the foundry smoke down by the river. In the corner, two vagrants whispered about a shadow they'd seen in Hobotown, a monstrous shadow that had twisted up from the very earth itself, butcher's knife in hand. Two younger men in hobnailed boots swapped "secret" details of the mutilations, each trying to outdo the other. A young mother gathered her two children closer and tried to stop up their ears, her eyes dark with fear.

Agnes was oblivious to the chaos she was causing, intent only on her day's appointments. Cure them by day; kill them by night. The fact that Agnes failed to see the irony—the perversity—of this only made it all the more delicious to the Nix. Of course, it would have been better if Agnes *could* share the irony with her, instead of trudging through the killings with all the joy of a factory worker putting in a twelve-hour shift. The Nix had held out every hope of converting Agnes, of introducing her to the joys of death and grief and chaos, but she knew now it would never happen, and if she kept pushing, this would be the first time she was evicted by her living partner. She wasn't ready for that—there was still much feasting to come. So she kept silent.

Agnes was in search of victim number thirteen . . . or so the Nix hoped. They'd finally found the decapitated man and woman Agnes had left in the East Ninth Street dump. At last, the city was in a true panic. To the Nix, there was no question what Agnes should do now. Strike again, while they were still reeling from the last killings. Make this one the worst yet, the most horrific, and she would not only have their attention, she'd own it.

Agnes didn't see it that way. Now that the city had noticed, she wanted to sit back and see whether they understood her message. For two days, they'd been arguing about this. Finally, the Nix had convinced Agnes to take this walk.

As they headed off the street, the Nix saw a shape flicker through the shadows.

"Over there," she said. "To your left. What's that?"

Agnes's gaze swept left so quickly the Nix saw only the flicker of a shadow. Frustration washed through her. For two days she'd been telling Agnes they were being followed. The hunter kept to the shadows, but the Nix had noticed that he failed to cast a shadow himself, which could only mean one thing—their stalker was a spirit. Probably an angel. One had followed her before, and she'd dispatched her easily enough, but the Nix wasn't fool enough to ignore the threat another would pose.

An angel had taken her to that supernatural hell dimension, where she'd spent two centuries, and could do so again with another swipe of those damnable swords. As a demi-demon she'd been impervious to the Sword of

Judgment, but she'd lost that immunity when she'd taken over a human form.

But Agnes had shrugged her off with a nonchalance that still sent waves of fury through the Nix. So long as the stalker wasn't coming for *her*, Agnes didn't care. This only confirmed the Nix's suspicion that she'd outlasted her usefulness to Agnes.

Agnes picked her way down a trash-strewn hill, then paused and inhaled.

"Smoke," the Nix murmured. "Something's burning over by Hobotown."

Agnes hurried forward, stumbling over piles of tin cans and scraps of lumber. When they rounded the next building, the sky turned orange. Distant flames lit the night sky.

"No," Agnes whispered. "No."

She rushed forward. Hobotown was afire, ringed by fire trucks. The firemen were just standing there, leaning on shovels, sitting on upturned buckets, watching the shantytown burn.

The Nix strained to hear the shrieks of dying men. For agony, there was nothing like burning alive. Yet all she heard were the shouts of the police and firemen, laughing and calling to one another as they enjoyed the spectacle. Finally she picked up the sweet sound of sobbing, and traced it to a line of police paddy wagons. Men were being loaded into the trucks.

A young man in an overcoat strode out from the line of paddy wagons. Eliot Ness. The Nix recognized him from the articles Agnes pored over.

"Burn them to the ground!" he shouted. "Leave them no place to return to. That will solve the problem."

"No," Agnes whispered.

She swayed on her feet. The Nix felt a sharp pain.

Agnes clutched her chest, gasping, and sank to the ground.

"No!" the Nix said. "Get up!"

Agnes lay on her back, mouth opening and closing, eyes wide and unseeing. The Nix let out a howl of frustration as she felt Agnes's life slipping away. Involuntarily, the Nix's spirit began to separate from Agnes's body. She tried to throw herself free but couldn't. As Agnes died, the Nix was trapped there, tethered to Agnes's earthly form. As she struggled, a figure stepped through the building beside them. A dark-haired, handsome man.

"No!" the Nix shrieked. "I will not go!"

She struggled harder, but was held fast. The man stopped, head tilted, studying her face. As she looked into his eyes, she realized, with a jolt, that he wasn't an angel.

He walked closer and hunkered down beside her spirit form.

"You appear to have a problem, pretty one," he said in Bulgarian.

The Nix snarled and writhed.

"I've been sent to capture you," he said. "And promised a nice reward for your return. All I have to do is call my angel partner, and it's over." He smiled. "Unless you can make me a more attractive offer." He lowered himself to the ground. "She appears to be taking a while to die. Shall we discuss my terms?"

16

I FELT A PANG OF GUILT AT HAVING LEFT THE JAIL BE-
fore I could find the little boy and say good-bye. Too late
to go back now. I hadn't left a marker, so it'd take me
hours to walk there again. I'd return and see him when
this was all done.

I found Kristof in my house, and told him what had
happened.

"Why not just kill her?" he said when I'd finished.

I threw my hands up. "Exactly. Why isn't this dead obvious to everyone but us?"

He put his legs up on the ottoman, resting his feet a
hairsbreadth from mine. "This Janah told you to find the latest partner. Is that because she's the only one you can use?"

"No, I think that was just because she'd be the easiest
one to find. With the others, who knows if they're still
alive . . ." My chin jerked up, eyes meeting his. "I see. If I
don't need to use the latest, then I can check out one
who's already passed over, and test my theory, see
whether they're connected to the Nix when she's on this
side. I'll just need to visit the Fates and get myself a visitor's pass to a dead partner's hell dimension." I looked
over at him. "Want to come along?"

He smiled. "I thought you'd never ask."

*   *   *

"No," the eldest Fate said, not even pausing in her spinning long enough to look at us. "You cannot go flitting about the other dimensions, bothering ghosts in purgatory."

"We can't *bother* ghosts in purgatory?" I said. "What the hell is purgatory for, then?"

The middle Fate took over before her sister could answer. "Most wouldn't speak to you anyway, Eve, and those that did would only try to lead you astray with lies and half-truths."

The youngest Fate cut in. "What about—?"

Her sisters cut her short, and the three of them flipped past as they discussed something. Then the middle Fate returned.

"We have a possibility," she said. "Someone who may be inclined to help you, and who will be truthful. However, like the others, she's not a supernatural, so she isn't within the realms we govern. We must make arrangements for you to speak to her, and this may take some time. Leave it with us."

The Fates sent us to my house. I stood on the front porch and looked at the pair of wicker rockers. I'd picked them up shortly after moving in. They conjured up images of lazy afternoons whiled away sipping mint juleps and reading trashy novels. And just as soon as I had time for lazy afternoons, mint juleps, and trashy novels, I'd use them. For now, though . . .

I looked over at Kris. "The Fates and Trsiel think this is all about following clues like tracks in the snow. But to catch your prey, you need to understand it."

"You want to better understand the Nix."

"Exactly." I waved him to the twin rockers. "I need to speak not to a partner, but someone else who was there, who saw what was happening. Someone who'd have a reason to talk to me. Maybe a victim . . ."

"Possibly, but outside of movies, I doubt many killers share their thoughts and motives with their victims. Those women the Fates showed you both had male partners. The first man is still alive, but the later one died in prison about ten years ago. From what I dimly recall of the trial, he and his wife didn't present the most united front. After his sentence was read, they dragged him out cursing her name."

I grinned. "So he might be up for a little tattletale payback?"

"Let's hope so."

Jaime lifted her eye mask to peer at me. "The first night off I've had in two weeks, and you're asking me to spend it in a cemetery five hundred miles away?"

I dropped onto the armchair and pulled my legs under me. "Forget the graveside version, then. Let's go for the long-distance ritual."

"You mean the one that will zap my powers for a week, and knock me flat on my back for three days? Even if I cared to do that—which I don't—the long-distance ritual never works on anyone who isn't in a normal afterlife dimension."

"Well, there is an alternative."

"Good."

"We could contact the ghost of Amanda Sullivan's

five-year-old daughter, ask her if she noticed anything strange about Mommy before she drowned her."

Jaime glowered at me, then plucked off her mask and tossed it across the room. "I'll pack."

It took me a couple of hours to get to the cemetery, first transporting as near as I could, then walking the rest of the way. While I waited for Jaime to arrive, I laid a marker and returned to the ghost world, to check on the Fates' progress. The wraith-clerk receptionist assured me the Fates were working on my request, but couldn't provide an ETA for results.

I popped over to Portland to check on Savannah. She was at school, poring over a math test. Math has never been her best subject, and I hovered there for a few minutes, trying to mentally communicate the answers, but the truth is that math was never my best subject, either. If I succeeded, I'd probably only guarantee her a failing grade. I kissed her for good luck, and went back to the cemetery to wait for Jaime.

It was a dark and stormy night . . .

Actually, the skies were crystal clear and, with the three-quarter moon overhead, it wasn't even that dark, but if you're going to conduct a graveside séance, you have to set the scene properly.

I'd been sitting on a grave marker for over an hour now. It was one of those double headstones, for a husband and wife . . . only the wife hadn't died yet, so the stone just bore her name and date of birth. Downright creepy, if you ask me. The woman's husband died twenty years ago.

Every time she came by to tend his grave, she had to see her name on a tombstone, that blank date-of-death space just itching to be filled in. Talk about a memento mori.

At least they had a tomb. I was buried somewhere in a forest in Maine. The upside to that, though, is that no necromancer could contact me unless they did it the hard way, which, as Jaime said, was damned hard, and rarely successful. So far my afterlife had been interference-free.

At the stroke of midnight, a cowled figure leapt over the cemetery fence. Well, okay, it was probably closer to twelve-thirty, she was wearing a full-length coat instead of a cape, and she more tumbled over the fence than leapt, but I'm really trying for atmosphere here.

Jaime spotted me and strode over, coat flapping. Under it, she wore a black bodysuit. It would have been a great disguise . . . if not for the flaming red hair that flashed through the darkness like a firebrand.

"Oooh, love the coat," I said as she drew closer. "Is that lambskin?" I looked down at my jersey and jeans. "Hmmm, underdressed as usual."

"I don't think you need to worry about being seen, except by our ghost."

"Ah, but that's the problem. If our ghost sees me dressed like this, he'll know right away that I'm a spook. Better not give him any clues."

I closed my eyes and changed into an all-black outfit—a turtleneck, snug-fitting jeans, cropped biker jacket, and knee-high boots. If you have to skulk around a cemetery, at least you can look good doing it.

* * *

I'd found Robin MacKenzie's grave earlier, so I led Jaime straight there and waited while she set up, then spent another hour waiting while she coaxed MacKenzie out. The Fates and their ilk keep a pretty tight lock on the nastier areas of the afterlife.

Finally, a ghost popped through. In my vision, I'd only seen MacKenzie from the back. This spook fit: average size, sandy brown hair, scrawnier than I remembered, but I guess a decade in prison took its toll.

"Robin MacKenzie?" Jaime said.

He looked around, deer-in-the-headlights stunned, then saw Jaime. He gave her a slow once-over, grin broadening by the second. Then his gaze slid to me and his grin widened.

"Hell-o, ladies," he said, running his hand through his hair.

"Robin MacKenzie?" Jaime repeated.

"Uh, yeah. Right." He shook himself and stretched. "Sorry if I'm a bit slow on the uptake. Never been called out by a necromancer before." He paused. "That is what you two ladies are, right? Necromancers?"

Jaime nodded.

"Sweet." He gave us each another once-over, his grin returning. "Very sweet. So . . . what can I do for you ladies? Looking for a little incubus action?"

I slipped off my tombstone and strolled over to him. "Is that what you think you're here for?"

"Well, heh-heh, let's just say it's what I'm *hoping* I'm here for. A little ghostly ménage à . . . uh, a three-some."

I kicked him in the back of the knees. As he crumbled, I grabbed his collar and threw him face-first into the dirt.

Kind of blew my cover, but it was a bit late to worry about that.

"Let me give you a hint," I said, leaning down to his ear. "This isn't foreplay."

He let out a gurgle, and tried to rise, but I ground his face into the dirt. He writhed and coughed.

"Stop faking it," I said. "You're dead—you can't choke. But there are a few other discomforts I can dream up. Any more ménage à trois notions, and we'll put my creative abilities to the test . . . right before I toss your murdering ass back down to hell. Got it?"

He sputtered, eyes saucer-wide. "Murdering . . . ? Look, ladies, I don't know who you're looking for—"

I glared at him. "You aren't Robin MacKenzie, are you?"

"Shit, no. I saw you ladies hanging around, trying to get hold of this Robin dude, and I figured if he doesn't want to answer, I will. I mean, shit . . ." His gaze traveled over me. "Can't blame a ghost for trying, right?"

I hauled him over to Jaime's altar, bent over her bowl of vervain, blew the smoke into his face, and watched him fade away. Then I turned to Jaime, who was sitting there, head in her hands.

"Sorry about that," I said.

When she lifted her head, she was sputtering with laughter. "Oh, that was too good. I need you around on all my séances."

"It might help if I looked more like I was trying to contact a spirit, and less like I was trying to pick one up." I closed my eyes and changed into a plain black T-shirt and pants. "There. Better?"

"Doesn't matter. Believe me, I've tried. I could shave my head and wear sackcloth and still attract a whole lot of ghostly wrong numbers. Makes me wonder whether there's some kind of ghost-necro porn industry down there."

"Séance Sluts III: Naughty Necros Caught on Film."

She grinned. "Probably. Okay, let's try again. And this time, we're checking ID."

17

AFTER ANOTHER FORTY MINUTES OF INDUCEMENTS, hell finally spit out Robin MacKenzie, and dumped him, sweating and shaking, on the ground. It was another fifteen minutes before he'd recovered the strength to hear our questions. Seems the hell dimension had been a bit rough on the guy. And I felt *so* bad about that.

For confirmation, we asked his wife's name. From the way he snarled the answer, I knew we had Robin MacKenzie.

He could only manage to rise onto his elbows. "Is she dead?" he asked, voice hoarse from disuse. "Please tell me she's dead."

"She is," I said.

His tongue slid across his cracked lips, eyes feverish. "Did she suffer?"

"We'll get to that," I said. "Not very happy with the missus, are you?"

"Do you know what she did to me?"

"No, but I'm sure you're going to tell me."

"It was her idea, all of it. Everything we did, she thought of it first. But when they caught us, she cut a deal. She told them I did it. That *she* was just another victim. The abused wife, forced to go along with everything I said. And they bought it. They bought it!"

"Of course they did. No one wants to believe a woman is capable of things like that."

He pulled himself upright. "That's it exactly! The evidence was right there, on the tapes, her laughing, egging me on."

"You got played," I said. "But I'm here to offer you a chance at another round. See, your wife is dead, right? But she's not in hell."

"What?"

"A serious injustice, I know. But you can set that right."

"You want me to prove she did it? I can—"

"No, we've already established that. What we need now is more detail, to give the celestial court a better picture of the defendant, her state of mind at the time of the crimes."

"State of mind? She was fucked-up. Crazy. Obsessed with that Scottish bitch—"

"What Scottish bitch?"

"Suzanne Simmons. She killed some kids back in the sixties."

Now, that sounded familiar. "This Simmons. Did she have a partner?"

"Yeah, her husband or boyfriend. They killed a bunch of kids and buried them out in these grasslands or something."

"And Cheri was interested in this case."

"Interested? She was fucking obsessed. Wouldn't stop talking about it. She'd always been into that kind of stuff, serial killers and shit. We both were. But then, all of a sudden, she starts going on and on about this Scottish chick, telling me all about her. It was spooky. Almost made me think maybe she was some kind of reincarnation of this Suzanne Simmons, but I looked it up, and Simmons was still alive."

"So Cheri talked about those murders."

"And talked and talked and talked. She kept going on about how this Simmons had found the key. That's what she called it. The key. We had to stop pissing around—talking about it, fantasizing about it—and do it."

"Kill someone."

"Only we couldn't just kill them. If we wanted this key, we had to do it a certain way."

"The way Suzanne Simmons had."

"See, that's what didn't make any sense. The stuff she said, it had nothing to do with Simmons. What we had to do was different. She had these instructions—"

"Is that what she called them?"

"Yeah. Instructions. Like she was reading out of some how-to book. At first, it was okay. The stuff she said, it was all things we'd talked about before. But then she started getting careless, and I said, if we keep doing this, we're going to get caught, but she insisted it was all part of the plan, and we were protected."

"Just like Suzanne Simmons, who was caught and sentenced to life in prison."

"Hey, don't look at me. I'm not stupid. But when I brought it up, Cheri said things went wrong with Simmons, but they were all fixed now."

"Uh-huh." I looked him up and down. "Fixed very well, I see."

"Look, that little cunt—"

"This key. What was it?"

"Oh, mystical bullshit. Magic powers and eternal life. Oh, and really great sex." He paused. "Can't say she was wrong on that last part. The sex was pretty damned good."

I remembered the scene from my vision, the girl crying for her mother. My hands balled into fists. Jaime shot me a warning look, but I didn't need it. MacKenzie was being forthcoming so I had no excuse to beat the answers out of him. Not yet.

I prodded his memory some more, but he just kept going in circles, babbling about the key and Suzanne Simmons and the instructions.

"After Cheri started in on this, how long did it take before you started killing?"

"She wanted to right away, but I held her back. I tried to reason with her."

"Uh-huh."

His head shot up, glare meeting mine. "I *did*. I said killing went too far. I just wanted to bring the girls home and have some fun."

My nails dug into my palms. "You mean you just wanted to rape them."

"Right. I'm no killer. So finally she says, okay, we'll take a girl and I can have some fun. But then, when we're done, she says we can't just let her go." MacKenzie paused. "I had to admit, she did have a point there."

Jaime laid a hand on my arm. Fat lot of good it would have done, since I couldn't even feel her touch, but I got the point and swallowed a snarl.

Before I could ask a new question, MacKenzie faded, becoming translucent. Jaime whispered an incantation and he popped back into 3-D.

"They're pulling him back, Eve," Jaime murmured.

"One last question." I walked to MacKenzie, towering

over him. "Do you like it where you are, Robin? Is it a happy place?"

"W—what? Are you kidding? Do you know where I am? They—"

"Stake you out on a rock in the desert and let buzzards pick the flesh from your bones? 'Cause that's what I'd do. In fact, I think I'll suggest they start doing that, because you're every bit as much a murdering piece of shit as your wife."

MacKenzie inched back. "No, you've got it wrong. I didn't—"

"Oh, and speaking of your wife, while I'm sure she'll get her comeuppance someday, I told a little fib earlier. She's not suffering. She's not even dead. But, you know what, she *is* enjoying that million-dollar life-insurance policy she took out on you before the trial."

"What?" He jumped up. "No way. No fucking way. I never signed—"

"One word for you, Robin: 'forgery.' " I bent down to the vervain bowl. "Oh, and one other word, too." I blew a puff of smoke on him and smiled. " 'Sucker.' "

Robin MacKenzie fell back into the ghost world, his screams still resounding through the cemetery long after he was gone.

"Slammed the door a little hard there, didn't you?" Jaime said. "Let's hope you don't want to talk to him again."

"I won't."

I watched Jaime leave, making sure she got back to her rental car okay. Sure, if someone *had* jumped her, there's not a damned thing I could have done about it. But I still felt better watching.

When she was gone, applause erupted behind me. I spun to see Kristof, leaning back against a tombstone.

"Now, *that* was a performance," he said. "Lying about his wife still being alive was good. But the life insurance bit? Truly inspired."

"A bit clichéd, don't you think?"

"It worked, didn't it? Added a few extra logs to his hell-fire." He backed onto the double gravestone and motioned for me to sit beside him. "So your Nix was giving Cheri both a role model and a road map."

"A road map unrelated to the role model, which seems strange." I leaned back and watched the moon duck behind a cloud. "Maybe that's the point. Repetition without duplication."

Kristof nodded. "Another young couple killing kids, but with enough differences to keep things interesting for the Nix."

"Interesting, yes. But maybe more than that. Not just changing the routine but improving on it. Cheri said things went wrong with Suzanne Simmons, but the problems had been fixed."

"Refining her method. So she goes from Simmons to Cheri MacKenzie to Amanda Sullivan, presumably with a few in between."

"Sullivan is a pinch-hitter," I said. "The Nix only stayed with her long enough to help her kill her children, then made sure she got caught. For chaos, comparing Cheri MacKenzie to Amanda Sullivan is like comparing a steak dinner to a Quarter Pounder."

"Fast-food murder."

I straightened. "That's it! When you're starving, you

grab what's available, no matter how bad it tastes. The Nix doesn't just want chaos, she *needs* it. Otherwise, why—"

A bluish fog floated past. Before I could brace myself, the Searchers sucked me under again.

18

I STOOD IN FRONT OF A PLAIN NARROW RECTANGLE OF a two-story house, white-sided with dark shutters.

"Doesn't look like the throne room," I muttered.

"Definitely not."

I started, and saw Kristof beside me.

"What am *I* doing here?" He shrugged. "My guess is as good as yours. Either the Searchers accidentally sucked me in along with you or the Fates want me to start pitching in."

We looked around. The sun had barely crested the horizon, but Mother Nature had turned the dial onto full this morning, and it blazed down, promising tropical conditions by noon. I glanced at the house. Every window was closed despite the heat. Air-conditioning? A horse and buggy trotted past behind me. Okay, probably not air-conditioning.

"Colonial America," Kris said. "Does that sound like any ghost-world regions you know?"

"Boston . . . but this doesn't look like Boston. And the ghost world is never this warm."

A door opened across the road and a man dressed in trousers and a long-sleeved white shirt hurried out, carrying a hat and a black bag. He had salt-and-pepper hair, a high forehead, and thin whiskers that joined his mustache to his sideburns.

He hurried to the street and, without so much as a glance either way, crossed . . . and walked right through me.

"Okay," I said. "If he's a ghost, too, how did he do that?"

The man pushed open the gate of the house I stood in front of, and strode through. He climbed the few steps to the front door and rapped. A man opened the door. He was tall and thin, with white hair and a beard. Despite the heat, he was dressed in a black suit, with his jacket buttoned. He grunted a surly hello at the younger man.

"Just stopped by to see if you folks are feeling any better," the neighbor said.

"Feeling better?"

"Yes, your wife came over this morning, said you'd both been up all night with stomach complaints. She thought someone might have put something in your food—"

"In our food? That's preposterous. Abby would never say—"

"Oh, you know how womenfolk are. They get to worrying sometimes. She seemed fine to me—"

"She *is* fine," the man said. "We're all fine, and if you go charging us for this visit—"

"Now, Andrew, you know I'd never—"

"You'd better not," Andrew said, and slammed the door.

The doctor shook his head, hefted his bag, turned, and walked through me again. There was a movement in one of the main-floor front windows, a young woman washing the glass. Her face was bright red from exertion and the heat. From her simple outfit and the size of the house, I assumed she was a maid.

"Crack open a window," I said. "You got rights, girl. No one should be working in this heat."

The young woman's eyes went round. She dropped the rag and bolted.

"Shit!" I said. "Am I not supposed to do that?"

An exterior door slammed. Kristof gestured toward it and we both took off, following the sound around the house, past the side stoop. There we found the maid puking into the back garden.

"Oh, geez, they really are sick," I said. "They're making her work when she feels like this? Isn't there a labor board in this town?"

"Not in *real* Colonial America," Kristof murmured. "Which is where I suspect we are."

"In the past?"

Before he could answer, the maid retched and hurled. I patted the poor kid's back, but I knew she couldn't feel it.

"You sick again, Bridget?" a voice asked.

Another young woman, also simply dressed, leaned over the side fence. She shook her head. "That's what you get, having to dump those slop buckets every morning. Bound to make anyone sick. Cheap old bugger. He can afford a water closet. Just too bloody cheap."

Bridget moaned and wiped her sleeve over her mouth. "It's not the slop buckets. It was supper last night. I told him that mutton stew wasn't no good no more. Not after three days sitting out in this heat. But he said—"

"Bridget?" A plain dumpling of a middle-aged woman appeared on the side stoop. "Bridget! What are you doing out there, chitchatting the day away? I want these windows cleaned."

"Yes, ma'am."

Bridget accepted a sympathetic nod from her colleague, and trudged back inside. Kristof and I followed, through the kitchen and into a room with a sofa, several chairs, and a fireplace. The man of the house—Andrew—adjusted his jacket and headed toward what I assumed was the front foyer. With a curt nod to his wife, and another to a round-faced, dark-haired woman on the sofa, he strode out the door, evidently unaffected by the bad stew.

I followed Bridget into a more formal version of the room we'd just left. The parlor. Until I'd moved into my Savannah house, I'd thought parlors were places that sold ice cream. Wiser spirit that I was, I now recognized a real parlor when I saw one.

Bridget picked up her discarded rag and resumed cleaning the front windows.

"What the heck am I supposed to be doing here?" I asked Kristof. "These people can't hear me, can't talk to me. What am I supposed to see, and why?"

I walked back into the other sitting area, where the two women were. The younger woman—the daughter?—continued to do needlepoint on the sofa, while the older woman, Abby, shook out a tablecloth from the side table.

The younger woman was definitely old enough to be married, especially in this time period, but I couldn't see a ring on her finger. As she worked, she kept her head bowed, and her shoulders pulled in—the natural posture of a woman who's accustomed to hiding from the world. Her light-blue dress had been washed too often, and she looked bleached out against the dark sofa. Yet, despite this outward timidity, she poked the needle through the fabric with quick, confident jabs.

Abby had moved on to dusting the mantel clock. Both

women worked without an exchanged word or glance, as if each was in the room alone. After a few minutes, Abby walked into the front foyer. Her shoes clacked up a flight of steps. The younger woman lifted her head, tilting it to follow the sound of Abby's shoes across the upstairs floor. As she tracked Abby's path, her eyes flicked past mine and I blinked. In that gaze I saw something as coolly confident as her strokes with the needle. She waited until Abby's footsteps stopped, then resumed her work.

"Okay, this is going nowhere," I said. "Maybe I was supposed to follow Andrew."

The young woman's eyes flicked up, gaze meeting mine for a split second. Then it dropped back to her needlework.

"Hey," I said. "Did you see—"

Bridget tore through the sitting room so fast I felt the breeze. She raced for the kitchen. The side door banged shut. A moment later, the retching began. The woman on the sofa shook her head and poked her needle through the fabric again; then, after the first stroke, she stopped. Her gaze lifted to the ceiling, where we could hear Abby bustling about. Then she tilted her head toward the back of the house. The sounds of Bridget's vomiting continued.

The woman cautiously rose to her feet, looked around again, laid down her needlepoint, and headed for the front hall.

"I swear she looked right at me a minute ago," I said to Kristof.

I hurried after her, with Kristof at my heels. In the hall, the woman stopped and latched the inner bolt. Then she turned and climbed the stairs.

"You!" I called after her. "Hold on!"

She didn't pause. At the top, she walked across the hall and through an open bedroom door where Abby was making the bed. A man's trousers hung over a chair, and shaving implements littered the bureau, next to a wash-basin filled with scum-and-whisker-coated water. On the floor was an open suitcase.

"Make yourself useful and dump that water, Lizzie," Abby said.

The younger woman—Lizzie—didn't move. "I heard Uncle John talking to Father last night."

"Eavesdropping?" Abby said.

"I hear Father is going to change his will."

"That's his business. Not yours."

Lizzie circled the bed, staying across the room from Abby. "But it is my business, isn't it? You don't think Emma and I know what you're doing? First persuading Father to let your sister stay in the house on Fourth Street, then persuading him to transfer ownership of that house to you, and now a new will."

"I don't know anything about a new will," Abby said.

Lizzie crossed the room and looked out the front window, turning her back on the woman I assumed was her stepmother. "So there is no new will?"

"No, there isn't. If your father has written one, he would have told me."

Lizzie nodded. She walked to the bureau and picked up the water basin. A few moments later, she returned the empty basin to the guest room. Then, without a word to her stepmother, she headed for a bedroom farther down.

Downstairs, the side door banged again. I looked toward Lizzie's bedroom, but whatever fire seemed to have been starting up here had sputtered out. Better check out the situation below.

We found Bridget back in the parlor, washing the side windows now. From upstairs came the sound of footsteps. Then a few muffled exchanges. Bridget paused her cleaning and looked toward the dining room, as if the voices came from in there.

"At least they're talking again," she murmured.

She hoisted the pail of wash water and headed through the sitting room and around to the side door. I trailed her outside and watched her dump the water over her puddle of vomit. Then she walked to a pump and refilled the bucket.

"Pumping your own water?" I said. "Thank God I was born in the twentieth century."

Kristof shrugged. "A hundred years from now people will probably be amazed that we cooked our own meals."

I jerked my chin at the house. "*They'd* be amazed that we cooked our own meals, too."

When we got back inside, someone was banging at the front door. Bridget hurried to answer it. She grabbed the door to pull it open and nearly fell over backward when it didn't budge. She grabbed it again and twisted.

"Bolted?" she murmured, reaching for the lock. "In the middle of the day?"

The banging grew louder. Bridget fumbled with the lock. The moment she got it undone, the door flew open and she toppled backward to the floor. A laugh floated down the stairs.

"That was quite a pratfall," Lizzie called from the top.

Andrew strode inside and handed Bridget his hat. Clutching a white parcel beneath his arm, he marched into the sitting room and took a key from on top of the mantel. As Lizzie watched him, she fixed a hook that had come unfastened on her dress.

"Back so soon, Father?" she said.

He grunted something about not feeling well, then walked through the kitchen to the side foyer. Instead of heading out the door, he climbed the rear steps. I followed. At the top of the stairs was a landing with a single door, then more steps leading to the attic level. Andrew unlocked the door and went into what was obviously his bedroom. After dropping off the parcel, he locked the door behind him and headed downstairs.

"Where's Abby?" he asked his daughter as he walked into the sitting room.

"She had a note from a sick friend and decided to pay a visit."

Andrew harrumphed and, without so much as loosening his tie, stretched out on the sofa and closed his eyes.

Note? Sick friend? When had this happened? Oh, wait, I'd been out back with Bridget for a few minutes before Andrew got home. Still, Abby must have left awfully fast . . .

Bridget walked in, carrying her bucket. Her gaze slid to Andrew. Lizzie shooed her into the dining room and followed, as did I. While Bridget washed the windows, Lizzie set up a board and began ironing handkerchiefs. They chatted quietly about whether Bridget was going out later that day, but Bridget confessed she was still feeling poorly. I only caught snatches of the conversation. My attention kept wandering back to the "note" and the "sick friend."

I left the two women, peeked in on Andrew, who was now snoring, and headed for the front stairs. The moment I got to the top of the stairs, I saw Abby. She was still in the guest room, and the door was still open. She was on the floor, facedown, as if she'd fallen to her knees, then slumped forward to the floor. A pool of blood surrounded her. Her head and shoulders had been . . . hacked. There was no other word for it. I've seen death before, and I've seen violent death, but this made even my gorge rise.

"Jesus," I swore. "How—what—?"

Kristof strode past me, and surveyed the room with a prosecutor's eye. As I walked inside, still struggling to understand what I was seeing, I nearly trampled a piece of Abby's scalp. I stepped over it, then looked down at the body.

The first blow must have killed her. If it hadn't, Abby would have cried out and Bridget or I would have heard her. But the killer hadn't stopped with one blow. There were ten, twenty, maybe more cuts, deep cuts. The fury that had gone into this killing, the absolute rage . . . I stood there, and I stared at the body, and I couldn't fathom the degree of hate that had done this.

"Who?" I said, wheeling on Kristof.

As his eyes met mine, I knew the answer was obvious. Dead obvious. But I thought of Lizzie, standing at the top of the stairs, laughing at Bridget's struggle with the door lock, then calmly ironing handkerchiefs while her dead stepmother lay one floor above them. To switch from this kind of rage to that kind of calm within minutes, well, it made no sense. What kind of monster—

I looked back at Abby. As I did, in my head I heard a skipping song from childhood.

Lizzie Borden took an axe
And gave her mother forty whacks;
When she saw what she had done—

"Oh shit!" I said, and raced for the steps.

I took them two at a time, turned at the bottom, and dove through the closed door.

Wearing her father's overcoat, Lizzie stood behind her sleeping father's head, with her back to me. She lifted a bloodied hatchet, then swung it down.

She gave her father forty-one.

19

WE STOOD THERE GAPING AS LIZZIE BORDEN HACKED apart her father's head. Then she laid down the hatchet. Her eyes closed, and her body went stiff as she rose onto her tiptoes.

Kristof nudged my arm.

"Look," he whispered.

There, on the sofa, lay Andrew Borden, intact and unbloodied, reading the morning paper. Lizzie had backed up to the doorway between the kitchen and the parlor. She blinked, then walked through, needlepoint appearing in her hand.

The doorbell rang.

"Who is it at this hour?" Andrew grouched, slamming his paper to the floor.

"I'll get it, Father."

"No. Go help your mother."

Lizzie nodded, then laid down her needlework and disappeared into the kitchen. In the front foyer, Andrew threw open the door, and barked a greeting at the man there—the doctor who'd come to the door before.

"Just stopped by to see if you folks are feeling any better," the doctor said.

"Feeling better?"

"Yes, your wife came over this morning, said you'd both been up all night with stomach complaints . . ."

The two continued, having the same conversation they'd had when we'd been watching from the front lawn.

"It's looping back to the start," I said. "Did we miss something? Are the Fates playing it again for me?"

"Someone is replaying it, but I don't think it's for you."

Andrew stormed back into the parlor, sniping to his wife and daughter. A moment later, Bridget rushed past, hand over her mouth. I started going after her, but Lizzie stood in the door, peering through the kitchen toward the back window. I kept going—and bumped into her, hitting so hard, I bounced back.

"She's real," I said, looking over my shoulder at Kristof. "Solid."

Without waiting for his reaction, I strode across the room, reaching out to both Abby and Andrew. My hand passed right through both. As with the doctor outside, I was the corporeal one here. They were the spirits.

"So Lizzie is real," I said. "But only her."

Kristof nodded, as if he'd reached this conclusion already.

"If she's real, then I can talk to her. I saw something in her eyes earlier—"

"She looked at you."

"Yes, but I think I also saw the Nix—or some leftover bit of her. Lizzie Borden must have been one of the Nix's partners. This must be the one the Fates wanted me to speak to, so let's—"

Kristof laid a hand on my arm.

"Don't rush her," he murmured. "Try it again when she's sitting down."

* * *

When Lizzie finally sat with her needlework, I plunked down beside her.

"I know you can hear me," I said.

She kept stitching, the needle sliding through the fabric, dragging a blue stream of thread after it.

"Look—" I began.

"Wait," she said.

She looked up at her father, who was adjusting his jacket, preparing to leave.

"Have a pleasant day at work, Father," she said.

He responded with an abrupt nod, and another for his wife, then walked out the front door. Abby and Lizzie worked in silence, as they had before. When Abby headed upstairs, Lizzie's eyes slanted toward me. My cue.

"Good," I said. "Now stop sewing."

"I cannot."

I glanced at Kristof. He motioned for me to ignore the needlework and continue.

"I need to talk to you."

She said nothing, just kept working with swift, determined strokes.

"Look, I am going to talk to you, whether you—"

"Hurry."

"What for? You're not going anywhere. Well, except to kill your parents again."

Her cheek twitched, eyes filling with genuine guilt and remorse, the kind Amanda Sullivan couldn't imagine, much less feel.

"So this is your punishment, then," I said, my voice softer.

"Punishment?" A confused glance my way. "This is what I deserve."

"A hell of her own making," Kristof murmured.

I looked up at him.

"I think this is her doing," he said. "She's created her own hell, and trapped herself in it. No need for anyone to punish her. She does it herself."

Lizzie had returned to her needlepoint, face expressionless. As much as I wanted to jump right in with direct questions, I knew I had to be careful. The Fates must have considered Lizzie Borden a credible witness, but that didn't mean she might not try to trick me, or tell me what I wanted to hear.

"Before you . . . did it," I said. "Did anything happen? Anything unusual. Maybe you . . . heard something."

"The voice, yes. I heard it."

"Telling you to kill them."

She kept her gaze down. "She didn't tell me to do anything."

"Encouraged you," I said, remembering Amanda Sullivan's confession.

"Yes, she did embolden me. But I wielded the hatchet. These fingers—"

She clenched her hands, the needle stabbing into her palm. When she opened her fists, a single drop of blood fell on her needlework. She stared at it, transfixed, as it disappeared into the fabric.

"The blame is mine," she said. "I'd thought of it, dreamed about it—killing them. No beau was ever good enough for my father. Those men weren't perfect. I know that. But they would have been kind to me, taken me out of this place. Except he wouldn't let me leave. And her—" She spit the word. "Always conniving. First she gave her half-sister the house that was supposed to be ours, Emma's and mine—"

She stopped, head dropping again.

"No excuses. It cannot be excused."

"Maybe, but I can see how—"

"No!" Her gaze shot to mine, filled with a vehemence approaching fanatical. "There is no excuse and no justification. Honor thy father and thy mother. Honor thy father and thy mother." She repeated the phrase, voice dropping to a mumble.

"Excuse me," she said, laying her needlework aside.

She headed into the foyer and up the stairs. I tried not to think about what was happening up there, but when I heard Abby's body hit the floor, I couldn't suppress a wince.

A few moments later, the scene with the locked front door replayed itself.

Lizzie and Andrew came into the parlor. Andrew took over the sofa, sprawling out and closing his eyes. Lizzie went into the dining room and set up an ironing board. The maid, Bridget, came in to begin cleaning.

"Are you going out today?" Lizzie asked her.

"I don't know. I'm not feeling very well."

"If you do leave, be sure to lock the front door behind you. Mrs. Borden has gone out on a sick call, and I might go out later as well."

Lizzie turned her attention to ironing handkerchiefs. As she worked, I stood beside her, Kristof staying across the room, listening but staying out of the conversation. Lizzie knew he was there, but had yet to say a word to him or even glance his way.

We returned to the subject of the Nix, and I asked Lizzie whether she ever sensed her or saw images of her.

"I see her . . . what she's done. Sometimes it stops for a

while, but when it starts again—" Her hands quivered. "When it starts again, there are always more."

More killings. The images stopped while the Nix was in the world of the living, then she returned bearing fresh nightmares for her dead partners.

I asked Lizzie what she'd seen recently, whether she had any idea where the Nix was or where she was headed.

"She seeks a teacher," Lizzie said. "A man named Luther Ross."

My head jerked up. "Luther Ross?"

"You know him?" Kris whispered.

I glanced over at him. "Heard of him. A poltergeist teacher."

Kristof snorted. "Another charlatan."

"No, Ross is actually . . ." I motioned that I'd explain later and turned back to Lizzie. "What does she want with this teacher?"

"I don't know. I never know. I only see."

Lizzie glanced over at Bridget, who was almost finished cleaning the dining room curtains.

"There's a sale on at Sargent's today," Lizzie said. "Dress material at eight cents a yard."

"Oh," Bridget said, smiling. "Then I will indeed be going out. I'm done here. May I leave now?"

"Certainly."

When Bridget was gone, Lizzie peeked into the living room, where her father had drifted off to sleep.

"Excuse me," she murmured.

While she went to get the hatchet, Kristof and I decided we'd learned all we could from Lizzie Borden, and transported ourselves out before the gore started to fly . . . again.

20

I LANDED IN A POOL OF WATER.

"Your aim, my dear, is excellent," Kristof said.

He was submerged up to his armpits in muddy water. He looked over at me, the water barely reaching my knees. As he opened his mouth, something jumped from the water, splashing a sheet of brown ooze over his face and into his mouth. I bit my cheek to keep from laughing.

"Sorry," I said as he spit the water out. "I told you I only have one travel code for Honduras."

He spit again, then swim-walked over to me. As he drew close, he gave a wet-dog shake, water spraying in all directions, including mine. I yelped, stumbled back, and fell flat on my ass, with a splash that drenched any part that hadn't fallen under the waterline. He grinned and held out a hand to help me up. I took it, and yanked him down beside me.

He rolled onto his side. His gaze traveled across my wet clothing, and his lips parted.

I cut him off. "If that sentence contains the words 'mud wrestling,' I'd strongly suggest you reconsider them."

"I wasn't going to say anything about mud wrestling. Now, mud bathing, that's a whole other matter. Plenty of people pay good money to do this." He lifted a handful of mud and squeezed it through his fingers. "It would be . . . interesting, don't you think? A new sensation. You always love a new sensation."

"So you're suggesting this for my benefit?"

"Of course. I won't touch you. Won't even try. I'll just watch." A quick grin. "That'll be enough."

I pushed to my feet.

"God, you're sexy when you're flustered," he said.

"Please. It would take more than you to fluster me, Kristof Nast."

"Oh?" He swung to his feet and sidestepped into my path. "Then, if you don't want to try a mud bath, you won't mind waiting while I do."

He unbuttoned the top of his shirt.

"You take that off, and I'm leaving," I said.

He grinned. "Flustered?"

"Exasperated. And too busy for games."

"Oh, you can spare a minute or two. You wait right here, watch me, and I'll be done before you know it." The grin broadened. "You know how much I liked it when you watched."

I turned fast, and slid in the mud. An overhanging vine slapped my face. With a muttered oath, I shoved the vine out of my way and stomped toward the shore.

"Flustered," Kris called after me.

As I turned to answer, something splashed beside me. On the bank lay a huge alligator.

"Enjoying the show?" I asked.

He blinked and gave a lazy flick of his tail. A mini–tidal wave of mud splattered over me. Kristof laughed. I glowered at the beast. He yawned, showing off teeth as big as bowie knives, and twice as sharp.

"Yeah, yeah," I said. "Very impressive. And I'd be even more impressed if you could use them, ghost-gator."

Once on the bank, I gave my head a shake. Mud flew everywhere, but when I stopped, every strand of hair fell into place—shiny, clean, and brushed. Gotta love the afterlife. I closed my eyes and murmured an incantation. When I opened them, I was dressed in worn jeans and a T-shirt. The alligator harrumphed. I flipped him the finger and started walking, leaving Kristof to catch up.

Luther Ross lived on the island of Roatan, just north of Honduras. Even in the ghost world, this is well off the beaten path, which is why someone like Ross would choose to live here. The ghost world, like any other, has its laws. Poltergeist activity breaks most of them.

A poltergeist reaches into the living world and manipulates objects. Fortunately for the Fates, it's not a major problem because few ghosts can do it. Most so-called poltergeist activity isn't ghosts at all—it's earth tremors and faulty construction and bad wiring and bored teens.

The few true poltergeist ghosts find their services in high demand as teachers. When something is rare, it's always cool to be one of the few who can do it. There's only one problem. Most poltergeists haven't learned their power at all; they're born with it.

Almost all poltergeists are really telekinetic half-demons. Something about the power of telekinesis allows it to transcend dimensions, so after death, some find that they can continue to mentally will objects to move in both the ghost world and the living world. Yet they can't pass on this power to a nontelekinetic any more than I can teach a binding spell to a non-spell-caster.

That doesn't keep telekinetic half-demons from selling their "services" on the black market. To disguise the true source of their powers, they pose as druidic or Vodoun priests, or other supernaturals with minor, easily faked abilities. They'll pretend to teach a student, all the while manipulating the objects themselves.

Luther Ross was different. When I first heard of him a year ago, I also heard that he was half-demon and dismissed him as someone too stupid to even hide the source of his powers. Then, a few weeks ago, I discovered that he was a Gelo, an ice demon, not a telekinetic. It's damned near impossible to fake the powers of a Gelo. So it would appear Luther Ross might be the real deal, someone who truly had learned how to move objects in the living-world dimension.

Getting into Ross's classes wasn't easy. To evade the Fates and their Searchers, he holed up in remote locations like Roatan, and gave out the transportation code only to students he personally approved. At least a dozen of my contacts had tried to get into his class, and failed, so I'd decided that when I had time to take his classes, I'd skip the application process. I'd tracked down someone who had directions to his latest school location, and I'd paid a pretty price in spells and transportation codes to get them.

I told Kristof all this as we trudged through the swamp, taking turns blasting the vines from our path. I skipped that part about bartering for the directions, though, and made it sound as if they were common knowledge. Kris wasn't fooled. He knew me, and he knew I must have been investigating Ross as a potential teacher, someone to help me in my quest to help Savannah. But he let the matter drop without comment. My "Savannah project" was one subject guaranteed to start fireworks, and neither of us wanted that. Not today.

We headed north, knowing we'd eventually reach the Caribbean. We came out near Puerto Cortez, or so we were informed by the first person we came across, a young man with the bleached-blond hair and dark tan of someone who'd spent his life near the ocean, and wasn't about to leave it after his death.

"Good surf?" I asked, pointing at his board.

"Nah. Great snorkeling, but no freaking surf unless you make it yourself." A quick flash of white teeth. "Good thing I can."

"Tempestras," I said.

"Whoa, you're good."

"Aspicio," I said, extending my hand.

He shook it sideways, fingers hooking around mine, thumb up. "Cool. You guys have the X-ray vision, right?"

"Something like that." I looked at his board. "So where do you conjure up your surf?"

"Over by Tela, near the National Park."

"Is that anywhere near Roatan? That's where we're heading . . . or trying to."

"Roatan?" His gaze flicked over Kristof and me, then he shrugged. "Whatever floats your boat. Easiest way would be to stick to the coastal route. Eventually you'll come to La Ceiba. That's the gateway to Roatan. Got quite a ways to go. Nice hike, though."

"Great. Thanks."

"No problem. You folks enjoy yourselves over there."

He started to leave, then stopped and gave us another once-over. "Just, uh, make sure you change before you get to La Ceiba. They like to keep the place, you know, pure."

After he left, I turned to Kristof.

"Pure?"

He shrugged. "Guess we'll find out."

I certainly wasn't about to catch up to the half-demon surfer and ask, no matter how friendly he'd seemed. I'd landed myself into trouble doing that before. In the ghost world, it's one thing to admit you don't quite know where you're going, but it's another to admit you don't know what to expect when you get there. Opens you up to a whole world of grief.

In my first year, I'd been given the name of a potential contact in Stanton, Texas, and so I'd asked the referrer what to expect there—what the period was. The guy told me Stanton was set in the Old West, and my contact lived in a brothel. Naturally, I showed up in a costume appropriate for the period and the setting, and found myself in a nineteenth-century Carmelite monastery dressed as a whore. Lucky to get my ass out of there· without a nice coating of tar and feathers. Oh, but the guy who sent me there had himself a good laugh. In a long and often monotonous afterlife, sometimes that's really all that counts.

I'm sure the scenery was lovely, but it had been ten miles since we'd seen any of it, trudging along in the darkness, under the glow of my light-ball spell. Finally, we saw another glow lighting the night sky.

"That's gotta be La Ceiba, but I think it's too late to get a boat to Roatan."

"Legally, yes. But there are bound to be plenty lying around."

"Good plan." I sniffed the air. "Do you smell that?"

"Wood burning. Campfires, I think."

"A Boy Scout town?"

"I wouldn't bet against it. They have everything else here. Just name your fetish."

I knocked his arm. "It's called an alternate afterlife-style choice, remember? Or did you sleep through that part of orientation?"

Kris snorted. "When you choose to spend your afterlife living in a Southern manor, that's a lifestyle choice. When you spend it playing Confederate soldier or Billy the Kid, it's a fetish."

"Hmmm. I seem to recall a certain someone playing Billy the Kid sixteen years ago."

"It was Pat Garrett," he said. "And one night is not a 'life'-style choice."

"No, it's a fetish."

He slapped me on the rear and growled, "Watch it."

"Hey, I said it was a fetish." I grinned over at him. "Didn't say I objected."

We crested a small rise. Just below, in the glow of moon-light, lay the town of La Ceiba, a ramshackle collection of houses that were little more than huts—and decrepit huts at that. From the town came the raucous laughs, whoops, and catcalls of men trying very hard to have a good time, and downing massive quantities of alcohol to help them find it. The waver of candlelight blazed from the windows of a few of the larger buildings. Wood-fire smoke hung in a blue-gray haze over the town.

"Nineteenth-century frat party?"

Kris shook his head and guided my gaze to the waterfront. There, crammed into the small harbor so tight they were double- and triple-parked, were a dozen or more boats. Not just boats, but spectacular wooden galleons, each with a dozen or more sails, and decks that were a veritable jungle of ropes. High atop the masts, flags fluttered in the breeze. From here, they looked like little more than brightly colored scraps of fabric. When I sharpened my sight, I could make out markings and designs—an arm bearing a scabbard, a skeleton raising a toast, several national flags, and on more than half, the ubiquitous skull and crossbones of the Jolly Roger.

Pirates.

21

THIS EXPLAINED LUTHER ROSS'S RELOCATION TO Roatan: the only route to the island was guarded by a pirate town. We now knew why that half-demon surfer had advised us to change our outfits before visiting La Ceiba. No part of the ghost world is off-limits, but just because you're allowed in doesn't mean you'll be encouraged to stay. Waltz into a themed afterlife town wearing your civvies, and you'll find yourself as welcome as a Mormon at Mardi Gras.

Themed afterlife towns were indeed a ghost-world Mardi Gras, a nonstop costumed paean to some romanticized bygone era. If you come to visit, you'd damned well better get yourself into the spirit of things . . . fast.

We slipped behind an abandoned hut on the outskirts of town and changed into more appropriate outfits. Kristof tried his damnedest to convince me to let him dress me, but I made him wait around the corner while I fashioned my own outfit.

"Still working on it?" Kristof called after a few minutes. "If you need help . . ."

I stepped around the corner. A slow grin swept over Kris's face. I'd dressed myself in hip-hugging calfskin breeches, knee-high boots, and a tight white laced bodice cinched at my waist with a jaunty black sash. Add oversize gold hoop earrings and a red bandanna, leaving my hair falling down my back, and I probably looked no more like the real Anne Bonney than Elizabeth Taylor looked like Cleopatra, but historical inaccuracy wasn't an issue—not in a place like this.

I surveyed Kristof's ensemble: a white linen shirt, black trousers tucked into low black boots, and a black naval jacket with brass buttons.

"Looks good," I said. "Now— Whoops. Forgot something."

I closed my eyes and conjured up two cutlasses.

"Hardware," I said, handing Kris one. I raised mine and sliced it through the air. "Think we'll get a chance to use them?"

"Only if we're lucky. But just in case we do, I'd better switch to this . . ." He closed his eyes and transformed the cutlass into a straight sword. He hefted it, spun it in his hand, then smiled, and lunged. "En garde."

"Uh, pirates, Kris, not the three musketeers."

"Close enough." He thrust the sword at an imaginary foe. "I always told my father those fencing lessons would come in handy someday."

"So you can really use that thing?"

He grinned. "Try me."

I raised my cutlass into something that vaguely resembled Kris's "en garde" position.

"Ready?" he asked.

I nodded. He lunged forward and knocked the cutlass so hard it flew from my hand, and left my wrist vibrating.

"Hey!"

I ducked to grab my cutlass, then stopped as I felt the

tip of his sword pressed against my throat. Still crouching, I looked up at Kristof.

"It would seem, sir, that you have me at a disadvantage."

"So it would."

He slid the sword tip down my throat to my chest, and traced a line down my cleavage, caught the edge of the bodice, and plucked it off my breast. The moment his attention was diverted, I flipped backward, grabbed my cutlass, and sprang to my feet. Kris lunged, sword raised. I feinted and swung around him, then lifted the cutlass blade to the back of his neck.

When he felt the blade shift, he ducked and spun, sword raised. We sparred for a few seconds. Then he caught the underside of my cutlass and knocked it from my hand. I quickstepped backward—and slammed into a wide tree. Kristof lifted his sword tip to my throat again.

"Mercy?" he asked.

"Never."

Kristof laughed and slid the blade down my chest again. This time, he snagged the first lace on the bodice, and sliced through it.

"Kris . . ."

He caught the second lace on his sword tip.

"Kris . . ."

"Oh, you know I won't do anything," he said. "Won't even try. Not until I know you're ready. I just like to . . ." A small smile as he pressed against me. "Remind you. In case you've forgotten what it was like."

That was one reminder I never needed. I'd had lovers before and after Kristof—never many, I was always too particular to share my body with just anyone—but Kris was the only man I'd ever lost control with, the only one

I'd never been able to get enough of. And now, feeling him hard against me . . .

Oh, to hell with this.

I tilted my hips up. Kris pressed closer, letting me lift my legs and wrap them around him. I wrapped my hands in his hair and kissed him. Kris moaned and slid his hands into my breeches, and grabbed my rear, pulling me tighter against him.

Then he tensed, resisting. After a moment's hesitation, he tugged my arms down and stepped back.

"You aren't ready," he murmured.

"No?"

I took his hand. He let me slide his fingers under my waistband, then jerked his hand away and took another step back.

"I don't mean ready for a five-minute bang against a tree, Eve. That's not good enough. I want you back. For now and forever. I mean that."

"Kris, I've told you—"

"You don't want that kind of relationship. Yes, you've said it. Over and over. We couldn't make it work the first time, so we shouldn't try again. A nice, pat excuse—"

"It's not—"

"Since when have you ever failed at something once and given up? It's an excuse, Eve—a simple excuse for avoiding the very complex problem that's you and me, and everything we did and didn't do once upon a time. You aren't ready yet. I know that. And I'll wait until you are." He gave a small smile. "It's not like I'm going to run out of time."

"I—"

"Speaking of time, though, you have a job to do, so I'd

suggest we stop screwing around—or talking about why we aren't screwing around—and get back to work."

Our goal was, of course, to get passage to Roatan, preferably that night. So we started down to the wharf. The first three pirates we passed did double-takes at my outfit, but only murmured greetings and kept walking. When we drew within twenty yards of the harbor, we had to pass a grizzled old salt with an eye patch. He heaved to his feet and blocked our path, hand on his sword. Unlike the others we'd seen—who'd had the look and dental work of men who'd never seen the Jolly Roger outside a movie theater—this guy could have been the real deal, with blackened teeth, swarthy battle-scarred skin, and serious hygiene issues . . . which probably explained why he'd been consigned to harbor duty.

"Avast!" he growled, voice thick with a near-impenetrable accent. "Who ye be?"

"Visitors," I said. "We just arrived, and we wanted to see the ships—"

"Not dressed like that, ye ain't, missy."

"Our outfits may be somewhat anachronistic," Kristof said. "Yet certainly no worse than others we've seen so far." He glanced over the pirate's stained and ragged ensemble. "Excepting your own fine attention to period detail, of course."

The pirate's lip curled. "Don't give a damn about *yer* britches, lad. It's hers that's t'problem. No wimmin pirates allowed here. Only wenches."

"Wenches?" I said.

"That may be your usual policy," Kristof said. "It may also explain the notable lack of female companionship available in your fine town. Might I suggest you reconsider—"

"I'm not *reconsidering* anything, lad. Either she changes herself into a proper wench, or ye best be *reconsidering* staying in La Ceiba."

Kristof opened his mouth to argue, but I shushed him with a look. Flexibility is the key to progress. So I slipped behind the nearest hut, and made a few minor alterations to my costume. The shirt, boots, and earrings stayed. The breeches gave way to a peasant skirt. A few necklaces and I looked as darned wenchy as I was getting. As for the cutlass, well, as much as I hated to part with it, I reminded myself that I could conjure it up anytime I felt the need.

I stepped from behind the hut.

The old pirate ogled me with a gap-toothed grin. "Now, that's more like it, ma beauty." He elbowed Kristof in the ribs. "Got yerself a damned fine wench there, lad."

"Uh, thank you."

"So, sir," I said. "Perhaps, if you have a moment, you'd be kind enough to tell us how we could get to Roatan."

"Roatan?" His face scrunched up. "Why ye want to go to Roatan? All t'action be here, on this side o' the bay."

"Perhaps," Kris said. "But we really must get to Roatan. Is there a ship we could charter?"

"This ain't t'yacht club, lad. Ye don't charter a pirate ship. Ye wants passage, ye gots t'earn it, by going on account."

"Going on account?"

The pirate slapped Kris on the back. "Joinin' a crew, lad. Joinin' a crew."

"I . . . see. Well, thank you very much for your time. Mind if we take a stroll along the harbor?"

"Stroll away. Ye wants to be joinin' a crew, now, ye lets me know, an' I'll set ye up." He slid a sly smile my way. "And I'll look after yer wench while yer at sea."

We thanked the old pirate and headed to the wharf. If we couldn't charter a ship, we'd need to steal one. Unfortunately, it quickly became obvious that every ship was guarded by at least two men, and the galleons were packed in so tight that the moment we boarded one, we'd be beset by attackers from the others.

I turned to Kristof. "They might not encourage rentals, but I bet we can find someone willing to bargain."

"Up to the taverns, then?"

I nodded.

We picked the largest of the three taverns along the main road. A sign at the door warned against the use of weapons, magic, and supernatural powers of all kinds. Kristof vaporized his sword, then pulled open the door and ushered me inside.

22

INSIDE, THE CLATTER OF STEEL MUGS COMPETED WITH the roar of voices raised in laughter and anger. The air was thick with cigar and wood smoke. Did pirates smoke cigars? Didn't look authentic, but obviously someone had decided it was, and that was good enough for them. A themed afterlife town should never be mistaken for a historical reconstruction. It's a theme-park version, like Disney's Pirates of the Caribbean ride . . . before they sanitized it for the age of political correctness.

As we stepped inside, all conversation near the door stopped. The silence rolled across the room until every mouth had closed, every eye turned to check out the new arrivals. They went first to the male half of the party, and the testosterone wafted up thicker than the cigar smoke. In a dive like this, when a new man walks through the door no one wonders what kind of conversationalist he'd make or sizes him up as a potential poker dupe. No one even wonders whether they could con him into buying a few rounds of grog. Instead, the thought going through every man's mind is "Hmm, wonder if I could take him in a fight." And, as most turned away without so much as a second once-over, the overwhelming decision was "yes." This wasn't a contender—good size, good structure, but too old, too soft, and, my God, look at those hands—is that a manicure? Only the smallest and oldest of the men let their gazes linger, but even those soon recognized a Wall Street wimp, no matter what costume he chose to cloak himself in.

Attention went next to the living, breathing piece of potential pirate booty. A few looked away after the briefest glance. They liked their women smaller, cuddlier, blonder. But most kept looking, a few perking up enough to slide off their stools.

"That yer wench?" barked a big man, spattering rum in his thick black beard as he spoke.

"Uh, er—" Kristof glanced at me, checking to see how much trouble this would get him into later, then responded with a gruff "Aye" and steered me toward the dark end of the bar.

"Bit tall, ain't she?" the man called after us.

"Not for me."

A tall, rangy blond with a red bandanna slid off his stool and dropped into Kristof's path. "Not for me, either."

Kris led me around him. As we passed, the man glided behind me and grabbed my ass. Didn't pinch and duck out of the way. Just grabbed with both hands and held on, chortling. I slowly looked over my shoulder, meeting the man's grin with a baleful stare.

"Uh-uh," Kris whispered by my ear. "Can't break character. Allow me. Please."

Kristof turned his best stare on the idiot. "Please remove your hands."

The guy just gave a big "make me" snigger.

"And apologize," Kris said.

A roar of guffaws rose from the audience.

"Hey, Pierre," a pock-faced man called. "Are ye shivering in yer boots yet? I know I am."

Another round of whoops and catcalls. Kristof waited for the laughter to wane, as calm and steady as a seasoned substitute teacher faced with an unruly class.

"One last time," he said. "Please remove your hands and then apologize to the lady."

"Oooh," someone called. "Better listen, Pierre. He might—"

Kristof grabbed Pierre by the collar and hurled him along the bar, sending rum bottles flying like bowling pins. For the next five seconds, numbed silence fell over the tavern as the men picked their jaws up off the ground. The pock-faced pirate recovered first, snatching the stool nearest him and charging. Kristof caught the stool and swung it. The man on the other end was a bit slow on the uptake, not letting go of the stool even when his feet left the ground. For a big guy, he sailed over the bar with remarkable grace, though his crash landing sounded pretty awkward.

By then, Pierre had rolled off the bar and was coming at Kris. Kris swung the stool into the side of Pierre's head. The pockmarked pirate stumbled from behind the bar and turned on Kristof, but a wiry old man jumped the pirate from behind, obviously deciding this seemed like a good opportunity for some personal payback.

Before you could say "bar brawl" the place erupted. I hopped onto the bar for a better view, using knock-back spells to stave off any stray bodies that flew my way.

As much as I prefer playing over spectating, there's something to be said for sitting back and enjoying a good brawl. Especially if Kris was doing the brawling. Diving, ducking, fists flying, bottles smashing, wood splintering, he plowed through the room, grinning like a kid in his first schoolyard dustup, grinning through every blow—delivered or received.

The fight petered out as most brawls do, the instigators sneaking away or being dragged off by friends, everyone else crashing from that first adrenaline explosion, unable to remember what dragged them into it in the first place. Kristof emerged from the fray. He sauntered toward me, hair rumpled, shirt torn, a wide "damn, that was fun" grin on his face. When I smiled back, he picked up his pace, then swooped me off the bar and onto a stool. As he pulled another intact stool from the debris, a tankard was slapped onto the bar and we both jumped.

There stood a plump, dark-haired woman a few years older than me, squeezed into a barmaid costume several sizes too small, her breasts barely contained by her tight bodice. She smiled and held out a second tankard and a dusty bottle of rum.

"House tradition," she said. "Victor gets the last bottle left unbroken."

Kris murmured his thanks as she opened it.

"Not bad fighting," she said. "For a sorcerer."

Since Kris hadn't cast any spells, there was only one way she could know he was a sorcerer.

"Blessed be, sister," I said.

Her grin broadened, revealing a missing canine. "Haven't heard that in a while. They still use that up there?"

I shook my head. "Only the humans."

"Well, blessed be, sister." She patted my hand. "Been a long time since I saw a witch, too." She glanced at Kristof. "So that's all over, then? The feud?"

"Between witches and sorcerers? Nah. They're just as

arrogant and nasty as they ever were." I smiled at Kristof. "But sometimes you can make an exception."

She poured our drinks.

I looked around the tavern. "Have you . . . been here long?"

She let out a long whoop of a laugh. "You mean, what the hell am I doing in a shit-hole like this?"

"I wasn't going to say it."

She leaned over the bar, lowering her voice. "You wanna know why I'm here, hon? Take a look around. See the male-to-female ratio? This place is Alaska without the snow." She capped the bottle. "So are you folks visiting? Or passing through?"

"Passing through. We were hoping to visit someone over on Roatan, but . . ." I glanced around. Most patrons had either scurried off into the night or were still finding a place to sit, free of broken glass and splintered chairs. No one was paying any attention to us. "Seems we've run into a problem renting a ship. I don't suppose you know any way we could rent—or 'borrow'—one."

"Borrowing's your best bet." She lowered her voice and set about wiping the counter. "Not easy, but there's one possibility. The *Trinity Bull.* Owned by Pierre, the half-demon with the wandering hands. He keeps it in a bay west of here, down the coast a bit. Secluded spot. Usually only one guard—a new guy."

We thanked her and she slipped away to tidy the bar, conjuring up a fresh stock of rum and making the broken bottles vanish.

As anxious as we were to get that ship, we couldn't seem to be in too much of a hurry to leave. So we hung around

for a half-hour before slipping out. We headed down to
the wharf, this time giving a wide berth to the triple-
parked galleons at the main dock, and instead slinking
through the empty huts lining the beach to the west. We
cut through a stand of tropical forest. On the other side,
we found the bay the barmaid had mentioned. In it was a
boat, not much bigger than Kristof's houseboat. Didn't
look much like a galleon. More like a yacht . . . with a
Jolly Roger flag on the mast. I sharpened my sight and
read the name on the side. The *Trinity Bull*.

The bay was a pretty place to dock your boat, if you
didn't mind the security risk. As I scanned the deck, I bit
back a laugh. There was indeed only a single guard, a
slight red-haired man sitting on a chair on the deck, his
feet propped on the rail, a bottle at his side.

"Easy pickings," I murmured to Kristof.

We advanced on the boat, sticking to the shadows.
When we drew close enough to see the deck without
Aspicio-boosted vision, we both stopped short. The
guard was talking. I saw no sign of another person.
Kristof motioned for me to listen.

". . . weeks in this fucking town and I'm still guarding
this fucking ship," the guard was saying. " 'Sorry, Danny-
boy, them's the rules.' Danny-boy." He let out a snarl.
"Next son-of-a-bitch who calls me that . . ."

The rant fell to a mutter. There was no one else on the
ship, just one very bored, very angry, slightly drunk guard.
So much for any hope of a sword fight.

Danny-boy leaned back in his chair, tipping the front
legs off the deck, and closed his eyes. Kristof and I crept
along the shore, keeping out of the guard's sight in case
he opened his eyes. I considered blinding him, but if he

did open his eyes, he'd panic and know something was wrong.

We reached the dock. The slap of the waves against the boat's hull covered our footsteps as we trod across the wooden boards. We made it all the way up the gangplank and the guard didn't so much as twitch.

"Asleep?" I mouthed to Kristof.

He waggled his hand, giving it fifty/fifty odds. Then he motioned for me to circle around and approach the guard from the rear. I had taken one step in that direction when the guard let out a soft sigh.

"Are you guys almost on deck?" he said, eyes still closed. "Take much longer and I really *will* fall asleep."

Kristof charged, sword raised. The guard sprang to his feet and feinted out of Kris's path. I swung behind the cabin before he saw me. As Kristof wheeled, the guard yanked his cutlass from his belt. He parried Kris's first thrust, but missed the second and danced out of the way seconds before being slashed.

The two men sparred for a minute. Kristof was obviously the better swordsman, but the smaller man had an easy agility that kept him out of sword's reach. Finally, when the guard's back was to me, I slid from my hiding place and pressed the tip of my cutlass between his shoulder blades.

"Take another step and I'll skewer you like a shish kebab," I said. "Won't hurt, but it could be damned uncomfortable."

He glanced over his shoulder, gave me a slow once-over, and smiled.

"Always was a sucker for a girl who can take care of herself," he said. "Let me guess, you two want this boat."

"Yes," Kristof said. "And either you let us or—"

"Take it."

When Kris hesitated, the man shrugged.

"What the fuck do I care? It's not mine. If you take the boat, I can take my leave of this dump, and believe me, I don't mind having the excuse. Don't mind seeing Pierre and his bunch lose this barge, either. Serves them right. Fucking pirates. Not nearly as much fun as you'd think."

"So you'll just leave . . . ?" I said.

"Sure. But I will ask for one favor, though. Give me twenty minutes before you cut 'er loose. Once you set sail, someone in town will see, and I want a good head start before Pierre and his buccaneers come after me."

Kris looked at me. I shrugged. We set the guard loose. True to his word, he loped off down the shore and disappeared into a patch of jungle. While Kris checked out the boat, I stood watch, making sure Danny-boy didn't circle back to town to warn the pirates.

"We good?" I asked Kristof when he returned to the deck.

"Very good. It's a modified cabin cruiser. No motor, of course, but she'll run fine on wind and spell-power. Dad bought me one just like it when I went to Harvard."

"You took a yacht to college? Most kids get a *car*, Kris."

"Oh, I got a car, too. Two, actually. The Lotus wasn't made for Northern winters."

I shook my head. "Can we shove off, then?"

"Just let me check a few things, then we'll—" He stopped and squinted into the darkness. "What's that?"

At first glance, all I saw was what he did—a flash of something running from the woods. I concentrated, invoking my night and distance vision, and saw that the "something" was a ginger-red dog running full out along the shore.

"Some kind of dog," I said, frowning. "Big one, too. More like a wolf. That couldn't be . . . Oh, shit! It's the guard!"

"He's a werewolf?" Kris squinted at the fast-approaching canine.

"Cut the ropes!" I yelled, running for the front of the ship.

"What?"

"The ropes, the lines, whatever. Cut them!"

Kristof hesitated only a second, then he lunged forward and sliced through the rope at the rear of the boat. I cut the one at the front. The boat didn't budge.

"It's anchored," Kris yelled, leaning over the side.

He grabbed hold of the anchor chain. I sailed across the deck and grabbed it from him. "I got this. You get the sails up and shove off, or whatever you need to do to get this baby moving."

As Kris raced around the cabin, the wolf reached the dock. The gangplank was still down. I dove for the ropes, seized them, and heaved. The wolf's forepaws landed on the edge of the gangplank, jerking the line from my grasp. I grabbed the rope, heaved again, and yanked the gangplank out from under him. He stumbled back, snarling.

"Double-crossing son of a bitch!" I shouted down at him.

Don't know whether he understood me, but it made me feel better.

The wolf gave a soft chuff of a sigh, and headed back down the dock.

"Yeah, you'd better run," I muttered.

I walked back to the anchor chain. I'd just gotten a good hold on it when a blur of motion caught my attention. I looked up to see the wolf tearing back down the dock, running hell-bent for the boat. Oh, shit. He was taking a run at it.

"Eve!" Kris shouted.

"I got it! You just get us moving!"

I wrapped the chain around my hands and pulled. The anchor barely budged. Where the hell was the windlass on these things? The wolf was almost at the end of the dock now, running full out, tongue hanging, green eyes fixed on the rail. I threw myself backward and felt the anchor lift just as the wolf launched himself. He shot toward the rail. I dropped to the deck, dragging the anchor higher.

A strong wind whipped around from the south—a magical wind. The sails billowed, the boat lurched from the dock, and the wolf's leap fell short. His front paws hooked the railing, but only for a second before the weight of his falling body sent him plummeting into the dark water below. I hauled the anchor over the side, then looked into the swirling dark water below.

"Hope you can swim, ya scurvy cur!" I shouted down at him.

Kristof laughed behind me. I waved at the wolf as he surfaced.

"Do you believe that?" I said. "He double-crossed us."

"Shocking. Absolutely shocking. Pretty clever, though."

"Damned clever . . . for a werewolf." I eased back against the railing. "So do you need to navigate this thing or what?"

"I've set her on a course for Roatan. My wind spell won't last long, but we'll get there."

"No rush. We can't visit Luther Ross until morning.

We should probably keep watch for a few minutes, though, make sure we aren't followed."

"I'll cover that, if you don't mind covering us with a fog spell."

I cast the sorcerer spell. Fog billowed up around the boat, and we sailed out to sea.

Edinburgh / 1962

THE NIX SAT ON A BARSTOOL, STARING AT THE BOTTLE of Scotch. Close enough to touch—to drink. In the old days, she'd never have considered such a thing. But now she was reduced to this, staring at a bottle of alcohol, imagining the burn of it down her throat, the pleasant numbing amnesia that followed.

She'd been inside plenty of partners with memories they'd wanted to forget, and most had indulged in alcohol to do it. She'd always despised them for such weakness. She'd suffered through the effects, with gritted teeth, hating every moment that her thoughts were dulled. And now she could think of nothing better than to partake of that same temporary oblivion.

She concentrated and reached for the bottle. Her fingers passed through the glass, through the amber liquid, leaving not so much as a drop of it on her skin. Once she'd have roared in frustration, cursed every demon she could name for not freeing her from this spirit prison. Now she only moaned and sank into her seat.

She hadn't fed properly since Dachev had left her. Oh, she'd taken partners, dined on her share of chaos, but it hadn't been the same. She'd come halfway around the world in search of something better, and hadn't found it. Every new partner was but a wretched substitute for him.

There would never be another like Andrei Dachev. A true partner of the soul. Though only a supernatural shade—and from an inferior race, at that—he'd understood the power of death and chaos the way only a demon usually could. More than that, he'd appreciated the craft of chaos more than most demons, and he'd opened her mind to possibilities she'd never considered, to the true beauty of physical and mental suffering.

He'd been content to watch, but they'd always talked of finding a way, not only to bring him inside her partners, but to impose their will on those partners, to force them to carry out Dachev's visionary ideas. Had they accomplished that, the Nix knew she would have felt an emotion she'd never experienced: happiness. The happiness of complete satisfaction.

If only she hadn't betrayed him.

She betrayed all her partners eventually, for that final satisfaction of seeing them fall. She'd told herself that was the reason she'd turned on Dachev, because she was so accustomed to doing so that she had acted without thinking. The truth was far more unforgivable. She had betrayed Dachev because she'd tasted another emotion she'd never encountered before: fear.

While she'd been inside a partner, an angel had come for Dachev—the same one who'd taken her soul from the Marquise's body and transported her to hell. She'd recognized him, but when Dachev saw the angel, dressed in contemporary clothing, acting human, he'd mistaken him for a corporeal being. She could have warned him. All she had to do was jump out of her partner. But to do so would have meant exposing herself. Fear had paralyzed her, and she'd left Dachev to his fate.

She'd had time to repent her cowardice. Fifteen years of finding only serviceable partners, nothing like Agnes or Jolynn or Lizzie, and certainly nothing like Andrei Dachev.

The pub door opened, and a boy crept in. As he slipped over to a table to deliver a message to his father, his gaze darted about, taking in everything about this forbidden place. A young blond woman across the room watched the boy. Nothing strange in that—everyone had turned to look at the child, the normal curiosity of the bored. It was the way this woman looked at him that caught the Nix's attention. There was a glint in her eye, not the hunger of a perverse human who lusts after children, but the truer lust of the predator.

The woman said something to her table-mate, a lankhaired young man. His gaze slid to the boy, and he smiled, his eyes lighting with a dimmer spark. Another predator, but a follower, a willing disciple. The woman was the leader. Interesting.

The Nix slid from her seat and moved closer. She hesitated, dreading the rush of disappointment that would come if she was mistaken. Finally, she met the young woman's gaze. And after only the briefest dip into her thoughts, the Nix knew her luck had changed.

23

ONCE BELOW DECK, WE DID THE SAME THINGS WE'D done almost every night for the past year—sat and talked. One would think that we'd have run out of topics months ago, but there always seemed to be something new to discuss, some subject, some opinion, some turn of mind left unexplored.

That night, a comment about the werewolf guard launched the discussion, which quickly led to an exchange of "werewolves I have known" war stories. Soon Kristof was telling me the long, convoluted tale of his encounter with a werewolf pack in Russia.

As I listened, my legs tucked under me and my head resting on my arm, the gentle rock of the boat and the familiar cadence of his voice conspired to tug me off to dreamland. Yet I resisted. Yes, my brain was in dire need of a sleep recharge. Yes, I could hear this story another time. And yes, it wasn't even all that interesting, but I could have listened for hours, curled up, comfortable, and sleepy, watching Kristof, his hands and eyes moving animatedly, voice rising and falling as the story slowed and restarted.

There'd been a time when I'd have given anything to be right here, listening to one of Kristof's stories. How many nights had I lain awake, just thinking of how good it would be to hear his voice? How many times had I considered picking up the phone and telling him about Savannah? Come morning, I was always horrified by the impulse, that I'd use my daughter as an excuse to get something I wanted. Now I could indulge myself without guilt or shame. So I stayed awake until the last bit of the tale was done, then let myself drift off to sleep.

When I awoke just past dawn, Kris was already on deck, navigating the boat to shore. We dropped anchor in a quiet cove and disembarked. We probably wouldn't need to use the boat again—our travel incantations would get us off the island—but it never hurt to have a backup plan. My guess was that all the pirates were back in La Ceiba. I never did figure out why they were guarding Roatan at all. A pretty enough island, but no different from a thousand other pretty islands in the ghost world. Maybe there was a hidden cache of treasure here somewhere . . . although I couldn't imagine what treasure ghosts would need to hoard. Or maybe it was simply a hideaway to protect, because that's what pirates did.

Following my directions, we found a vine-choked path heading into the jungle. From the hills, we could see a gorgeous white-sand beach hugging an aquamarine Caribbean sea, pink coral reefs visible beneath the crystal clear water . . . but of course, our path didn't take us anywhere near there. After about a quarter-mile of fighting through thick jungle, we came to an open stretch. I stopped and shaded my eyes to look south. There, on the other side of the clearing, was the next landmark, a huge slab boulder. An easier path wound past the boulder and through a semicleared gully.

A half-mile later, a simple white clapboard house came into view. Kristof waved for me to move in for a better look while he lurked in a coconut grove.

I circled the house and peered at the rear windows, invoking my built-in zoom. Once I was certain no one was watching from a window, I cast a blur spell and hurried onto the rear wraparound porch. With a combination of blur and cover spells, I was able to sneak a look in each window. It wasn't until I hit the last one that I found Luther Ross.

I had no physical description to work with, but I didn't need it. There were five people in the living room. Four of them were twentyish, female, and varying shades of blond. The fifth was a tall, dark-haired man in his early forties, with a Vandyke beard, mischievous gray eyes, and a hand planted on the ass of one of the blondes as he leaned over her shoulder and pointed at a vase. The girl's face screwed up in concentration as she tried to displace the vase. When it didn't so much as wiggle, he patted her rear and waved her to a chair.

Unbelievable. Give a guy the power to move objects across cosmic dimensions and what does he use it for? Screwing cute coeds. No wonder Ross hid out on Roatan—it wasn't so much about evading the Searchers as limiting his classes to a select type of clientele, those he could handpick and give the transportation code. He probably took on the occasional legitimate student, to maintain his reputation, but if this was an example of his average class, then I understood why he hadn't been more successful in passing along his skills. From the looks of these girls, they'd be lucky if they could pronounce telekinesis. Nymphs probably. If you'd asked me in life what a nymph's powers were, I couldn't have told you. And now that I'd met some in the ghost world, I still wasn't sure.

Whatever special abilities nymphs once possessed had vanished generations ago, and they'd fully assimilated into the human race, where they could be found filling the ranks of cheerleader squads everywhere. Almost no one in the living supernatural world even knew they existed. Hell, *they* didn't know they existed until they popped up here after they died and went, "Wow, we're, like, magical."

The supernatural dimensions of the ghost world were filled with extinct races like elves and dryads, beings who'd lost their powers centuries ago but came to our realms after death. I suppose it wasn't easy, arriving here and finding yourself surrounded by people who could cast spells, change into wolves, manipulate the elements, and more. Not surprising, then, that these extinct races kept the ghost-world black market in business as they desperately tried to find some power, any power, to call their own.

I went back to Kristof and told him what I'd seen.

"Looks like a job for you," he said. "I'll stand guard out here."

I changed into the short black dress I'd worn with the haunters, and left my hair straight. Maybe not Ross's style, but at least he wouldn't mistake me for one of his nymphs.

I walked to the front door, opened it, and strode inside.

As I entered the living room, every nymph jumped. Ross looked over at me. Then he looked at me some more.

"Well, well," he said. "A new student, I presume?"

I made a show of looking at each nymph, then cocked a "not likely" brow-arch at Ross.

"You can't just walk in here—" the girl in the chair began.

Ross lifted a finger and she stopped in mid-squeak.

"It's a business call," I said. "I would have phoned but . . ."

He smiled. "Not that easy in this world, is it? So you're looking for lessons? Maybe . . . private lessons?"

I turned a slow smile on him and shrugged. As I strolled closer, his eyes widened briefly, that look of surprise most men get when they realize how tall I am.

When he looked me full in the face, his lips pursed. "I know you, don't I?"

"Do you think you'd forget if you did?"

He chuckled, and reached to touch my hair, but I swept it out of his reach. His smile only broadened. Around me, the nymphs fairly growled.

"Mind if I sit?" I asked.

"Please," he said.

I walked to the nymph in the chair and finger-waved for her to get up. She glowered at me.

"Annette . . ." Ross said.

"Let her find her own chair." She looked around the room, which had no empty seats, then smirked at me. "Whoops, guess you'll just have to go home."

I murmured a spell under my breath. When I finger-waved again, the motion yanked Annette out of her chair. I flicked my fingers and she tumbled to the floor. From the couch came a mixed chorus of gasps and giggles. I swept my skirt under me and sat, then looked up to see Ross grinning.

"Eve Levine, I presume?" he said.

I arched my brows.

"Your reputation precedes you," he said. "It just took me a moment to make all the connections. Girls, this is Eve Levine. Aspicio half-demon and spell-caster extraordinaire."

One of the nymphs from the couch crossed her arms and thumped back into the cushions. "That's not funny, Luther. We aren't stupid, you know. Half-demons can't cast spells."

"True," I said. "But even half-demons have two parents."

The nymph frowned as she struggled to digest this.

"You girls go on upstairs," Ross said. "Ms. Levine and I have business to discuss."

It took more coaxing than that, but he finally cleared the room. Then he took a seat in the chair across from mine.

"So, lessons . . ." His gaze traveled up my bare legs. "I believe that could be arranged."

"There's some other business I need to discuss first."

"Ah." A twitch of disappointment as he eased back into the chair.

"Have you ever heard of something called a Nix?"

He paused, eyes rolling back as if peering into his memory banks. "Demi-demon, isn't it?" Another pause, lips pursing, then he shook his head. "That's all I'm coming up with."

I gave him a brief rundown. He listened, motionless, gaze on mine, never interrupting, never so much as blinking as he absorbed my words. When I finished, he stroked his beard.

"And do you know *why* she'd be looking for me?"

"No idea. Do you do anything besides poltergeist lessons?"

He shook his head. "My one and only claim to fame, I'm afraid."

We talked for a few more minutes, but I could see no other reason why the Nix would come to Luther Ross. And why visit a poltergeist teacher when you can cohabit with the living?

When we finished, Ross thanked me for the warning. "So you expect she'll show up here?"

"She was on her way."

"In that case, perhaps you shouldn't be in too much of a rush to leave. Why don't you stay for a while? Pose as a student . . . if, indeed, you were serious about those lessons."

"I was. And that might not be a bad idea. What would you take in exchange for lessons? Transportation codes, contact names—"

"I was thinking of something more"—his teeth flashed against his dark beard—"personal."

"Oh, I'm sure you get enough of that from your nymph harem. No room on the mattress for me, I'll bet."

His smile broadened to a grin. "Some nights it can get a bit crowded. But for you, I'd clear it out. Even put on fresh sheets." He caught my look and sighed. "Or I suppose I could settle for a few prime transportation codes."

24

"PSST!" SOMEONE HISSED AS I STEPPED ONTO THE front porch.

I looked to see a girl with a heart-shaped face, long blond hair, and doelike brown eyes. Typical nymph. She looked as if she should be sprinting through the woods, clothed only in a few strategically placed leaves.

"Yes?" I said.

She motioned for me to follow, then scampered off to the woods, as silent and nimble as a deer. I looked around. Kris hailed me with a raised hand. I gestured toward the nymph. He nodded, and I took off after her.

When I got to the edge of the woods, I slowed. Last thing I needed was to get attacked by one of Luther Ross's jealous students.

I found the girl hovering by a tree. She looked around nervously.

"He's lying," she whispered. When I frowned, she hurried on, "Mr. Ross. He's lying about the Nix. She was here. I saw her. I heard them talking. Is she really—" She shivered. "Is she really as bad as you said? She kills people?"

" 'Fraid so. Is she here now?"

"She left last night. I can't believe I was in the same room as her. I talked to her! Do you think—do you think she might have done something to me? Made me evil, too?" A whimper. "I've never killed anyone. I did some bad stuff when I was alive, but it wasn't my fault. I always picked the wrong kind of friends. Do you think she infected me? Turned me into a murderer?"

"She can't turn anyone here into a murderer."

The nymph turned her wide eyes up to mine. "Are you sure?"

"The only people in the ghost world are dead, hon. You can't kill them."

"Oh, right." Her shoulders relaxed. "That is such a relief."

"I'm sure it is. Now, you overheard Ross and the Nix talking . . ."

She nodded. "They were discussing a plan. Mr. Ross said—"

Something crackled in the undergrowth. The nymph jumped like she'd been shot. I scanned the jungle, but saw nothing.

"No one's here," I said. "It was probably an animal."

"What kind of animal? Oh!" She shivered and looked back to the house. "I shouldn't be doing this. If Mr. Ross found out he could—he knows some scary stuff."

"So do I. Now, you were saying?"

Her fingers wrapped around my forearm, tugging me farther into the jungle. When I hesitated, her lower lip wobbled and her eyes filled, as if she might cry from sheer terror. Obviously she wasn't talking until she felt safe, so I let her lead me. After a few steps, she mumbled something.

"Hmm?" I said.

She kept muttering, her face forward as she pulled me

into the forest. I caught a couple words of Latin and knew she wasn't talking to herself. She was casting.

I yanked my arm back. Her grip only tightened.

"Hey!" I said.

I tried to shake her off, but she just looked over her shoulder, fixing me with eyes that had lost every trace of girlish innocence. Her lips kept moving in their cast. Once more I tried to fling her off, unable to believe this sudden show of bionic strength. She yanked back, and I flipped forward, nearly falling.

As I twisted up again, I snarled my own cast. A binding spell. I finished it . . . and she only smiled, her own incantation still flowing. I started a knock-back spell, but the first words had barely left my mouth when the air around me started to shimmer. The unmistakable first sign of an opening portal. Shit! Again I struggled to pull my arm from her grasp, but couldn't budge. Demonic strength. Only thing with demonic strength was a demon. Or a demi-demon.

I mentally shouted for Trsiel. While I'd have loved to hog-tie the Nix myself and present her to the Fates, I knew better. A demi-demon was too strong, and immune to spells and demonic shows of power. This was a job for an angel.

The portal split open, a black hole to nowhere.

I threw myself in the other direction, but the Nix jerked me back, and I flew off my feet. I saw the portal. Saw it yawning before me, knew I was about to fly into it . . . and there wasn't a damned thing I could do about it.

Then something hit the Nix from behind and her grip went slack. I sailed across the clearing, hit the ground rolling, and sprang up. I wheeled to face the Nix. She was charging Kristof. I threw myself at her, but Kris dove out of her way in time. As she wheeled, she snarled at him, lips curling, teeth bared. Something in that snarl sent ice water through my veins and I froze, just long enough for her to lunge at Kristof again. He feinted. I cast an energy bolt. It passed right through her. She spun on Kris and flew at him. He ducked, but this time she managed to snag his arm. She swung him off his feet, and whipped him toward the portal.

My gut went cold. I pitched forward and hit Kristof in the side just as his feet passed into the portal. The Nix lost her grip, and Kris and I tumbled to the ground. As I hit, I remembered a spell that might work, an incantation to protect the unwary spell-caster who summoned something she couldn't handle.

As I ran through the spell, I braced myself. The moment the final words left my lips, a thousand-watt jolt ripped through me and I collapsed, writhing and convulsing. Had the Nix attacked me in that moment, I'd be helpless to fight back. But as my body jerked and shuddered, I caught sight of her on the ground across the clearing, racked by a seizure double the strength of what I was feeling. Then Kristof's arms went around me, lifting me up, his face ashen.

"S'okay," I managed as the last twitches rippled through me. "Anti-demon spell. Nasty side effect. Damned demon blood."

As he lifted me, the Nix struggled to her feet, still unsteady.

"A demon witch." She spit the words with a sneer, but made no move to come closer. "Half-demon, I should say. A substandard demon from a substandard race of spell-casters. I suppose the Fates grew weary of wasting their angels on me. Perhaps they've given up trying to catch me and now seek only to annoy me. Go away, little gnat. This isn't a game for you."

"No? But I'm doing so well. Found you faster than those angels ever did, I'll bet."

She laughed. "Found me? I found you. And almost sent you into the great beyond."

"Yeah, great plan. Too bad you fucked up, huh? Foiled by a half-demon witch. That's gotta sting." *Come on, Trsiel! Where the hell are you?*

The Nix's face clouded and I readied another anti-demon spell and hoped I still had enough power to cast it.

"Do you think that portal is the worst I can do? You really are a fool, witch. And the only way to teach a fool is with a demonstration."

She lifted her hands . . . and disappeared.

"Shit!" I said, rushing forward.

Kristof strode up beside me, frowning as he scanned the forest.

"You called?" said a melodic voice behind us.

I wheeled to see Trsiel, standing there as nonchalantly as if he'd been summoned to tea.

"You!" I said. "Where the hell were you? She was here—the Nix—I called you."

His lips formed a soundless word that I'm sure was a very unangelic oath. I explained what had happened.

"So now she's in this nymph's body—"

"That's not a nymph. It's the Nix. That's her form in this world."

"What? You knew what she looked like? When the hell were you going to tell me?"

"You've seen the books, haven't you? The pictures? There wasn't one of her specifically, but they all resemble one another."

"I've seen *human* renderings of *mythological* Nixen. And, yes, they looked like nymphs, but they were paintings, done by humans. What kind of idiot would assume that's what the damned things really looked like?"

"Er, well, yes, I guess that makes sense."

"You guess?" Kristof strode over to Trsiel. "What are you people playing at? Eve nearly got herself thrown into a hell portal because she doesn't know how to stop this Nix. Or was she supposed to read that in some book, too?"

Trsiel's eyes hooded and he looked over at me. "Who is this?"

"Kristof Nast. Kris, meet Trsiel."

From Trsiel's expression, he knew who Kris was, or maybe he just knew who the Nasts were. Either way, he was not impressed. He gave Kris a slow stare, turned on his heel, and marched out of glowering range.

"That's your guardian angel?" Kris said, jerking his thumb at Trsiel.

I nodded.

"He's doing a hell of a job so far. Time to apply for a replacement, if you ask me."

"No," Trsiel said. "I don't believe she did. Eve?" He motioned me aside.

I shook my head. "If you have something to say, you can say it in front of Kris."

"I'd rather not."

"Eve?" Kris said.

I looked at him. He, too, waved me over for a personal conference. As I walked toward Kris, Trsiel's jaw tightened.

"I'd better leave you to handle this," Kristof murmured. "Otherwise, I'll be sorely tempted to slug this idiot, and I don't think that'll go over well with the Fates. Would you like me to go have a chat with our poltergeist friend?"

I nodded. "Please. If he did double-cross me—"

"I doubt it. You're a good judge of character."

"Yeah? I did a great job last night with that wolf-pirate."

A tiny smile. "Ah, but you *didn't* trust him, remember? You just gave him the benefit of the doubt. No, I'm sure Ross will be as surprised as we were to find he had the Nix in his midst. But I'll test that theory with a little . . . interrogation."

"Thanks." Before he could leave, I reached for his arm. "And Kris?"

"Hmm?"

"Thanks for earlier. With the Nix."

He smiled. "Anytime."

I watched Kristof go. As he rounded the corner of the house, a jolt of alarm ran through me. Would Ross tell him about the poltergeist lessons we'd arranged? Shit. I hoped not. Kris had bit his tongue the day before, not asking why I knew so much about Ross. He didn't need his suspicions confirmed now . . . and we didn't need a reason to start arguing about Savannah again.

"Where is he going?" Trsiel asked.

"To interr—talk to Luther Ross. See whether he knew he was tutoring a Nix."

Trsiel shook his head, anger falling from his face. "This isn't a good idea, Eve. I know Kristof is your daughter's father, and you're obviously still close, but this is your quest. He can't help. The Fates should have explained this to you."

"The Fates sent Kris along to Lizzie Borden's house with me. They must think it's more important for me to catch this Nix, using whatever resources I have, rather than insist I fulfill my debt by myself."

"It's not that, Eve. It's—you can't—when you ascend—" He bit the rest off. "I'll speak to them. In the meantime, Kristof is right. You do need to know how to hold this Nix until I can capture her. The problem is that, as far as I know, the only thing that can bind her is this."

He lifted his right hand, said a few words, and a gleaming sword appeared, his hand already in the grip. He lowered it and held it out for me. I leaned over for a better look. I'd seen Janah's sword so this one shouldn't hold any great fascination, but the moment it appeared, I couldn't rip my gaze away. My fingers clenched, as if imagining the feel of the hilt in my hand. I remembered how it felt and a shiver raced through me.

"So that would stop her," I said. "But I can't have one, can I?"

"Not until you're an angel. Perhaps, though . . ." He hefted the sword and looked at me. "I wonder if you could use mine."

"Sure—I mean, if you don't need it."

"Not anymore." His eyes clouded. "Not lately, at least."

He held it out. I lifted my hands, with every intention of casually reaching for it. Instead, I fairly snatched it from his hands. He chuckled. I gasped as the white-hot heat licked down my arms.

He grabbed for it. "I'm sorry. Here, let me—"

"No." I stepped back, hands still on the sword. "Hurts like hell, but I can handle it." I managed a wry smile. "Don't get much pain in this world anymore. Feels very strange. Is this what normally happens if a nonangel touches it? Or is it my demon blood?"

"I'm not sure. I've never had any reason to let anyone hold it before."

I lifted the sword, expecting to feel the strain on my wrist muscles, but it flung upward as if it was made of aluminum instead of steel.

"Wow."

Trsiel gave a soft laugh. "You like that, don't you?" He stepped back and looked at me, his lips curving in a mischievous smile. "It suits you."

I gripped the hilt tighter. In my hands, I held what might very well prove to be the answer to my problem with Savannah. If Trsiel was right, and I was being tested for angel-hood . . .

I rearranged my fingers, staring at the light filtering through them, almost hypnotized by the glow. There would be strings attached to this beautiful piece of weaponry. Responsibility, for one thing. Big responsibility. If I brought in the Nix, and the Fates offered to reward me with angel-hood, I couldn't just say "Thanks for the cosmic makeover" and run. To get those powers, I'd have to promise to use them for the purpose for which they were intended. I'd need to join the ranks of the celestial bounty-hunters.

A big price . . . for a big reward.

I tore my gaze from the sword. All hypothetical right now. Even if Trsiel was right about the Fates' plans, I still had the catch the damn Nix.

"If it hurts too much—" Trsiel began as my grip slackened.

"It's fine. But will it work for me?"

"Only one way to find out. Swing it at me."

"At you?"

"At me, through me, whatever. Slice away. Can't do

any damage, but I'll be able to tell whether it's working as it should."

I stepped back and sized up Trsiel, then hefted the sword a few times, getting a feel for it. A practice swing, testing the arc. Then a readjustment and another trial run.

"You're not trying to decapitate me, Eve. Just take a swing."

I did, executing a samurai-worthy slash. The blade sliced through his torso and shot, bloodless, out the other side.

"Still a bit upset with me, I see," he said, rubbing the side of his abdomen.

"Did it hurt?"

"Will you be disappointed if I say no? I felt it, but, no, I don't think it hurt."

"You don't *think* it did?"

"Having never been human, I'd hardly recognize pain if I felt it. I can say, though, that it didn't work. In your hands, the sword won't incapacitate the Nix. Not until you become—"

"An angel, which I can't become until I finish this quest. Love those catch-22s." I glanced over at him. "Do you think that's really what they have in mind? Testing me for angel-hood?"

"Ah, so after she holds the really big sword, she begins to think ascension doesn't sound so bad after all." He smiled. "Yes, I'm ninety-nine percent sure that's what the Fates intend, and I'm holding back that final percent only to preserve my dignity, in the unthinkable event that I'm wrong." He reached out and touched the sword. It evaporated. "Best way to find out for sure? Complete this quest. First, we need to go back to that penitentiary. If the Nix intends to show you something, it'll be in the living world."

"A death," I said. "Or deaths. Let's go, then. We have to—"

Trsiel put his hand on my shoulder. His touch was almost as hot as the sword. "Slow down. This is what she wants, for you to rush off after her."

I hesitated, my gut telling me to ignore him, move fast, head her off. Another classic Eve Levine error-in-judgment in the making.

"She may succeed," Trsiel said. "She probably will. You have to be prepared for that."

"She'll kill someone, you mean. Take a partner before I can intercede." I nodded. "I know. But if I'm going to move cautiously, then the first thing I need to do is make damned sure that the Fates don't have any tips to help me contain her. Could you visit Amanda Sullivan by yourself?"

"You want us to split up again," he said with a soft sigh.

"This is the best use of our resources. Now, give me an hour—or do you guys keep time?"

"We can." He hesitated, then nodded. "Let me give you a code. Someplace safe you can wait."

I waited until he was gone, then headed to the house to meet up with Kristof.

25

ROSS HADN'T KNOWN ANYTHING ABOUT THE NIX, AND he was pretty damned freaked out to learn she'd been under his nose—and in his bed—for several days. It was enough to make a guy swear off nymphs for good . . . or at least for a few weeks. The Luther Ross Poltergeist School for Nymphs was closing its doors until the Nix was captured, and in the meantime, its headmaster was packing his bags. As for those poltergeist lessons, the subject never came up in front of Kristof . . . thankfully.

"Trsiel has been here," the middle Fate said as soon as we appeared. "He has some concerns about Kristof's involvement."

"And didn't waste any time voicing them," Kristof muttered.

"We believe he may have a point." She lifted a hand against Kris's protest. "Hear us out. This Nix, having now met Eve, clearly feels this is personal, and we fear she may lash out at Eve by hurting someone close—"

My gut went cold. "Savannah. Oh, my God."

Kristof's head shot up, eyes wide with alarm. The Fate lifted both hands this time.

"To go after Savannah, the Nix would need to know who you are, and what is important to you. She's a demi-demon. She has no patience for that—not when she's already found one way to hurt you."

I saw the Nix whipping Kristof toward that open portal, felt my gut go cold again. One look my way at that moment, and she'd know exactly how to get to me.

"While I appreciate your concern, ladies," Kristof murmured. "I believe that, ultimately, the risk is mine to accept or decline."

The oldest Fate shot in. "Is it?"

Kris snuck a glance my way. "Well, of course Eve can voice her opinion, but if I feel I can help, I will."

"If that Nix opens another portal and tries to toss you into it, I'm sure Eve will say, 'That was his decision,' and let you go while she captures the Nix."

Kristof looked at me again. "Very well. I'll step aside. But if you need me, Eve—"

Before he could finish, the Searchers whisked him away.

It turned out that the Fates didn't know a way for me to contain the Nix, so I used Trsiel's code and teleported into a room that looked as if it had been carved out of pearl, with iridescent walls that glimmered with streaks of pink and blue. The wall looked as hard and solid as pearl, but felt like loosely wadded silk. As I stepped back, my feet sank into what felt like plush carpet, yet the floor appeared to be made of the same material as the walls. From somewhere came the softest strain of music, almost an undercurrent of the air itself.

Typical angel quarters? Hardly the way I'd want to

spend my afterlife. But places like these would be for full-bloods like Trsiel. I wondered where the ascendeds lived. In the ghost world? Keeping their angelic identities a secret? Another of a million questions I'd need to ask . . . if Trsiel was right that the Fates intended to offer me angel-hood.

"Where the hell did you send me?" I muttered. "A celestial waiting room? Damned angels—"

A discreet cough. I turned to see a man and a woman standing half-turned toward me, as if I'd interrupted their conversation.

He was tall and dark-skinned, and she was also tall, with strawberry blond hair. Neither would have been out of place on the cover of any fashion magazine . . . if they wore something more fashionable. But both wore garments of a diaphanous fabric the same luminous pearl white as the walls. The woman wore a toga that left one shoulder bare, while the man was dressed in a loose-fitting shirt and billowing pants. I've heard of people looking so healthy they glowed, but these two literally did; their skin gave off an unearthly shimmer.

"Eve," the woman said, her beautiful voice leaving no doubt that she was a full-blooded angel.

"Uh, yes," I said, suddenly flustered. "I'm looking—"

"For Trsiel," the man said. "He gave you the code to come here?"

When I nodded, the two exchanged a look that I was sure was more than a look. They were speaking to each other telepathically, like the wraith-clerks did. Did full-blooded angels naturally communicate by telepathy? I'd never considered that with Trsiel, but then, except for the voice and picture-perfect beauty, he and these two seemed like members of different species.

"Is Trsiel . . . around?" I asked. "He was supposed to meet me here but—"

"But he is late."

The woman gave the barest shake of her head, as if this wasn't surprising. She looked at the man and they communicated something. The man looked over at me.

"I will find him," he said.

"Find who?" Trsiel swung through the doorway, still dressed in the cargo pants and jersey he'd been wearing earlier.

"We need to get you a watch," I said.

He grinned, eyes glinting. "At least this time you aren't dueling anyone." He saw the others. Dismay flickered across his face, but he forced it back with another jaunty smile. "Have you guys been introduced?"

"No, we *guys* have not," the woman said.

"Eve, this is Shekinah." He gestured at the woman, then nodded at the man. "And Balthial. Eve is—"

"We are well aware of who Eve is and what she is doing," Shekinah said, voice rippling with annoyance. "We are also aware, Trsiel, that you have been having some . . . difficulty helping her with that task."

"Difficulty?" Trsiel's jaw twitched. "I haven't had any—"

"Eve found the Nix and you failed to capture her. You were late, and—"

"He wasn't late," I cut in. "The Nix took off as soon as I summoned him."

As soon as I said this I wished I hadn't. Shekinah shook her head as if to say, "What's the universe coming to, a ghost defending an angel?" When her gaze met Trsiel's, I'm sure that's pretty much what she *did* say to him, telepathically.

"We should be going," I said. "We have a lot to do—"

"Of course you do," Balthial said. "It was a pleasure meeting you, Eve, and I am looking forward to renewing the acquaintance when you ascend."

"Yes," Shekinah said. "It was indeed a pleasure. And if you require any assistance with this quest, any assistance you might not be currently receiving, you may contact either Balthial or myself through the Fates."

At that, Trsiel's jaw set so hard I feared he'd start snapping teeth. The other angels nodded a farewell, as serene and composed as ever, and faded away.

"What the hell is her problem?" I muttered when they were gone.

Trsiel's jaw relaxed into a crooked smile. "Shekinah and I have some . . . philosophical differences. Balthial and I do, too, but he's better at hiding it."

"Seems like there's more than *philosophical* differences between you and them."

Trsiel tensed. His gaze studied mine, as if trying to interpret my meaning. Then he relaxed again and reached for my hand.

"Let's go see Amanda Sullivan," he said. "I'll explain on the way."

"So the Nix has resurfaced in the living world?"

He nodded. I laid my hand in his, and he teleported us there.

26

WE EMERGED IN A DARK, DANK ROOM THAT STANK OF something indescribably awful.

"Guano," Trsiel said in response to my gagging. When I gave him a "huh?" look, he translated. "Bat shit."

"There's a special name for it? Can't imagine why that never entered my vocabulary before. What's guano doing in—"

I stopped as my brain made an abrupt logical click. Where there's bat shit, there must be . . . I looked up, way up, and saw rows of little bodies suspended from the ceiling. I shuddered and wrapped my arms around my chest.

Trsiel smiled. "You'll wrest a burning sword from an angel, but you're afraid of bats?"

"I'm not afraid of them. I just don't like them. They're . . . furry. Flying things shouldn't be furry. It's not right. And if I ever meet the Creator, I'm taking that one up with him."

Trsiel laughed. "That I'd like to see. Your one and possibly only chance to get the answer to every question in the universe, and you'll ask, 'Why are bats furry?'"

"I will. You just wait."

As Trsiel prodded me forward, I tried hard not to

glance up. Judging by the damp chill and the flying rodents, we were either in a cave or a really lousy basement. The stacks of moldering boxes suggested option two.

"I thought we were going to the jail," I said.

"We are."

I scanned the room. "I think your teleport skills need a tune-up, Trsiel."

"Close enough."

He led me through a door and into a cleaner part of the basement. As we walked, he made good on his promise to explain about Shekinah and Balthial.

Earlier, Trsiel had mentioned a structural reorganization in the angels' ranks, whereby only ascended angels went out into the world on missions. The full-bloods did other tasks, higher tasks. Most of the full-bloods were more than happy to leave the daily grind as "divine instruments of justice" to the ascendeds. A few, though, like Trsiel, chafed at this new world order like career beat cops assigned to desk duty. Can't say I blamed him. Give me the down-and-dirty life of a warrior over a sanitized office job any day.

That, Trsiel explained, was part of his "philosophical difference" with Shekinah and Balthial. They were glad to be out of the trenches, away from the taint of humanity, while Trsiel embraced that "taint," and all that went with it.

"It's not that I want to be human," he said as he led me through the basement. "It's just that I don't see anything inherently *wrong* with being human. Wait—oh, this way." He swerved around a corner. "It comes down to one question. Who do angels serve? We serve the Creator, the Fates, and the other divine powers. That's a given. But do we also serve humanity? I think we do."

"And they disagree?"

"Vehemently." He paused at the bottom of a rotted set of unused stairs, then took my elbow and guided me up them. "So that's part of the problem. The other part, not unrelated, is that I'm younger than they are."

"So you weren't all created together?"

"For full-bloods, there were three waves. As the human race grew and expanded, the Creator saw the need for more angels. I'm from the third wave, the last one. Since then, the ranks have been increased by recruited ghosts. The ascended angels."

"So how old are you?"

"Only about a thousand years."

I sputtered a laugh. "A mere tot."

He tossed me a smile. "Well, according to the old ones, that's exactly what I am. A child—a willful, uncouth, in-experienced child—one who definitely shouldn't have been assigned this job."

"Seems to me you're doing just fine."

Another smile, broader. "Thanks."

We found Amanda Sullivan sleeping fitfully in her cell, jerking and moaning with dreams . . . or visions of the Nix. I hoped they gave her nightmares, horrible night-mares, the kind that disturb sleep for months and scar the psyche forever.

Again, Trsiel offered to scan Sullivan's brain for me. I refused.

Since he'd been here only minutes before, he knew ex-actly where to look for the visions, and zipped me over to that part of her sleeping brain without so much as a glimpse at the putrid wasteland elsewhere.

As we coasted to a stop, I braced myself. Colors and sounds flickered past. A man's face twisted in anger. Ripples of simmering frustration. A pang of envy. A woman's taunting laugh. A newspaper clipping. More clippings, like a scrapbook. A grainy photo of a sprawled body. An announcer's voice with feigned gravitas, words cutting in and out. "Deaths." "Wounded." "Notorious." "Manhunt." A wave of excitement. Then harsh words raining down like hail. "Stupid." "Ugly." "Useless." "Wasted space."

The images flipped faster, out of focus, like a movie reel hitting the end. Then nothing. I waited, straining for voices, but nothing came. After about ten minutes of this, Trsiel pulled me out. When I opened my eyes, I saw Sullivan on the cot, sleeping soundly.

"So that's it?" I said. "She's gone?"

"It seems so. Her old partners aren't connected to her all the time."

"We can't sit around here, popping in and out of this woman's brain, hoping she links up with this new partner again."

"And what would you suggest? Unless you noticed more than I did, there wasn't anything to go on. Only a few news articles with no solid connection to the partner herself."

"No? What are they, then? Random images?"

Trsiel shook his head. "The Nix is plucking them out of her memory, showing them to her, hoping to incite a reaction."

I slumped against the wall. "So we have nothing, then."

"Be patient. More will come."

* * *

We spent the rest of that night in Sullivan's cell, with
Trsiel logging in to her brain every five minutes, checking
for fresh data. At about four, he suggested I go hunt down
the little boy, George, see how he was doing. Very considerate . . . though I suspect he was just tired of watching
me pace.

Morning came, and a guard roused the women for
breakfast. Sullivan stayed in bed. The other women were
released from the cells, but no one even stopped at
Sullivan's door. Maybe she wasn't a breakfast person.

After every other woman had filed out, Sullivan rose,
groggy and sulky, and yanked on her clothing. A few minutes later, a guard brought her a food tray.

"It's cold," Sullivan whined, without even taking a bite.
"It's always cold."

"That so?" the guard said, hands on her broad hips.
"Well, Miss Sullen, we could always let you go down and
eat with the rest of them again. Would you like that?"

As Sullivan turned away, her hair tumbled off her
shoulder, revealing a slice across her neck that had yet to
scab over.

"Didn't think so," the guard said. "Be thankful for the
room service."

The guard strode away.

"Fat cow," Sullivan muttered.

She scooped a spoonful of oatmeal, then stopped,
spoon partway to her mouth. Carefully, she lowered the
spoon, head moving from side to side with the wariness
of one who's learned she has reason to be wary.

"Who's there?" she whispered.

When no one answered, she rose, noiselessly laying
the tray aside, and glided to the cell door. A long, careful

look each way, head tilted to listen. The cell block was empty.

"I can hear you," she said. "I hear you singing. Who is it?"

I looked at Trsiel. The same thought passed between us. If Sullivan was hearing voices in an empty cell block, they could only come from one place. Trsiel reached for my hand and transported me back into her mind.

I came to a stop in a pit of darkness. Sure enough, after only a moment, I picked up the whisper of a voice. Someone humming off-tune. Then words. I'm usually damned good with songs, but it took me a moment to place this one, probably because the singer kept mangling the lyrics.

"Invisible" by . . . someone. Didn't matter. The voice only sung a few lines from the refrain, and when she hit the end of those lines, she started over again. Something about being treated like you were invisible.

I vaguely remember the song, probably because it had always triggered a childhood memory of the neighborhood grocer. I'd stood head and shoulders above all my friends, but the grocer always served all of them first, then served every other customer in the store, only taking my money when I tossed it onto the counter and walked away with my candy bar. I figure now it was anti-Semitism—East Falls being the kind of small town where even Catholics are eyed with suspicion. My mother never talked to me about stuff like that; she preferred to pretend it didn't exist. When I told her about the grocer, she'd said I was imagining things. I knew I wasn't, and being unable to put a label to his dislike, I had assumed it was my fault. Like my teacher, Mrs.

Appleton, he saw something bad in me, something no one else noticed.

"Invisible," the woman crooned. "Oh, yeah, I'm invisible." A sudden shriek of laughter sent me jumping like a scorched cat.

"That's me," the woman chortled, voice shrill with manic glee. "Miss Invisible. They treat me like I'm not even there. And they sure as hell don't care. Dah-dah-dah-dah. Miss Invisible."

Another voice, the soft, insidious tones of the Nix. "And what are you going to do about it?"

"Make 'em notice me, of course. Make 'em stand up and salute. All hail, Miss Invisible." The woman's laughter screeched like nails down a blackboard, drunken bitterness infused with a teaspoon of madness. "Gonna show them that I'm somebody. Somebody important. Somebody who can make them tremble in their pretty little Pradas."

The darkness cleared and I found myself in the young woman's memory, inside her body, looking out her eyes, as I had with Sullivan and the death-row inmate. I stood in a long hallway, sweeping the floor with a wide, industrial-size broom. Two well-dressed women walked past, chatting and laughing. One unwrapped a stick of gum and dropped the wrapper. Dropped it right where I'd just finished sweeping. The woman laughed.

Laughing at me—at the stupid, ugly cleaning girl. No need to find a garbage can. Not when Lily is right there. That's her job. Make her earn her pay.

If the Nix was retrieving this memory for Lily, it had to be important. I struggled to pull myself away from Lily's thoughts, to look around for myself. Long hallway. Well-dressed women. An office building? *Look, Eve. Look harder. You'll need to find this place.* Farther down the hall, sheets of paper dotted the walls. Notices of some kind. Dog-eared and brightly colored. Not very businesslike.

"Hey!" a young man's voice shouted. "Hey, that's mine!"

Three giggling girls streaked past, nearly knocking me—the woman, Lily—flying. They kept going without so much as a "Sorry," not surprising, considering they were about thirteen and being chased by a boy their age.

Bitches. Stuck-up little bitches, just like their mommies. Too good to say "Excuse me." Why bother? It's only the hired help. The cleaning lady.

I squirmed free of Lily's thoughts. The three girls ran shrieking down the hall, plowing past the two women without an apology, either, but Lily didn't notice that, didn't care about that. One of the girls lifted something and waved it like a flag as she ran. A boy's bathing suit.

"Give me that!" her pursuer yelled.

They threw open a door and zoomed through. The barest whiff of chlorine wafted back.

As the boy skidded after them, my gaze went back to those distant sheets on the wall. I honed in on them, concentrating, but was only able to invoke half my usual power, just enough to make out a few of the headings. SPRING FLING. TUTORS WANTED. MARCH BREAK MADNESS.

Two men strode in front of the bulletins, coming toward us. Both were in their early twenties, both dressed in sweat-drenched shorts and tank tops, both damned fine-looking. My pulse quickened, heart tripping, a slow burn of longing plunging through me— pretty creepy, considering these boys were about half my age. Fortunately, since I had neither a pulse nor a heartbeat, I knew this lust attack wasn't mine.

Brett. The name fluttered through Lily's mind. Her

gaze lingered on the shorter of the two, following him up the hallway.

"Next week is going to be my week," Brett said to his companion. "You just watch. I will beat you so badly, you'll—"

"Die of shock?"

Brett cuffed the other man and they bounced down the hall like overgrown puppies.

Look at me, Brett. I'm right here.

The two men passed Lily without a glance her way.

I'll make you look, Brett. I'll make you see me. Just wait—

An alarm wailed. Lily shot up, blinking fast, heart racing. The bedside clock-radio continued to screech. She slammed the Off button, then stared at the blurry red digits. Seven-thirty.

"I owe, I owe, it's off to work I go," she muttered.

"Oh, but today will be different," the Nix whispered.

Lily chortled and reached for her glasses. "Oh, yeah, today will be much different."

With her glasses in place, the room came into focus. She leaned over and opened the nightstand drawer. Inside were a few dog-eared magazines. She reached underneath, fingers closing on metal. She pulled out her prize. A semiautomatic.

The scene faded to black.

After a few minutes, Trsiel pulled me out.

"Is that it?" I said. "I need more. Did you see the flyers on the wall?"

"I saw papers, but I couldn't get a good look. I'm restricted to what she sees."

I started to pace. "So was I, but I could zoom in a bit. It was a community center. Indoor pool, ball courts, bulletins for a dance and March Break activities—she works in a community center. And that's where she's headed now. With a gun."

As I passed Trsiel, he grasped my shoulder, forcing me to stop pacing.

"Eve, we need to—"

"Slow down and think. I know that. But I think better when I'm moving."

He let me go. I wheeled and strode across the cell.

"Let's see what we have," Trsiel said. "Her name is Lily and she works at a community center as part of the cleaning staff."

"Yeah, yeah." Still walking, I rubbed my hands over my face. "Okay, she just woke up, so it'll take her a while to get to work. It was seven— Wait. What time is it now?"

Trsiel walked through the cell bars and looked around. "This clock says just past nine-thirty."

"Then we've got a two-hour time difference. That means she's somewhere west of Colorado. American accents, so definitely in the country."

"Upper West Coast accents," Trsiel said. "North of California."

"Right. Thanks. I'll talk to Jaime. We'll search the Internet for community centers on the upper West Coast with mentions of a Spring Fling and March Break Madness. Once we've narrowed it down, she can see whether any have a janitor named Lily." I stopped pacing. "A game plan. Good. But it'll take some time. With any luck, that guy she's after won't be heading to the community center for a while today."

I paused, then looked at Trsiel. "So she wants to kill this guy because he doesn't notice her. Besides the seriously fucked-up logic behind that, there's one thing I don't get. What is this boy to me?"

Trsiel frowned.

"The Nix is doing this for my benefit, right? A demonstration of her power. A lesson for me. So—" I stopped and met his gaze. "Look, if she succeeds in killing this kid, I'll feel bad. Anyone would, right? But it won't—well, I don't know him. If this is a lesson, either I'm missing the point or this Nix has me pegged all wrong, thinks I'll fall apart over the death of a stranger."

"She knows you're working on something usually reserved for angels—"

"So she probably assumes I'm typical angel material— protect the innocent no matter who they are. Makes sense." I glanced at Sullivan. "Should we check in her skull one last time? If I could get a better look at the flyers in that hall—"

As I said the words, I pictured the flyers again and my words froze in my throat. The pink poster. TUTORS WANTED. I'd seen that before. Months ago. My memory pulled up an image—a soft, pretty hand reaching for the tabs along the bottom of the flyer, ripping one off, silver rings flashing. A deep sigh sounded somewhere to the left.

"Literacy tutors? Oh, please. Don't you do enough of that crap already?"

"It's not crap. And it's only an hour a month."

"Like you've got an hour to spare! Geez, Paige—"

I spun on Trsiel. "Portland. The community center is in Portland. My daughter—oh, God, Savannah goes there."

27

I RECITED A TRANSPORT INCANTATION. AT THE LAST second, Trsiel realized what I was doing and grabbed my hand. We landed a few blocks from Paige and Lucas's house. The community center was a couple miles in the opposite direction.

"Can you get us any closer?" I asked.

"I'd need to find out exactly where we're going. A map, a street address—"

"No time."

I started to run. Trsiel shot up beside me.

"She's not going after your daughter, Eve," he said. "She can't."

"Can't?" I said, still running. "Can't how?"

"The Nix can't choose her partner's victims. They make the choice. They pull the trigger. She can give them the resolve to pull it, but she can't aim it for them."

I rounded a corner, not slowing.

"This Lily is going after that young man," Trsiel said. "He must have a connection to your daughter. That's how she's going to hurt you. By hurting Savannah—emotionally."

I eased down to a jog, giving my brain a chance to digest this. Could this Brett guy have a connection to my daughter? Sure. He played basketball—so did Savannah. Had he coached her? Maybe played some one-on-one with Savannah and her friends? Or had she just seen him around the courts, thought he was good-looking, developed a crush?

There had to be a connection, but it did no good to stand around pondering the possibilities. We still had two miles to go, and no idea what time Lily started work.

We arrived at the community center just past nine. The massive two-story building was filling fast. A steady stream of cars and minivans drove through the drop-off circle, disgorging kids toting knapsacks and duffel bags. As the children and teens climbed the stairs, they merged with the current of adults flowing in from the parking lot, heading to the gym, a class, or a club. A typical Saturday for an urban family—twice as busy as any weekday.

We hurried up the front steps, through the congestion, and into the bright foyer. I looked around. We were at the junction of four hallways and a double set of stairs. Ribbons of people wended their way in every direction.

"We should start with the janitor's room," I called back to Trsiel, yelling to be heard over the cacophony of laughs, shouts, and greetings.

"Good idea. Where is it?"

"I have no idea. I've only been here once, and only to the basketball courts. Maybe we should check there instead. Brett was coming off the courts."

"Which doesn't mean that's where he is today. Better to find Lily. Then it won't matter *where* her target is."

"Right. So where—"

"Just a sec."

Trsiel disappeared.

"Hey! What—"

He zipped back before I could finish. "There's a basement."

"Then that's where we'll start."

We found a suite of janitorial rooms downstairs, everything from storage closets to an office to a lunchroom. All were empty. Two jackets hung in the office. A man's and a woman's.

We spent the next two hours combing the building. The problem was that, in a place like this, nobody stayed still. Kids raced from swimming lessons to the lunchroom to model-building classes. Adults hurried from the treadmills to their child's floor-hockey game to the coffee shop. Walk into any room, then return an hour later and ninety percent of the faces had changed.

Eventually, we found one of the janitors—an elderly man. But there was no sign of his female counterpart.

After our fourth sweep of the building, we stopped in the second-level child-care center, by the window overlooking the front entrance. Below, the flow of traffic dropping off children had slowed as noon approached. A brief break for lunchtime, then it would start all over again.

"So is Lily not here?" I said to Trsiel. "Or do we just keep missing her?"

"We haven't seen a female janitor yet. And that was definitely a woman's jacket downstairs."

"But is it from today? It's spring. Come to work in a

winter coat and by afternoon it can be hot enough that you forget to take it home. Damn it! What if—"

I caught a glimpse of a motorcycle pulling out of the drop-off circle, and turned for a better look, invoking my long-range sight. One glance, and I was flying out the door.

"What is it?" Trsiel asked, hurrying after me.

"That bike. The motorcycle. It's Lucas's. Lucas Cortez. Savannah's guardian. She's here. Savannah's here."

Trsiel grasped my shoulder, but I shrugged him off, plowing through people as I made my way to the stairs.

"Don't panic, Eve," Trsiel said, jogging at my heels. "Maybe it looks like his motorcycle—"

"It *is* his motorcycle. It's an antique. Very rare. He restores them."

"Maybe he was dropping off his wife, Paige. You said she comes here—"

"There was no helmet on the back of the bike."

"What?"

"Paige would have left her helmet. Savannah's fifteen. She'd carry it inside with her."

From Trsiel's silence, I knew this didn't answer his question, but I wasn't wasting my breath explaining the adolescent coolness quotient of toting around a motorcycle helmet. I cut through the solid wall of kids heading up to the lunchroom, and bounded down the stairs so fast I tripped. Trsiel grabbed me. I righted myself, shook him off, and kept going. A few steps from the bottom I stopped. I peered out over the sea of heads. People kept walking through me, blocking my view. I climbed onto the railing for a better look.

"Eve," Trsiel said, laying his hand on my leg to steady

me. "If we find Lily, she can't hurt anyone, including Savannah."

"You go after Lily, then. I'll find—"

"I need your eyes, Eve."

A shape shimmered below, on the other side of the railing. Kristof appeared, looking up at me.

"Oh, thank God," I whispered. "Kris! It's Sav—"

"I know," he said, putting out his arms to help me down. "I'll find her." He lowered me onto the floor. "You find the Nix."

I squeezed his hand. "Thank you."

Trsiel wheeled through the crowd, grabbed my elbow, and tugged me away.

"The basketball court," I called back to Kristof. I gestured to the north end of the building. "It's that way."

Kris nodded and jogged off.

We started our search where we'd begun—in the janitorial rooms below. As we hurried down the hall toward the lunchroom and office, something clattered to the floor in one of the storage rooms, like a broom or mop falling over. I veered toward it. Then, from the end of the hall came the muffled sound of a phone ringing. Someone answered after the first ring, with a reedy, feminine-sounding "Hello."

Trsiel changed course. I darted ahead of him and ran through the closed office door. On the other side, back to us, stood a slight, pale-haired figure. Tinny music wafted from a cheap radio on the desk, the rise and fall of the music cutting into the phone conversation. I took a step closer, then saw the gnarled hand clutching the receiver. The elderly male janitor.

As I turned to leave, the song on the radio ended, and the janitor's words became clear.

". . . exit door shouldn't be locked. I opened them all myself this morning." Pause. "Which room is it?" Pause. A sigh. "I'll send Lily." He hung up, then muttered, "If I can find her. Damned girl is making herself scarcer than usual today."

He lifted the walkie-talkie. Trsiel and I stayed where we were, hoping to catch the room number so we could head off Lily there. The janitor pushed the Call button four times, but only static responded.

"Lazy kids," he grumbled.

He stalked to the door and yanked. It didn't open. Another pull, but it stayed shut.

"Goddamn it!" he said as he yanked on the door.

I stepped through to the other side. A broom had been jammed through the handle. Trsiel and I looked at each other, then dashed for the stairs.

On the main level, doors all along the corridor banged open and slammed shut as kids raced out of classes. We headed for the gym. As we turned the corner, a shriek cut through the din. I leapt through the wall and came out in the boy's changing room. Two ten-year-olds were whipping each other with wet towels, dancing out of the way, and screeching with laughter.

We walked through the next wall and found ourselves in the men's shower room.

"Circle around back to the hall," Trsiel said. "But keep your eyes open in here for that young man Brett."

As we stepped into the changing area, a loud pop sounded. A man leaning into a locker jumped, head clanging against the metal shelf.

"Damn it!" he said. "Did those boys get hold of caps again?"

"Nah, that came from the classrooms. Science club, I'll bet," another man said with a laugh. "Those kids. Remember when they made that—"

Three more pops. Then a scream. As Trsiel and I ran for the hall, one of the men shouted, "Someone's shooting. Oh, my God! Brooke! Brooke!"

We raced through the wall, into the women's changing area. Inside, women were shouting their children's names as they ran, half-dressed, for the door. Others grabbed their cell phones to call 911, while more raced to a rear emergency exit, only to find it locked.

"Fire alarm!" someone yelled. "Pull the fire alarm!"

A teenage girl dove into our path, racing for the alarm, but it sounded before she reached it.

The hall was now jammed with people, all trying to get to the front door. I thought I heard a shot, but the screams and shouts all around us were too loud for me to tell, much less pinpoint a direction. I soon lost sight of Trsiel. I didn't stop to look, just kept plowing forward through people.

Trsiel's hand grabbed mine, tugging me backward.

"This way," he said. "The first shots came from over here."

One of the distant screams took on a shriller note, filled with more than panic. Screams of pain.

We followed the sounds into a room of stationary bikes. A woman lay huddled in the corner, screaming as an elderly woman tied a tourniquet around her thigh, trying to stanch the flow of blood. Jaunty music played, then a man's chipper recorded voice came on, enjoining listeners to "pedal faster, but not too fast—save your strength for the big hill at the end."

Across the room a woman my age still sat on a bike, pedaling erratically, stopping, then restarting, eyes wide with shock. Blood dribbled from a bullet nick under her arm. More blood, mixed with flecks of gore, spattered her face. That blood came not from her, but from the man in front of her. He lay backward over his bike, feet still trapped in the pedal straps, a hole through his eye socket.

Behind them, a young woman lay on the floor, convulsing, as a young man in sweats hunched over her, telling her, "It'll be all right, honey, just hold on, honey, help's on the way."

As I looked around the room, I remembered those newspaper clippings I'd seen in Lily's memory. Not single murders, but killing sprees. Lily said she wanted to be noticed. She wanted to be remembered. This wasn't about killing one man who ignored her. It was about killing everyone who ignored her, and that meant everyone she met, everyone she could hit.

"Savannah!"

Trsiel grabbed my arm.

"No!" I said, trying to yank free.

His grip only tightened, as firm and unyielding as the Nix's. "Go and make sure Savannah is safe. Then start hunting. If you see Lily—if you even *think* you see her—call me. Don't try to stop her. You can't."

"I know."

He released my arm and I tore off in the direction of the gym.

28

THE HALL HAD CLEARED AS EVERYONE JAMMED INTO the section near the narrow front doors. The panicked screams had given way to sobbing and angry shouts of "Move!" and "Get out of my way!" Through the commotion, though, the sound *I* heard loudest was the softest— the whimper of frightened children. I tried not to think about them, packed into that seething mob. People knew there were kids here—they wouldn't let panic override caution. Or so I told myself. It was the only way I could keep going in the opposite direction.

"Eve!"

I was almost at the gym when Kristof hailed me. I looked across the scattering of people to see his blond head cutting through them.

"Savannah," I said, rushing to him. "Where is she?"

"I can't find her."

"Here, I'll—"

He grabbed my arm as I raced past, toward the gym. "She's not there, Eve. The courts are empty. They closed for lunch hour. She must be in the cafeteria. Where is it?"

"No, Lucas just dropped her off. If her class was after lunch, she'd have eaten at home. She— Art! She has art class on Saturdays. They were downtown last year, but they must be here now. The studios are up the hall."

I turned and ran in the other direction, passing through the logjam at the front door and racing to the studios on the other side. Distant sirens blared. Then a shot. Another. More screams behind us.

The first studio door was closed, the room dark and empty. In the next, we found the remains of a class—a half-dozen adults huddled behind tables, a few whaling at the locked exit door. Unfinished sketches papered the floor. One middle-aged man grabbed an upended easel and threw it at the window, but it only bounced off the thick glass. A younger man raced for the hall.

"No!" a woman screamed after him. "It's blocked. Stay here!"

My gaze swept across the faces, seeing no Savannah, no one even close to her age. As I turned, I caught a shimmer in the corner—like a portal, but much weaker, the glimmer so slight only a practiced eye could see it.

"There!" I said, pointing. "She's cast a cover spell."

I raced across the room and knelt beside the empty spot.

"Good girl," I whispered. "Smart girl. Stay there. Stay right there."

A shot sounded in the hall. A young woman to my left screamed. A figure wheeled through the door. Another young woman—skeletal-thin, all jutting bones, with greasy brown hair and an acne-pocked face.

She lifted a gun.

I started to call Trsiel. The woman beside me dove to the floor, sailing through me and knocking against Savannah. The cover spell broke, and Trsiel's name died on my lips.

Savannah lifted her head. She saw Lily. Saw the gun.

"Cast, baby," I said. "Cast it again. Hide!"

Her lips started to move . . . in a binding spell.

"No! Hide. Just hide!"

Lily turned toward Savannah. Something flickered in her eyes, something I recognized from the day before. The Nix. Her gaze fixed on Savannah, and her eyes flashed with jubilation.

Lily swung the gun in Savannah's direction.

"Trsiel!" I screamed.

The gun fired. Kristof leapt into the bullet's path, but it shot right through him. Savannah had no time to duck, no time to finish her cast. I threw myself over her, knowing even as I did that it would do no good, that my gesture was as futile as Kristof's.

Someone gasped. Someone behind me. I twisted to see the other young woman, the one who'd hit the floor beside us. She was lying on her side, face contorted with pain and shock, hands on her stomach, blood flowing through her fingers.

I looked back at Lily. She stood there, a tiny smile on her face, gaze and gun fixed on her intended target—the dying woman, not Savannah. The Nix's rage flashed behind her eyes. The air around Lily rippled, as a formless vapor flowed from her body.

Trsiel sailed through the doorway, sword raised. With a perfect lunge, he swung it and the sword cleaved through Lily. It passed right through her, bloodless, as it had when I'd used it on him. But Lily felt it. Her eyes went huge, hands dropping the gun as she clenched her heart.

"Trsiel!" I yelled, pointing behind Lily.

He saw the vapor, now taking on the faintest outline of

the Nix. He charged, sword raised, and slashed at her, but she vanished before the blade made contact.

Lily slumped to the ground, slack-jawed, dead.

"Theresa? Theresa!"

Savannah was crouched over the young woman on the floor. As she cast a healing spell, her hands fumbled at the woman's shirt, ripping it away from her stomach. The woman's eyes stared, empty, at the ceiling. Savannah pressed her hands to the woman's neck, feeling for a pulse.

"She's gone, baby," I said.

I reached for Savannah. My hands passed through her as she lowered her mouth to perform CPR. I tried again, tried with everything I had, to touch her, to hold her, but my fingers just slid through her body, my words tumbling out unheard.

I screamed with rage and frustration. Kristof's arms wrapped around me, and he hugged me tight as we watched our daughter desperately try to resuscitate a dead woman.

"They're coming," Kris said, striding back into the studio. "Lucas dropped Paige off at the door. He's parking the car now, and she's running in." He knelt beside Savannah. "Come over to the window, sweetheart. You can see Paige. She's on her way."

Savannah just kept rocking, her bloodied hands wrapped around her knees, gaze straight ahead. Two medics had arrived and were tending to Lily and the other woman, but no one had time for Savannah. Her classmates had fled the moment Lily dropped the gun, leaving Savannah alone with two dead bodies.

"Wasn't fast enough," Savannah mumbled, mouth pressed against her knees. "Should have picked another spell. A faster one."

"You did fine, sweetheart," Kris said. He reached for her hands, lips twitching as his fingers grasped only air. He threw a glare over his shoulder. "Where's Paige?"

I walked to the window. From there, I could see the drop-off circle, now hastily taped off. Paige was stuck on the other side, arguing with a young officer. Her face was taut, eyes simmering, and I knew she longed to knock the officer flying over his yellow tape with a knock-back spell, and charge in here after Savannah. But I also knew she wouldn't, not until she'd exhausted all the safe routes.

A young man strode up behind Paige. Tall, thin, Latino, wearing wire-rimmed glasses and a battered leather jacket.

"Lucas," I breathed. "Thank God. You tell them."

"He will," Kris said from across the room.

Even from here I could see Lucas's quiet demeanor fall away as he drew himself up, snapping orders with the air of authority only a Cabal son can muster. As he spoke, he eased sideways, pulling the officer's attention with him. Paige sidestepped in the other direction, then darted under the tape and ran for the building.

"She's coming," I said.

I hurried into the hall to coax Paige along. Even if she could have heard me, she didn't need the encouragement. She made a beeline for the studio, flying through the door and across the room, then dropped to embrace Savannah.

Savannah melted in Paige's arms, sobbing against her shoulder. Lucas wheeled through the doorway a minute later. He left Savannah where she was, still clinging to Paige, face buried, but took her hand. With his free hand, he reached into Paige's purse, dug out a tissue, and gingerly began to clean the blood from Savannah's fingers. As I watched them, my heart ached. Part of me was happy, knowing that my daughter had the best guardians I could want for her. And yet another part of me hurt so bad seeing them there together—a family that didn't include me and never would.

"I couldn't help her," I whispered. "I couldn't do anything. I tried—I've been trying so hard. I thought maybe, just maybe—but I was wrong. I can't do anything."

Kristof's arms went around me and I collapsed into them.

Paige and Lucas took Savannah home a few minutes later. Kristof led me around the back of the building and we walked the trails there for about an hour, saying nothing. I couldn't stop thinking about that moment in the art room when Lily had lifted the gun, playing it and replaying it as I searched for a solution, something I could have done. There was an answer. One answer. Become an angel.

As I turned to Kristof, the words were on my lips. *I could protect her, Kris. If I became an angel, I could protect her. I could have stopped Lily and the Nix.* But as I imagined saying it, I knew his response. He'd see it not as the perfect solution, but as another step down into the quagmire—giving up my afterlife to serve as an angel so I could protect our daughter.

So instead I said, "Maybe I can't help Savannah, but I

can show the Nix that this little 'demonstration' hasn't done anything but piss me off."

A tiny smile. "And that's never good."

"Which she is about to find out." I glanced back toward the community center. "I'd better go find Trsiel." I looked at Kristof. "I guess this is good-bye again, for a little while."

"I'm never far," he said. "You need me, I'll be there. You know that."

I squeezed his hand. "I do."

Heartfelt vows of vengeance are easy to make, but rarely easy to carry out. I roared back into hunt mode, ready to track down this demon-bitch and send her soul to the deepest, darkest hell I could find. Instead, I found myself billeted to Lizzie Borden's living room, while Trsiel hung out with Amanda Sullivan.

Trsiel did his best to placate me, reminding me that so long as Amanda Sullivan saw nothing, the Nix wasn't in the living world. Fat lot of reassurance that was—the last time Sullivan saw a vision, it'd taken less than six hours for the Nix to persuade her partner to act—less than six hours before three people were dead.

I couldn't imagine how she'd accomplished that— finding a partner so quickly. Not just any partner, but one who would be in the same building as my daughter that day. Was it that easy to find someone with a motive for murder? Someone who lacked only the guts to follow through on their impulses?

Trsiel's theory was that the Nix hadn't been nearly as surprised to find me tracking her as she'd pretended, that she'd known I'd been on her trail, found out who I was, and scouted a few potential partners in the periphery of Savannah's life, women she could leap into if I got too close and needed a demonstration of her power.

There was no way I was hanging out with Lizzie Borden, not while I still had leads to pursue. We'd questioned Luther Ross, but I still felt as if I'd missed something there, some insight into the Nix and her motivations. Ross had said he hadn't known why she'd come to his school, and I doubted he was lying, but if I asked the right questions, maybe I could figure out her motive for myself.

Before we'd left Luther Ross, Kris had given him a "safe house" transportation code, sending him to a remote location where he could lie low and, more importantly, where we could track him down if need be. Now I wanted to speak to him again. So as soon as Trsiel dropped me off at Lizzie's house, I did a quick check-in with her, then zipped off after Kristof.

29

I FOUND KRISTOF IN HIS OFFICE AT THE COURTHOUSE, talking to a toga-clad client. The moment I peeked around the corner, Kris scuttled his client off.

"I need to find a certain nymphomaniac," I said, perching on the edge of his desk.

"Nymph—?" Kris laughed. "Ah, and never has that word been more apt. Mr. Ross, I presume."

"So where'd you tuck him away?"

Kris's fingers closed over mine. "Let me show you."

We touched down in a field of white. For a second, I thought the Fates had diverted us to a throne-room waiting area. Then I saw a distant line of trees and, behind them, a mountain range. As I turned to look for Kristof, the ground under my sneaker crunched like broken glass. I knelt and reached down. My fingers sank into something soft and faintly cold.

A white ball struck my shoulder, and exploded on contact. I looked over my shoulder to see Kristof packing a second missile.

"Throw that at your peril."

The snowball glanced off the top of my head, showering

me with snow. I glared at him, spun on my heel, and started to march away. As I walked, I cast a blur spell. The last words left my mouth, then I wheeled, raced behind Kristof, and knocked him flying off his feet. When he hit the ground, I jumped on his back and rubbed his face in the snow.

He sputtered, bucked, and managed to flip me off his back. We tussled for a few minutes, both armed with fist-fuls of snow, trying unsuccessfully to give the other a face-washing. Finally, we fell onto our backs, laughing.

Overhead was a faint greenish arch. As I watched, other threads of colored light appeared, reds and blues and yellows, dancing and weaving against the black sky.

"Are you doing that?" I asked.

"Wish I could take credit. It's the Northern Lights."

"Wow."

For a few minutes, we watched the lights dance. The night was so silent I could hear the distant crackle of breaking ice and the occasional hoot of an owl. The air was pleasantly cool, like a brisk fall day.

"So where are we?" I murmured, reluctant to disturb the quiet.

"Remember that witch barmaid in La Ceiba? Said the pirate town was like—"

"Alaska without the snow." I choked back a laugh. "You sent Luther Ross to Alaska?"

Kristof tilted his head to the side. "You don't think he'll like it?"

"Naughty boy. We'll be lucky if he'll talk to us after this." I looked back up at the sky. "So how come you never brought me here?"

"I was saving it. For a special occasion, I guess." Another glance my way. "You like it?"

I closed my eyes. I could still see the Northern Lights dancing. "Mmm. You'll have to bring me back."

His fingers found mine, enclosing them in a sudden surge of warmth. "I will."

A shout, and we bolted upright. I concentrated and the darkness lifted enough for me to make out two orange jackets moving from a stand of trees.

"*Never* shoot anything around here," a man said, voice carrying in the stillness. "The drop-off point's there, remember? That's fine welcome for a new visitor—getting shot the moment he touches down."

"But I saw something over there," a younger voice said. "In the woods, not near the drop-off."

"Doesn't matter. You don't shoot anywhere near here."

Kristof leaned toward my ear. "Time to make some new friends. See if they've encountered your pedagogically inclined nymphomaniac." He pushed to his feet. "Hullo!"

The older voice hailed him and two hands rose in greeting. As I brushed the snow from my jeans, the men approached. Their voices had suggested an older man and a younger one, but I couldn't have guessed which was which. Both were bundled in parkas, with fur-lined hoods drawn tight over their bearded faces, as if it really was subzero out here. Matching hunting vests topped their parkas. Each man carried a modified rifle.

"Well, hello there," the man with the older voice boomed. "Welcome to Deerhurst, Alaska. Population: a few thousand." He winked. "But only a handful of 'em human."

"Beautiful place," I said, looking around. I snuck a glance at Kristof. "You, uh, must get a lot of visitors."

"Nope," the man said. "The transportation code is

damned obscure, which is how we like it. Just enough visitors to keep things interesting."

"So I bet you haven't seen another visitor in . . . weeks."

"Not that long, actually. Had a party come through just this morning." He thumped the younger man on the back. "Billy here came with them. Now, let's get you folks back to the lodge. It's getting nippy out." He shivered for effect. "Time for a hot cocoa and brandy by the fire. A proper Alaskan welcome." He started to lead us away, then turned. "Damn it, I've been out in the bush too long. Always forgetting my manners. I'm Charles. You can call me Chuck, Charlie, Chas, whatever you like . . . though, given the choice, I'll stick with Charles."

We introduced ourselves, then followed Charles across the snowy field.

As hunting lodges went, this one was damned near perfect: a two-story log chalet nestled among snowcapped evergreens, wood-perfumed smoke spiraling lazily into the night sky. Icicles from the second-floor balcony glistened in the moonlight. When Charles pushed open the thick wooden door, a wave of heat rushed out, carried on a current of laughter. Inside, a half-dozen men sat around a huge stone fireplace that took up the entire north wall.

"Got two more," Charles called as he led us in.

While the men called greetings and introductions, an oversize pet door on the east wall swung open and a gray-brown wolf pushed its way inside.

"Hey, Marcello," Charles called. "Good hunting?"

The wolf gave a grumbling growl, walked over, and turned, presenting us with a flank splattered in still-wet orange paint.

"Lemme guess," Charles said as a wave of guffaws rose from the fireplace crowd. "New guy?"

A middle-aged man rose from his chair. "How was I supposed to know he was a werewolf? He should be wearing a collar or something."

Marcello chuffed and tossed a baleful glare at the man, then strode to the fireplace and stretched out in front of it.

"Marcello prefers his wolf form," Charles whispered. "Hardly ever changes back. Won't hear us complaining, though. I had scores of hunting dogs in my day, but none of them compared to Marcello."

I looked at Charles's rifle as he laid it down. "So you guys hunt with paint balls?"

He laughed. "The Fates won't let us use bullets, that's for sure. Not that we can kill anything here anyway. Doesn't matter to me. I like it better this way. More sporting . . . and you never run out of targets." He looked over at Marcello and lowered his voice again. "He can make that paint disappear with a good shake. He's just leaving it on to razz the new guy."

"So . . ." Kris said as we moved into the room. "How many new guys do you have?"

"Four. All first-timers. Real keen on hunting, though, and that's the important thing."

That certainly didn't sound like Luther Ross. He'd probably touched down, taken one look around, and teleported out again.

A few minutes later, I was on a sofa by the fireplace, legs stretched over Kris's lap, enjoying a hot chocolate with marshmallows as Kristof chatted up the hunters, trying to discreetly find out if anyone had spotted Ross. I was only half-listening, having already decided Ross was long gone, and was furiously trying to think up a new plan . . . one that didn't involve sitting with Lizzie Borden.

I had gotten about halfway through my drink, and nowhere near a good backup plan, when the door swung open, blasting us with cool air. In walked Luther Ross, a pained smile pasted on his face. A young man followed him in and patted his back.

"Got ourselves a real hunter here, boys," he said. "Could barely drag him back in, even when I promised him brandy and venison stew."

Ross's gaze darted about, searching for an escape route.

"Hey, Luther," Charles called. "Got someone you might like to meet. You know how you were asking if we ever got any ladies up here? Well, you're in luck. One just landed."

Ross's gaze followed Charles's wave almost reluctantly, as if afraid of what he'd see. When he saw me, he blinked. Then a slow smile lit up his eyes.

"Well, hello," he said.

"Uh, one problem," Charles said as the others chuckled around him. " 'Fraid she didn't come alone."

Ross's gaze slid to Kristof and his eyes narrowed.

"Told you you're in trouble," I murmured. "Better let me handle this one."

It took a few minutes, but I was finally able to excuse myself from the group. Upstairs, I made a beeline for the balcony. I'd been outside only a few moments when Ross joined me.

I should have known he'd still be in Alaska—he'd have let us send him to Siberia if it meant he'd be safe from the Nix. The old saw about being "a lover, not a fighter" fit Ross to a tee. There was probably a good dose of "yellow-bellied coward" behind that, but I'm sure he would have preferred the first cliché.

I blamed the poor choice of safe house on a transportation-code mix-up, and promised to find him something more suitable . . . as soon as he answered a few questions. He agreed, and Kristof joined us.

Ross said he'd never asked the Nix anything about herself, including why she'd shown up at his door. There's a Luther Ross in every bar every night of the week—guys who are willing to sit across from a pretty girl for hours, look deep into her eyes, and entreat her, with near-perfect sincerity, to tell him everything about herself, her thoughts, her fears, her hopes and dreams. But, hey, if you'd rather just hop straight into bed, then your private life is your own, sugar.

So I focused on what *she'd* asked *him*. And that answer did surprise me. The Nix had asked Ross absolutely nothing that didn't relate to telekinesis and poltergeists. During lessons, she was a little keener, always volunteering to try a new technique, always persevering in the face of failure. Though she hadn't succeeded in actually moving anything telekinetically, Ross was certain that, had she stuck with the lessons, she would have become one of his success stories.

When teaching sessions ended, the Nix would always withdraw from the group, find a quiet corner to practice in, and keep working. Yes, she had shared Ross's bed on her last night there, but the postcoital chitchat had been purely business, and she'd apparently used the sex only to get some one-on-one training time.

"Speaking of one-on-one training," Ross said as we finished. "Send me someplace decent this time, preferably warm, preferably female-friendly, and definitely safe, and you can forget about owing me for those poltergeist lessons."

"Er, right." I resisted the urge to sneak a look Kristof's way, but I could feel his gaze boring into me. "So how about we send you—"

"What I don't get, though," Ross cut in, "is why someone like you even wants poltergeist lessons. Not that I'm complaining." A quick grin. "But, let's face it, you're powerful enough to get whatever you want without resorting to parlor tricks."

"Being able to manipulate objects in the living world would help me solve a problem."

His brow crinkled. "With the Nix?"

"No," Kris murmured. "It has nothing to do with the Nix . . . or anything in this life."

"It's to help my"—I glanced at Kris—"our daughter."

"Ah," Ross said. "Well, now, that I can see. But I'm not sure how much good poltergeisting would be. What you really need is that demon amulet."

"Demon—"

Kristof cut in. "It's a legend. A myth."

I glanced at him. "You've heard of it? What does—?"

"There is no amulet, Eve."

We exchanged glares. Then his gaze softened, and his eyes begged me to let it go.

I tore my gaze away and looked at Ross. "This amulet—"

Kristof strode out. I murmured an apology to Ross, and a promise to return, then hurried after Kristof.

I found Kris on the front lawn, standing behind a tree, face lifted to the sky. He couldn't have missed the sound of my shoes in the snow, but he didn't call to me, didn't even look at me when I found him.

"Kris?"

"Do you think you're the only parent who worries about her children?" he asked quietly.

"No, of course not—"

"Do you think you're the only one who made mistakes? Who isn't haunted by those mistakes? Who wouldn't do anything to turn back time or reach into the living world and set them right?"

I stepped toward him, hand going to touch his arm, but he moved away.

His gaze swung down to meet mine. "My younger son is poised to ruin his life following a path he hates, because he thinks it's what I would have wanted, and my eldest is trapped between betraying himself and alienating the only family he has left."

"So you know—"

"That Sean's gay? I'm his father, Eve. I probably knew it before he did. I saw him struggling, trying to find his way, and I decided I had to let him find it himself. When he figured it out, I'd be there for him. Only I wasn't, was I? Now he's left wondering how I would have reacted, and I can't help him, can't support him. Just like I can't tell Bryce that I never wanted him to follow in my footsteps. That life made me miserable, cost me the only woman I loved, and I thanked God every day that Bryce had the guts I didn't have."

I tried to say something, but my voice dried up in my throat.

He continued, "Even with Savannah, I made mistakes. I was so afraid of facing her, of seeing you in her, so afraid that she'd hate me, that I let Gabriel Sandford go to

Boston in my place. His mistakes were my mistakes, and all the hell Savannah suffered because of him is my fault."

"It wasn't—"

"Do you know what I don't regret, though? Going into that basement after her. Even if I couldn't protect her, even if she accidentally killed me, I have not one regret about that. Do you know why? Because it brought me here. To you."

"Kris—"

"So maybe I screwed up in my life. Maybe I can't undo any of that. But coming here gave me the chance to fix the biggest mistake I ever made: letting go of you."

I opened my mouth but, again, nothing came out.

"This is our chance to start over, Eve. Yours and mine. Forget everything we did before and start over. Not just with each other—that's only part of it. Maybe you didn't need a new life the way I did, but you got one, and there's no going back now, no matter how hard you try."

"You want me to choose," I whispered. "You or Savannah."

He turned so fast he startled me. "Goddamn it, are you even listening? I'm not saying forget Savannah, and I'm not saying start up again with me. I'm saying start living a life. Any life. I thought—" He swallowed. "I thought with this Nix thing, maybe you were finally moving on, finding a place for yourself here, but then I see you in there, talking about Savannah and poltergeist lessons and that amulet, and I can see in your face that you haven't moved on at all. When you're done, you'll go right back to where you were, living in your own limbo, no better than one of those damned earth-spooks." He paused, voice lowering. "And I'm not sure how much longer I can stand to watch you do it."

His eyes met mine. For a minute, we just looked at each other. Then his lips moved in a few silent words, and he disappeared.

I stood there, feet rooted to the ground, my brain whirring, refusing to think, afraid that if I started thinking about it, I wouldn't be able to stop. Was I really losing him? My gut went cold at the thought. I'd fix this. I would . . . soon.

For now, I headed back inside to ask Ross about the amulet.

It was only when I returned to Ross, and saw his smug smile of triumph, that I realized my mistake. I know; it should have been obvious to me long before that. One second I'm worrying about losing Kristof's friendship, the next I'm plowing forward with the very action that brought things to a head in the first place. Typical—barreling toward my own destruction even as the warning signs flew up around me.

As long as I was there, though, it wouldn't hurt to know about the amulet. If Kristof was right, and it was only a myth, then it didn't matter. I knew his objection was not to me hearing about the amulet, but to the relentless obsession it symbolized. But . . . well, I could think about that later.

I told myself I'd only stay long enough to hear what this amulet did, but as soon as I heard that, I needed to know everything Ross could tell me about it. This amulet, if it existed, could solve my quest to help Savannah . . . with none of those pesky angelic responsibilities. According to Ross, the necklace, known as Dantalian's Amulet, together with the incantation inscribed on it, would grant the wearer the ability to possess a living person. The only catch? The wearer had to have demon blood. It was almost too good to be true.

Problem was, the amulet's function was all Ross knew. He didn't even realize "Dantalian" was the name of a demon. I didn't enlighten him now—as a half-demon, he'd be able to use such an amulet just as easily as I would, so I wasn't giving him any help finding it. Not that I thought it could be found, but . . . Well, it bore thought, and maybe a little investigation, when I was done with this Nix quest.

When I was almost done picking Ross's brain, I heard a noise in the hall, the creak of a floorboard. I slipped out, but no one was there. If it had been Kristof, he'd probably heard all he needed to hear. That thought spurred me to bring my talk with Ross to a quick conclusion. I gave him a transportation code more to his liking, then was saying good-bye when I heard the floorboards creak again. This time, I cast a blur spell and rushed out, hoping to catch Kris eavesdropping. Instead, I ran smack into Trsiel.

"Er, hello," I said. "Fancy meeting you here."

He glowered at me. "A long way from Massachusetts, isn't it, Eve?"

Before I could answer, he took my arm and teleported us out.

30

I'D HOPED TRSIEL'S ARRIVAL MEANT HE HAD A NEW LEAD
for us to follow, but he was only checking up on me. After
escorting me back to the Borden residence, he returned
to Amanda Sullivan's cell. I spent the next ten hours at
the Bordens', rehashing what I knew and trying to find a
fresh direction. I kept hoping Kristof would pop by, but
he didn't.

In the eleventh hour, an angel appeared.

It was just Trsiel, but by that point, it seemed like divine intervention nonetheless. A sparkling conversationalist Lizzie Borden was not.

"Got a lead," he said.

"Oh, thank God," I said, leaping to my feet. "When can
we go? Now? Please?"

He laughed, took hold of my hand, and teleported me
away.

Seems Sullivan finally had a vision of the Nix. She was
still in spirit form, but on the move. Through Sullivan's

dreams, Trsiel had pinpointed her last stopover: here. Wherever "here" was.

We were tramping across a dark meadow. A wispy fog had settled, a wet lace that smelled of heather and something not nearly so pleasant.

I wrinkled my nose. "Wet dog?"

As I said the words, a hairy red-brown lump appeared in my path. I stumbled back with an oath. The lump turned and fixed me with big bovine eyes. Then it shook its head, long curved horns flashing.

"What the hell is that?" I said. "A yak?"

"Highland cattle, I believe."

"Highland . . . We're in Scotland?"

"Near Dundee."

"And the Nix was here? Doing what? Cattle-herding?"

"No, visiting *that*."

He pointed to a forest. Seemed a strange place to visit, but before I made a fool of myself by asking, I narrowed my eyes and concentrated on sharpening my night vision. After a moment, I could see a building soaring above the treetops. Spires ringed the huge, flat roof.

"Looks like a castle," I said.

"Glamis Castle."

"Glamis thou art, and Cawdor; and shalt be What thou art promised. Yet do I fear thy nature; It is too full o' the milk of human kindness."

One of the cows mooed appreciatively. Trsiel arched his brows.

"What?" I said. "You recognize Bogart and Bacall but not the Immortal Bard?"

A shrug and a half-smile. "I've always been more of a cinematic angel. Shakespeare told some great stories, but I could never get past the boys in drag playing

Juliet. As for the quote, judging by the locale, I'm guessing *Macbeth*."

"Bingo. My one and only high school drama starring role: Lady Macbeth. I was a natural."

Trsiel started to laugh.

I turned on him, finger raised. "Don't say it."

Trsiel grinned. "I don't need to."

I started forward again, still staring at those majestic spires, black against the blue-gray night. "So this is *that* Glamis?"

"This is the Glamis Castle that Shakespeare wrote about, though it had nothing to do with the historical Macbeth."

We walked through a barbed-wire fence and onto a path.

"What's the Nix doing here?"

"I'm not sure," Trsiel said. "I saw the images through Amanda Sullivan, and I recognized the castle, but the only connection I can make is that it's reputed to be the most haunted in Scotland."

"Oooh, a haunted castle. I've always wanted to visit one of those. What's the story?"

He smiled. "Which one?"

"The best one. The bone-chilling-est one."

"Well, the best one, I'm afraid, doesn't involve a ghost at all, but a living, breathing monster. As for ghosts—"

"No, tell me the monster one."

He glanced over his shoulder at me.

"Oh, come on," I said. "Unless you can teleport us over to the castle, we have another mile to walk. I've spent ten hours sitting with Lizzie Borden. Entertain me. Please."

He smiled. "All right, then. But I warn you, storytelling

is definitely not an area of angel expertise. So, how to start . . . hmmm."

"Once upon a time?"

He shot me a look. "Even I can do better than that. Let's see . . ." He cleared his throat. "No castle would be a proper castle without a secret room or two. Glamis being a castle among castles, has three. There's the one where Earl Beardie spends eternity playing cards with the Devil. And there's the one where a Lord Glamis walled up a band of Ogilvies. But the best, and most . . . bone-chilling-est, is the one that contains the cursed Glamis monster."

"Oooh, I love a good curse."

"You want to tell the story?"

I grinned. "Sorry. Please continue."

"Well, legend has it that the Glamis family is cursed, as all the best families are. That curse was born, quite literally, in the form of a child. The first son born to the eleventh earl, a child so deformed, so hideous that every wet nurse brought to his crib took one look and the milk dried up in her breast."

"Really?"

"No, but the story's a bit short, and we still have a half-mile to go. I'm livening it up. Now shush."

"Sorry."

"The worst of it, though, was that the family was doomed to care for this child, not only through his lifetime, but for eternity because he was immortal. So they locked him up in a secret room, and it became the duty of each succeeding generation to care for him, and to keep him a secret from all, even those they loved. However, the bonds of matrimony permit no room for secrets, and one enterprising young Lady Glamis grew weary of hearing these rumors and not knowing the truth behind them. One night, while her husband was away, she held a dinner party, and conveyed an ingenious plan to her guests. They would take towels and hang them from each window of the castle. They did. Then they went outside and circled the castle, looking for the window with no towel, for this would be the secret room. And there it was, high up on the third floor. A tiny window . . . with no towel. So Lady Glamis rushed into the castle, up the stairs, down the hall, and threw open the door of the room nearest the secret one. Then she knocked along the wall, listening for the hollow spot where a hidden door might be. She knocked once, took a step, knocked again, took a step, knocked a third time . . . and something within knocked back."

Trsiel stepped onto the winding drive, and kept walking.

"Then what?" I said finally.

"Well, that's it. According to legend, before she could investigate further, her husband came home, found out what she'd done, and gave her hell. Soon after that, she left him."

"I don't blame her. But it's still a lousy ending."

"You want me to do better?"

"Please."

He gave a deep sigh. "The things I'm asked to do on this mission. Okay, better ending coming up. So . . . something within knocked back. Then, at a noise behind her, Lady Glamis turned to see her husband there. In his hand was a rusted metal key. He grabbed her, but before she could cry out for help, the secret door sprang open. A horrible moan came from within. Lady Glamis screamed then, screamed as loud as she could, but Lord Glamis shoved her through the door, slammed it shut, and locked her inside—locked forever with the monster, there to serve him for all eternity."

I lifted a brow. "Serve him how?"

He looked at me, then sputtered a laugh. "Not like that! This is a G-rated ghost story, woman. Don't be messing with it."

"A G-rated story? About taking some deformed baby and locking him up? And if it was true, and this poor guy had been locked up in there for decades, and someone threw in a perfectly good woman, what the hell do you think he'd do with her? Play Parcheesi?"

"You've corrupted my story."

"Believe me, it was corrupted long before I got hold of it."

As we rounded the corner, I looked up and stopped. Looming above us, embraced by threads of fog, was Glamis Castle.

"Holy shit," I whispered. "You know, when I hear stories like that, about hidden rooms, I always think they're obviously bullshit. How can you have a room and not know about it? But with a place like this . . . ? I bet you could have a dozen of them." I looked the castle over again. "It's supposed to be haunted? Doesn't surprise me. Hell, *I* wouldn't mind hanging out here for a while. Is there a dungeon?"

"No, just a crypt."

"That'll do. But I don't see the Nix as the sightseeing type. She's after something here, but there's a hell of a lot of *here* to search. Did Sullivan's vision give you any clues?"

"Just random snippets of various castle rooms."

"Like she was looking for something."

He nodded. "And I suspect she's come and gone."

"Meaning we're probably looking, not for the Nix, but for what drew her here. Could be a wild-goose chase. But if the castle's haunted, then it's likely related to—"

"Well, that's the thing. It *isn't* haunted."

"Huh?"

"One hundred percent spook-free."

I frowned. "Places this old are always haunted. Maybe not 'moaning specters and clanging chains' haunted, but with real ghosts. The ones caught between dimensions and the ones who just like to soak up a little spooky atmosphere."

"Normally that's true. But not here."

"Why not?"

Trsiel shook his head. "I have no idea. One of the ascendeds was assigned to investigate it last century, but then something more important came up, and he was never sent back. Nothing bad ever happens here. No unexplained murders. No demonic activity. No real reason to investigate further. If haunters don't want to set up shop here, well, that's not a bad thing. We have enough trouble with them as it is."

"But something must make this place unpopular with ghosts. And maybe that something has to do with the Nix's visit."

We slid into the castle through a side wall, emerging in a huge dining room with a table set for twelve and portraits lining the paneled walls.

The moment I stepped inside, a tingle raced down my spine—an indefinable prickling, like something in me perking up.

"You feel that?" Trsiel whispered. He had his back to

me, scanning the room, body held tight. As I stepped up beside him, he continued, "I told Katsuo—the angel who investigated—that I've felt something here, but he swore he didn't."

I stared at Trsiel, not so much because of what he said as how he said it. His lips never moved, yet I heard him clearly. He caught me staring.

"Sorry," he said, still speaking telepathically. "Should have warned you. Is this okay?"

I nodded.

"Keeps things quiet. If you need to talk, just think the words."

"Like this?"

He nodded. "And don't worry, I can't read your mind. It has to be a distinct thought aimed at me."

"Like a communication spell."

"That's right." He looked around, tensing again. "I don't know how Katsuo couldn't feel this."

"You've been here before?" I asked.

A shrug. "Once or twice. Sightseeing."

I doubted that.

"Split up?" I said.

He gave me a look that needed no telepathic explanation. I sighed. It was going to be a slow search.

As we headed deeper into the castle, my sense of disquiet grew, wavering between unease and something almost like anticipation. It wasn't what I'd call a negative vibe . . . certainly not negative enough to scare away any ghost with an ounce of backbone. Still, it was unsettling. As we searched for what drew the Nix to the castle, Trsiel did his best to keep us both calm with a running telepathic commentary, part castle tour, part historical ghostwalk.

From the dining room, we went into the Great Hall, a long tunnel-shaped room with an ornate plaster ceiling and more paintings of family members, including some guy wearing a really strange-looking flesh-colored suit of armor.

Adjacent to the Great Hall was the chapel . . . and still more paintings of dead guys. These, I think, were the disciples, though my knowledge of Christianity is a bit sketchy. In the center of the wall, over a candle-covered table, was a painting of Jesus on the cross. *That* one I knew. What really caught my eye, though, were the paintings on the ceiling. Fifteen of them, showing various religious scenes and at least one winged cherub.

"Doesn't look a thing like you."

Trsiel smiled. "Ah, but you haven't seen my baby pictures." He looked around. "Now, this, in case you didn't guess, is the chapel. Listen closely, and you might hear the scratching of a vampire, trapped forever within these walls."

"There's a lot trapped in these walls, isn't there?"

"It's a popular place. Do you want to hear about the vampire?"

"Let me guess, he infiltrated the castle as a servant or something, then they found him sucking the blood of some poor schmuck, and walled him up in here."

"No, they walled *her* up in here." He glanced over at me. "But, otherwise, you're right. Standard vampire lore. On to the billiard room."

We walked through a doorway into yet another oversize room, with yet more paintings. Glass-cased bookshelves lined one wall.

"Looks more like a library," I said.

Trsiel pointed at a table in the middle.

"Billiards, and a decent segue into my next story. The second earl of Glamis, known as Earl Beardie, was an inveterate card player. One Saturday night, he and his friend, the Earl of Crawford, played for so long that a servant came in to tell him it was nearly midnight, and to beg him to stop playing, for it was sacrilege to play cards on the Sabbath. Beardie sent him out, saying, 'I'll play with the Devil himself if I like.' A few minutes later, there came a knock at the door. There stood a man, dressed all in black, asking to join the game. The earls agreed and, that night, wagered and lost their souls. When Beardie died five years later, his family began hearing the sound of curses and rattling dice coming from that same room where Beardie had played. They walled it up, but the noises continued."

"More walling up? Geez, they must have employed full-time bricklayers in this place."

We continued on our walk. A few minutes later, he led me into a sitting room.

"And here is a bit of history closer to your time. The Queen Mother's sitting room. This was her ancestral home. She grew up here, and Princess Margaret was born here—well, not in this room, but in the castle."

"So the Queen Mother grew up and had a child in a castle known for ghosts, vampires, visits from the Devil, murderous revolts, executions, and torture? You know, this may explain a few things about the British royal family."

As we continued up a wide set of winding stone stairs to the clock tower, I saw a young woman in a long white dress standing at the landing window. My first thought was not "Ack, a ghost!" but "Hmmm, these Scots wear some pretty strange jammies." As Trsiel had said, the castle was still the private residence of the latest Lord Glamis, with the family and their staff living in a wing off-limits to the daily tours. But then the woman turned, and it was obviously not a nightgown, but a formal white dress.

She turned from the window, her eyes wide with horror. "They come!"

She snatched up her skirt and raced toward the stairs, passing right through an urn.

I glanced over at Trsiel. "I thought you said there were no ghosts here."

"That's a residual."

"A residual what?"

"A residual image of a past event. Some traumatic events burn images of themselves into a place. Like a holographic sequence. When triggered, the sequence replays. Any ghost or necromancer, and some sensitive humans, can trigger them." He paused. "You *have* seen these before, haven't you?"

I thought of the crying woman in Paige and Lucas's home.

"Er, right. I just . . . didn't know they were called that."

Trisel grinned. "You thought they were ghosts?"

"Of course not. I—"

He threw back his head and laughed. "What did you do? Try to talk to them? Entreat them to go into the light?"

I glared and stalked past him up the stairs.

After two rooms of being ignored, Trsiel offered an olive branch by way of a story, one about the woman I'd just seen. The White Lady. Ghost hunters can be the most ingenious breed when it comes to inventing ghastly tales, but ask them to think up a name for the ghost of a woman dressed in white, and they give you "the White Lady."

She was Janet Douglas, widow of the sixth Lord Glamis. She'd been burned at the stake for witchcraft, accused of conspiring to poison King James V. Her true "crime" was being the sister of Archibald Douglas, who'd expelled the young king's mother from Scotland years before. Political revenge—with a pretty, popular young widow for a pawn.

Last stop: the crypt.

I expected to descend into some dark, dank basement. Instead, Trsiel led me back to the main entrance at the foot of the clock tower, through a door to a set of narrow stairs that led *up*. We climbed the stairs into a long narrow room with a rounded ceiling.

"What's at the other end?" I asked.

"The dining room."

"Oooh, a dining room just off the crypt. Now, that's a feature you don't see very often these days." I looked around. "Okay, where are the stiffs? I really hope they didn't stick them in those suits of armor."

"This is actually the servants' hall. Where they originally ate and slept."

"And they called it the crypt? That can't be good."

Trsiel shook his head and prodded me forward.

"What? I'm not moving fast enough?"

I stopped. If I were a cat, my fur would have stood on end. I looked around, but all I saw was a mishmash of antiques, and two small windows at the end of the half-tunnel room.

"It's strong here, isn't it?" Trsiel said. "The strongest point, though, is in there." He pointed to the wall. "There's a room on the other side. Legend has it that Lord Glamis walled up a group of Scottish clansmen inside, sealed it, and left them to starve to death."

"Is it true?"

He nodded. "That one, I'm afraid, is more than a tall tale."

"So what we're feeling is another kind of residual. A negative energy instead of a physical form."

Trsiel went silent, cocking his head to look at the wall, eyes narrowing as if he could invoke an Aspicio power of his own and look within.

"That can happen," he said slowly. "And it would make sense in a place with such a violent history. Only one problem with the theory. Residual *emotion* only affects the living. The infamous 'cold spot.' Ghosts don't feel it. Neither do angels."

"If the Nix was here, I bet her visit had something to do with whatever is making us jumpy—whatever is on the other side of that wall."

"There's nothing there. I've been—"

"Doesn't hurt to check again, does it?"

"It isn't—it's not pleasant in there, Eve. There are—"

"Skeletons, right? People die, they leave bones. Nothing I haven't seen before."

He opened his mouth to argue. I stepped through the wall.

31

HALFWAY THROUGH THE WALL, I STOPPED, EYE TO EYE socket with a skull. With an oath, I wheeled to see a skeleton leaning against the wall, face-first, hands raised, dark brown streaks above every finger bone . . . as if he'd died trying to claw his way out.

I turned and saw another skeleton. And another. A half-dozen of them were propped against the wall. At the foot of that wall lay piles of bones. Splotches of dried blood streaked the brick and plaster.

Walled in.

My gaze tripped over a pile of bones in the corner, neatly disarticulated and deliberately piled, each marred with scratches. Gnaw marks.

A movement to my left—Trsiel, reaching to steady me. I shook my head and strode farther into the room. The moment I did, all thoughts of those skeletons vanished as my brain and body kicked into hyperalert mode, every muscle tensing, ears straining, gaze darting about. I definitely sensed something here. Felt it—a heavy, palpable warmth, like a dry-heat sauna.

"Was I not clear enough the first time?"

The words whipped past me on a blast of hot air. The demon-repelling spell flew to my lips, but I bit it back.

This wasn't the Nix—the voice was male, deep, and resonant. Unsettlingly hypnotic, like the angel's . . . and yet not like it.

"Impertinent imp," the voice said. "Did you think—"

The voice stopped, and a warm current caressed my face. I stood my ground, and started the spell. A low chuckle breezed by my right ear.

"That will hurt you more than it will hurt me. I see you are not the same as the first. Two demon bloods in one day. What have I done to deserve this?"

"Two?" I paused. "Someone was here earlier, someone with demon blood. A Nix."

The voice drifted to the back of the room, as if settling onto the moth-eaten sofa there.

"Hmmm, a half-demon ghost. I can't recall the last time one of your kind has come this way. Who's your sire?"

"Answer my questions and I'll answer yours."

A faint snarl. "As impudent as the other. Do they not teach you respect these days, whelp?"

"Tell me who it is I'm supposed to be showing respect to and I'll consider it."

"If you don't know already, then I'm not about to tell—"

A noise from Trsiel, whom I'd almost forgotten was there, still by the wall. When I turned, he beckoned, backing it up with a telepathic "Let's go."

A sharp laugh sounded across the room.

"A third?" the voice said. "Truly I am blessed. And an angel, no less. Forgive me if I don't prostrate myself."

Trsiel marched into the middle of the room, chin up, trepidation falling away. "Identify yourself, demon."

"Demon?" I hissed under my breath. "I thought you said there was no demonic activity here."

Trsiel pulled his chin up higher. "I said, identify your-self—"

"Oh, I heard you, and I decline the invitation . . . Trsiel."

Trsiel's jaw tightened.

"Okay, forget the introduction," I said. "You said some-one else with demon blood was here today. What did she want from you?"

The demon's chuckle wafted around me. "You honestly expect me to answer that, whelp?"

"Not for free, no."

"Ah, you wish to bargain for your answer?"

"No, Eve," Trsiel said. "Not with him. We'll find an-other way."

"I don't believe she was asking your opinion, *half-blood*."

Trsiel stiffened. A long raucous laugh swirled around us.

"Don't like that, do you?"

"I am a full-blood," Trsiel said.

"So you've been told, and so you wish to believe, but you know better, don't you? You are no more akin to the full-bloods than this pretty half-demon whelp is to me."

"Come on, Eve," Trsiel said, wheeling. "He'll tell you nothing but lies."

"I'm not the one who's lied to you, Trsiel. Oh, but your Creator hasn't lied, has He? He never *said* you were a full-blooded angel. He just doesn't care to correct that misconception. No sense sowing more dissension in the ranks. Quite enough of that already—"

"Eve," Trsiel said, voice sharpening.

"Why don't you ask Him, Trsiel?" the demon contin-ued. "Ask Him what you are. Or does this great warrior of truth prefer the comfort of lies?"

I turned to Trsiel. "Don't listen to him. He wants you to leave—wants us both to leave."

"Oh, but I don't want you *both* to leave. Just him. Get out, mongrel. Thy presence doth offend me."

Trsiel strode back to the center of the room and planted himself there.

"See?" the demon said, chortling. "Your defiance gives you away, half-blood. No true angel would have so much pride."

When Trsiel said nothing, a current of hot air snaked from the couch and encircled me, wending its way up my legs, over my torso, and to my ear.

"You wish to bargain with me, whelp?" the demon whispered.

"Perhaps," I said. "Do you wish to bargain, demon?"

"Your Nix annoyed me. You seem, if not properly respectful, at least courteous."

"Or perhaps you just wish to cause trouble," Trsiel said. "By giving her false information."

"And what, sweet mongrel, would be the fun in that? There is no 'trouble' to be found in watching a half-breed demon and a half-breed angel pursue an arrogant Nix. The trouble comes when they *catch* her."

"You can't trust him, Eve," Trsiel said. "You know you can't."

When I hesitated, the demon only chuckled, hot breath tickling my ear.

"When you're ready to bargain, you'll know where to find me."

A blast of tropical heat, and he was gone.

* * *

We finished searching the castle, but we'd already found what had enticed the Nix here. As for the demon's offer, the cardinal rule of bargaining is to never let your opponent know how badly you want what he has. And the encounter with the demon had left Trsiel unsettled. Better to let him cool off before I raised the subject again.

Outside the walls, Trsiel turned to me. "The Fates will want us to sit with Lizzie and Sullivan again. If you have a better idea . . ." He gave a distracted half-shrug. "I'm sure you do, so go ahead and do that. I'll cover the babysitting. If you need me . . ."

I grinned. "I'll whistle."

He nodded, unsmiling.

I looked over at him. "I have no idea what that demon was needling you about, but it obviously got to you, and if you want to talk about it, I'm a pretty good listener."

His eyes met mine, and I saw a loneliness and a sadness there that jolted through me.

"I appreciate the offer," he said softly. "But I won't take you up on it—not yet."

I did indeed have a fresh plan. Thinking of Lizzie made me realize that I had to speak to another partner, one who'd enjoyed the relationship with the Nix. Getting her to talk would be a challenge, but I had an idea.

Given Jaime's response when I asked her to summon Robin MacKenzie, I knew she'd be less than thrilled at the prospect of traveling across the ocean to summon another serial killer. And she did grumble, but it seemed more a token complaint. She didn't have any shows scheduled for the rest of the week, so a trip to Edinburgh wasn't a complete inconvenience. She decided to make a tax-deductible "research" vacation out of it, called her travel agent, and managed to get a last-minute ticket for a flight leaving from O'Hare in two hours.

When I met Jaime at the cemetery gates, it was almost noon.

"I don't suppose this can wait until tonight," she said as we wove through a posse of dog walkers.

"Hey, you're getting better at that."

"At what?"

"Talking without moving your lips."

A tiny smile. "I'm a woman of many talents."

"And if the showbiz spiritualist thing doesn't work out for you, there's always ventriloquism."

She shook her head and ducked around an elderly couple bearing wreaths of plastic flowers. "Is there something going on today? Or is it always this busy?"

"I think it doubles as the neighborhood park." I looked around at the treed landscape, dotted with people out enjoying a rare day of early-spring sun. "The way it should be, really. Otherwise, it's just a waste of good land. It's not like the spooks care whether you Rollerblade over their graves." I glanced at a dog squatting next to a cenotaph. "Although that might cross the line. Hey, you! Don't pretend you didn't see him do that. Get back here and scoop!"

Jaime laughed. "Sic 'em, Eve."

"I could spook the dog, but that's not fair. Well, not unless I could spook him so he drags his owner right through that steamy pile o' shit."

"Speaking of alternate careers, there's one for *you*."

"Yeah, and if I don't catch the Nix, that's probably what I'll get: celestial poop-and-scoop enforcer. Probably wouldn't even get a sword. Just a big shiny shovel."

"Sword?"

"Don't ask." I instinctively moved aside for a pram parade. "So are we going to be able to do this during the day?"

"That was my question. Remember? Possibilities of postponement?"

"Next to none, I'm afraid."

"Damn."

32

CONDUCTING A MIDDAY SÉANCE IN A CROWDED cemetery . . . I'm sure it appeared near the top of the list of "don'ts" in the necromancer handbook.

After we tossed around a few suggestions, we decided she'd pretend to be meditating, which let her sit cross-legged on the ground, close her eyes, and mumble without attracting attention. Well, without attracting too much attention, although more than once she had to stop mid-incantation when some curious passerby stopped to ask whether she was trying to communicate with the dead.

Jaime sat about ten feet away from Suzanne Simmons's grave, with her back to it. Meditating in a cemetery was strange enough—doing it right at the foot of the grave of a notorious serial killer would be asking for trouble. Because Jaime's back was to Simmons's headstone, I had to stand watch, to let her know when Simmons popped up. It took nearly two hours. More than once Jaime snuck a look my way, as if maybe she'd raised Simmons and I'd somehow failed to notice.

Unlike Robin MacKenzie, Suzanne Simmons didn't just drop into our plane. It took at least ten minutes for her to fully materialize. When she did, there was no question of asking for ID. I'd seen her full-on in the vision the Fates gave me, and I'd never forget that face. She was still wearing prison hospital garb. The beehive hairdo from the vision was gone, and her dirty-blond hair hung about her shoulders, lanky and unwashed, as if no one bothered with that nicety while she'd lingered on her deathbed. Her feet were bare. That was the first thing she noticed—her feet. She stared down at them, lifting one, then the other, toes scrunching as if gripping the grass. Then she smiled. Eyes closed, she lifted her head and took a long, deep breath.

Jaime turned, mouth opening to speak, but I cut her short and motioned for her to wait. Wait and watch.

Simmons opened her eyes and looked around. Her gaze crossed the tombstone. A blink. She tilted her head to read the text. A tiny nod, as if the confirmation of her death was neither unexpected nor terribly alarming.

As she turned, I sidestepped, staying out of her field of vision. Her gaze passed right over Jaime, and she surveyed the cemetery grounds, gaze flickering from person to person, a slight frown as she looked out on a world that was familiar . . . and yet not familiar.

Two teens whooshed along the path on Rollerblades, lips and brows a patchwork of metal studs that glinted in the sunlight. The girl yapped into a cell phone while the young man skated beside her, eyes half-closed, immersed in the thumps from his headphones. As they approached, Simmons reached out. The girl on the cell phone passed right through her fingers. Simmons nodded, as if this, too, was not unexpected.

"Welcome home, Suzanne," I said.

She turned, hands going up as if to ward off a blow. I

leaned back against a neighboring tombstone, my hands
shoved in my pockets.

"Are you a ghost?" she asked.

I reached down into the bouquet of flowers at the
grave's base and plucked the one I'd conjured there earlier. I held it up.

"Does it look like it?" I asked.

"Then how—?"

"Necromancy," I said. "Ever heard of it?"

A pause, then a slow shake of her head. "No."

"Well, necromancers can contact the dead."

"And that's what you are?"

"Nah." I waved at Jaime. "That's what she is. I'm just
the client."

Simmons looked Jaime up and down, then stepped
toward her. Jaime struggled to hide her distaste, but it
seeped out. Simmons cocked her head, gaze boring into
Jaime's, then took another slow step toward her, and
watched the necromancer inch back.

Simmons smiled, a tiny little Mona Lisa smile. "Your
friend doesn't like me."

"Employee, not friend. Like I said, I'm the client. I
hired her to set you free."

"Free?" Simmons's head jerked up.

I smiled. "You like that word, don't you?"

She shuttered her excitement and shrugged. "It's
not . . . unpleasant. But I suspect this act of generosity
comes with a price tag."

"That it does. No sense pretending otherwise. I
brought you back to ask your advice on something. I—"

Simmons's attention was riveted to a young boy strolling
past. Her eyes gleamed like a hawk spotting a mouse.

Jaime's lips twisted. Simmons turned on her. Jaime stood her ground, arms crossed, and glared back.

Simmons turned to me. "Make her leave."

I looked from Jaime to Simmons. It was obvious Jaime wasn't going to be able to control her contempt—and probably wouldn't even try. Not the most conducive atmosphere for a friendly girl-to-girl chitchat.

"Just a sec," I murmured to Simmons, then led Jaime aside, pretending to grip her arm and tug her away.

"I'm not leaving you alone with her," Jaime said. "So don't ask."

"Because you're afraid she'll do something to me? She can't—"

"That's not what I'm worried about."

"Oh. I see. So you think this is all part of my master plan to release a league of murderers back into the world?"

"No, but I set her free. She's my responsibility."

"She's not going anywhere unless I let her. She runs, I can take her down. You know I can. I'm not asking you to leave. Just back off a bit. Better yet, let us back off. We'll take a walk, but stay within sight."

Jaime agreed, and I returned to Simmons and led her onto the path, being careful to avoid body contact with her, and to avoid walking through anything that should be solid.

"It's about the Nix," I said.

Another Mona Lisa smile. "I thought it might be."

"She's approached me with an offer. Sounds good, but so does 'prime real estate in the heart of sunny Florida' until you realize you've bought a hundred acres of swamp."

"Caveat emptor."

"Exactly, so I'm doing my homework. She gave me your name as a reference."

The corners of her mouth twitched. "Ah, yes. She does like to do that. Praised me to the heavens with that other one."

"Cheri MacKenzie."

A small roll of the eyes. "Whatever her name was. Quite desperate of the Nix, really. Like a man who picks up a piece of street meat because she reminds him of his dead wife."

"She did kind of look like you."

"You noticed it, too."

I circled a large oak, skirting the picnickers beneath, and headed back in Jaime's direction.

"Is that a 'no' for the recommendation?" I said.

"Not at all. As a partner, the Nix was splendid. I would have traded Eric for her, if I could have."

"So she's straight-up, then. I can trust her not to betray me."

Simmons laughed, a tinkling, girlish laugh. "Oh, of course she'll betray you. Or she'll try to. She betrays us all."

I looked over at her. "You don't seem to hold a grudge about it."

"I don't blame her for trying. I knew she would. As soon as I started spreading my wings, wanting to do things my way, I knew she'd turn on me. I saw it coming and avoided it. Not that it did any good in my case. That idiot, Eric, loused it up for us. As for the Nix, she delivered what she promised. I reaped the rewards . . ." She smiled at me. "And I still reap them."

"Through the visions."

Her smile broadened. "She takes good care of us. Special little treats that make the torment almost sweet."

Something to the left caught her attention. I turned to
see a child crouched on the ground, poking a finger at
something. A little girl with short, wild red hair and bright
blue eyes, her jeans and sneakers filthy the way only a
five-year-old can make them. She poked again and a toad
jumped. With a gap-toothed grin, she shuffled forward,
still crouching, finger outstretched.

A figure moved behind her and I glanced up to see
Simmons there, having slid over while I'd been watching
the child. Simmons bent and stroked her hand over the
girl's head, as if smoothing down her hair. When she
looked up at me, her eyes glistened with the same ec-
stasy I'd seen in my vision, when she'd watched Eric bury
the boy.

"Do you like children?" she asked, smiling.

I swallowed hard. I tried to smile back, but it took
every bit of acting ability I possessed just to stand there,
watch her stroke the girl's hair, and do nothing.

"So the—" I sucked in air, choking back my rage. "So
the Nix betrays *all* her partners."

Simmons gave the girl one last lingering look, then
straightened. "All of them. As I said, it's not personal.
Look how she speaks so highly of me. She even betrayed
Dachev, and he was her favorite."

"He?" I frowned. "The Nix told me she only takes
women as partners."

A tiny, secret smile. "True, she can only inhabit women.
But Dachev . . . he was special. They were truly a team.
Kindred spirits, so to speak."

"Dachev was a ghost."

A momentary pause, as if surprised that I'd figured out
her meaning so quickly. Then she fluttered her fingers,

gaze traveling across the cemetery. "Ask her about him. If she wants to tell you, she will."

I tried the question from a few more angles, but only began to annoy her, so I switched gears and asked more about the Nix. She didn't tell me anything I didn't already know.

I signaled Jaime that it was time to send Simmons back, then steered Simmons in her direction. Two kids ran past, a boy on the cusp of puberty chasing a girl the same age. Simmons watched them, the tip of her tongue pressed between her teeth.

"One last question before I go," I said.

She kept watching the kids. "Hmmm?"

"If the Nix returns to her hell, you won't see any more visions, will you?"

She glanced back at me, gaze turning thoughtful. "No, I suppose not, but there's nothing to worry about. They've sent three after her already and she's still free."

"True, but you know what they say." I grinned at her, baring my teeth. "Fourth time's the charm."

She stared at me. Then comprehension dawned, and she sprang. I wheeled out of the way, and waved as she fell back into hell.

33

AT THE JAIL, AMANDA SULLIVAN LAY ON HER COT, reading *Redbook*. She was alone.

"Trsiel?" I leaned into the hall and called louder, "Trsiel?"

A small face popped out from a cell farther down.

I smiled. "Hey, George. Have you seen Trsiel? The man who was here with me before? He's about this tall—"

George grabbed my hand and dragged me out of the cell, then dropped it and scampered off toward the end of the row. Again he led me down the old ladder into the basement, past the cells, and along the narrow hall leading to his treasure room. I began to suspect that was where we were heading, and was just about to ask about Trsiel again when George stopped. He looked each way, then ducked into some kind of ventilation shaft. There was no way I was fitting in there, but for his sake, I faked it, rather than walk straight through the wall.

We came out at the bottom of a set of stairs, in the basement room where Trsiel had "misteleported" us earlier. If the sight of the room wasn't familiar, the smell of bat shit certainly was. George feigned opening a door to the left. Then he turned to me and flourished his hand toward the room beyond, grinning broadly. There, with his back to us, was Trsiel.

Before I could thank George, he brushed past me and darted off again, returning to whatever adventure I'd disrupted.

I looked over at Trsiel. He was pacing the empty room, eyes downcast, hands stuffed in his pockets, shoulders hunched forward. When he turned to pace back, he saw me and stopped short. For a moment, he just stood there, looking at me. Then he took a slow step forward.

"Eve?"

Granted, the lighting down there was next to nil, but I was standing less than a yard away.

"Uh, yeah," I said, waving my hand in front of his face. "Have I changed that much in the last day?"

"Uh, no. Sorry. I, uh . . ." He looked over my shoulder.

"Expecting someone else?"

"I, uh—" He blinked as if snapping out of a fog, then took me by the elbow. "You should check in with Lizzie."

"Uh-huh. Not very good at subterfuge, are you? Let me give you a tip. If you want to get rid of someone, the worst thing you can do is *act* like you're trying to get rid of them. Subtlety is the key. Lying helps, but you might be stuck there. Can angels lie?"

"Eve, really, you have to—"

"Leave? Uh-uh. We need to talk. Starting with 'Who is Dachev?' "

"Dach—" His brow furrowed as his brain switched back from whatever track it had been on, he blinked, and his gaze slid away from mine. "I know hundreds, if not thousands, of people by that name. It's a common surname in—"

"You know which one I mean. The one connected to

the Nix. The one you'd rather not talk about. Now spill it or—"

"Trsiel," said a voice from the doorway.

I'll admit, I almost expected that voice to be female. Anytime a guy is that eager to get rid of you, it usually involves a woman. Well, it *can* involve a man, but the meaning is the same. With Trsiel, though, the chances of him interrupting a mission for a romantic liaison—with someone of either sex—were pretty much zero.

The voice was male, with an angel's rich timbre. I turned to see a man about my age, sandy blond hair, well built, wearing trousers, a short-sleeved dress shirt, and a tie. Clearly lacking Trsiel's sense of casual style, but a damn sight less unnerving than those iridescent outfits the other full-bloods had worn.

The man walked into the room and looked around. "The abandoned basement of a penitentiary." He looked down. "Dirt floor, rat turds and all. You do know how to make a fellow feel welcome."

He looked around, then stopped, as if seeing me for the first time. His eyes were a clear neon blue, even brighter than Kristof's. As he turned toward me, Trsiel tensed. Before he could react, the man was right there, less than six inches from my face, eyes boring into mine. Trsiel's eyes widened, genuine fear flickering behind them, and he jerked forward, but the other man lifted a hand to stop him, then stepped away from me.

"Eve Levine," he said, with the barest bow of his head. "A pleasure. Your father speaks very highly of you."

My father? Before I could ask, the man clasped my hand. His grip was firm . . . and as hot as the blade of Trsiel's sword. A few degrees hotter than Trsiel's own touch. None of the angels I'd met had eyes with that familiar inner glow.

"I am Aratron," he said. "Since Trsiel seems to have temporarily forgotten his good manners."

I realized who I was speaking to and straightened. The demon at Glamis might have expected my respect, but this one got it. Aratron was a eudemon—a nonchaotic demon, and a high-ranking one. I dipped my head in greeting.

Aratron smiled, then looked from Trsiel to me. "Now, what is Balam's daughter doing with an angel?"

Trsiel shrugged, hands still stuffed in his pockets. He reminded me of the Cabal kids who'd come to me for black-market spells, making their first foray into the underworld, furtive and nervous, like college kids meeting their first drug dealer.

When Aratron lifted his brows, Trsiel mumbled, "Working."

"So you're back in the field? Good. I don't know why they ever took you out of it in the first place. You were one of the best—far better than most of those ascendeds."

Trsiel lifted his gaze to search Aratron's, looking for the insult or insinuation behind the words, but Aratron's eyes were clear, his tone free of sarcasm.

"It's . . . temporary," Trsiel said.

Aratron looked from him to me again. "A full-blooded angel temporarily working with a supernatural ghost. That sounds an awful lot like training." He paused, then threw back his head and laughed. "Ah, those Fates are innovative gals, aren't they? This is one of their most original ideas yet. And deviously clever, if I might say so myself. If you want a good warrior against evil, you need one who understands what she's chasing. You'll make an excellent angel, Eve . . . though I can imagine your father won't be quite so pleased."

"I have something to ask of you," Trsiel said. "You said that you owed me—"

"A favor. And I do . . . though, I'll admit, it's one marker I never expected to be called in. What's it been now, three hundred years?"

"Er, yes, well, being out of the field, I haven't needed—"

"You haven't wanted to call it in. I'm a demon. A eudemon, perhaps, but still a demon, and such a contact— even professionally—is expressly forbidden." He tilted his head, lips pursing. "Well, perhaps not expressly, but certainly implicitly. Your new partner, however, sees things differently—more pragmatically—and has persuaded you to call in this marker."

Trsiel snuck a look at me. "Er, uh—"

"That's right," I said. "It was my idea, and if it blows up in our faces, I'm in deep shit with Trsiel, so I'm really hoping you can help us. What we need is . . ." I glanced at Trsiel, lobbing the ball to him.

"To know who the demon at Glamis Castle is," Trsiel said.

I blinked back my surprise. Seems Trsiel hadn't been sitting on his hands waiting for something to happen after all.

"Ah," Aratron said. "The monster of Glamis." He smiled. "You've heard the stories, I suppose. The deformed immortal child locked in a secret room? The earl and the Devil playing cards for eternity? The clansmen being walled up and left to starve? Humans can be amazingly inventive sometimes, can't they? What they can't understand, they explain with stories, spiced up with bits of truth, like raisins in a sweet-cake. The real monster of Glamis, as you've discovered, wasn't that poor child, but a demon. Not trapped for eternity, but imprisoned for a few hundred years, just long enough to teach him a lesson. As for who it is . . ." He looked at me and smiled. "I'm sure Eve could make a few guesses."

"Demons who've been off the radar for a few hundred years?" I said. "Hmm. Amduscias, Focalor, Dantalian—" I stopped, my gut going cold.

Aratron didn't notice my reaction. "There are more than a few of them, aren't there? It's one of Baal's favorite punishments for underlords who incur his wrath—something, I'm afraid, that isn't very difficult to do."

"It's Dantalian, isn't it?"

He smiled. "Well done."

I struggled not to make the obvious connection, to think of anything but that, hurrying on with more questions. "What did Baal lock him up for? It has to do with that room, doesn't it? With walling in those men?"

Trsiel snorted. "I doubt *that* was his crime."

Aratron shook his head. "Your prejudices are showing, Trsiel. A cacodemon could indeed be punished for such a thing, though not for the reason you'd find the deed objectionable. Had Dantalian walled up those men against his lord's wishes, he would be punished for his insolence. That, however, was not his error." He looked at me, eyes twinkling. "I doubt it will help your cause, but do you want to hear the story?"

I nodded, brain still numb.

"Excellent. Curiosity for the sake of curiosity is the mark of a true student." He glanced at Trsiel, eyes still sparkling. "You can move closer, Trsiel. I know you want to hear this as much as she does."

Trsiel shrugged, but when Aratron looked away, he slid next to me.

"Now, one of the earls of Glamis was a half-demon. Baal's own child. As Eve knows, even the lord demons have little contact with their offspring. That doesn't keep them from watching from afar, as Balam does, but it is rare for any cacodemon to play a role in his child's life. Glamis, though, sought out that contact, and made a very persuasive argument for Baal to do otherwise, providing him with sacrifices and proving as dutiful a son as any father could want. Eventually, Baal took notice, and when Glamis had his father's attention, he asked for a boon. He would sacrifice a dozen men to Baal, not just killing them, but walling them up. As modes of death go, the only thing more terrible than being buried alive is being buried with others. The . . . animal instinct eventually asserts itself, providing a veritable feast of chaos."

I remembered those skeletons in the room, and the teeth marks on the bones. When I shuddered, Aratron studied my reaction with the impassive curiosity of a scientist.

"The boon," Trsiel said. "What did he ask in return?"

"Ah, well, it had to do with a lady, as these things often do. A married lady who was proving most resistant to his advances. Glamis, being an avid student of Arthurian lore, took his solution from there."

"He wanted to be able to assume the form of the lady's husband," I said. "That's where Dantalian came in. His specialty is transmigration. Not assuming another form, but possessing one."

Aratron smiled. "That's it exactly. Baal went to Dantalian and demanded that he create something to allow Glamis to inhabit another man's body. This is, of course, a skill every demon possesses." He waved a hand at his current form—probably that of a prison guard. "But for a half-demon it is impossible. Baal charged Dantalian with the task of making it possible. And he did. He created a piece of jewelry."

"An amulet," I whispered. "One that would allow anyone with demon blood to fully possess the body of any living person."

"Very good. You've heard of it, then?"

Before I could answer, Trsiel cut in. "But if Dantalian made the amulet, why did Baal imprison him?"

"Because Glamis never got that necklace. As for why, I fear that is a question only Dantalian and Baal could answer. Some say Dantalian had a follower among the Ogilvies—the clan Glamis walled up. Some say Baal denied him a share of the sacrifice. Whatever the reason, Dantalian changed his mind and secreted away the amulet, and for that, Baal sentenced him to spend five hundred and fifty-five years walled up in that room with the Ogilvies."

"That's what the Nix wants," I said, turning to Trsiel. "Dantalian's Amulet."

And I'd been the one who'd told her about it.

Once we'd taken our leave of Aratron, we returned to Amanda Sullivan's cell and I made my confession to Trsiel.

"That's why she came to Glamis," I said as I finished. "All along I've been trying to figure out what's motivating her, and it's been staring me in the face the whole time. She wants what I want. To be able to act within the living world. She's tired of relying on her partners for her food.

That's why she went to Luther Ross. Same reason I've been interested in him, as a way of breaking through that barrier. But that's nothing compared to what she could do with Dantalian's Amulet. And I led her straight to it."

"We don't know that," he said softly.

I didn't argue, but we both knew it was no coincidence. I remembered the young hunter saying he'd seen something move in the woods near where we'd landed, and I remembered the creak in the hallway before Trsiel arrived. She'd been following me, and I'd rewarded her efforts beyond her wildest dreams. As soon as she'd heard of the amulet, who'd made it, and what it did, she'd headed straight for Glamis, where she'd know Dantalian had been exiled.

"If she gets the amulet, that'll make our job tougher," Trsiel said. "But I doubt that will happen. Dantalian isn't about to tell her where it is."

"No? He may not like her very much, but how long do you think it'll take before he decides that telling her— and watching the havoc she'll wreak in human form—is more rewarding than turning her down? We need to find it first."

He nodded. "But the only one who knows where it is—"

"Is the only person we can ask."

"We are *not* bargaining with a demon." He glanced over at me. "And don't tell me I already have. My deal with Aratron was one-sided. I did something once that, unintentionally, benefited him, and he promised me a favor in return. It wasn't a bargain."

"We aren't going to bargain with Dantalian."

"Good, because—"

"Kristof is. He's a skilled demon negotiator."

Trsiel rolled his eyes, as if this didn't come as a surprise.

"It may not be your way, but we use whatever—and whoever—proves useful."

"If you've done it before, then you can do it. No need to bring in anyone else."

"I said I've dealt with them. I've never negotiated with them. For that, I hired professionals. If you do it right, it's an honest transaction. If you do it wrong, well, then you're screwed, because there isn't a demon alive who won't take advantage of stupidity or naivety. Kris can do it right."

Trsiel leaned against the wall, arms crossed. After a few minutes, he shook his head. "Go and find him, then."

34

I FOUND KRISTOF IN HIS OFFICE AGAIN, THIS TIME alone and hard at work, which seemed the perfect excuse to slip off and find another demon mediator. But, as always, the moment I arrived, he knew I was there, and when I tried to retreat, he called me back. His welcome cooled when he realized I was there on business.

Of course, I had to tell him everything, and this confession was ten times tougher than it had been with Trsiel. As much as it hurt to admit to Kristof that, after everything he'd said, I'd turned around and gone back in to ask about the amulet, what hurt worse was the look on his face: raw pain, but not a trace of surprise.

When I finished, I stood there, mouth still half-open, wanting to say so much, but unable to form the thoughts into words. Instead, all that came out was "I fucked up, Kris."

For a minute, he just looked at me, eyes searching mine. Then he gave a tiny nod.

"Let's see what we can do to fix it, then," he murmured.

* * *

Dantalian was somewhat put out that we'd engaged professional negotiation services. It's so much more fun dealing with amateurs.

"So you want to know what the Nix was after," he said, his tone bordering on bored.

"We know that," I said. "The amulet you made for Lord Glamis."

A moment's pause, then he continued, sounding a bit more interested now. "Clever whelp. You did your homework. Then you know who I am?"

"Dantalian, Master of Transmigration, Duke of Baal."

A warm breeze encircled my legs, wound up my body, around my neck, then slithered away. I knew he was still there, probably hovering right in front of my face.

"Say it again," he murmured.

"Dantalian, Master of Transmigration, Duke of Baal."

"Hmmm, yes, I suppose that will do. Lacking the proper degree of respect, yet not *dis*respectful. At least it's better than fawning. That's what she tried when she returned."

"The Nix? She came back?"

"Of course she did. After she amended her attitude."

"Uh-huh."

He laughed, blasting me with heat. "My reaction, precisely, whelp. The only thing worse than fawning is fake fawning. As if I were some vain fool of a potentate, willing to grant any wish in return for a few strokes of my ego."

"So you sent her away again? She'll be back, then. All we have to do is wait—"

"Oh, I didn't send her away. What would be the fun in that? Far better for me to set her on the trail . . . and then set you on it after her."

"Great," I muttered. "How long of a head start does she have?"

"A half-day. Which would be a problem . . . had I sent her to the right place. A little lesson in humility for an imp in sore need of it."

"And now you'll tell us where to find her."

"Certainly . . . but I believe there was mention of a bargain?"

"Not now," Trsiel said, stepping forward. "You just admitted you intended to set us on the trail, so we certainly aren't about to bargain for—"

I lifted a hand to cut him off, then looked at him. "I'd *rather* bargain. Otherwise, I owe him a favor."

Kristof then went through the formal rituals that tested a demon's sincerity, to ensure Dantalian wouldn't do to us what he'd done to the Nix. Dantalian suffered through this with the exasperated patience of someone having a grocery clerk examine his cash to see if it's real.

"I want two things," Dantalian said when Kristof was finished. "First, you will ensure that your Nix knows I intentionally set her on the wrong path. If she doesn't, then the lesson is incomplete."

"Done," I said. "And part two?"

"Hmmm, part two . . . I'm still working on that one. Give me a few moments."

I sighed.

"Impatient . . . or eager to get back on the trail?"

Dantalian's voice seemed to come from all sides. I looked around, trying to track it, but he only chuckled. Neither Trsiel or Kristof seemed to notice.

"They can't hear me," Dantalian said. "This part of the negotiation is for you and me alone. I must admit that seeing a half-demon has reminded me of at least one of the pleasures of freedom I've been missing. It's been over five hundred years since I fathered a whelp myself."

"Uh-huh," I thought the words, as I had with Trsiel. "Can't help you there. No babies coming from this shade."

"Oh, but it's not entirely the passing on of my genes that I miss." Tendrils of heat slid along my bare arm, like hot fingers stroking my skin. "The process of doing so wasn't entirely unpleasant, either. Of course, I'd need to inhabit a more hospitable form. Perhaps your lover wouldn't mind taking a more . . . active role in negotiations."

My head jerked up. Kristof looked over at me when I jumped, but he said nothing, just lifted his brows.

Dantalian laughed. "Your relationship is obvious to anyone with eyes, and most without. How is that for a bargain, then? Allow me to take over his body and reap the benefits of a more corporeal form."

"Moving right along to option two . . ."

"Well, there is another option standing alongside the first. The angel. I could—"

"No."

He chuckled. "Not even going to hear me out? Or afraid, if you do, it might prove a more enticing offer than you'd like to admit? He is an intriguing one, isn't he? So old and yet, in so many ways, such a child, a sweet, confused, beguiling child. How much of a child is he?" Another chuckle. "I'm sure you've wondered that as well."

"Are you trying to lead me into temptation?" I said. "Or just annoy the piss out of me?"

Kristof glanced over at me. "Has he gotten to the sex part yet, or is he still working up to it?"

I sputtered a laugh.

Trsiel strode over, eyes going wide. "What's going—"

"Dantalian is attempting private negotiations with Eve," Kristof said, stifling a yawn. "Private negotiations of a private nature, I'm sure."

Trsiel's cheeks reddened. "That's not—he can't—"

"Oh, he could, but he won't. And before you take offense, Dantalian, that's no reflection on you. Many have tried. None succeed. Eve doesn't whore herself for any cause."

"This is going nowhere," Trsiel said. "Asking for sex . . . ? If he can't come up with something better than that—"

"There *is* something better than that?" Dantalian said. "My dear boy, your innocence is showing. Surely you—"

"Ignore him," I said. "This isn't about sex. It's about causing trouble. Sex is just a tool for achieving it. If I were a man, he'd ask me to go out and lop off a few heads in his name. Same destination. Different path."

"Would you prefer lopping off heads?" Dantalian murmured. "I hadn't considered that, but, yes, now that you mention it, I see how my request could be considered quite inappropriate for a woman of your nature. Lopping off heads would be more your style, so perhaps—"

"No lopping heads. No giving head. I'm not doing anything that would get you off . . . in any way."

A moment of silence. "Well, that limits things, doesn't it?"

"Eve . . ." Trsiel said.

When I looked at him, he jerked his head toward the door. I glanced at Kristof. He discreetly lifted a finger, telling me to wait.

"Those are her terms," Kristof said. "She will do nothing to cause chaos. If that is unacceptable, then I'm afraid our negotiations are—"

"She will visit me," Dantalian said.

I cast a frown in the direction of his voice.

"I have but a few years left on my sentence. She will visit me for a half-day each month until it ends."

"If this is heading back to the sex thing—" I began.

"It's not. I ask only for a visit."

Trsiel wheeled as Dantalian's voice glided past. "So you can spit poison in her ear? Try to turn her to your—"

"Evil ways?" Dantalian laughed. "Such melodrama. You do like your stories, don't you, Trsiel? The virtuous angel warrior and the nefarious demon battling for the soul of the innocent. Yet she's not so innocent. And you're not so angelic. Perhaps I'm not so demonic. But that spoils a good story, doesn't it?"

"He's not going to woo me over to the dark side, Trsiel," I said. "No more than you can bring me over to the light. I like it right where I am." I glanced back in Dantalian's direction. "Once a year."

"Every two months."

"Only an hour, then. An hour every two months or a half-day every six."

"A half-day every six, then."

I looked at Kristof. He nodded and I waved for him to begin the binding ceremony that would tie us both to our sides of the bargain.

35

"WHAT DO YOU WANT TO KNOW FIRST?" DANTALIAN asked. "Where the amulet is? Or where your Nix thinks it is?"

"Back up," Trsiel said. "This amulet. If by some chance she gets it, will it work?"

"Of course it will work. I designed—"

"I meant will it work for *her*?"

"For anyone with demon blood."

"And if she fails to get it, is there any other way she can achieve her goal and take on human form? Some rite or mystical object she can use? When she first made the leap, she used a witch spell—"

I interjected, "Which will no longer work or she'd have used it long ago. Likely a side effect of her now being a ghost."

"Yes," Dantalian said. "As a ghost, she is restricted to ghost methods of possession. Without the amulet, she could only use full spiritual possession, through a necromancer."

I nodded. "Which any necromancer who's powerful enough to perform is also smart enough *not* to perform. So she's stuck with the amulet. Good. Well, then we should go after the amulet . . ." I hesitated. "No, the Nix is our primary target. If we get her, we don't need to worry about her getting the amulet or finding some other way to dimension-jump. We'll get her, and then . . ." I steeled myself, knowing what I needed to say, but having to force the words out. "And then Trsiel can retrieve the amulet and put it away for safekeeping. I—we don't need it."

I could feel Kristof's gaze on me. I didn't look, but knew that if I did, I'd see not relief, but skepticism, as he searched my face and tone, trying to figure out whether I was telling the truth or saying what he wanted to hear. I wasn't sure which it was, either.

"Okay," I said, facing the demon—or his direction— again. "So where is she?"

"I sent her to a building, one that once housed half a million scrolls, which later were said to have fed the fires at the public baths; a thousand years of knowledge destroyed to keep bathwater warm. And one wonders why humans—"

"The Great Library of Alexandria."

His laugh boomed through the room like a furnace blast. "You are quick. And that's where you'll find your Nix, in the ghost-world Great Library, searching madly for my amulet among those half-million scrolls."

"And the amulet?" I said.

"Oh, that's closer. Much closer. There's a tunnel under Glamis, connecting it to Castle Huntly. It's—"

"A legend," Trsiel said. "The tunnel doesn't exist."

"Nor does this room, my dear mongrel angel. Your sorcerer has bound me to tell the truth. If I say the amulet is in that tunnel—"

"Then it is," I finished. "But if it leads to another castle, I'm guessing there's a fair bit of tunnel to travel."

"Fifteen miles."

"Uh-huh. Care to be more specific, then?"

"Not really."

"You gave your word," Kristof said.

Dantalian's sigh fluttered around us. "That I did, and I will keep it. But she asked whether I *cared* to be—"

"*Be* more specific," I said. "Please."

"It's in a room, inside a drawer. I cannot be more specific than that. There are many rooms down there. When I hid it, I had no time for drawing maps. Search and you'll find it."

A soft laugh fluttered from behind us. A feminine laugh.

"Thank you, Dantalian," a lilting voice said. "I intend to."

I wheeled to see the Nix, her face pushed through the wall across the room, where she'd been listening on the other side. Dantalian roared. Trsiel's hands shot up, the sword invocation flying from his lips. The Nix pulled back to the other side. Kristof and I both raced into the hall, Trsiel at our heels, but the Nix was gone.

"Downstairs," I said to Trsiel. "To the tunnel. Kris . . ."

Our eyes met.

"Go," he said. "And be careful."

"Wait someplace safe."

"I will."

Trsiel and I hurried down the stone steps to the basement, and came out in . . .

"A cafeteria?" I said. "This is the castle catacombs?"

"You'd prefer a dungeon maybe? A few skeletons chained to the wall?"

"Well, yeah. What's a castle without a dungeon?"

As we talked, we walked in opposite directions, each

scanning a side of the cafeteria. There was no sign of the Nix.

"Washrooms, kitchen, cloakroom," I said, reading the signs. " 'This way to the tunnel' would be too much to ask for, wouldn't it?"

"There is no tunnel," Trsiel said as he walked through a storage closet door. A second later, he returned, still talking. "It was a hoax. In 1939, the last owner of Huntly, a Colonel Paterson, claimed to have unearthed a tunnel linking Glamis to Huntly while carrying out renovations on his castle. No evidence of it has ever been found to support that claim."

"Which makes it false? What happened to this Paterson guy?"

"Drowned a year later, in a boating accident."

"Aha," I said, as I ducked my head into a closet. "I smell conspiracy. Who owns Castle Huntly now?"

"The state. It's a prison."

"And they claim there's no tunnel leading out of it? Very convenient." I glanced over at Trsiel. "I know you're convinced Dantalian found a way to lie to us, but humor me. Which direction is Huntly?"

He paused. "North."

Trsiel headed for that side of the room, but I waved him back.

"Keep checking these rooms," I said. "If we're searching for the tunnel, so is she. You look for her. I'll look for it."

"Don't go anywhere—"

"Without you. I know. I don't need to. X-ray vision, remember?"

I used my Aspicio power all along the north side of the room and up a short hall. It took another twenty minutes, but I finally looked through a section of stonework and saw something besides solid dirt on the other side.

"Got it," I said.

He took my hand. "Lead on."

We stepped into the wall and darkness enveloped us. Using my sight, I led us through the dirt and into the empty space beyond. After a moment in there, my night-vision kicked in, and I could make out a dirt tunnel, no more than four feet wide. I took a step and banged my forehead on a chunk of soil.

"These medieval Scots . . . not that tall, were they?"

"Apparently not," Trsiel said, ducking as he stepped up beside me. "It looks like it gets shallower still."

"So you can see okay?"

He nodded.

"Does that mean she can, too?"

"Probably. It's a common demonic power."

I hesitated. "I suppose her hearing works fine in the dark, too."

A soft laugh. "Yes, we'd better switch to telepathy."

I ducked and started forward again. After a few feet, I scraped the top, and got a soil shower.

"Uh, Trsiel?" I said, mentally forming the words. "Why are we hitting the ceiling?"

He glanced back at me, brows lifting. "Because we're tall?"

I socked him in the arm and motioned for him to continue walking. "I'm serious. Why are we hitting the ceiling instead of walking through it?"

"You're right. Huh. That's strange."

"That's not the answer I'm looking for."

"Well, uh . . ." He looked around. "This kind of thing

happens sometimes. It's an interdimensional warp in the fabric of time and space."

"You have no idea, do you?"

"No, but that sounded good when they said it on *Star Trek*. Honestly, I can't explain it. But I know it does happen. Either this tunnel has somehow vanished in the living world, which explains why it hasn't been found, or it does exist, but is under some kind of demonic influence."

"Which would explain how Dantalian, a noncorporeal demon, could open a drawer and drop off the amulet."

"Right. I think."

"Works for me. And speaking of hiding places, here's the first room."

I cast a light-ball inside. The room was crammed with stuff—the kind of stuff someone must have considered worth hiding, but was now garage-sale reject trash—moldering carpets, rotted wooden furniture, mildewed paintings, and more.

"Got four words for the Glamis family," I murmured. " 'Climate-controlled storage units.' So now what? Search for the Nix or the amulet?"

"Let's keep going."

In less than a mile of tunnel, we hit two more jam-packed rooms. Fourteen miles to go. Shit. No wonder Dantalian didn't remember where he'd put the amulet.

All these rooms were filled with furnishings. Knowing we were hot on her trail, the Nix must have raced past these, looking for more amulet-friendly storage. But if you want to hide jewelry, is it better to put it in a room filled with other treasures? Or stuff it in a desk drawer?

When I mentioned this to Trsiel, he agreed that the amulet might very well be in one of these home-decor-packed rooms. Since we knew the Nix would be moving forward, there was no harm in me lagging behind to search for the amulet. So I started to look while Trsiel took off in search of the Nix.

Dantalian said he'd put the amulet in a drawer. That gave me a place to start. With the stuff crammed in so tight, some drawers had no room to open, and others were stuck shut by swollen wood or rusted hardware. I gave each one a tug, but the moment they resisted, I didn't waste time yanking, just used my Aspicio powers to look inside.

With both the light-ball spell and the X-ray vision to help, I whipped through the first room in about ten minutes. The only drawer that wasn't empty held only the crumpled remains of papers. Probably ancient letters detailing some illicit royal affair, or the deed to some misappropriated property, now lost to history forever.

I was in the fourth room when I peered into a stuck drawer and finally saw a glitter of silver. I tried to get a better look, but the angle was wrong, and all I could see was what looked like a length of chain. I tugged on the drawer, but it wouldn't budge. Bracing both feet against the front of the chest, I grabbed the drawer handle, then yanked as hard as I could . . . and fell flat on my back, holding the broken handle.

"Goddamn it," I muttered.

I looked around, then crawled over a dismantled bed and tugged a metal hanging rod from a tapestry. Back at the drawer, I wedged the narrow end of the rod into the top gap. The bar was slightly too thick, and it took some work to shove it in there, but finally I had enough through. Then I moved alongside the bar, put both hands on it, and slammed the bar down. Wood cracked. The drawer gave way, and I stumbled forward, catching myself before I fell. I looked back, to see the drawer still in place—but the front panel lying on the floor.

"That'll work, too," I murmured.

I reached into the drawer. My fingers clasped metal. I pulled it out . . . and found myself holding nothing but a silver chain.

"Goddamn it!" I whipped the chain across the room. "After all that . . ."

I cursed again, spun on my heel to stomp out, then stopped. *Slow down and be sure.* I turned back to the chest, crouched, and peered into the dark depths of the broken drawer. Empty. *No—be absolutely sure.*

I waved my light-ball down. As it moved, the light glinted off something in the very back of the drawer. I reached inside. My fingers found the top edge of a disk wedged in the back of the drawer. I traced my index finger over a half-circle of cool metal. The rest of it was stuck in the crack between the drawer's rear panel and base.

Resisting the urge to rip the drawer apart, I carefully worked the piece out. Finally it came free, and the drawer popped open. I wrapped my hand around the metal disk and pulled it out. It had better not be a worthless old coin, or I was going to scream loud enough to bring both Trsiel and the Nix running.

I straightened, then slowly opened my hand. There, on my palm, lay what did indeed look like a cheap coin, a plain silver disk with writing around the edges. Yet I didn't even need to glance at the inscription to know that this was the amulet. I could feel it, the power of it, pulsating against my skin.

The power of transmigration. The power to inhabit a corporeal being, to fully occupy and control that body, to enact one's will on the living world. This was what I'd been searching for. I was half-demon. I could use this amulet. I could see my daughter, be with her, speak to her, touch her. Protect her.

If I'd had this that day in the community center, I could have protected her, instead of being forced to stand by, helpless.

And what would you have done? whispered Kristof's voice. *Leapt into the nearest person, jumped into the bullet's path, and killed your host, only to discover Savannah wasn't even in danger? And how will you make sure you're there if something like that ever happens again? Do you plan to follow her around every hour of every day, a spectral guard dog, always at her heels?*

I shivered. I couldn't be there all the time. I didn't *want* to be there all the time. I wanted . . .

I squeezed my hand tight around the amulet and closed my eyes.

I wanted my own life. Here. In this world.

Eyes still closed, I put in a mental call to Trsiel. Almost immediately, I heard soft footfalls in the tunnel.

"Thank God," I murmured.

I hurried to the door. I stepped out and saw a dim figure down the corridor—a figure far too small and too blond to be Trsiel. The Nix.

36

I BACKPEDALED BEFORE SHE SAW ME. AFTER ONE MORE mental shout to Trsiel, I looked down at the amulet in my hand. If she found me, she'd better not find this. She'd heard Dantalian say it was in a drawer, so I shoved my hand into a roll of carpet and dropped the amulet inside. Then I took two steps back and cast a cover spell.

The Nix's footsteps drew closer. They stopped outside the room.

"Someone's made a mess in here," she murmured. She walked to the middle of the room and looked around. "Did they find what they were looking for? Let's hope not."

She opened the nearest drawer, then stopped, gaze catching on the broken drawer panel on the ground . . . on the ground at my feet. She moved toward it. Shit! A couple more steps and she'd smack right into me, breaking my cover spell.

I waited until she was close enough to reach out and touch. Then I let loose a front kick that caught her square in the jaw, and sent her sailing across the room. Before she could recover, I slammed her with a round-house kick to the gut then, as she crumpled forward, an uppercut to the jaw knocked her off her feet and flipped her backward, her head cracking against a marble bust.

As she staggered back up, I darted behind her and kicked her in the ass, knocking her face-first to the dirt floor.

"Come on," I said. "Get up again. Please."

She pushed up to all fours, then lifted her head and glared at me.

"Oh, come on," I said. "I can't kick you when you're down. That's not fair."

When she didn't move, I whirled and slammed a front kick into her the bottom of her jaw, toppling her over onto her back.

"Screw fair," I said. "This is too much fun."

Yet, as much fun as it was, I knew I couldn't keep it up forever. Where the hell was Trsiel? As a last resort, I put my fingers in my mouth and whistled as loud as I could. As I did, the Nix sprang to her feet. I kicked. Her hand shot out, grabbing for my foot. I managed to abort the kick just as her fingers grazed my ankle. I danced away, out of reach of that iron grip.

"You think you're clever, don't you, witch?" she said. "But the harder you hit, the harder I'll hit back. Haven't you learned that yet?"

She lunged for me. I sidestepped out of the way, pivoted fast, and aimed a roundhouse kick at the back of her knees. My foot connected with a *crack* and she dropped to her knees.

As I kicked again, the Nix ducked in time, then grabbed at my foot, getting just enough of a grip to pull me off balance. I twisted away and rebounded with a side kick that knocked her into the wall, dirt raining down.

"You want the amulet, witch?" she said. "You keep it. I'll go the other route. Less satisfying in the long run but—" She smiled. "Temporarily, perhaps very satisfying indeed, if done right. So why don't . . ."

She flew at me, hoping to catch me off guard, but I veered out of her path and wheeled to face her again. Running footsteps pounded in the tunnel. Trsiel. Finally.

The Nix started an incantation. A portal, or so I assumed. But the words sounded familiar . . . and I didn't know any portal-opening spells. It didn't matter. Whatever she was casting, I wasn't about to let her finish.

I spun and kicked, but the Nix backed out of my way. She lifted both hands, then fluttered them down. A spell with hand gestures? Had to be sorcerer magic. As I readied another kick, she stopped casting. I braced myself, but nothing happened.

"As good a spell-caster as a fighter, I see," I said . . . and dropped her with a front kick.

Trsiel flew through the doorway. I was off to the side, up near the door, so when he came through, his back was to me and all he saw was the Nix sprawled across the floor.

She lifted her head.

"Trsiel!" she said. "Look out! Behind you!"

He swung around, sword raised. Then he saw me and stopped.

"Trsiel!" the Nix shouted. "It's her. She cast a glamour spell."

Glamour? Oh, shit! That's what the Nix had cast. A sorcerer glamour spell . . . to make herself look like me. A protest flew to my lips, but Trsiel's sword was already sheering toward me, too fast for me to say anything . . . or to dive out of the way.

At the last second, our eyes met, and his filled with horrified realization. He tried to stop, but the momentum of his swing was too great and all he could do was divert the sword's course, swinging down away from my torso.

The blade hit me in the upper thigh. I heard an inhuman scream, then felt the sound ripping from my own throat as the pain—the indescribable pain—tore through me. I pitched forward. Trsiel dove to catch me. The sword clattered to the floor.

As I fell, I blacked out, coming to only as another flash of agony knifed through me. Trsiel's arms tightened around me as he lowered me to the floor. His mouth opened, but I heard only the sound of my own screaming. Behind him, the Nix was running—not at us, but off to our side. I blinked, then comprehension hit.

"Trsiel," I gasped. "Sword. She—"

He shot up just as the Nix dove for the sword. Too late to grab it, Trsiel kicked it aside and threw himself at the Nix. He caught her by the shoulders and they went down.

I struggled to focus on them, but pain pulsed through me, each throb bringing a split-second blackout. I fought to stay conscious. Across the room. Trsiel almost had the Nix pinned, but she wriggled out of his grip, rolled, then darted toward the sword. Trsiel took her down again.

I forced my body to turn, and tried to see the sword through the flashes of darkness. There! By the door. Biting my lip, I managed to push up on all fours, then stumbled toward it. When I was still a few feet away, I felt my limbs tremor, threatening to give way. I threw myself forward, onto the sword. I felt the heat of it burn through my shirt. Then everything went dark.

I awoke in something like a bed, soft and comfortable. Trsiel leaned over me. I struggled to sit, but white-hot pain forced me down again.

"Nix," I whispered.

"Gone," he said. "She teleported out as soon as I had a good hold on her."

"Amulet. Found—"

"It's right here."

"Good. Wh—" I gasped as fresh pain ripped through me.

Trsiel's arms went around me, one sliding under me, and his hands moved up to my neck. I gasped again. His hands were nearly as hot as the sword. As soon as his fingers touched my skin, the pain ebbed. He massaged the back of my neck, and I slowly relaxed into the bed as the pain gave way to soft waves of soothing heat. I felt myself drifting toward sleep, only dimly aware that he was talking. I struggled to listen, but could make out only the hypnotic sound of his voice as he reverted to his angelic tone.

"Better?" he whispered.

"Ummm. Getting better."

A soft chuckle. "I'll keep at it, then." His voice sobered. "I can't tell you how sorry—"

"S'okay."

I stretched, then lifted my head and looked around. I was lying on a divan. He'd pulled up a chair beside it. Both were big chunky pieces, postmodern furniture, more comfortable than they looked. Two more chairs flanked a fireplace, and another two were by a window overlooking a cityscape. Art gallery and museum posters decorated the walls. Across the room was a floor-to-ceiling bookcase, crammed to overflowing, with books shoved into every space and more piled on the floor underneath. On my right, magazines covered a low-slung table.

"Your room?" I said.

He nodded. "Not much like the other angel quarters, is it?"

I picked up a copy of *Entertainment Weekly.* "Not much."

His cheeks heated.

"I'm teasing you," I said. "Your room is much nicer. That other one? Kinda creepy."

He gave a soft laugh. I continued flipping through the stack of magazines. Some, like *Time* and *National Geographic,* I recognized. Others, I wasn't even sure what language they were written in.

"I suppose this answers the question," he said, sweeping a hand around the room. "Though I'm sure you already knew it."

"Hmm?"

"What Dantalian meant. About me. His . . . insults. You said you didn't know what he meant, but I know you do."

I flipped onto my back and looked up at him. "That you're part human. Or so he says."

"He's right. Which you also know. Not that I can prove it." He swept a lock of my hair off the pillow, fingers sliding to the end, his gaze fixed on this diversion as he continued, "I told you I'm from the last group of full-bloods. The Creator—He saw problems with the older ones, the first angels and even the seconds. As the world grew, they couldn't keep up. They went from thousands of years of watching over hunters and gatherers to a world that seemed to change every time they blinked. When we— the last group—were created, we were taught to immerse ourselves in the human world—to keep up with its traditions, its language, even its fashions, so that we could better understand those we served."

"Then that's the explanation, isn't it? The training. Not that you're part human."

He shook his head. "That's the rationale, not the reason. We all know it. Some of the older ones try to be more like us, and some of us try to be more like them, but it doesn't work. The difference goes deeper."

"So you think the Creator gave you some human blood? To make you more human?"

Trsiel released my hair from his fingers and nodded. "And when Dantalian brought it up, I saw my reaction, and I hated myself for it, for what you must have thought of me."

"I don't—"

"What a hypocrite, right? One minute I'm telling you I see nothing wrong with humans, and the next I'm flying into a rage when some demon accuses me of having human blood." He shook his head fiercely, eyes blazing. "What a damnable—"

I pulled myself up. "I don't think you're a hypocrite, Trsiel. I saw how those other angels treated you. *That's* the problem, isn't it? Not having human blood, but having them think you do."

"I care about what it makes me in their eyes. I know I shouldn't—"

I ducked to meet his gaze. "It's okay. You don't have to explain it to me." I gave a small smile. "I'm a witch, remember? I know all about being treated like a second-class citizen when you know you aren't."

I pulled myself up. "But, blood or training aside, whatever the experiment, it obviously worked. You understand and fit into human culture far better than those other angels could, so why the ascendeds?"

"Not all the angels in the last wave are like me. Most aren't. They . . . assimilated."

"Succumbed to the pressure to fit in. But you didn't."

"It's more like 'couldn't.' It isn't in my nature. And I'm certainly not the only one. There are a few like me."

"Just not enough to fight this new 'only ascended angels in the field' rule."

A slow nod, gaze shuttering, but not before I saw the sadness there.

"But if I ascend," I said. "If I do this quest, and they offer me angel-hood, I'd need someone to teach me the ropes, and Zak . . . Zaf—"

"Zadkiel."

"Isn't around, so that would be you."

He hesitated, then nodded. "Yes, that's what I'm hoping. Meaning you're not the only one who needs to prove something on this quest. Unfortunately, you seem to be making your case a lot better than I am."

"Hey, you got the amulet, right?"

"I'd rather have the Nix. Preferably decorating my sword."

I laughed. "We'll get her for you, don't you worry. Then we'll finally find out whether all this supposition has been for naught. My luck, I'll finally decide I want to be an angel, and find out the offer isn't even on the table, that it never was."

A look passed through his eyes.

"You already know, don't you?" I said.

He stood, crossed the room, grabbed an apple off the counter. "We should work on our next move."

"No, you should work on your diversionary tactics. That one's as obvious as trying to send me to check on Lizzie before Aratron arrived." I got to my feet. "You've talked to the Fates, haven't you? You sneaky . . . When did you—what did they say?"

He lobbed the apple from one palm to the other. "It's not my place to discuss this, Eve."

I grabbed the apple from him. "Well, obviously, if you're still worried about proving you could mentor me, the answer was yes. They want me to be an angel."

I took a bite and chewed slowly, turning the thought over in my mind. Like a magnet, it both repelled and attracted, depending on which way I turned it. But, still, no matter how much it might change my life, it would take care of my problem with Savannah . . .

I took another chomp of the apple and walked back to the divan.

"Why me?" I said.

When Trsiel didn't respond, I sighed and glanced over my shoulder at him. "Okay, hypothetically, *if* the Fates have a space to fill, why pick me? There must be dozens of supernaturals more worthy of the honor."

"Becoming an angel isn't a reward for goodness," he said, taking the chair next to the divan again. "It's a job, and like any job, it has requirements."

"Such as?"

"Each realm has its own team of ascendeds, pulled from that realm, who tend to matters involving the ghosts in that realm and the living who will eventually come to that realm. The Fates, having guardianship of the smaller supernatural realms, are permitted fewer ascendeds, and have a smaller pool to choose from. So they must choose more carefully and have developed a rather unique, and creative, system for picking angels."

"They're inventive, like Aratron said."

Trsiel nodded. "Every ascended on the Fates' team has

been chosen for what new skills or personality traits he or she can add to it. Janah, for example, was the first, and she was a priestess, a very devout woman eager to serve on the side of righteousness. Katsuo—who investigated Glamis—was a samurai, making him a powerful warrior who will obey without question. Marius is a warrior of another kind, a gladiator who led an uprising against the Romans. Unlike Katsuo, Marius has never met an authority figure he didn't challenge, but give him a case of injustice to solve, and no one fights harder."

"Different angels, different strengths. Different weapons for different battles."

"But when it came to the Nix, the Fates realized something was missing from their weapon case."

"Someone who could understand a creature like the Nix."

"I can't speak for the Fates, but I suspect it's that, plus a combination of other factors, that made them—or *would* make them—see you as a good candidate." He snuck a look my way. "You do want it, don't you? At first, I wasn't sure, but then you seemed to warm to the idea."

"I did," I said, turning the half-eaten apple over in my hands. "But now . . . I'm not sure. There's a lot to think about."

He was quiet for a moment, then looked at me. "It's Kristof, isn't it?"

"He . . ." I leaned back against the divan cushions and fixed my gaze on the bookshelf. "A few days ago he said I need a purpose in my life, and he's right. This hunt—this quest—it's made me feel . . ." A small smile. "I'd say 'alive,' if that didn't sound so silly."

"It doesn't."

"In a way, 'alive' really does make sense. Since I died, I've been . . . well, 'dead,' hovering in limbo, obsessing about my daughter, surfacing now and then to see Kristof, but he's been the only thing that brings me out of it. I need more than that, and he knows it. I need a job." I laughed. "Isn't that rich? Spent my life proud of the fact that I never held a proper job, never paid a dime in income taxes, and now that I'm dead, that's exactly what I want."

Trsiel smiled. "Well, I hate to break it to you, but angels don't pay taxes. Don't collect a salary, either."

"You know what I mean."

"You want a purpose, and you think this might be it. Your calling."

I made a gagging noise.

He grinned. "Okay, *career*, not calling. But there's still the problem with Kristof. Obviously he means a lot to you . . ."

"And in taking his advice and taking this 'job,' I might screw things up completely. Become an angel, and I'll finally realize my dream of being able to protect Savannah. Instead of finding a new purpose in my life, I might be opening the door to furthering *that* obsession. So what could be the best thing for me might end up being the worst. If that happens, Kris is gone. Guy's got the tenacity of a bulldog, but even a bulldog eventually realizes it's latched onto something it'll never pull free."

Trsiel said nothing. When I glanced over, he was just staring at me.

"You don't know, do you?" he said softly.

"Don't know what?"

"When you ascend . . . Eve, you can't . . ." He rubbed his hand over his mouth. "I thought you knew."

"Knew what?"

"When you ascend, you have to break all ties with the ghost world."

The room seemed to darken and tilt.

"You mean, I couldn't live there, right?" I said slowly. "I'd have to move up here or something, but I could still visit the ghost world—"

"I mean you'd have to leave. Forever."

I don't know what I said next. I felt my lips moving, heard something like words coming from them, vaguely saw Trsiel nod and say something in return, then felt myself recite a transportation code. The room darkened, then disappeared.

37

I STOOD IN KRISTOF'S HOUSEBOAT, IN FRONT OF THE tiny writing desk beside the bunk. Over the desk was a shelf crammed with photos. Memory shots, we called them in the ghost world. We didn't have cameras or access to old pictures, but we didn't need them. If we could pluck an image from memory, we could make a photograph of it, as I'd done with Amanda Sullivan's picture.

On Kristof's shelf, he had photos of what was important to him. His parents, brothers, nephews, and, of course, his sons. Plus two shots of Savannah, one as she'd been when he met her, and one as she was now. All pictures of family. Then there was a scattering of shots near the middle, of the two of us, memory shots of things we'd done together fifteen years ago, then after our deaths. Off to the side were two more pictures of me, one goofy face-pulling pose, and one of me laughing, curled up in a chair at my house. Then there was the picture he'd had to ask me for: something he'd never had the chance to see, Savannah and me together.

Two days ago, I'd accused him of making me choose between him and our daughter. Now I stared at those pictures, and I realized I'd almost made that choice, however unwillingly. I'd like to say that I would never have become an angel without knowing all the facts, but that would be like saying I'd never have taken Savannah from Kristof without first asking whether he cared. Or like saying I'd never have tried to escape that compound without first making sure my plan was foolproof. Act now, ask questions later, and pay the price forever—that was my path through life. Had Trsiel not told me the cost of angel-hood, I might very well have found myself in an afterlife where I'd chosen Savannah over Kristof—chosen the illusion of a relationship with Savannah over the reality of one with Kristof.

I tore myself away from the photos and headed onto the dock, brain still spinning. When I looked up, I saw Kristof striding down the hill, gaze down, thoughts clearly elsewhere. Then he looked up. As he saw me, his frown evaporated in a wide smile, pace picking up to a jog, a shout of greeting cutting through the soft thump of the waves against the hull.

As I walked out to meet him, Kris's grin faltered. He said nothing, just walked faster. I stopped at the edge of the wooden dock. My mouth opened and I wanted to tell him I'd found the amulet, regale him with the story of how I'd swiped it from under the Nix's nose and given her a good ass-kicking in the process. But all I could think about was how close I'd come to throwing away the only real thing I had in this afterlife.

I lifted my hand and touched his cheek. Why does skin still feel warm here, long after the blood that gives it heat is gone? Maybe it's the memory of warmth that we feel, or maybe it's something deeper than biology.

Kristof put his hand over mine, and pressed it against his cheek. Then he pulled my hand over to his mouth and kissed my palm, the touch so light it sent a shiver through me. I looked around, but there was no one here to see us. There was never anyone but the occasional seagull or tern winging past overhead.

I pulled my hand from Kristof's grasp and undid the first button on his shirt. Closing my eyes, I slid my hands to his chest, and traced my fingers over his collarbone. No need to look; my fingers knew the way, as they did over every part of him, neural pathways etched into my brain, tread and retread and committed to memory years before, as if I'd known from the start that someday I'd need to rely on my memories to see him.

"I used to dream about you," I said, undoing the rest of the shirt as I trailed my fingers down his chest. "Long after I left. Right up to the end. Twelve years gone, and I'd still wake up in the night, thinking you'd just left the room, certain I could smell you there. Even the mattress felt warm."

I undid his pants and pushed them down over his hips. "Some nights it was just that, dreaming you were sleeping there beside me. Other nights . . ." I shivered and slipped one hand into his shorts, while the other tugged them off. "Other nights I'd wake up aching for you, sweating, so wet I barely needed to touch myself to come. I could never remember what I'd been dreaming, but I knew it was about you, even when I told myself it wasn't."

I slid my hands down his hips, then ran my fingertips down the inside of his thighs. "I used to fantasize about you. I tried not to. I'd start imagining someone else, anyone else, but it always turned into you. I'd close my eyes and remember what you smelled like, what you tasted like. Sometimes it wasn't enough, and I'd call your office and listen to your voice on the machine. It never sounded like you—not the real you—but if I concentrated just right, and tuned out the words, I could hear your voice, and that always worked."

"I used to see you," he said, tugging my shirt out of my jeans. "Everywhere. The street, the office, at home, even sitting beside me in the car. Out of the corner of my eye I'd see something and, for a second, I'd forget you were gone and I . . ."

He inhaled sharply and buried his head against my shoulder. After a moment, he kissed the side of my neck, and started pushing down my jeans.

"Sometimes it was a smell," he murmured. "The smell of a food we'd eaten or a place we'd been. Other times it was a laugh. I'd swear I heard your laugh, and I could see you there, in bed, grinning at me, head turned just so, hair falling over your breasts." Another sharp inhale, and he brushed his fingers along my hair, tickling it over my breast. "That's what did it for me. Hearing that laugh. Sometimes at the most inconvenient times. But, once in a while, that wasn't enough."

He traced his fingers down my sides, and across my stomach, inching lower. "I found one of your apartments once. I stayed away until you were gone. After you moved out, I went there, just to . . ." He shrugged, eyes lowered. "Just to look. To be there. I found a pillowcase you'd left, fell behind the bed. I could still smell you on it. That's what I used, when remembering wasn't enough."

I put my arms around his neck. "I want you back, Kris. For now and forever."

He lowered me to the dock.

* * *

Afterward, we stretched out, enjoying the faint heat of the sun and the slap of the surf. Kristof's fingers slid up my thigh, then stopped. He frowned and looked down at my leg. His frown deepened. I followed his gaze to a paper-thin raised welt encircling my thigh where Trsiel's sword had passed through.

I told him what had happened.

Kristof shook his head. "That man has serious sword-control problems."

I sputtered a laugh. "You think?"

"If he's not slow getting it out, he's sticking it in where it doesn't belong."

As my laugh died, I pressed my face against his shoulder. After a moment, Kristof stroked the back of my head. "What else happened?"

Until now, I'd said nothing about Trsiel's hints that my quest was really a stepping stone to angel-hood. When I told Kristof that, I expected him to burst out laughing. I guess I should have known better. Instead, he listened, then gave a slow nod.

"That makes sense," he said.

"It does?" I smiled. "I swear, Kris, you're the only person in the universe who could hear that I'm a candidate for angel-hood and say, 'That makes sense.'"

"But it does. You may not be the most obvious choice, but if they haven't caught this Nix in over a hundred years, I'd say the obvious choices aren't working out so well." He paused, thoughtful. "I know this may not be the path you had in mind for your afterlife, but you may want to give the offer some serious thought. You've been . . . well, you've been better than I've seen you in a long time, happier, more . . . there. First, of course, you'd have to have a very long talk with the Fates, find out exactly what this deal would entail."

"I—I've done that, Kris."

His brows arched.

I managed a twist of a smile. "Surprised at my foresight? Don't be. Trsiel told me the catch. And good thing he did, because . . ." My throat went tight. "Because I came very close to making a very big mistake. I'm not going to be an angel, Kris. The price is too high."

"Savannah," he murmured. "You couldn't watch her anymore."

"No, that's not it. If anything, Savannah was the biggest plus to this whole offer." I caught his gaze. "Becoming an angel would mean I could protect her, that I could have stopped Lily, just like Trsiel did. And, ever since Trsiel told me I might be a candidate, that's all I've been able to think about, how it would help me with Savannah. But then, after you talked to me in Alaska, I wasn't so sure that was the right path anymore. Then, today, I found out something that clinched it. Become an angel, and they send me off to angel-land. A one-way, one-passenger ticket."

His brow crinkled, then a blink of surprise, quickly stifled. "You'd have to leave the ghost world, you mean, and you like it here—"

I cut him off with a fierce kiss. "You know what I mean, so stop playing dumb. I don't care about the damned ghost world. It's you I won't leave."

A slow smile, then he leaned over and kissed me back. A few minutes of that—too few minutes for my taste—and he pulled away.

"So no halo and wings for Eve." He grinned. "I have to

admit, that particular outfit wasn't one I've ever imagined you in."

"One of very few, I'm sure." I shifted closer to him, belly to belly, feeling a fresh wave of heat. "I will find a job. That much I've realized. I need to do something in this life. Maybe we can spend some time thinking about it. I can try on different uniforms, see if any catch your fancy . . ."

He laughed and slid his hand around to my rear, pulling me against him. "I'm sure most will catch my fancy, at least for a night or two. Perhaps we can start with the nurse . . ." He closed his eyes, lips moving in a soft oath.

"Kris?"

"Sorry, just the practical part of my brain, reminding me that I'm distracting you from something more important than nurse fantasies." His gaze slid down my body. "I could shut it off, if you like . . ."

I laughed as I sat up. "You're right, I do have work to do, and we'll have all of eternity to play dress-up when I'm done. Now give me a hand brainstorming my next move. As partners go, Trsiel's a good guy, but when it comes to plotting, our brains operate on completely different wavelengths."

"Won't let you kill anyone, will he?"

"Won't even consider it. No killing, no stealing, no lying. I think I've caught him swearing once or twice, but I can't be sure."

"I'm taller, too."

I sputtered a laugh. "You're what?"

"Taller." He snuck a grin at me. "He's better-looking, thinner, still has all his hair . . . but I'm taller. By at least an inch."

"Not only do you support me in my moral bankruptcy, but you're taller? What more could any woman want?"

"So she didn't get the amulet," Kris said after I'd recapped my last Nix encounter.

"Right, but she said she had another way. A less satisfactory way."

"Spiritual possession," he said. "And for that she'd need not just any necromancer. What did you say back at the castle? Few necros who are powerful enough to perform it—"

"Would be stupid enough to perform it."

"A powerful necro . . . who's somewhat lacking in mental agility." His brows arched. "Sound like anyone you've worked with recently?"

"Jaime's not stupid. She doesn't come off as the brightest bulb, but, hey, I know all about the benefits of acting dumber than you are. In her case, there are some emotional issues there, too. Acting like a ditzy celebrity might be her way of dealing with things."

"True, but, as you say, she doesn't come off as the brightest bulb. What's important is what she *appears* to be. The Nix did make some cryptic comment about her secondary choice having some effect on you, that it'd be 'temporarily' very satisfying, probably meaning something that would hurt you. If she knows that you know Jaime—"

"Shit!" I scrambled up. "I need to warn Jaime."

Kris got to his feet as I conjured fresh clothing. "I'm right beside you. But even if the Nix does get to Jaime before we do, Jaime's not about to volunteer her body for full spirit possession, certainly not to an unknown spirit."

*   *   *

Finding Jaime wouldn't be a problem. Because of her erratic schedule, we'd already worked out a system so I could track her down if I needed help. If she was out, she'd leave me a note on her desk, where I could read it.

I recalled Jaime mentioning earlier that she'd be in Sacramento for a couple of shows this week, and when we got to her apartment, the note she'd left confirmed she was already gone. She'd even penciled in her schedule in both local and Pacific time, to avoid confusion.

"Very considerate," Kris said.

"Unless she thinks *I'm* the one lacking a few brain cells."

He laughed. "There are probably misconceptions on both sides." He peered down at the paper. "So her show finished an hour ago, with nothing scheduled before or after. Either she's still at the theater, or she's headed back to her hotel."

"For which we have a name, but no room number, which she probably didn't know at the time. She says it'll be a suite on one of the top floors. That should narrow it down . . . I hope."

"Do you want to take that, then? And I'll search the theater."

I agreed, and we left.

38

BEING A GHOST SEARCHING THROUGH HOTEL ROOMS at eleven P.M. has its drawbacks—namely unwitting voyeurism. It wouldn't be so bad if I could have picked up something useful—a new technique, a new position, a new game—but it was all pretty pedestrian stuff. Even the businessmen who'd sprung for high-class hookers weren't doing anything that they probably couldn't have done at home with their wives. That made me wonder how many halves—or wholes—of these copulating couples had a wife or husband or lover at home, and what they thought they were doing, risking that relationship simply for a momentary change of pace . . . and change of face.

I finished the first floor of suites, climbed to the second, stepped into the first room . . . and found the Nix and Jaime kneeling across from each other, a host of necromancy implements between them.

"Hey!" I said, racing toward them. "What the hell are you doing?"

The Nix's gaze flicked my way, then turned back to Jaime, who was nibbling her lower lip, staring down at the necromantic altar.

"I'm not—I'm really uncomfortable with this," Jaime said.

"No shit!" I said, planting myself over the altar. "If this is what it looks like— Damn it, Jaime, that's the Nix—the demi-demon I've been chasing."

Jaime kept chewing her lip. I reached to shake her shoulder, but, of course, my fingers passed right through. So I got in her face—literally—ducking down and putting my face a scant inch from hers.

"Hello! Anybody in there?"

The Nix laughed.

Jaime's head shot up. "What?"

"You're sitting with a murdering demi-demon, that's what—" I began.

"Nothing," the Nix said. "I was just thinking that I don't blame you for not trusting me. Hell, I don't blame *anyone* for not trusting me."

"No shit," I said. "That's what happens when you're an evil—"

"I did a lot of horrible things in my life," the Nix continued. "But I did one good thing, too—"

"Bullshit."

"—and that good thing is all that matters to me now."

"Savannah," Jaime said with a soft sigh.

My gut went cold.

"I need to protect her, Jaime," the Nix continued. "And I would love to be able to do that on my own, but I can't. I tried. God knows, I've tried."

I stared at the Nix and, for a moment, hearing those words, I saw myself sitting there . . . which was exactly what Jaime was seeing. The glamour spell. Shit!

"Trsiel!" I shouted.

The Nix fought back a smile.

Jaime exhaled a deep sigh. "Okay, let's get this over with. But if you double-cross me, Eve—"

"I won't," the Nix said. "Give me your body long enough to catch this bitch, and I'll give it to you with all the spook-busting credits you'll ever want."

I lunged at the Nix. Yet even though she was in spirit form, I passed right through her and landed across the floor.

I mentally called for Trsiel again, then recited a quick communication spell, putting in a desperate call to Kristof. I knew it wouldn't work—he'd never been able to master this piece of high-level witch magic—but I had to try anyway. The Nix had erected some kind of barrier against me, but maybe Kris could get through and either warn Jaime or stop the ritual.

Jaime had barely finished the first invocation when Kristof popped into the room, facing Jaime and the Nix, his back to me.

"You rang?" he began, then stopped. "What the hell?"

"That's not me," I said as I hurried up beside him.

"Of course it isn't," he said. "It's the Nix, but what—"

"She's cast a glamour spell to look like me, and convinced Jaime to let me—her—possess her. I can't stop them, and Jaime can't hear me. Some kind of spell—"

"Jaime," Kristof said sharply as he strode toward the two. She didn't turn.

"Jaime!" he said, then bent over her and looked into her eyes. "Goddamn it!"

He turned to me, opened his mouth to say something, then twisted fast and launched himself at the Nix, trying to catch her off guard. He flew through her and tumbled to the floor.

"What kind of spell has she—?" I began.

"Not the Nix. It's Jaime—she's put up a necromantic barrier to block interference from other spirits. The Nix probably told her to."

"So what can we—"

"Do?" Jaime said, rising to her feet. "Nothing, witch. You can do nothing."

I blinked. The Nix had disappeared—into Jaime.

"Where is she?" I said. "If you've—"

"Oh, don't worry about the necromancer. This isn't about her."

Before I could answer, Trsiel appeared, landing in front of me with his back to Jaime—the Nix. His gaze darted first to Kristof, then to me.

"Ah, the angel," the Nix said. "Better late than never, hmmm?"

Trsiel spun, saw Jaime, and frowned back at me. "What's she—?"

"I was just about to tell Eve what I'm doing with this body," the Nix said. "Of course, I could surprise her, but that would quite ruin things. How much better that she should know exactly what I have in mind . . . so when it comes to pass, she can know that she failed to stop me."

"Trsiel!" I said. "That's the—"

"Nix," she said. "He knows, witch, and he'll do nothing about it. He won't interfere even when I wrap my hands around their necks. Yes, *their* necks. Those whose lives you made this bargain to save. Ironic, I think."

"Paige and Lucas?" I said. "Don't you dare—"

"Not only will I kill them but, with a little ingenuity, I can take an even sweeter revenge. What could be worse than your poor daughter losing her perfect guardians? Thinking she killed them herself."

I started to lunge at the Nix, then remembered it

would do no good and spun to face Trsiel, shouting his name. But he didn't move.

"Goddamn you!" Kristof said, turning on Trsiel. "If you don't—"

The Nix's laugh cut him off. She lifted a hand, waved, and walked out the door. With a roar, Kristof rushed Trsiel. He grabbed him by the shirtfront and threw him toward the door.

"Get out there and do your goddamned job!" Kristof snarled. "Stop her!"

"I can't," Trsiel said softly.

Kristof bore down on Trsiel again. He grabbed him by the shirt, then rammed him against the wall. He locked his forearm under the angel's chin.

"You've tricked Eve, haven't you?" Kris said. "Betrayed her to that . . ." His mouth worked, unable to find the right word. He lowered his face to Trsiel's. "If you've had something to do with this, no Fate is going to save—"

I laid a hand on Kris's shoulder. He stopped, jaw still working as he eased back.

"Trsiel? You said you can't," I said. "Why can't you?"

"Because I'd kill Jaime."

"And your point is?" Kristof said.

Trsiel's gaze hardened as it rose to meet Kristof's. "My point is that Jaime Vegas is an innocent party. I don't know how the Nix got into her body, but unless she's a willing participant—"

"She's not," I said softly. "The Nix tricked her. Jaime thinks she's helping me save Savannah from the Nix. Which means Trsiel's right. We can't kill her . . . not if there's another way. The Nix can't teleport while she's in Jaime, so we have some time before she gets to Portland."

Kris stepped back and rolled his shoulders. A moment's

hesitation, as he slipped back into character. "I would suggest, then, that we not waste time trying to figure this out ourselves. We'll see what the Fates have to say."

"Trsiel is right," the middle Fate said. "He cannot kill her."

We stood in the throne room. Kristof and I, that is. Trsiel stayed outside, probably having decided he was better off keeping away from Kris for a while.

"Fine," I said. "He can't kill an innocent. We get that, and so long as we still have a chance of stopping the Nix before she kills Paige or Lucas, I don't want Jaime hurt any more than you do."

The Fate shook her head. "I don't think you understand, Eve. Trsiel cannot kill her. Not now. Not ever . . . even as a last resort."

"What?"

"Hold on." Kris stepped forward, hands raised. "You mean to tell me that you'll let this Nix kill those kids, and you won't interfere? What kind of justice is that?"

The oldest Fate slid into her sister's place and fixed Kris with a glare. "Is her life worth less than theirs?"

"Yes. There's no question about that, is there? No disrespect to Jaime Vegas, but this is a woman who whores her—"

"Kristof—"

Kris met the Fate's gaze. "*Whores* her talents to the highest bidder, while Lucas and Paige are down there doing your work, fighting on your side. You cannot compare her to them."

The middle Fate took over. "It's not our place to judge the value of a human life, Kristof."

"Then whose is it? Because I want to talk to him."

"No one has that power . . . or that right."

Kristof shook his head in disgust. "Fine, then. Maybe you can't compare lives, but I'm sure you can count, and two lives lost plus one destroyed must be worth more than a single loss."

The youngest Fate appeared. "We can count, Kristof. Even me. It's you who needs a lesson. Not in math, but in English. We didn't say Trsiel *may* not kill the Nix while she's in Jaime's body, or that he *will* not. We said *can* not."

"You mean it's not possible," I said. "Because Jaime's innocent."

The Fate nodded. "The Sword of Judgment cannot bring to justice the soul of an innocent."

"But the *soul* isn't innocent," Kristof said. "The Nix—"

"The soul of the body still belongs to Jaime."

"So now what?" I said. "Where does that leave us?"

"Exactly where you were," the girl said. Then her lips twisted in a rueful semismile. "Only without the backup plan."

"Great."

The Fates called Trsiel in to join us then. The more brains we had working on this problem, the better.

The most obvious solution was to treat this as a normal case of spirit possession, and contact a few living necros to perform an exorcism. Problem was, as the Fates reminded us, this wasn't a normal case of spirit possession because the Nix wasn't a normal spirit. They were ninety-nine percent sure it would fail. By the time we tracked down and prepped a necromancer for the exorcism, if it didn't work, it would be too late to try something else.

As long as we stayed in the throne room, plotting, we

were operating on the Fates' time, and only minutes would pass in the living world. But the moment we stepped into the living world, we were on our own, clock ticking.

"So we need to find a way to separate the Nix's spirit from the body of her living partner," I said. "And the only way to reliably do that is to use an angel's sword . . . which won't work in this case. So how the hell—?"

"There is another way," the child Fate said.

"What?"

The young Fate began to shimmer, her body lengthening and aging, morphing into her middle sister, but in slow motion, as if fighting the change. A split-second burst of light, and the child stood there again, her face a grim mask of childish determination.

"There's another way," she said, words spilling out almost too fast to understand. "It's been done before. The second seeker—"

"No!" Trsiel said. "We agreed—"

"You agreed what?" I said. "Are you telling me that after all this, you know another way?"

"No, I don't." He shot a scowl at the child Fate. "And neither does she."

"But the other one does," she said, chin lifting. "The second seeker."

"You mean the angel you sent the second time?" I began, then stopped. "No, it wasn't an angel, was it? It was a ghost. A man named Dachev. You sent him after the Nix and he caught her. Then she cut a deal, persuaded him to join her instead of turning her in."

The youngest Fate's mouth opened, but her middle sister took over before she could confirm it. I didn't need that confirmation, though. One look at Trsiel's face, and I knew I'd put the pieces in the right place.

I continued, "And if he wasn't an angel, then he must have managed to separate the Nix's spirit from her body *without* a Sword of Judgment. How?"

The Fate shook her head. "We don't know, Eve. We only know that he did . . . and that things became much worse after that."

"A problem some of us foresaw," Trsiel said.

The Fate nodded. "Yes, Trsiel. We should have listened to those with a better understanding of such matters. We made a mistake, and we have paid for it."

"Such matters . . ." I said. "You mean evil. This Dachev, the Nix didn't tempt him into a partnership, did she? It was his idea." I looked up at her. "Send a killer to catch a killer . . . and I'm not the first killer you've sent."

39

IT SEEMS THAT AFTER JANAH'S SANITY-BUSTING BRUSH with the Nix, the Fates had decided that they needed a bounty-hunter with a better understanding of the Nix's mind. So they'd reached into their darkest hell dimension, and plucked out a likely candidate, a supernatural serial killer who'd expressed contrition and remorse for his crimes. Andrei Dachev.

They then struck a deal with Dachev. If he caught the Nix for them, he would be rewarded. Not by becoming an angel—that was never an option. Instead, he would be transferred to a medium-security afterlife, one worse than my own but much better than his hell dimension. A fine and fair deal. Unfortunately, once freed, he took it upon himself to renegotiate . . . without consulting the Fates.

Like me, he had been assigned an angel liaison—not Trsiel, but another of the full-bloods. It had taken him all of two days to ditch the guardian and strike out on his own. Of course, he'd been bright enough not to just cut and run, probably because the Fates had been bright enough to fit him with the mystical equivalent of an anklet tracking device. Instead, he'd proven to them that he worked better on his own. When he needed an angel, he'd call. Until then, he'd report back daily with updates. After four months, he caught up with the Nix. Only he didn't call for backup. He separated her from her partner's body all by himself. Then, rather than drag his prize back to the Fates and collect his reward, he cut a new deal . . . with the Nix.

"Okay," I said when the middle Fate finished her explanation. "So he's still in this serial-killer hell, right? I mean, he hasn't, you know . . . escaped."

"No, Eve. Our security isn't that poor. The Nix was—"

"A special case. Yeah, I know. But if this guy's still down there, what are we waiting for? Throw open the gates to hell, 'cause I'm coming in."

"That's a very, uh, noble sentiment, Eve," Trsiel began.

"Noble, my ass. I just want to see this bitch's face when I rip her out of Jaime's body."

A soft chuckle from Kristof.

Trsiel shook his head. "It's not that easy—"

"Yeah, I know, this guy's a killer, and he's in a hell dimension, but I didn't lead a sheltered life. If this guy knows how to catch the Nix, I'll get it out of him. I know how to reason with guys like that. If I can't, I'll kick his ass from hell to Honolulu."

Kris grinned. "And I'll be there to help . . . in the persuasion phase." He shot the grin my way. "If it comes down to ass-kicking, I'll just watch."

The Fate let out a heartfelt sigh and shook her head.

"Great plan," Trsiel said. "One small problem."

"What?" I said.

"He lies."

"Huh?"

"Dachev can't be trusted. Shocking, really, but—"

"Stuff the sarcasm, Trsiel," I said. "We're here to solve a problem, and I don't hear you offering to help—"

"Which, track record considered, may be a blessing," Kristof murmured.

Trsiel shot him a glare, but before he could come up with a retort, I carried on.

"If you don't have a solution of your own, at least don't mock ours," I said. "Obviously this guy can't be trusted to tell the truth about how he stopped the Nix, but if I can apply enough pressure—"

"You can't," the Fate said. "There is only one way to compel him to tell the truth. The Sword of Judgment. If he could be made to tell what he did, while laying his hands on it, he'd be forced to tell the truth."

Trsiel looked at Kristof. "And before you ask why I haven't done so myself, I cannot enter that place. *Can* not, not will not or may not. No full-blooded angel can enter a true hell. The ascendeds can . . . and we've already sent Katsuo, the only one who'd volunteer."

"So the only way I can force him to speak the truth is to become an angel." I looked from Trsiel to the Fates. "Convenient."

Kristof wheeled on Trsiel. "You scheming son-of-a-bitch."

I laid my hand on his arm. "If anyone's scheming here, I doubt it's Trsiel. So far, he's been the only one who's been—or tried to be—honest with me about this whole angel thing." I fixed my gaze on the Fates. "Anything you ladies want to tell me about this quest?"

The middle-aged Fate nodded. "Yes, Eve, we have selected you as a candidate for ascension. Trsiel has told us that you figured that out . . ." A reproachful look his way. "With a little help from him. While it's not the way we wanted you to learn of our plans, we will not deny it. However, it will always be your decision to make. We would never force you to ascend."

"But the point is moot anyway, considering I can't get that sword until I've completed this quest . . . and if I've completed the quest, I don't need Dachev."

"The inaugural quest is not an entrance exam. It is an assessment of your training requirements. We have chosen you, and although we're supposed to wait until after the quest to let you ascend, in this case the Creator would grant an exception. There is, however, another, less reliable way. If you do not wish to become an angel—"

"I don't."

She glanced from Kristof to me. "Your . . . attachment to this world has changed, then?"

"It has."

She nodded. "Then perhaps that will be what you needed. As I said, the choice was yours, and we will not press the matter further, although we may find other tasks for you from time to time."

"That's fine. Thank you. Now what's this other way?"

"You know there are magics for testing the sincerity of a demon. Something I believe you've tested fairly recently." Her gaze shunted to Kristof. "There are also magics to do the same with a spirit. This spell would test Dachev's words, but couldn't force him to speak those words."

"In other words, I need to trick him into telling me."

She shook her head. "This spell requires his active participation. He must recite part of the incantation, and you cannot 'trick' him into doing that."

"Okay, so I have to persuade a psychopath trapped in

hell to voluntarily tell me how to catch his former partner—"

"There's more."

"Of course there is."

Kristof walked behind me and put his arms around my waist, letting me lean against him. I felt his warmth against my back and relaxed.

"He can hurt you," the Fate said.

"Who? Dachev? But I'm a—"

"A ghost, yes. But in that world—it's part of the magic there. Physical pain is possible, and there's nothing we can do to shield you from it. He can't kill you, of course, but he can hurt you . . . and we may not be able to erase all the damage."

"Uh-huh. Well, I didn't really need both my arms anyway."

Kristof chuckled against my ear.

The Fate frowned at me. "I don't think you're taking this seriously, Eve."

"Look, compared to what you've already suggested, I'm willing to take the risk, okay?"

"*We're* willing," Kris murmured against my ear. "I'll be right beside you."

"No, Kristof," the Fate said.

He opened his mouth to object, but the Fate lifted her hand.

"We will not let you go with Eve. That is an absolute, so do not argue the matter or you'll only delay her. As for why we won't allow it, I'm sure you already know. Perhaps you could help her, but you will also hinder her. Anyone we sent with her, even Katsuo, could prove a dangerous distraction. In a place like that, she must look to her own safety at all times."

"I'll go alone," I said. "That's best. One question: If I can hurt, he can hurt, right?"

"Yes, but . . ." She hesitated. "I have said that I will respect your decision not to ascend, and I am loath to do anything that could be seen as pushing you toward that choice, and yet . . ." She gripped the side of the spinning wheel and leaned forward. "This much I *must* say, if only because it would unpardonable to omit it. Were you to find yourself in a situation where no other escape is possible, ascension is still an option. You need only to wish for it, and the Creator will grant it immediately. You would then be impervious to harm and would be able to use the sword. But, know this, Eve, if you ascend, we cannot reverse the process, however much we may wish to."

"I understand. Now tell me more about this Dachev. If he's in your realms, that makes him a supernatural."

"He's a magician."

I thumped my head back against Kristof's shoulder and sighed. "Of course he is."

Magicians were related to sorcerers, and they had even more reason than their brethren to hate witches. Magicians are a substandard form of spell-casters. I say that with no snobbery. Sorcerers and witches can argue over which race is less powerful, but even a sorcerer would admit, albeit grudgingly, that a witch outranked a magician any day.

For centuries, there had been no distinction between male spell-casters—they were all sorcerers, and all inferior to witches. At the time, their magic was limited to simple illusions and sleight of hand, the kind of magic you can see at a kid's birthday party these days. Then witches, being the generous fools they often are, decided it was time to join forces, a drive for sexual equality a thousand years before the suffragettes hit the streets.

Witches taught the sorcerers how to strengthen their skills with stronger magic and incantations. All went just dandy for a few hundred years, until the Inquisition hit, and sorcerers turned on the witches. But that's ancient history . . . even if it doesn't keep either race from holding a grudge five hundred years later.

Back to the original racial integration. There were some sorcerers who couldn't cut it. They didn't have the supernatural juice to learn what the witches were teaching them. So, as any group with an ounce of ingenuity and pride does when it can't fit into the larger society, these sorcerers reinvented themselves, breaking away from their brothers and declaring themselves a new race: magicians. Rather than fight a losing battle to learn higher magic, they would concentrate on the lesser skills of illusion and sleight of hand, and be happy with what they were.

A very noble plan of modern-day self-affirmation. Unfortunately, as they soon discovered, those lesser skills weren't good for a whole helluva lot. Magicians ended up forming two factions: entertainers and con artists—and the lines between the two weren't always that clear. Today, almost all the magicians who remain fall into the latter category. In a world accustomed to David Copperfield no one will pay to see a guy pull a quarter from behind your ear.

In Bulgaria, circa 1926, though, things were different and, as the Fates explained, that's where Andrei Dachev had made a name for himself with his sideshow acts, traveling from town to town, bringing light entertainment to a country still reeling from the Balkan conflict and the

First World War. Although Dachev was an accomplished magician, the real attraction at his circus was the freak show. And I don't mean sword swallowers or fire-breathers. Dachev's freaks were the type that children would dare one another to look at, then suffer weeks of nightmares if they did. His freaks were born severely deformed or had been mutilated in horrific accidents, and all were young women, adding to the titillation value.

For three years Dachev toured Bulgaria and surrounding countries, sticking to the rural areas, avoiding cities and larger urban areas where his freaks might be less welcome. And if, over those three years, the occasional girl disappeared from a town he passed through, well, Dachev was a handsome charmer, with an eye for the ladies, and these things happened.

Eventually, though, one of these missing girls had a beau who didn't buy this "ran away with the circus" explanation. He followed Dachev. Soon, he discovered that the circus freaks hadn't suffered a cruel twist of genetics or accidental fate. They were man-made. Though he managed to rescue his fiancée before Dachev started in on her, when it came to the other half-dozen victims, the authorities decided to quietly provide them with a fast-acting poison and allow them to make their own decision. All chose death, and Andrei Dachev was executed as a serial killer.

"And you unleashed this . . . this *thing* back into the world?" I said.

The eldest Fate appeared, mouth a thin, tight line. "We did not unleash—"

"Yeah, he was a ghost. Powerless. Found a way around that one, though, didn't he? What the hell do you think he's been doing down there all these years? Hail Marys?

He's been reliving his glory days, just itching for the chance to—"

"No, he has not."

"Oh, and you know that because—"

"Because he cannot." She paused, and her middle sister took over. "Andrei Dachev has no memories of the atrocities he committed, Eve. That is part of their punishment. We take away all memory of their lives before they died. They can't relive their crimes, their fantasies, even their impulses. It's all gone. Then they are cast into a plane where, when their urges and impulses resurface, they have no possible outlet."

"Because they're in a world of killers."

She nodded. "A world without victims, without even those that they might see as a potential victim, no female killers, no weaker males—"

"All predators and no prey. Okay, so he can't remember his crimes. But those impulses you mentioned? First time he sees a pretty girl, even if he can't remember *ever* seeing one—"

"The memory loss sometimes has a second, reformatory effect. Erasing their memories may erase the source of some of their urges. If their lives were warped by extreme circumstances, such as early abuse, then—"

"When they can't remember the abuse, they become a different person, someone who isn't a killer?"

"Which, granted, happens very, very rarely," the Fate said. "But it does happen. That's what we believed had happened here. For ten years, Andrei Dachev gave no sign of having any of the urges that possessed him to commit these crimes."

"He played model prisoner."

"Played. Yes, most likely, though every test we gave him

indicated that he had indeed reformed. Perhaps even he thought he had."

"Until he went into the world again."

She gave a slow, sad nod.

"His memory," I said. "It wasn't erased after his capture, right?"

"We can't do that. We can only erase living memories. I suppose, though, that's a blessing now."

"Or else he wouldn't know how he'd caught the Nix. So I need to persuade him to tell me, by descending into a hell filled with serial killers, for most of whom I'll be the first woman—and potential victim—they've ever seen." I sighed. "Well, at least they can feel pain. Please tell me I can use my spells and my Aspicio powers."

When she didn't answer, I groaned. "Let me guess. Because they're all supernaturals, it's a magic-free zone—wipes out any racial advantages."

The little girl appeared. "Well, it's *supposed* to be magic-free, but if a person went in there who possessed a type of magic none of the inhabitants should be able to possess . . ."

"Such as a female-only variety. Like witch magic."

"Magic blocking is tough enough. No sense doing it for a type of magic that no one there will ever use."

"Hmmm. I'd rather have my sorcerer spells, but witch magic is better than nothing. Now, I guess it doesn't matter what supernatural race these other killers are, if they're power-free, but I should ask anyway."

The Fate rattled off the various races in this particular supernatural serial-killers hell. Mostly half-demons, with one necromancer and one werewolf. No sorcerers, which was all I really cared about, in case they were still able to recognize a witch. Bad enough I might have to deal with that problem with Dachev.

Next, the Fates explained how I'd get out of the hell. I couldn't just walk out or recite a teleport code—it was locked too tight for that. Instead, they'd give me a hells-bane potion. Swallow it, and I'll be hell-free.

Finally, the Fates wanted me to do some practice runs with the sincerity-testing spell. As anxious as I was to get moving, I knew time in the throne room areas was slowed to a crawl. An hour spent testing the spell could save me a lot of grief later, and it would only take seconds of "real-world" time.

"Give me the spell and I'll get testing." I glanced over my shoulder at Kristof. "I could use a partner for that."

He smiled. "But of course. A magical lie detector. Just what every good relationship needs."

40

DESPITE KRIS'S JOKE, I DIDN'T USE THE SPELL FOR RE-vealing his deepest, darkest secrets. What would be the point? I knew them already.

Without the obvious ways to test the spell, I had to get inventive.

"Ginger or Mary Ann?" I asked.

He pulled a face. "Neither."

His eyes stayed blue, which meant he was telling the truth. If he'd lied, they go black. A growing nose would have been more fun, but apparently the spell's creator hadn't been properly schooled in fairy tales.

I recast the spell.

"The Rolling Stones or the Beatles?" I asked.

"The Stones, which I'm sure you could have guessed, if you didn't already know." He uncrossed his legs, stretched them out, and leaned back against the wall. "See, that's the problem. If you know the answer, then you'll know if I lie, even without the spell."

"Ah, I've got one. Would you rather be smart or good-looking?"

He rolled his eyes, but I held up my hand to cut off his answer.

"Hold on," I said. "There's a codicil. If you pick smart, you can't be good-looking. And vice versa."

He pursed his lips. "Define 'not good-looking.'"

"Triple paper-bag ugly. But Nobel Prize–winner brilliant. And dumb as a stump, but drop-dead gorgeous."

He laughed. "You first."

"Option B. Gorgeous and stupid."

"Oh, now, that'd fail the test."

"Try it and see."

He cast the spell. When I repeated my answer, he leaned forward to look in my eyes, then nearly toppled backward laughing.

"I don't believe it. You *are* serious. Either that, or my casting is off, and I think that must be it, because I can't imagine you'd ever pick beauty over brains."

"No? Think about it. If you pick brains, you'd be smart enough to know exactly how ugly you were. But if you picked beauty, you'd be too dumb to know the difference. I'd rather be happy than miserable. And I'm sure the sex would be better, too. Well, a lot more plentiful at least. Go with option A, and you might as well join the priesthood."

He shook his head, still chuckling. "Well, I'm sticking with option A. Brains over beauty for me any day."

His eyes darkened.

I sputtered a laugh. "Liar."

He sighed. "You got me with the celibacy angle."

I laughed. He lifted me onto his lap and kissed me.

After a moment, he pulled back slowly. "I need you to promise me something, Eve."

"Hmm?"

"If things go wrong in there—badly wrong, and you get into a situation you can't get out of . . ." He hesitated, then wrapped his hand around mine. "The Fates said if you change your mind, at any point, and you need to become an angel—"

"No."

He took my chin in his hand and lifted my face to his.

I shook my head. "I'll find another way, Kris. There's always another way. I'll have the hellsbane potion, remember? Anything goes wrong, I gulp that, and I'm home free faster than the Creator could make me an angel."

"But if you ever *did* get stuck—if that was the only way out, I need to know you'll take it." When I hesitated, he stroked his finger across my cheek. "If it did come to that, Eve, we'd find a way. I'd find one for us. For now and forever. I say it and I mean it. I backed down once, and I'll never do it again."

"Backed down? You never—"

"I didn't have any say in your leaving last time, but I had years to fight your decision, twelve years to say 'I want you back and I don't care if it means giving up everything else to get you.' But I never did. Not because I didn't love you, or I didn't love you enough, but because I was a coward."

"You weren't—"

"I was afraid you wouldn't want me back. So I told myself that I'd wait, give you time to come to me, and when you didn't I convinced myself that my fears were well-founded, that you'd only wanted me for who I was and what I could give you . . . and even that wasn't worth staying with me for."

"Kris, I never—"

"I know. Even then, I think I saw that for what it was—self-pitying bullshit. But it made my cowardice easier to justify. Then I came here, and found you, and I knew I was wrong." He smiled. "Even as you were telling me to go to hell, and trying to send me there with an energy bolt, I knew I'd been wrong. So I vowed I'd get you back, and when I did, I'd make damn sure nothing got in the way again, not your obsession with protecting Savannah, not ghost-world bounty-hunter duty, not even impossibly good-looking angel mentors."

"But you're taller."

He grinned. "See? You did notice."

I laughed. When I finished, he touched my chin, turning my face to his.

"The point is that I'm not leaving, and no one can make me. No matter what happens, I'll fight. If you get stuck in there, absolutely stuck, you don't quit on me, either— you fight, even if it means you need that damned sword to do it."

I hesitated, then nodded. "I will."

When I was ready, Trsiel took me away, to escort me into Dachev's hell. As we walked through the complex, he gave me some tips about Dachev himself, based on his own encounters with him. I drilled him on that, getting everything he knew about Dachev, from concrete facts to behavioral interpretations to general impressions. Then I declared myself ready.

"He's right through that door," Trsiel said.

"Door?" I followed his finger to see a narrow door behind me. "He's through there?"

"His hell is, at least. You'll have to find Dachev himself. I don't know what's in . . ." He shook his head. "This won't work. You need more details. Let me try tracking down Katsuo again. He's been there—"

"Don't," I said. "If I start stalling, I won't stop. If Dachev's in there, I'll find him."

Trsiel nodded. "But be careful. Remember what I said—"

"I know."

"Don't forget, the . . . men down there, they haven't seen a woman—"

"I know."

"They can hurt you, Eve. Really hurt you. You have to be—"

"I know." I reached out and squeezed his hand. "I know, Trsiel."

He hesitated, as if there was so much more he wanted to say, a hundred more warnings he wanted to impart, but instead he returned the squeeze and, with his free hand, pulled a vial from his pocket.

"Ah, the hellsbane potion," I said. "Don't want to forget that."

"If you did, or if you lost it, we'd send someone after you. You don't need to worry about that. No matter what happens there, you aren't trapped. But try not to lose it. Time is slowed in the hells, so we can afford to give you all the time you need to talk to Dachev. That means, though, that if something goes wrong, it could feel like days before we realized it and came to get you out. It—it wouldn't be a pleasant stay—"

"I have deep pockets," I said.

"Good. Put this in the deepest. Now, one last thing—or two last . . ." He shook his head. "Never mind. Just . . . just . . ."

"Go," I said, smiling.

"And be careful."

"I will," I said, then turned and opened the door.

41

I STEPPED INTO A SAGE-AND-GOLD MEADOW POLKA-
dotted with jewel-toned wildflowers dipping and swaying
in a warm summer's breeze. Overhead, the sun shone
from a perfect aquamarine sky, marshmallow clouds
drifting past, but never blocking its bright rays. Birds
sang from the treetops. A butterfly fluttered past.

"Serial-killer hell, huh?" I muttered. I started turning
around. "Trsiel! You sent me to the wrong—"

The door was gone. In its place was a dirt road, lined
with tall grass and more wildflowers. The road led to a
cluster of picture-perfect stone cottages.

"Trsiel," I sighed. "When you screw up, you go all the
way, don't you?"

I took the vial of hellsbane potion from my pocket and
peered at the clumps of tarlike ooze suspended in a
muddy brown liquid. Yummy. I'd really rather not drink
this stuff, only to have Trsiel do a mental forehead smack
ten seconds later, realize his mistake, and reopen the
door. In the meantime, no harm in checking out this village, seeing what kind of afterlife he *had* sent me to.

As I approached the village, I was struck by the stillness of it. Though the birds continued to chirp and trill,
not a glimmer of movement came from the collection of

tiny houses. I shivered, reminded of some long-forgotten TV movie from the seventies, one of those Cold War nuclear-disaster flicks. After the bomb went off, the camera had panned around a pretty little town, devoid of life, only the cheerful tinkle of wind chimes breaking the silence.

That's what this looked like. A ghost town. Only not like any real ghost town I'd ever seen. Walk down any street in our world and, even if you happened to arrive at the rare moment when no one was out-of-doors, you saw signs of life everywhere: a folded paperback under a shade tree, a pair of gardening gloves draped over a bush, an empty coffee mug on a porch railing. But here I saw none of that.

I walked past the first pair of houses, gaze tripping from one to the other. The houses stared back with empty eyes, windows with no curtains or blinds, no hanging plants or gaudy sun-catchers . . . just blank, dead stares.

I counted eight houses on this street, four to a side, perfectly spaced on postage-stamp lawns. There were no side roads, just this street petering out after a hundred feet to either side of the village, one side ending in the meadow, the other in a forest.

I turned to the house on my left and narrowed my eyes to zoom in on the front windows. Nothing happened. I tried again. Still nothing. Damn.

I looked around, but the caution was more instinctive than intentional; there was no one here. I headed up the walk. The house sat at ground level, with no front porch or patio, just a gravel path leading to a door flanked with empty gardens. Above each garden was a single window. I tramped across the dirt garden and peered inside the left one. A bedroom . . . or so I assumed from the furnishings. Make that furnishing—singular. The only thing in the room was a twin-size bed. Not much of a bed, either, just a bare mattress on a frame. Cozy.

I walked to the window on the other side of the front door. A living room–dining room combo, with a sofa, a dinette table, and a single chair. A crumpled throw rug in the corner caught my eye. No, not a rug . . . bedding. A sheet and a blanket lay near the corner, rumpled into a makeshift sleeping place, like a dog's bed.

I looked back at the street. If there had been any dogs here, they were long gone. Not just the dogs, but all animals. The ghost world was like most urban areas—not obviously teeming with animal life, but if you looked close enough, you always saw it—a rabbit darting across a lawn, a gopher peeking from a ditch, a dog stretched out on a front stoop. But here there wasn't so much as a phantom squirrel scampering past. I could still hear the birds, but caught only the occasional glimpse of one, high above in a tree. An empty world. Maybe an afterlife town in the making, awaiting a population spurt, some disaster in the living world. Yet that didn't explain that nest of bedding . . .

As I turned back to the house, I thought I saw a face reflected in a window of the house across the street. I swung around, but there was nothing there. Instinctively I tried to sharpen my sight, then swore when it didn't work. I scanned the two windows, watching for a shadow, a flicker of movement. Nothing.

Where the hell was Trsiel? I reached into my pocket. As my fingers closed around the vial of hellsbane potion, something rustled beside me. I spun to see a big ornamental bush at the corner of the house, a couple of yards away. The breeze whispered through the leaves. Was that what I'd heard? Must have been, but—

A floorboard creaked. My head shot up and I peered into the house. No way I'd hear a floorboard creak through those thick stone walls. So where . . . ? My gaze traveled to the wooden porch on the neighboring house. Empty. I listened, body tense, but I heard nothing. Nothing. Not even the birds. I turned toward the window again.

"Was sie sind?"

I wheeled. A man stood behind me, a small man, no taller than five foot four, and thin, with skin that looked like it had been left out in the sun and shrunk, tanned and leathery, stretched taut against his bones. His face was a flesh-colored skull topped with sparse tufts of iron gray hair. As he studied me, he tilted his head to one side, then the other, the movement jerky, birdlike. His eyes lifted to mine, dull gray disks, like worn metal washers. He stared at me, unblinking, head jerking up and down now, taking me in from head to toe.

"Was sie sind?" he said. "Answer. Now. What are you?"

I blinked. As the words switched to English, his lips didn't follow, moving out of sync, like a badly dubbed movie.

At a noise behind me, I glanced over my shoulder and found a man standing in the living room window. Average height, young—no more than early twenties—with dirty-blond hair that flopped over hooded blue eyes. Those eyes traveled over me, then up to mine, and his upper lips curled back to reveal canines filed to points. He ran his tongue over his teeth.

Another rustle to my left, and a third man stepped off the porch of the neighboring house. He was chubby and baby-faced, with large brown eyes, a small nose, and a receding chin. A huge carved wooden club dangled from his hand. He lifted the club and smiled at me.

"Guess Trsiel didn't screw up after all," I muttered.

The bird-man struck first, leaping onto my side, one arm hooking around my neck to pull me down. A jab in the ribs foiled that plan, and he fell off with a shriek.

"It fights," the man with the club said as he strolled across the lawn. "How well does it fight?"

"Pretty damned well," I said. "But I suppose you aren't going to take my word for it."

He broke into a run, club swinging over his head. At the same moment, bird-man flew at me again. I wheeled out of bird-man's path, and front-kicked club-man. My foot caught him square in the groin . . . and a blow that would have sent most men to their knees barely tottered him back a step. Obviously that particular vulnerability no longer worked here. Damn.

Out of the corner of my eye, I saw bird-man coming again. I side-kicked him out of the way, then drove my fist into club-man's gut. As he doubled over, I wrenched the club from his hand and whipped it aside.

"You use weapons and I will, too," I said. "And you won't like the ones I've got."

As club-man recovered, I saw a shape move to my left and wheeled to see another man circling us, head cocked to the side, frowning as he watched me, trying to figure out what I was. I turned on club-man . . . and an arm grabbed me from behind. I flew off my feet. Teeth clamped into my right shoulder. I yelped, more from the shock of feeling pain than from the pain itself.

The teeth dug in harder. I slammed my fist into my attacker's face. His head flew back, taking a chunk of my shoulder with it. As pain coursed through me, my attacker leapt at me again. I grabbed him and flipped him off me. It was the man from inside the cottage—the young one with the sharpened teeth.

I quickstepped back against the door, keeping my opponents where I could see them. Four now . . . and a fifth was slowly approaching from the far end of the road.

"*Qu'est-ce que c'est?*" asked the man who'd been circling us. "And what can we do with it?"

"That noise," the club-man said, licking his lips. "The loud noise. Make it do that again."

The fourth man's mouth stretched in a thin smile and he slid something from the back of his waistband . . . a blade lashed with a dried vine onto a wooden handle. The blade was stone, chiseled into a knifepoint, like something an archeologist would dig up. How deeply did the need have to go to fashion such a weapon?

The young man with the sharpened canines growled. The werewolf—I knew that now. Unable to change forms, but the wolf's instinct still running so deep that he slept in a dog's bed and sharpened his teeth to fangs, making the brand of weapon he understood. What supernatural instincts had the others retained?

As this thought flew through my brain, the werewolf lunged. I dove to the side. The other man's knife slammed into my open hand, and pinned it to the wooden door. For a second, I could only stare at it in disbelief. Then I realized I'd turned my attention away, and whipped it back to the men. Too late. The werewolf struck me first, fangs sinking into my shoulder. Grimacing, I wrenched my hand from the door, the knife still embedded in my palm.

I yanked the knife out and sliced it at the werewolf. It

would have been a great move . . . had I been right-handed. As it was, the knife barely nicked him. I tried to flip it over to my wounded left hand, but he knocked it from my fingers.

As the werewolf came at me again, I instinctively cast an energy-bolt spell. A sorcerer spell. Too late, I realized my mistake. The club-man grabbed my hair and whipped me back. I sailed off my feet, fire searing through my scalp as he spun me around by my hair. I squelched the instinct to struggle, and cast a binding spell. As the club-man froze, his grip loosened, and I flew free, hitting the ground hard. The men rushed toward me. I backflipped out of the way and cast a cover spell. They stopped dead.

"Where did it go?" the club-man said. His lips quivered. "Is it gone?"

The werewolf walked over to where I'd been and, for the millionth time in my life, I cursed the limitations of witch magic. Because the moment he bumped into me, the spell broke, and there wasn't a damn thing I could have done about it. As he leapt at me, I sprang to my feet and cast a binding spell. Caught him. And caught the bird-man but, again, hit the limitations of the spell as number three came at me. Still holding the other two in a binding spell, I front-kicked club-man in the gut. He went down, but right behind him was the man with the knife. His hand rose, and I was in the midst of trying to decide whether to transfer my binding spell from the werewolf or bird-man when a hand clamped down on the other man's shoulder.

Behind him stood the man who'd been slowly making his way here, a dark-haired bearded man in his thirties, slender, with the kind of easy grin that made hearts flip. His eyes met mine, and I saw in them not the animal cunning of the others, but something more complex, a level of awareness the others had lost. I also saw that he was a sorcerer . . . or had sorcerer-based blood. And there was only one of those here.

He said a few words in a language I didn't recognize, then the translation kicked in. "I believe our pretty guest has come for me," he said, eyes never leaving mine. "Am I correct?"

"You are," I said.

His gaze slid over me and he smiled. "When the angels send me a woman, they don't skimp, do they?"

To my left, the werewolf snarled, his hooded gaze fixed on Dachev.

"Your fun is over, pets," Dachev said. "Go back to your lairs."

They hesitated but, after a mutter here, a grumble there, started to fall back.

"Come," Dachev said to me. "We'll speak at my house."

"No, we'll speak over there," I said, waving at the meadow.

He nodded and tried to motion me forward, but I pointed at the road and, with a small smile, he took the lead.

42

AS I WALKED BEHIND DACHEV, I KEPT GLANCING OVER my shoulder. None of the others followed us. Dachev must wield some power here—like the first man to travel beyond his prehistoric village and discover the existence of a greater world. Unlike those early explorers, I doubted Dachev shared his knowledge with his comrades, instead retaining that false edge of superiority for as long as he could.

When we reached the meadow, I led Dachev to a spot in the middle. Then I had a decision to make—turn my back to the village, to the forest at the other end, or to the meadow stretching off to either side. I chose the forest; it was far enough away that no one could leap out of it un-noticed, and I wanted to keep both eyes on that village.

As I turned to Dachev, I found him studying me, not with the insolent leer from earlier, but an academic stare, accompanied by a slight frown.

"We have met, have we not?" he said. "You appear fa-miliar . . . and yet . . ." His frown flipped into a broad grin. "I'm quite certain I wouldn't forget such an angel. So much prettier than the other one they sent. He wasn't my type at all."

"We've never met," I said. "The last time you were top-side, I hadn't even been born."

He gave me another once-over, pausing at my eyes, his confusion obvious. He recognized something there . . . just wasn't sure what it was. Too bad. If he didn't know I was a witch, I wasn't enlightening him about that, any more than I was letting him know I wasn't an angel.

"Do you have a name, pretty one?" he asked.

"Everyone does."

He waited. When I said nothing, his lips tweaked in a smile.

"The exchange of names is the first part of any polite conversation," he said.

"Yep," I said. "It is."

When I didn't continue, he laughed. "Not even going to humor me, are you? The other one did. He was very polite. Very . . . understanding. And most companion-able. I think he wanted to be my friend."

"I'm sure he did."

Dachev's brows lifted as he tried to suppress a grin. "You doubt his sincerity? Oh, but he was *so* sincere. He didn't make me stand in this meadow. He accepted my invitation, came right to my house, to prove how much he trusted me. Don't you trust me?"

"No."

Another barely contained grin. "You should. It makes things so much more pleasant. The other angel sat right at my table and told me he understood that I'd been tempted and succumbed. After all, I was human . . . just as he'd been, so he understood temptation. What the Fates did to me was wrong, putting this poor sinner in such a situation, into contact with one such as the Nix. She tempted me, and I fell from grace."

"Uh-huh. Moving right along. You know why I'm here, so—"

"See? Now you're being rude. Katsuo was so much nicer. He wasn't in a hurry. He listened to me, listened most intently as I confessed my sins and told him what the Nix and I had done. Then I told him what I wished I'd done . . . in beautiful, intricate detail, everything I wished I could have done to those women, if only it had been me in those killers' bodies. I described every cut I would have made, every degradation I would have inflicted." Dachev's face gathered in a mock frown. "That's when he left. Left without even saying good-bye." He looked over at me. "Do you think Katsuo remembers me? Perhaps in his dreams?" He flashed a wide smile. "I hope so."

I said nothing.

"Do angels dream?" he said. "Can they have nightmares? Or are they all dreams like this?" He waved a dismissive hand around the meadow. "Visions of wildflowers and sunny skies. We dream, you know. When we sleep, the cracks in our memory open, just enough to let out a flash here, a glimpse there. And there are no wildflowers and sunny skies in our dreams. Sometimes I hear the others screaming. They keep me awake at night."

"Damned shame."

A shark-toothed smile. "A damned shame indeed. You aren't even going to feign sympathy, are you?"

"If you want sympathy, I'll send Katsuo. If you want to cut a deal, you're stuck with me."

"A deal? I do like the sound of that. Let me see . . . what should I ask for? Well, first, of course, I want out of here."

I laughed.

"Oh, not permanently. Just a visit, under escort, of course. I—"

"No. I couldn't arrange it even if I wanted to."

"Pictures, then."

"Huh?"

"When I was out there, with the Nix, whenever we killed someone, the police took so many pictures. Click, click, click. Every angle, every close-up." He closed his eyes and sighed. "Such attention to detail. Even I was impressed."

"You want those photos?" I said.

"No, no. Those I remember. And they weren't truly mine. I want mine—the ones I don't remember. I found newspaper clippings of what I'd done, but there were no pictures. So disappointing."

"Cops didn't take crime photos back then," I lied.

"No?"

I looked him in the eye. "No."

"I see. In that case, I will settle for descriptions. Those who reported on my case were most stingy with the details. Not so much as a single word about precisely what I did, only the broadest hints. I want—"

"Detail," I said. "I get it. But you *won't* get it, because I don't know the details, and the only offer on the table here is one I can provide."

"Use your imagination, then. Tell me what you *think* I did to those girls. Or, perhaps, I'll tell you what I think I did, what I see when I close my eyes."

"Sure, let's do that. You tell me what you think you might have done, and I'll listen. You have an hour. At the end of that, if I'm still here, haven't tossed my cookies or bolted out the door, you'll tell me how you caught the

Nix. And you'll tell me while I'm casting a lie-detection spell."

Disappointment seeped into his face, then hardened into a petulant scowl as he realized this deal wouldn't be nearly as rewarding as he'd hoped. I might not want to hear his sadistic fantasies, but I'd listen, and I'd listen without giving him the reaction he craved. After all, they were just words, words unrelated to me, words not even grounded in fact, just the fantasies of a sick fuck who'd never have an opportunity to enact them.

"Never mind that," he said at last. "I have something better. A game for two."

"Let me guess. Hide-and-seek. And I don't get to be 'it.'"

A glimmer of confusion, then he smiled. "Yes, hide-and-seek, as you say. You will run. When I catch you . . ." His gaze slithered down me, eyes darkening. "I may do as I wish. And then I will tell you what you want to know."

"Uh-uh. *If* you catch me, fine, we'll do it your way. But if you don't, you forfeit and tell me how to catch the Nix."

He shook his head. "If that's how you wish to play, then if I catch you, *you* forfeit. You allow me to do as I wish, and I tell you nothing."

"Fine."

He arched a brow. "You're quite sure of yourself, aren't you?"

"I'm quite sure you aren't going to agree to my terms, and I don't feel like pointless arguing. We'll set a time limit," I said. "The sun's starting to go down, so let's say that if you don't catch me by—"

"Not a time limit. A goal. There's a book in my house. Katsuo brought it as a hospitality gift. Poetry of some sort. I have little use for it, but it may come in handy someday, so I've stowed it in the crawl space under my house. Find it—"

"Where?" I said. "Be more specific. Otherwise, you'll probably nab me while I'm still searching. Where's the crawl-space hatch, and where exactly down there is the book?"

He told me.

"Good. Now, which house is yours?"

He laughed. "I'm not giving you *everything*."

"Fine. I'll find it myself. Now I'm going to cast a spell, and you're going to say a few words of it. You'll repeat the deal and tell me that you will abide by its terms."

He sighed and grumbled about my lack of trust, but did as I said. His eyes stayed green.

But that was the last bit of truth he told. After I'd ended the spell, he promised me a five-minute head start—and gave me less than three.

I made it to the forest, then my legs tried to shut down. They'd had enough of this "running away" crap. It was time to turn around and fight. The idea of being prey, even of playing at it for a while, brought a wave of bile to my throat. But if I was going to outwit Dachev, I needed to give him what he wanted . . . for now.

If cornered, I'd fight, but I already had a hole in my hand, a chunk out of my shoulder, and whole hanks of hair missing. I wasn't too worried about the hand and shoulder scarring, but I really hoped the hair would grow back. In the meantime, the less damage I took, the better.

There was a path through the forest. It might seem like the smart thing to do would be to veer off that path and cut through the woods, but my goal was speed, not stealth. If I'd had my blur spell, that would have made things much easier, but I was trying hard not to bemoan what I lacked.

If I needed to hide, witch spells were perfect. Plus, since my death I had learned a few nasty offensive ones, the sort even spell-hungry Paige might deem too dangerous. They took time to cast properly—time I hadn't had back in that village. If I needed them, I'd make the time to do them properly.

As I raced along the path, I kept glancing over my shoulder. The first time I saw Dachev, he was less than fifty feet behind me, but within a quarter-mile he'd dropped to well over a hundred feet back. Not accustomed to chasing former track stars obviously.

To my right, I caught glimpses of houses as the path circled behind the village. When I hit the far side of the village, the path divided, one branch heading back to town, the other going deeper into the forest. I took the village route. At the midway point between the fork and the path's end, I dove into the woods and cast a cover spell. Then I waited. A minute later, Dachev appeared at the fork. He looked both ways.

"Did you keep running?" he murmured. "Or are you trying for the prize already?"

A moment's hesitation, then he walked past me, into the village, and vanished. I considered slipping out and finding a better vantage point, so I could see which house he chose, but that was too risky. When I'd first seen him, he'd been coming from the far end of the road, meaning one of the last two houses was probably his. I suspected I'd know which house he occupied the moment I peeked through its window. No sleeping mats on the floor for that ghost.

After about ten minutes he returned to the path, walking fast. Again, he passed me. This time, when he hit the fork, he headed back the same way he'd come. Strange, but I wasn't about to question his sense of direction.

When his footfalls faded to silence, I slid from my hiding spot and crept closer to the village. As tempting as it was to race in and find the book, it wasn't safe, not in daylight, when the others were almost certainly still watching for me. The sky was growing dark already.

When I was close enough to see the village, I found a suitable tree, climbed to a sturdy branch, cast a cover spell, and settled in to wait for dark.

For nearly an hour Dachev hunted for me, twice coming to the edge of the forest and scanning the village to be sure I hadn't returned. The third time he left the forest, looked around, then hurried to the last house on the left.

"Thank you," I thought. "One problem down; one to go."

When he emerged from his house, he surveyed the village again, peering into the gathering night. Then he walked to a stand of bushes by the forest's edge. After less than ten seconds of contemplation, he strode back toward the road. A man like Dachev fancies himself a purist—a predator who catches his prey by running it to the ground, not by skulking in bushes, hoping it'll run past.

Down the street, two other residents stepped from their homes. When they made a move to come closer and see what he was doing, he snarled something, then stalked into the woods. One followed. The bird-man—darting back and forth, weaving his way there, sticking close to trees and bushes, ready to dodge behind one at the first sign of Dachev.

Dachev had disappeared into the darkening forest

before bird-man even got to the edge. Bird-man stepped into the forest, hesitant, head high, body tense. He took a few steps, then strained forward, obviously unwilling to go in any deeper.

He dropped to his haunches at the edge of the path and crouched there. Dachev returned roughly a half-hour later, which must have been how long it took him to scour the small patch of woods. I hoped his return would scare off the bird-man, but he darted into a thicket and waited for him to pass, then peered out after him.

Dachev surveyed the village once, then headed back into the woods. Bird-man stayed where he was. Wonderful. It was almost dark now, and from the blackness of the village, I guessed these guys didn't have candles. Although a full moon shone overhead, it barely pierced the forest. One more once-over and Dachev would have to return to his house and wait for me there. Time for a new plan.

I eased along my branch and grabbed a vine looped around the tree trunk. When I yanked hard, the vine snapped in two. I shimmied down a branch and found a thicker one, which held no matter how hard I whaled on it. I unwound it from the branch, then found a second piece for backup.

After coiling the vines into balls, I started to put one into my pocket, then felt the hellsbane potion vial and stopped, envisioning myself yanking out the vines and the bottle tumbling into the undergrowth and forgotten. Instead, I tied them around my calf. Next I took off a sock and stuffed it into my empty pocket.

I shimmied down the tree until I reached the lowest branch that would hold me. I inched out as far as I dared. The leafy cover of the lower branches hid me well enough. I broke off a twig and dropped it. It caught in the lowest branch. I pulled off another, reached out as far as I could, and dropped it. This one hit the dry undergrowth and sent up a crackle that seemed as loud as a gunshot. Bird-man popped up from his hiding place. He looked around, gaze on the ground, head jerking as he searched. I let loose another twig. He took a step my way. Then another. A third step, and I dropped onto him.

As I fell onto his back, I slammed my forearm into his mouth. He bit down, hard enough to make me wonder whether I was going to lose another chunk. It took some wrangling, but I managed to get my flesh out of his mouth, and replace it with my sock. Once I'd bound him, I lashed him to the tree trunk with the loose end of the vine. Eventually his moaning and thrashing would alert Dachev, but I'd have a few minutes.

I followed the forest as close to Dachev's house as I could. With the full moon, I didn't dare go around to the front door, so I crept up to the open side window. As I crawled through, I heard someone moving through the forest. I somersaulted inside, hitting the floor with a *boom,* then sprang to my feet. I was in the living room. Dachev said the crawl-space hatch was under his bed. I ran through the only doorway, and into the bedroom, grabbed the bed frame, and yanked. No rollers, of course. I dragged the bed aside, then grasped the edge of the hatch. Running footsteps thumped along the dirt road. I yanked open the hatch and jumped through.

43

TO CALL DACHEV'S BASEMENT A CRAWL SPACE WOULD imply that it was big enough to crawl in. To even turn around, I had to scrunch down and duck my head.

Although the full moon had illuminated enough upstairs to see by, even with the open hatch, it was pitch black down here. I cast a light-ball spell. It lasted less than a second, just long enough to stamp an impression of dirt walls on my retinas before sputtering out. I cast it again. Same thing. I'd always thought of this as a child's spell, and had used it so little that I hadn't even bothered passing it on to Savannah. Since arriving in the nonelectrical ghost world, though, I'd used the spell regularly, so there must have been something about the conditions underground that were making the light go out. I tried it twice more, then gave up.

Dachev had said the book was on a shelf to the left, immediately under the hatch. The only thing I could feel there was a web of thin roots. As I ran my hands over them, the front door slammed. I wriggled around as fast as I could, and swept my hands across the right side, then the end wall. My fingers snagged on the roots and my nails filled with dirt, but I could feel nothing like a shelf or a book.

I cast the light-ball spell again. Then again. And again. Each time I cast, I got a split-second snapshot, all revealing the same thing—an unbroken expanse of dirt and roots.

Footsteps crossed the living room. I twisted around and scrambled to the other end, looking about wildly, hands running over the walls, knocking off clumps of dank earth, the stink of it filling my nostrils.

"Do you have the book?" Dachev's voice reverberated through the room above.

I skimmed my hands over the roof. Splinters bit into my palms. It was a solid sheet of wooden planks.

"There is no book," I said, teeth gritted.

Dachev's laughter floated down.

"You said—" I began.

He lowered his head into the crawl space and peered around, then pulled back. "I said I would tell you the secret if you retrieved the book . . . which I would have, had there been a book to retrieve."

I clenched my teeth and forced myself to be quiet. When I didn't respond, he ducked his head back in, trying again, unsuccessfully, to see me.

"You might as well come out of there," he said. "There's no place to go."

As he spoke, I crept forward, then stopped when he did. He sighed.

"Cowering in that hole does not become you. Or are you sulking?"

I made it halfway across this time. As he paused, I itched to creep another few steps, but didn't dare. Even the whisper of my clothes as I moved was too loud. When he started talking, I started moving.

"I will count to five, and then I will come in there after you, and drag you out by that pretty, long hair."

I waited, barely a foot from his face, holding myself as still as I could.

"Five . . . four—"

I hooked him around the neck and yanked. He tumbled into the hole. He scrambled onto me and tried to pin my arms. When he couldn't get a grip on them, he seized my hair. I slammed my open palm into the bottom of his jaw. He grunted, and fell back.

I slid out from under him. He reached for me again, but I scrambled out of the way, and grabbed the edge of the hatch, hoisting myself up. When he came at me, I kicked him in the face. He stumbled back. I dropped into the hole and fell on him.

He bucked to throw me off, but I managed to flip him onto his stomach. I kneeled as best I could on his back. Then I grasped his hands and held them and, with my teeth, untied the extra piece of vine. He rocked and wriggled and cursed, but after a few tries, I got the vine tied around his wrists and ankles.

"You think you're clever?" he snarled. "One scream from me and every one of those beasties up there will come running—"

"Whoops, almost forgot. Thanks."

I stuffed my other sock into his mouth. Then I paid him the same honor he'd promised me: I grabbed him by the hair and hauled him out of the crawl space.

"So," I said as I dumped him on the bedroom floor. "Are you going to tell me how to catch the Nix?"

He only narrowed his eyes, a "fuck you" in any language.

"Fine," I said. "I'll come back in a couple of days, see whether you've changed your mind."

As I walked toward the living room, Dachev made a guttural sound behind his gag.

"Oh, no, don't worry," I said. "I'm not going to abandon you. You'll have plenty of company . . . just as soon as I tell your comrades where you are."

He let me get as far as the front door, then banged his shoulder against the floor to get my attention. I peeked around the bedroom doorway.

"Yes?"

He grunted and gnashed at his gag. I yanked the sock from his mouth.

"Ready to talk?" I said.

"Untie me first."

I laughed.

"Then no deal. You'll take what you want and leave me like this."

"No, I won't, but since you don't know me well enough to trust my word, I'll meet you halfway. I'll untie your feet now. Then, if I do betray you, at least you can run."

He let out a stream of obscenities, at least one of which lost something in the translation to English.

"Keep that up and I'll stick the sock back in." I cast the lie-detection spell. "Now start talking or I start walking."

He snarled, but, after a moment, spat out his part of the incantation.

"How can the Nix be caught?" I asked.

Another hesitation, then, "By killing the host body."

"I know *that*. But you did it without the sword. How?"

For at least a minute, the only sound was the grinding of his teeth, as he struggled to think of some other way out of this. Finally, he said, "By killing . . . and yet not killing."

"I don't do riddles."

He leaned back to look up at me. "No? Why? Because they require you to use more than your fists and your feet? Not much in that pretty head of yours, is there?"

"No. Just enough to trick you."

His eyes narrowed.

"Can we skip the insult toss?" I said. "The sooner I'm out of here, the sooner we'll both be much happier."

"She must be killed, but not allowed to die."

"Deliver a mortal blow, you mean." I paused, thinking it through. "If the host is still alive, she can jump free. If the host is dead, she can jump free . . . unless she's skewered on the end of an angel sword first. But during that time between life and death, she's stuck, isn't she?"

Dachev glared at me.

"Yes or no," I said. "Is she trapped in the host when it's stuck between life and death?"

"Yes."

"But how do you pull her out? A spell?"

"No." He paused then, but I could tell he wanted this over with, so after a moment, he said, "Her spirit starts to separate as the host dies. You'll see it. At that point, she's powerless—she can't transport herself and she doesn't have her demonic strength."

I remembered the community center, when the Nix had escaped from her partner's body before Trsiel could deliver the life-ending blow. I'd seen her spirit oozing out from Lily. Only one problem with this scenario. The life-ending-blow part. For a split-second, I mentally panicked, certain I was right back where I'd started, and there was no way to catch the Nix except by killing Jaime, and if the Fates wouldn't allow that, then how the hell—

"But the host *didn't* die," I said. "She was resuscitated, wasn't she?"

Dachev's jaw locked. Another opportunity to mock me lost. After a moment, he answered with a nod.

"Out loud," I said.

"Yes," he said through his teeth. "She was brought back to life. People were nearby. Someone found her—"

"And resuscitated her." I walked to his side. "Where did you find out how to do this? Is there a book?"

A short laugh. "Book? Books are for those who lack the mental capacity to think for themselves. I figured it out by myself."

His eyes darkened.

"Uh, wanna try that one again?" I asked.

He let out another stream of profanity. I paused, thinking, then laughed loud enough that the sudden noise made him jump.

"It was an accident, wasn't it?" I said. "You were tracking the Nix. You found her, and as you were trying to figure out what to do next, her partner almost died. You saw the Nix's spirit and you cut her a deal. Help you escape from the Fates or you'd sic an angel on her. It wasn't planned. It was pure, dumb luck."

Dachev snarled, then spat on the floor.

"No need to answer that one," I said.

I untied his bindings.

"There, freed as promise—"

He lunged to his feet and hit me, knocking me back. I recovered, but before I could retaliate, he'd backed off. He crossed the room, hands clenched, then turned to face me.

"You have what you came for," he said. "Now drink your hellsbane potion and go."

"Oh, don't worry, I will."

A tiny smile tweaked his lips. "No, pretty one, I don't think so."

He lifted his hand, fist clenched, turning up palm up, like a magician about to reveal the hidden quarter. When he opened his hand, I knew what would be in it. I started to run even before I saw the vial of hellsbane potion. I was three-quarters of the way across the room when he turned the uncapped bottle upside down. The potion spilled onto the floorboards.

My body hit his, slamming him into the wall. I snatched the bottle from him, but it was empty.

Dachev grabbed my arm and threw me down. As I fell, I tried to snag his leg and pull him off balance, but missed. I hit the floor hard with him on top of me. I tried to roll out from under him, but he had his full weight on me.

"Don't struggle, pretty one," he murmured. "Struggling only makes it hurt more. I'm so sorry about your potion. But I have a present for you. Something to replace it."

Still atop me, he reached down into his pocket, took something out, then brought it up to my face. It was one of the other man's chiseled stone knives.

"I think we'll have fun with this," he said. "Much more fun than we'd have with your potion."

I started to cast a binding spell. The moment the first words left my mouth, his eyes widened, with confusion, then fury. I saw my mistake, and tried to rush through the incantation. His fist slammed into my cheek. Bone crackled and a tooth pinged into my throat. I wheezed a cough and the tooth flew out on a string of spittle. I started to cast again, but Dachev slammed his hand down on my throat.

"A witch?" he snarled, bringing his face to mine. "So that is what I recognized. You didn't care to enlighten me. You didn't dare, did you?"

Again, I tried to push him off, but he had me perfectly pinned, so I couldn't do more than glance awkward blows off his back.

"Do you think I don't know how to hold you, witch?" he said. "At my trial, some thought I used a sedative on my victims. Others believed I knocked them unconscious. But I didn't. What is the pleasure in cutting an unfeeling carcass?"

I narrowed my eyes, hoping to summon some bit of my Aspicio powers and blind him.

"Don't give me that look, witch," he said with a chuckle. "I don't shock you. I can see it in your eyes. You remind me of her, you know. My Nix."

He lifted the knife. "That's not to say I'll spare you. After all, she did betray me. I forgive her. But that doesn't keep me from imagining how I'd like to betray her. Love and hate. The same impulse, the same passion."

I flicked my fingers in a knock-back spell, managing to gasp the single word needed to cast the sorcerer spell. Nothing happened.

"Useless without your spells, aren't you, witch?" He smiled. "Well, without your spells and your kicks and your punches. You do know how to fight. None of my other victims did. Quite disappointing."

I started to narrow my eyes again, to retry blinding him, then stopped myself. *Give it up and stick with what will work.* I had to choose carefully, though. The more powerful the spell, the more spell-power it required. If I cast something big and it didn't incapacitate him, I'd be screwed—unable to cast anything stronger than a cover spell. I emptied my brain and began the mental preparation for a high-level witch spell.

Dachev continued, "I think I will let you fight. But first, I should let you know what fate you are fighting. We'll start with a sampling. Nothing too disabling. Not an arm or a leg. Perhaps a finger or two? No. That might still impede you, and give me unfair advantage. Let's say an ear. Or perhaps the nose. Yes, that's it. I'll cut off your ear or split open your nose." He leaned into my face, lips pulling back from his teeth as he smiled. "Your choice."

I feigned struggling, to buy more time to prep the spell. Dachev pinned me easily.

"Enough of that," he said. "If you don't choose, and choose quickly, I'll do both."

I mouthed something.

He frowned. "What was that?"

Again, I opened my mouth, as if struggling to speak, but only a choked gasp came out.

He eased back on my throat. Mouth slightly open, I whispered a few words of the incantation, but knew I didn't have enough time to finish.

"Ear," I said. "Take my ear."

I managed to get out another line before his arm clamped down on my throat again. I closed my eyes as the knife went to my ear. The blade sliced into the tender skin between my earlobe and my face, and began cutting up, through the soft lobe. When he hit cartilage, he shifted forward for a better cutting angle. As he did, the pressure lessened on my throat, and I managed to whisper the last line of the incantation.

Dachev screamed, an eardrum-piercing wail. I shot

out from under him and leapt up. He stayed on the floor, doubled up, screaming as if his guts were on fire. Which they were. I'd used a fireball spell, conjuring the same simple, nearly useless fireball that Paige used. With one important difference. This fireball was conjured in the belly of the target, producing a few moments of blistering agony, followed by a quick death. Unless you were already dead, that is.

Dachev rolled on the floor, clutching his stomach. I walked over to him, bent down, and snatched the knife from his hand.

"If you can hear me, it'll be over in a minute," I said. "The fire, that is. The burning, well, that'll take a while to heal." I leaned over him and smiled down. "In the meantime, you'll need plenty of bed rest. I think I can help with that."

I knelt behind Dachev. I grabbed his leg with one hand, the knife in the other, preparing to cut his hamstrings. If I was stuck here until someone rescued me, I damned well wasn't giving Dachev any chance of payback. As he writhed and screamed, in too much pain to try to escape—or even know what I was doing—I cut away his pant leg.

"What did it do to him?" asked a voice behind me.

The club-man stood in the doorway, weapon in hand. He stared at Dachev, baby-smooth brow wrinkling. His gaze turned to me, and he smiled, showing off an orthodontist's wet dream worth of crooked teeth.

"I thought it was gone," he said as he stepped into the room, club thumping against his leg.

"Maybe it stayed to play." The knife-man walked in, a homemade blade in each hand. "Does it want to play some more?"

Still gripping the knife, I leapt to my feet.

"Do you see how I play?" I said, waving at Dachev, who was still moaning and writhing. "I don't think I'm the kind of playmate you're looking for. But if you both leave now, I'll forget I saw you and—"

The club-man rushed me. I cast a binding spell, but my powers were too weakened, and it only trapped him for a split second before he broke free. Right behind him came the knife-man, the werewolf, and a redhead I hadn't seen earlier. Another shadow slid in through the door, but I didn't stay to see who it was.

I wheeled, ran, and smashed headfirst through the window. Quite the dramatic exit . . . though I'd rather not have been exiting at all. As much as I hated running away, I'd had enough practice rounds with these guys earlier to know I couldn't stave them off for long in a fight, not without any spell-power. Better to get my ass back in those woods until I figured out how I was getting it back to my dimension.

As I tore around to the back of the house, running footsteps sounded behind me. I glanced over my shoulder. Knife-guy was already out. He swung back his arm . . . and I ran smack into a giant air-bag.

As I stumbled back, I caught sight of my air-bag obstacle—a man with three chins and a gut that could house a full-term pregnancy.

"Going somewhere?" he rumbled.

A blade sank into my shoulder blade. I twisted and kicked the knife-man off my back. The big guy grabbed me by the shoulders. I wriggled out of his grasp, and danced away . . . only to find myself surrounded. Even the bird-man had now joined the group, vines still dangling from his wrists, flat gray eyes simmering with fury.

"Six against one?" I said. "Now, that's hardly fair. Tell you what, you guys pick a champion, and the rest of you just sit back—"

Bird-man, the werewolf, and the big guy all ran at me. I whirled out of the way, but the others closed in to block my escape routes. I looked around, found the clearest spot, then dove for it, casting a cover spell as I flew.

When I hit the ground, I vanished. Again, everyone stopped to stare in momentary confusion. Before they could recover, I sprang to my feet and ran for the forest.

44

WHEN I STARTED RUNNING, THE MEN WERE RIGHT BE-
hind me, but soon they began to drop back, unable to
keep up the pace. I kept waiting—hoping—for the footfalls to peter out, but I should have known they wouldn't.
These guys hadn't seen a victim in decades, even centuries; they sure as hell weren't going to give up the moment their first one took off.

I couldn't take them all on. Trsiel had said the Fates
would send someone after me if I didn't return. The only
thing I hated worse than running away was hanging
around waiting to be rescued, but this wasn't the time for
a show of independence. The smart thing to do was hide
and wait. Stung like hell, but the alternative would hurt a
lot worse. Stand and fight, and there might not be
enough of me left to rescue. It was my fault I needed rescue in the first place. Suckered by a magician's pick-
pocket trick. I could say it was an all-time personal low,
but I'd be lying.

As I ran deeper into the forest, the night took over, en-
veloping me in black. I tried my light-ball spell again. This
time it took hold—dim but steady. Dim was good,
though. At full strength, it would have been like running
with an Olympic torch, an obvious target for my pursuers.

My night vision would have been even better, but I didn't even hope for that to kick in.

When I hit the fork in the path, I veered down the right-hand branch, heading deeper into the woods. After a few minutes, I caught a glimpse of a clearing to my right. Instinctively I focused my long-range vision. Of course, that failed. Without slowing, I swung my light-ball in that direction. Through the trees, I could make out the dim shapes of houses. Shit! More villages? Why not. Maybe that's what this dimension was, not a single smattering of houses, but a whole world of villages, each with its own mob of killers.

I hit a thin patch of woods where someone had cut down a handful of trees, clearing an unintentional window to the village beyond. I'd seen this same open patch before, this same pattern of cut trunks. As I raced past the clearing and looked through to the village, I knew what I'd see. The stone houses I'd just left.

It was the same village. The seemingly endless forest was an illusion. Walk north from the village, and you'd find yourself at the south end. That was why Dachev headed back the way he'd come when he thought I'd kept running down the path earlier—so he could head me off when I unintentionally looped back around. The moment I thought this, I saw a shape moving through the trees ahead. I glanced over my shoulder. More shapes running that way.

I dove into the forest on the left. Even as I crashed through the bushes, hearing nothing behind me, I knew I wouldn't get far. Not only had I lost the advantage of speed, but I was cutting their path for them. Any minute now, they'd be close enough to see.

I stopped running, dowsed my light-ball, slipped off to

the left, and cast a cover spell. A moment later, the forest erupted in crashes and curses, as they stumbled through the dark looking for me. Should I stay here, covered, until the cavalry rode in? I was relatively safe, but would my rescue team know where to find me? I had to trust that they would . . . or that I'd hear them. So long as I was hidden here, with the killers fumbling in the dark—

· A light flickered to my right. As I strained my eyes in that direction, I saw orange flame bouncing through the darkness, approaching from the west. A torch. Someone had gone back to the village for a torch. Within moments, all of them carried a lit tree branch, swinging it about and peering into the darkness.

"She's using magic," Dachev called. "She can make herself invisible, but she cannot move. If you bump into her, she will reappear."

A few grunts of satisfaction.

"There are two ways we can do this," Dachev continued, voice ringing over the shuffle of footsteps and the spit of the torches. "Competition or cooperation."

"I help no one," club-man's voice rumbled. "I find it, it is mine."

"Then you do that. Those who want to help me find her, come here and we'll split up, do this systematically."

"And then you will take her," someone said.

A chorus of agreement.

"No, then I will let you have her. All who help me will get a turn. And when you are done, she is mine. If that sounds fair to you, come over here. The rest, search on your own."

Several shapes moved toward Dachev, while others headed farther off, beginning to hunt. I waited until the lights dimmed, then began to creep away. There was no sense continuing west. If Dachev had come that way with the torch, that meant that he'd come from the village. This world was spherical. Keep walking in any direction and you'd end up back where you started. The deepest part of the woods, then, would be that strip to the north and south. That's where I headed.

I moved as fast as I dared. Once I was far enough, I'd find a tree and try that trick again. At least that would make it impossible for one of the searchers to stumble into me and snap my cover spell. But what if they bumped the tree? Would that vibration be enough to break my cover?

I should stop and fight. Lure them away, one by one, and disable them. Sure, great plan . . . provided I could outwit and outfight every last one of these bastards, with my spell-casting still drained from the fireball spell. *Don't be stupid. Just find a tree and hide.* But what if the bird-man had seen me jump from that tree, and told Dachev my trick?

In the midst of this internal debate, a hillock appeared in my path and, only a few yards to my right, a boulder blocked a blob of darkness deeper than that of the hillside. Some kind of hole. I walked over and peered in the narrow slit above the boulder. Beyond it, the darkness stretched as far as my light-ball illuminated. Not a hole, but a cave. Oho. Now, that's what I needed.

I moved to the side of the boulder and pushed. My pierced hand flared again. I grabbed a handful of leaves from the nearest tree and, using them for padding, put my hands back on the boulder, dug in my feet, and heaved. The rock didn't budge. Okay, not so perfect. Or was it? If I couldn't move the rock, they'd never think to look behind it. With proper leverage and a telekinesis spell, I should be able to shift it aside enough to squeeze through.

I found a thick branch and used it to pry the rock as I pushed and cast a telekinesis spell. The spell was intended to displace small objects, but many witches used it as an added muscle boost for moving heavy objects, like pushing out the fridge to clean behind it. Practical magic.

With the spell, my pry-bar branch, and a hefty dose of push power, I managed to move the rock about a foot, giving me an eighteen-inch gap to squeeze through. Problem was, the rock had been there so long, it had sunk into the ground, so I was prying it up from a hole. The moment I let go, it would roll back into place—and block the entrance again. I could try pushing it right out of the depression, but that meant going inside and leaving the door wide-open. First guy who walked by and saw the cave opening would know exactly where I was hiding.

So I squeezed through, yanked the branch in with me, and let the boulder tumble into place. Then I recast my light-ball spell and looked around.

The tunnel extended as far as I could see, the floor angling downward, like the entrance to a subterranean passageway—like the one that had linked the two castles. Had someone dug this one, too? Maybe that would explain the rock, put there by the Fates to keep the inmates of this dimension in the village where they belonged.

I looked from the entrance into the cave depths. The deeper I went, the safer I'd be, so no one passing by would see the glow of my light-ball. If I didn't have to cower under a cover spell, I wasn't about to. Better to find a place, hunker down, and take stock of my injuries. Pushing that rock had set my punctured hand and shoulder ablaze.

Then there was my ear. I could feel the half-severed lobe tickling my neck as I moved, but hadn't yet reached up to assess the damage, not really sure I wanted to know how close it was to falling off.

If I could stop, I could tear strips from my shirt and bind that ear and my hand. Nothing was bleeding—one advantage to being a ghost—but I'd be able to use my hand better if the wound was covered and cushioned. As for the ear, while losing a lobe would solve the problem of misplacing half a pair of earrings, I'd really rather keep it intact and hope the Fates could stitch it back up.

About twenty feet down the tunnel, what looked like a room branched off the right side. The main passage continued back as far as I could see. Was there an exit under the village? A chill ran through me, but I dowsed it with common sense. First, the village was at least a quarter-mile away. Second, even if the tunnel did extend that far, it wasn't being used—that entrance boulder had been in place long enough to grow moss. Still, best to play it safe and duck into this room, rather than continue on.

As I walked into the room, the floor dipped and my light-ball dimmed. Great. It must be a subterranean effect of the anti-magic barrier on this place. I hoped I wasn't going to lose the light altogether, like I had in Dachev's crawl space. I really didn't relish sitting in the dark for hours.

I took another step and kicked something—softer than a rock, but solid enough to nearly trip me. I glanced down to see a long pale cylinder. A tree branch. I went to step over it, then stopped. There was something covering the branch, and it didn't look like bark.

I swung my light-ball over and saw an arm lying in front of my foot. A human arm, still encased in a sleeve. I hunkered down for a better look. The arm had been ripped from its socket. Not that I've seen a lot of that sort of thing, but the torn and jagged flesh around the uncut bone certainly looked more like a rip than a saw job.

I hadn't noticed any of the men in the village missing an arm, but I hadn't taken a good look at a couple of them. Wouldn't surprise me if one of them had done this to a fellow villager. Put a group of killers together and eventually someone's going to start losing body parts. It kind of surprised me that they hadn't done worse.

I started to straighten, then stopped. A half-dozen paces away lay a jean-clad leg. Okay, now *that* I would have noticed. They looked about the same size, probably from the same person. Maybe they weren't real. They certainly didn't look real. The torn flesh was clean and bloodless, like a movie prop before someone splashes on the fake gore. I bent to touch the hand. Cold, but definitely flesh.

As I took a step toward the leg, I let out an oath. A second leg lay behind the first, and, a few feet away, the other arm. Okay, now I was creeped out. What the hell had happened down here? I was better off not knowing, not thinking about it. And if I stayed in this room, that was exactly what I would do. Time to find a new hiding place.

Turning to leave, my gaze swept the left side of the room. A bowling-ball-shaped rock rested by the wall. Yeah, a rock, that's it. Bullshit. I knew exactly what it was. And I knew what had happened here. They'd done this— the villagers—turned on one of their own and ripped him apart. Then they hid the body in here, and sealed it up, hoping the Fates wouldn't notice.

With a shiver, I turned away. As I did, I heard a faint

clacking. It came from the direction of the head. I turned, more instinct than intent, swinging the light-ball that way. The head of a dark-haired man lay there, blue eyes staring at me, blank and unseeing. Then he blinked.

"Jesus fucking—!" I yelped, jumping back.

The man's eyes focused and his mouth opened wide, as if to scream, showing a bloodless stump where his tongue had been. He clacked his teeth together. Beneath his neck, something long and white snapped against the dirt—his spine, the only thing still attached to his head, twisting and jerking like a macabre tail.

I ran out of that room faster than I'd ever run from anything in my life. Once back in the tunnel, I leaned against the wall and rubbed my face, trying to rub the image from my mind. I couldn't, of course, no more than I could stop my brain from churning through the implications of that image. I should have known he was still alive. He was a ghost. He couldn't die. The true horror of that hadn't struck me until now. If you couldn't die, but you could feel pain, you could be ripped apart and still live.

With a growl, I shook the picture from my head. I had to concentrate on staying hidden and safe, not on what they could do to me if I failed.

I looked along the tunnel. Staying in that room was out of the question. I needed to go deeper, find a better place to—

A noise cut my thoughts short. Even as I glanced back toward that room, I knew it hadn't come from there. The sound came again, a dull *thump*. Then a harsh whisper, like something being dragged through the dirt. Another thump, and another drag.

Without thinking, I wheeled around the corner, back

into the room. As I moved, my brain screamed for me to stop, stay where I was, and cast a cover spell. Whatever happened, I did not want to be stuck in the same room as that *thing*. But it was too late. By the time I ducked into the room, the noise in the tunnel was too close for me to risk going back out. Time to cast a cover— Shit! The light-ball. I dowsed it, then cast my cover spell.

As I recited the incantation, I could feel *it* watching me. Was it watching? Could it still think, feel, a full consciousness trapped within—

Goddamn it, stop that! He's a fucking psychopath. Otherwise he wouldn't have been down here. I'd do the same to the rest if I could. But it wasn't him I was worried about; it was the thought of him, what it could portend for me. When the Fates said I was in danger, I sure as hell never thought—

Don't think. Turn it off and pay attention.

The noise was close enough now for me to hear something else accentuating the thumps and drags—a low, wordless mumble. A shape passed the doorway. With only the sliver of distant light from around the boulder to illuminate the passage, I saw little more than a shape, but I could tell it was human, a squat lump of a man, one leg dragging as he shuffled along.

He was midway past the room door when he stopped, head whipping around so fast I nearly jumped and broke my cover spell. His face hovered there, a thin pale streak in the darkness. He snuffled, as if sniffing the air. After a low mumble of unintelligible gibberish, he crouched and peered at the ground. He traced his fingers in the dirt, then chortled and clumped forward, still squatting as he followed something in the dirt. Followed my footprints.

I held myself still, but my thoughts whirred. Would my

binding spell work yet? Could I outrun him? And run where? I'd locked myself in. Wait, there had to be another exit, the one he'd come through. The moment I thought this, I knew he hadn't come through anywhere. If he could see my footprints in the dirt, in this darkness, that could only mean that his eyesight had adapted to this near-blackness. And that meant he'd been here a helluva lot longer than a few minutes.

The men in the village hadn't ripped their fellow inmate apart. He had—this man—this creature lumbering toward me, mumbling in a language that had long since sunk below any standard of human communication. He'd ripped his victim limb from limb and they'd locked them both in here. And now I'd locked myself in with them.

Goddamn it, don't just stand here and wait for him to bump into you! Cast something. Launch the damn fireball spell. No, better yet, the gouging spell, explode his eyes from their sockets, see how well he can track you without them. Blind him, then get that tree limb and beat the living shit—

Stop that! Stop and think. I hadn't recovered enough for a foolproof binding spell yet. Cast anything stronger and I'd end up in pieces on the floor, still alive, trapped in—

Stop that!

I could smell him now, a sickly sweet smell like rotting meat. Where was that smell coming from? His breath? Did he eat—?

I gritted my teeth and fought to shut my brain down, to concentrate on the moment. He kept shambling forward, still crouched, pale fingers glowing as they traced my steps in the dirt.

I'd have to risk the binding spell. It should hold for at least a few seconds, long enough for me to get past him and run like hell farther into the cave. With that bad leg, he couldn't catch me.

He stopped. After a moment's hesitation, he veered to the right, following my original tracks into the room. He scuttled to the arm where I'd first paused. At a noise across the room he leapt to his feet. He looked around, head low, sniffing the air. Another noise—the click of teeth. With a roar, he lunged forward and kicked the head into the wall. It hit with a *splat*, but rolled back again, spine still jumping. He kicked it again, still bellowing, frustrated by his inability to end its life.

After a few more kicks, rage sated, he looked around the room, then strode out. He'd forgotten me. Thank—

Grunts drifted from the main passage, near the entrance, as he tried to move the boulder. He hadn't forgotten me, he'd just changed tack and gone to see how I'd gotten in . . . and whether he could get out.

How long had he been in this cave? How long had this other thing—this head—I couldn't think of it as a man, that just started my brain spinning—how long had it been here? Like that?

This was the true hell of this dimension. Not the thing on the cave floor, but the never-ending possibility of it. Trapped for eternity in a world of other killers, any of whom could, at any moment, do this to you. All you can do is trust that they won't, trust that if you don't touch them, they won't touch you, rely on honor and decency from men who have none. And when they do exactly what you fear they'll do, you band together and lock them up with their victim, barricade them in and leave them there, alone . . . until some goddamn idiot walks up, goes, "Hmmm, what's this boulder doing here?" moves it, and barricades herself inside with them.

I squeezed my eyes closed and chased the thoughts away. Panic. So that's what it felt like.

After a few shoves on the boulder, the man gave a snarl that resounded through the cavern. Those dragging foot-steps resumed and, seconds later, he appeared at the room entrance. He stepped inside and peered around, head low, snuffling and muttering. Then he wheeled and strode out the door, heading for the tunnel depths. Thank God. Now I could— Wait. Shit! When he'd turned, there'd been something in his hand. It was still too dark for me to see more than shapes, but I knew he hadn't been carrying anything earlier, and the only long, narrow object he could have picked up on his way to the entrance was the tree limb I'd left there—the one I needed to get out of this place.

Slow down. Take it slow and think. There has to be something else here you can use. As I looked around the room, my gaze slid over the four limbs. Arm bones would be too short. A leg bone might work, but first I'd have to get the flesh off of it. I knew a spell for flaying, but it only removed the skin layer and wouldn't do anything for the tissue beneath.

If only I still had Dachev's knife. I should have gone back for it. Carelessness. Pure carelessness. I was too ac-customed to relying on spells.

I crept over to the nearest leg and bent down, running through my list of witch spells. Behind me, the thing on the floor chattered and made a strangled hissing sound, as if sensing what I was considering. I ignored it. Wasn't like he was going to need this anymore, and if I could use it, that's all that mattered.

After another moment's consideration, I shook my head and straightened. There was no easy way to deflesh the bone. Either I tried to move the stone without a pry bar or I went deeper into the cave in search of another tool. As the chattering continued behind me, I quickly rejected option two. No way in hell I was going anyplace that might bring me into contact with the creature who'd done this. I wasn't that brave . . . or that stupid.

45

AT THE DOORWAY, I STRAINED TO HEAR THOSE DRAG-ging footsteps, and picked up distant echoes of them. Good. At least I knew where he was—and that he wasn't anywhere near me.

I hurried to the entrance, then cast my cover spell, my back to the tunnel. Again I listened. The footsteps were still faint. I cast my telekinesis spell, leaned into the boulder, and heaved. It didn't move.

Before I could push again, I heard the man coming back. I sidestepped to the wall, and pressed against it. I closed my eyes before casting the cover spell. If I needed to cast a binding spell, I'd stand a better chance of success if I could fully concentrate on it. More than that, I closed my eyes because I knew if I kept them open and saw that limping figure drawing closer, I'd panic.

As the footsteps approached, I tensed, mentally recit-ing the binding spell, ready to cast it if he bumped me. What if it didn't work? What if I let him get that close, and I couldn't stop him? And if I *could* bind him? Where would I go? This had to be the only exit. I could bind him and still be trapped, just waiting for the spell to snap—

The smell of rotting meat washed over me. The foot-steps had stopped. Where was he? Right in front of me?

Why the hell had I closed my eyes? He could be right there, looking at me, cover spell blown, and I wouldn't know it. Of all the stupid—!

A grunt. So close that the exhaled air tickled my torn ear. Shit! The moment he moved so much as an inch, he would bump me and my cover would break. I had to act now. I was about to open my mouth to cast the binding spell, when I realized, even if it worked, I was trapped. I'd backed myself into the corner and he was blocking that corner. To get past him, I'd need to shove him aside, and that would break the binding spell. Goddamn it! How could I be so monumentally—

Stop!

Get past him first, then cast the binding spell. Have a fireball ready to distract him—the external kind, easy to cast. I tensed, ready to leap. Then, with another grunt, he turned and walked back into the cave.

The moment his footsteps receded as far as the doorway to that chamber of horrors, I opened my eyes, then recast the cover spell. He stopped at the room entrance, did a quick visual sweep, then, muttering away again, continued down the main passage.

I looked at the boulder. No time for fooling around with low-level magic. I needed to use the major telekinetic spell. It would drain my power supply completely, meaning if it wasn't enough to move this rock and he came back, I was screwed. Might as well just hand him a limb and let him start ripping.

Oh, stop that. Just because you'd be spell-powerless, doesn't make you powerless. If he comes back, you'll do what you'd do in any situation like that. Fight and run, run and fight. He's a man. Nothing more. You'll fight and you'll run and you'll pray that someone comes to get you out of this hell before it's too late.

Pep talk over, I rubbed my hands over my face, pushing past the lingering wisps of panic. Then I put my hands against the boulder, dug my feet into the dirt floor, cast the major telekinesis spell, and heaved.

The rock shuddered. I kept pushing. Another shudder, then it began to move, inching up from the depression.

A noise behind me. *Thump. Drag. Thump. Drag.*

A cover spell flew to my lips, but I forced it back. If I broke the telekinesis cast, it would be an hour or more before I could recast it, and even something as low-voltage as a cover spell might not work now, with my power level so low.

Keep pushing.

A grunt echoed down the corridor behind me. A different kind of grunt. One of surprise. Then the footsteps sped up. A roar of exultation. He could see me. *Shit! Turn and run. It's your only chance.*

No! Push harder. Cast the spell again and push like your life depends on it.

I closed my eyes, cast the telekinesis spell, and threw everything I had into one final shove. The rock shuddered, then jumped out of the hole. Fingers grabbed my shoulder. I whirled, kicking blindly. A sharp grunt as my foot connected. I twisted, dove for the narrow opening, and pushed my arms and torso through. One leg made it out. Then fingers dug into my other ankle. A tremendous wrench. I flew back, hitting the dirt of the hillside, wedged now, one leg in, one out. He pulled again. Pain ripped through me as my legs scissored, hips threatening to dislocate.

In that moment, the option I'd been trying so hard to

fight sprang unbidden into my head. I heard Kristof's voice.

If you get stuck in there, absolutely stuck, you don't quit on me, either—you fight, even if it means you need that damned sword to do it.

I'd promised him I'd do that, and I would, if it came to that. But it hadn't yet. Not just yet.

I held myself as still as I could, struggling against the urge to claw my way out. The second his grip relaxed, as he braced for another heave, I kicked the leg trapped in his hands, not pulling it out, but kicking back, at him. Another grunt of surprise, and his grip loosened. I jerked my leg back again, and his grip slid along my ankle, tightening again around my sneaker. One big heave, and my foot flew free of my shoe and I sailed face-first to the ground.

A roar from the cavern. As I scrambled up, I saw his arms flailing through the opening, clawing at the air as he tried to push himself through the narrow gap. I didn't stay to see whether he'd succeed. The second I was on my feet again, I was off and running.

For the first few minutes, I ran blindly, tree branches whipping my face, stumbling as undergrowth caught my feet, tripping along in one shoe, fumbling through the inky blackness. As the cave fell farther behind, I slowed enough to listen for sounds of pursuit. Nothing. On the heels of that relief came a mental curse. What the hell was I doing charging through the forest like a panicked deer? Had I forgotten the others? Six or seven more killers combing the woods, searching for me?

I stopped to get my bearings. The forest was silent. After another moment, I shook myself, bent down, and removed my other shoe. Easier to run in none than one. I tucked the shoe under a bush—no sense giving my trackers any clues. Then I straightened and cast a light-ball. Nothing happened. Was I that low? Dumb question, really. I knew I was that low on spell-power. I could feel it, a barely-there pulse in my head where normally there was a steady stream of energy.

I closed my eyes, leaned against a tree, and waited. After a few minutes, I cast again. The light-ball appeared for a couple of seconds, then fizzled out with a faint *pop*. I swallowed a growl of frustration and rolled my shoulders, trying to relax. No sense running in complete darkness. Wait for the spell.

A twig cracked behind me. As I pushed forward from the tree, a sharp point dug into my shoulder, in the same spot knife-man had stabbed me, and I bit back a yelp.

"Thank you so much for that flare," Dachev whispered in my torn ear. "Most kind of you to let me know where you were."

I back-kicked and caught him in the shins. The torch flew from his hand. As he went down, he slashed the knife. The stone blade sliced through the back of my thigh and I stumbled. He leapt at me. I twisted out of the way, but he stabbed again, this time cutting through my other calf. I roundhoused with my right leg. Pain shot through the split thigh muscle, but I kicked with everything I had and caught him in the gut. He flew back into the tree. As he hit, the knife fell from his hand. I wanted that knife. God, how I wanted it. But I knew if I lunged for it, he'd jump me. So I did the next best thing and kicked it as it fell, sending it sailing into the darkness.

Dachev pitched forward and hit me in the side. As I wheeled around, catching my balance, a sound from deep in the forest stopped me cold. Running footsteps.

Multiple sets of running footsteps. The others could hear us and they were coming.

In a spell-free fight, I could probably have bested Dachev. *Wounded* and in a spell-free fight, that "probably" had already dropped to a "hopefully." My chances of taking on Dachev plus all the others, while in this condition, were nil. Absolutely nil and I wasn't fool enough to pretend otherwise.

So I ran.

I cast my light-ball. This time it held, as dim as an almost-dead flashlight, but steady enough that I could see by. And, yes, as Dachev tore after me, I knew the light-ball was giving him a beacon to follow, but I couldn't worry about that. Stumble around in the dark forest and I'd be dead the moment the others arrived with their torches.

I managed to stay ahead of Dachev, but not easily. Nor did I put any more distance between us. I was barefoot, with one injured thigh and one injured calf. It was only determination that kept me running at all. Determination and the knowledge that if I stopped running, I'd hurt a hell of a lot worse than I did right now.

A noise sounded ahead of me. Shit! Had someone circled around? The noise wafted through the night air. A low mumbling. Oh, goddamn it! The caveman. He *had* made it past that boulder. In my headlong rush to escape Dachev, I'd taken the clearest path I'd found—and that path had been the clearest because I'd cleared it earlier. I'd retraced my steps right back to that goddamned cave. Of all the idiotic things I'd done tonight, this topped them all.

No, wait. Maybe not so stupid. Maybe damned clever . . . if unintentionally so. It was a risk. A big one.

And if I failed— *Don't think of that. Concentrate on the moment.*

I pinpointed the cave monster's location. Off to my left. Then I veered toward it.

A few moments later, I could make out his shuffling shape against the trees. His face flashed, pale against the blackness as he looked up, seeing my light. Then he saw me. His eyes lit up and he lumbered forward.

I cast the binding spell. He kept moving. I started to swerve. Then he stopped, frozen in place. I balled up all my courage and ran right past him, so close that the rotting meat smell of him filled my nostrils.

I tore past and listened. From behind me came a gasp. Then an oath and the sound of feet skidding in the dirt, trying to stop.

I broke the binding spell. The cave man roared. Dachev screamed. And I kept running. As for what happened next—didn't know, didn't care. If Dachev suffered the same fate as that thing in the cave, well, I'm sure none of his victims would have judged the punishment too harsh.

I kept running until I found myself in the village. Seemed the safest place to be, if everyone else was out in the forest looking for me. I'd just hide out here and—

A knife flew from the darkness and buried itself between my ribs. As I doubled over, I saw knife-man step from the shadows. He smiled and lifted another blade. I yanked the first one out and spun out of the way. Or at least I tried to spin, but ended up more stumbling in a half-circle, legs ready to give way, fresh pain now slicing through my torso. I managed to avoid the knife throw, though, and that was all that mattered.

Knife-man ran at me. As I recovered my balance,

another man ran toward the road—Asian, about my age, short and muscular, with modern clothes. Shit! How many were there?

Knife-man whacked a fist into the side of my rib cage. I stumbled, then caught myself and whirled around, blade in my hand. The knife hit him in the shoulder. His eyes widened. As he fell back, my first thought was "Hmmm, didn't think I hit him *that* hard." Then another blade flashed in the moonlight. A sword, slicing up, as knife-man fell back, screaming.

I followed the sword to the hand of the newcomer.

He met my gaze, and brandished a wide smile. "Katsuo."

"Oh, thank God," I murmured. "Please tell me you have hellsbane potion."

He laughed. "For two."

At a noise from the end of the road, we both turned to see four shapes running at us.

"And not a moment too soon, it seems," Katsuo said. "Catch."

He tossed the vial. I caught it just as knife-man struggled to his feet. I kicked him back, then uncapped my vial. Both bird-man and the werewolf rushed me from opposite sides.

"Sorry, guys," I said. "Gotta run."

I dumped the potion into my mouth.

I LANDED BACK IN THAT LITTLE ROOM WITH THE DOOR that led to the killers' hell. Trsiel was there waiting for me. I knew he'd been worried, and he'd want to know what had happened, but I wasn't ready for that yet. I brushed past him with a murmured "I got it." He tried to follow, telling me I needed healing, but I hurried down the hall to another room. When I opened the door, Kristof was there, right where I'd left him.

For a moment, I just stood in the doorway, legs trembling, ready to give way under me. Kristof crossed the room in two long strides, scooped me up, and gave me a fierce hug. Then he closed the door behind us, carried me across the room, and lowered me to the floor.

I huddled there against him, shivering, unable to speak. I wished I could have strode through that door and shouted a triumphant "I did it," forgetting everything that had happened. But I couldn't. And this was the one place where I knew I wouldn't have to, the one person who wouldn't think any the less of me for sitting here, shivering, a heartbeat away from breaking down and bawling like a baby.

Kristof took my left hand and traced his thumb around the stab wound through my palm. His lips moved. I strained to hear what he was saying, then picked up a few words of Greek and recognized a minor healing incantation. A witch spell, one of the few he knew. I'd taught it to him when we'd been together, a little something for his boys, to make the cuts and bruises of childhood easier. He'd struggled with the spell, but had insisted on perfecting it, practicing more than he ever would for any spell of true power.

When he finished, he glanced up at me sheepishly. "Guess you need something stronger than that."

My eyes filled. "No, that was perfect. Thank you."

I leaned forward and pressed my lips against his, closing my eyes as the warmth of his skin chased away the last niggling bits of cold from that place. I put my hands to his cheeks as I kissed him and the heat radiated through, as soothing as Trsiel's healing touch, maybe more.

He wrapped his hands in my hair and kissed me back, and I tasted my own fear mingling with his, knew how worried, how frightened he'd been for me. How many times in my life would I have given anything for this, to come home after something awful and have someone there waiting for me. To have Kris there.

"I need to finish this," I said, pulling back to look up at Kristof. "I put Savannah in danger, and I need to get her out of it. But after that, it has to stop. This one last thing, and it's over. I'll let her go."

His arms tightened around me and he pulled me to him. "You don't have to let her go, Eve. You just need to step back, trust that she'll be okay, and look after yourself."

"I know."

We sat there for another couple of minutes. Then it

was time to let him know what I'd found, and figure out what to do about it.

Before I began, Kristof decided we should called Trsiel in. Trsiel insisted on healing me before we got to work. Any pain from my injuries was gone. The hair would grow back. The missing tooth wouldn't. As for the ear and other open wounds, he could close them, but warned me they'd likely scar, a reminder of the price I'd nearly paid to stop this Nix.

As I finished telling them how Dachev had captured the Nix, Kristof paced the tiny room.

He shook his head. "I had hoped that when this Dachev caught the Nix, he'd both initiated and carried out the capture, but it's now obvious that he only took advantage of a preexisting circumstance."

"One that's going to be damned difficult to replicate," I said. "We're in the same position as Dachev. Pretty much impotent when it comes to killing anyone in the living world. But that's exactly what we need to do." I glanced over at Trsiel. "Not kill Jaime—just deliver a mortal blow and resuscitate her. The question is, how?"

Trsiel gave a slow shake of his head. "It doesn't solve the original problem. Delivering a mortal blow—"

"And resuscitating. We're going to find a situation where she has a damned good chance of being resuscitated."

"A damned good chance isn't good enough, Eve. No matter how carefully you set it up, there's no possible way to guarantee that she would survive."

Kristof wheeled on him. "What the hell do you want from us?"

Trsiel stepped back, blinking. "I'm not—"

"You're not doing a damned thing, Trsiel. That's the problem. Eve just went to hell and back to get you this information. Now you're telling her that it was for nothing?"

"I'm not saying that. I'm just saying that if there's another way—"

"There are other ways," I said. "Of course there are. But none that stand a better chance of us catching the Nix without killing Jaime."

"You don't need to convince me, Eve," Trsiel said. "I get it. I really do. I'm not telling you that I disagree. But the fact remains that Jaime is an innocent, and therefore, no angel's sword can strike that fatal blow."

"But Eve isn't an angel," Kristof said.

Trsiel threw up his hands. "Which is why she can't even use the sword to touch Jaime. And if she can't touch her, or cast magic on her, she can no more attempt to kill her than I can."

"Do you still have Dantalian's Amulet?" Kristof asked.

"The soul-transference one? Yes, but it only works on—" Trsiel stopped and looked at me. "Someone with demon blood."

Two days ago, I'd have jumped at this chance. It was everything I'd wanted, everything I'd dreamed of. But now, after I'd come to a decision about moving forward with my life, about breaking away from Savannah . . . ?

I looked at Kris, and I knew it wasn't a matter of whether I should risk it. You don't test your swim strokes by sticking to the shallow end. Kristof studied me for a long minute, then scooped me out of the deep end . . . and plunked me down into the center of the shark-infested ocean.

"She should transfer into Paige," Kris said.

"Oh, hold on," Trsiel said. "That's not—"

"It has to be Paige," Kris continued. "She's right there, on the scene. She can get next to the Nix easily, without arousing suspicion. She's a witch, which means Eve should be able to use her own spell-casting skills through her. And Eve knows Paige. Knows her well enough that she should be able to, temporarily, fool Savannah and Lucas." Kris's eyes met mine. "Because that's what she'll have to do. She can't tell them what's going on."

I swallowed, then nodded. "Or I triple the chance that one of us will screw up, and the Nix will know something's wrong. So I can't . . . I can't reveal myself to Savannah."

"Are you going to be able to do that, Eve?" Trsiel asked softly.

I lifted my chin and looked at him. "If it means saving her from spending her life thinking she killed Paige and Lucas? Absolutely."

Next we had to discuss a more detailed plan of action. As for the "killing Jaime and bringing her back to life" part, we were leaving that for now, knowing it was better to let me suss out the situation first, and build a plan of action on the fly rather than preplot when I didn't yet know all the variables involved.

Instead, we discussed what could go wrong and backup plans. Although I knew CPR—having learned it when Savannah was young—I'd never had any opportunity to use it. Not that I'd never seen anyone in need of it, but, well, let's just say I never felt inclined to reverse the process. I could try CPR with Jaime, but I'd also make sure that Lucas was close enough to help. As for whether Lucas knew CPR, that was a given. CPR, first aid, Heimlich maneuver—this was a guy who'd know it all. Saving people was his business.

It was far from a complete plan, but before we went a step further, we needed to subject it to the acid test.

"That might work," the middle Fate said slowly.

"Might?"

"There are many variables to consider, Eve, not the least of which is the danger posed to Jaime's life."

"We—"

"You will take every precaution to avoid endangering her. Yes, I know that, and I believe that you will carry through with that intent. Given the danger the Nix poses to the living world, we have agreed that some slight risk to Jaime, however repugnant to us, is unavoidable. Even if you do nothing, and the Nix attacks Lucas and Paige, Jaime's life would still be in danger, assuming they would fight back."

"Good, so I can—"

"The other concern is that Trsiel may not be able to capture her."

Trsiel stepped forward, eyes blazing. "I'm perfectly capable of doing that. I'll be there, waiting, the whole time she's on the other side."

"I'm not questioning your competence, Trsiel," the Fate said. "However, consider the circumstances. Had the Nix entered Jaime by demonic possession, or through the spell she used with the Marquise, then I have no doubt you could capture her. But necromantic possession is different. The Nix has entered Jaime, not as a demon, but as a ghost. Once Jaime's body dies, the Sword of Judgment should work, but while the Nix is trapped between worlds . . . it may not. No angel has ever been sent to retrieve a soul under those circumstances."

"What if I was on the living side?" Trsiel said. "We could see whether the amulet works on me. I could leap into Lucas Cortez and—"

"You couldn't pull it off," I said. "Not in front of Paige and Savannah. You don't know them well enough." I looked at the Fate. "So we don't know for certain that Trsiel can trap the Nix from this side. But we can still try, right? At worst, we'll scare her out of Jaime—then Paige, Lucas, and Savannah will be safe, and I'll just resume the hunt. We'd be no worse off than we were before she leapt into Jaime."

The Fate hesitated, then gave a slow nod.

Next they transported Trsiel, Kristof, and me to Paige's office, where she was hard at work answering e-mails. She looked like she'd be there for a while, so we tele-ported to the ghost-world version of her office to say our good-byes.

Trsiel promised to stay at my side after I crossed over, ready to help me end this. Then he handed me the amulet, and left Kristof and me alone.

When Trsiel was gone, Kris took the amulet from my hands and put it around my neck.

"Looks good," he said with a wry smile. "Just don't get used to it."

I answered him with a kiss, my hands going to his hair, letting the silky fine strands slide through my fingers. His arms went around me, rib-crushing tight, and I pressed myself against him, getting as close as I could. After a minute, he pulled his head back.

"I trust that's not a good-bye kiss," he said.

"You know it isn't. I'm coming back, and when I do, it'll be for good. Both feet planted on this side finally."

We kissed again. When we finished, he slid his hands to my cheeks, holding my face within kissing distance of his.

"Trsiel won't be the only one at your side," he said. "I won't be able to do anything. But I'll be there. I'll always be there."

"I know you will." I squeezed his hand, then touched the amulet. "Let's try this thing."

There are many ways to activate an amulet. Most require an incantation, usually the one conveniently inscribed on the piece itself, as this one was. As fluent as I am in Hebrew, the first time I ran through the spell I knew it wouldn't work. I didn't expect it to. With a new spell, you need at least a few trial runs to get the gist and the cadence of it. By the fourth try, I knew I had it right. Yet Paige continued to click away at her computer, fingers flying over the keyboard.

"Maybe I need to be closer," I said, stepping up behind her.

"It's only your fourth try. Now, if it were me, we'd be here all day, but even you might need a few—"

Kristof went quiet.

"A few what?" I said.

My voice had taken on a deep contralto pitch, and an accent I'd lost a decade ago. In front of me was a half-finished e-mail message.

"Holy shit," I muttered.

As I spoke, there was an odd catch to my words, a

vibration in my chest. It took a second to realize what it was, and when I did, I couldn't stifle a laugh. I was breathing. I looked down at my hands, still resting on the keyboard, awaiting commands. I saw fingers decorated with silver rings and a white-gold wedding band. Each nail was a quarter-moon sliver, kept practical—short and unpolished.

A car started in the drive below. I jumped up and almost tripped as my knees caught the fabric of a skirt. I looked down. A casual A-line dress, beautifully tailored from soft cotton, and oh-so-feminine. I laughed again. For Paige's third birthday, I'd bought her the cutest little pair of jean overalls . . . and the horror on her face had been priceless. After the party, I'd slipped the overalls from the neatly folded pile of gifts, taken them to the store, and exchanged them for a red wool coat with a fake-fur collar and matching muff, and earned myself a heartfelt hug and a grin I'd never forget.

I hurried to the window and looked down just in time to see Paige's car pull from the driveway. I couldn't see the driver—presumably Lucas—but when the passenger glanced back toward the house, my heart skipped—and for the first time in three years, I *felt* it skip.

"Hi, baby," I whispered.

I pressed my fingertips to the cool windowpane. Savannah glanced up, attention caught by the motion or the figure in the window. She squinted up through the car window, then smiled and waved.

"Alone at last," said a voice behind me.

Arms wrapped around my waist and swung me in the air. I twisted, right hook at the ready, then saw my attacker.

"Lucas," I said. "What—uh—" I wriggled out of his

grasp and stepped backward. "I thought you were— Good to see you."

He arched one brow. "Good to see you, too."

"Sorry," I said with a tiny laugh. "You just caught me off guard. I was thinking."

He eased back against the file cabinet. "About what?"

"Er, things. Work. Boring stuff."

My God, I was short. Of all the things I should have been thinking at that moment, this probably ranked near the bottom, but I couldn't help it. Lucas wasn't any taller than I was—the real me—but he was a damned sight taller than Paige, who barely hit five foot two. The sensation of having to look up at someone was so disorienting that my brain snagged on it and wouldn't let go. And while I was thinking this, Lucas was giving me a look that told me I had to do something—something Paige-like— fast.

I slid forward, smiled, and grabbed his hand, then leaned up against the file cabinet beside him, my side touching his.

"So," I said . . . and then couldn't think of anything to go with it.

"About that gift."

"Gift?"

He smiled down at me. "The one you are trying very hard to pretend you've forgotten about."

"Ah . . . that gift. The one from . . . your trip."

He nodded, and I mentally high-fived myself. Lucas always brought Paige something home from his trips.

"So what is it?" I asked.

He arched a brow again, a clear "You have to ask?" and I knew I was losing ground fast.

"Now, let me see." I grinned and stepped away, letting

his hand fall. "What could it be? A fur coat? Noooo. A Lamborghini? Noooo."

He shook his head, but didn't smile. Okay, joking wasn't going to get me out of this. Think harder—what would Lucas bring Paige as a gift . . . ?

"Magic!" I said. "You brought me a, uh, a spell or a spellbook. Right?"

His brow furrowed. I knew I'd got the answer right, but I think my delivery had been a bit off. I grabbed his hand again and grinned at him.

"Okay, Cortez," I said. "Stop goofing, and tell me what you brought me. Is it a spell? A new one? What does it do?"

He laughed, and I breathed a mental sigh of relief. Only Paige called Lucas by his last name, and her enthusiasm for new magic matched my own.

"I told you yesterday that I was picking option twelve," he said. "But I lied."

"You . . . did?" Option twelve? What the hell was option twelve and what did it have to do with a new spell?

His lips twitched in a grin that lit up his eyes and made him almost handsome. "Yes, I apologize for my dissembling, but I wished to conceal my true intentions until such time as we were able to execute them without fear of interruption."

"English, Cortez."

His grin grew. "I wanted to wait until we were alone. The truth is that I have come up with an option of my own." He caught my look of confusion and laughed. "Yes, I know, my previous efforts in that regard were underwhelming, and I'll admit that I still lack your particular brand of creativity in such matters, but I believe I may redeem myself with this one." His eyes sparked with a wicked grin. "This time, I had help. Namely the *Cinsel Büyücülük*."

"The *Cinsel Büyücülük?* Isn't that a sex—" I dropped his hand and backpedaled. "Damn, Lucas. I'm so sorry. I would love to, but . . ." I waved at the computer screen. "My in-box is overflowing. How about a rain check?"

He gave a slow nod. "I understand."

I smiled. "Thanks. You're so sweet." I turned to the computer. "How about I get a few of these done, then I'll make us some tea and—"

A hand flew around my throat, fingers digging in so hard I gasped.

"Move and I will crush your windpipe," Lucas murmured behind me, his voice low, tone conversational. "You have two minutes to tell me what I want to know, starting with: Where is my wife?"

47

I GRABBED AT LUCAS'S HAND, AND TRIED TO PRY IT free, but it wouldn't budge.

"What is wrong with you today, Cortez?" I gasped.

An edge crept into his voice. "Don't call me that."

"Don't call—? Lucas? It's me."

His grip tightened.

"Lucas?" I twisted, injecting fear into my voice. "Lucas, please. You're scaring me."

"Don't."

"Lucas? It's me—"

"Don't!" He leaned over my back. "You are not Paige, and the more you try to deny that, the more angry I'm going to become. Now, who are you?"

Damn it! I'd been here less than ten minutes, and I'd already screwed up. I thought of Jaime's hotel room, when Kristof had seen through the Nix's glamour spell without a moment's hesitation. He'd known she wasn't me. So how the hell had I thought I could fool Lucas about Paige?

I had two options—keep pushing and hope he backed off, or come clean. The success of the first depended on how gullible Lucas was . . . which made the decision pretty darned easy.

"Eve. Eve Levine. Savannah's—"

"I know who Eve Levine is."

"Right, we met. Ninety-eight, ninety-nine, maybe. God, you were just a kid. You had balls, though, coming to take those grimoires away from me. I admired that. Didn't keep me from kicking your ass, but I admired it."

His hand stayed locked around my throat.

"Er, you do remember that, right?" I said.

"Yes."

"But you don't think I'm really Eve—"

"No, I never questioned that. Now, where is Paige?"

His tone cut through me, as cold and emotionless as it had been when he started. Not that I expected a big hug of welcome, but, well, I suppose I expected something. I thought of all the hours we'd spent together, all the times I watched out for him, even rooted for him. And as we stood there, his hand wrapped around my throat, I became keenly aware of the one-sidedness of this relationship.

His grip tightened. "Where is Paige? You may be Savannah's mother, Eve, but don't think I won't—"

"Don't! This is Paige's body. If you hurt me, you'll hurt her. She won't feel it, but when she comes back—and she is coming back. I promise you that, Lucas. This is just temporary."

"Is it?"

"Absolutely. I'd never do anything to hurt Paige. I used to babysit her when she was little. Did she tell you that?"

"She told me that you said that . . . though she has no recollection of it."

"Still?" I couldn't hide the disappointment in my voice. "I wonder if her mother blocked the memories after I left the Coven. Not that I can imagine Ruth doing such a thing—but, well, I can't imagine Paige would just forget me on her own. I taught Paige her first spell. An unlock spell, because her mom kept locking up her favorite toys—"

"Paige told me something else," Lucas cut in. "When she met you in the ghost world, you said a few things that concerned her. She said you were trying to find a way to help Savannah, and you seemed very determined to do so."

"Hey, I didn't mean any disrespect to you guys. You're doing a great job—" I stopped. "You think that's what I'm doing? That I took over Paige's body to come back? Whoa. No, no, no." I twisted, trying to look at him, but he held my throat, keeping my face turned from his. "I'm back to do something very specific, very short-term, very important. Then I'm gone. I'm not even telling Savannah that I'm here."

He hesitated, then said, "What exactly is this 'something'?"

"Can I sit down? Please?"

Another hesitation, longer this time. Then his fingers relaxed on my neck. As I rubbed my throat, I gave him a brief rundown of the situation, leaving out as many details as possible, since I wasn't sure how much I should or could tell.

"So you are telling me that Jaime Vegas is planning to kill Paige and me, and blame Savannah?"

"Right."

He picked up the cordless phone from the desk. "You have one minute to return Paige to her body, or I will, within an hour, have the best necromancer in the country here to exorcise you . . . a process that I promise you will find most unpleasant."

"Er, I think I'd better give you the expanded version."

He held up the phone. "Two minutes."

When I finished, his eyes met mine, his expression unreadable.

"So what happened at the community center, the shooting. That was this Nix."

I nodded, but I knew I'd failed, that my story was too preposterous and he wasn't—

"We were worried that it was somehow connected to Savannah," he said quietly. "We tried to convince ourselves we were being paranoid but—" His head shot up. "This Nix is in Jaime? Right now?"

"Yeah, but don't worry. We'll head her off before she gets near—"

Lucas was already on his feet and flying out the door. I jumped off my chair and tore after him.

"Hey!" I called as he bounded down the stairs.

He didn't even slow. He hit the bottom step and wheeled through the dining room doorway, disappearing. I ran into the dining room just as he flew through the kitchen, pausing only to grab his keys.

"Oh, shit!" I said. "She's already here, isn't she? That's who's with Savannah."

I caught up with Lucas in the lean-to, as he yanked the cover off his motorcycle.

"Hold on," I said. When he didn't listen, I snatched the keys from his hand. "Lucas, hold on! She's not after Savannah, and if you go tearing off to wherever they've gone, she'll know we're on to her. Given the choice between killing Savannah and abandoning her revenge altogether, I sure as hell know which one she'll pick."

He turned to me, mouth opening to say something, then stopping as he saw me, a look of disconcertment passing behind his eyes.

"Cast the glamour spell," I said.

"Hmmm?"

"This is making you uncomfortable—me looking like Paige. You know what I really look like, so cast the glamour spell, so you'll see that instead."

He nodded, and cast it. When he finished, his eyes darted my way, shoulders tense, as if bracing himself. Then he relaxed.

"Better?" I said.

He nodded. "Thank you."

"You'll have to uncast it when they come back, so you remember who I'm *supposed* to be. So when did Jaime get here?"

"This morning. Savannah, of course, was thrilled to see her, and Paige and I—" He shook his head. "We were just as happy, thinking it was exactly what Savannah needed, how thoughtful it was . . ." Another sharp shake of his head.

"She didn't seem at all . . . odd?"

"Had it been anyone else, I'm sure I would have thought so. But Jaime's moods—and behavior—can be . . . erratic. She called after she heard about the shooting, and was concerned about Savannah, so for her to get a sudden notion to visit wasn't abnormal, not for Jaime."

He looked back at the keys in my hand. I clasped my hand around them, hiding them.

"Trust me," I said. "I want to go after her at least as much as you do, but so long as you don't have the keys, and I can't drive a motorcycle, we're pretty darned safe. So where'd they go? Will they be gone long?"

"They're just going to the video store, and picking up a few groceries. They should be back any moment." He walked out of the lean-to, and peered down the driveway. "Perhaps I should call on my cell—"

"Good idea. Tell them you forgot you're out of milk or something."

He nodded and called. From his voice, I knew he'd phoned Savannah. I don't think I could have made that call without betraying something, if not screaming for her to get out of the car and run back here as fast as she could. Lucas handled it as calmly as if he'd really been calling to ask her to pick up something else.

"She's fine," he said when he hung up. "They're finishing up at the store now, meaning we have about ten minutes to devise a plan."

We came up with a decent basic premise. Well, Lucas came up with most of it, but that was his thing, so I left him to it and refined as necessary. It was still impossible to plot a complete strategy like "when she comes in the house, you send her upstairs, and I'll hide, then . . ."

The moment the Nix realized she'd been led into a trap, she'd jump free from Jaime's body. So the mortal blow had to come as a surprise. Or, as we decided, maybe not as such a surprise. There was one time when we could battle the Nix without her realizing what was happening and leap clear: when she was the one who initiated the fight. In other words, we had to wait until she made her move to kill one of us. She'd expect us to fight then.

"Quickly," he said, as the car sounded in the drive. "Get upstairs, back into Paige's office, and close the door. I'll tell them that a client's Web site crashed, and you're not to be disturbed. I'll bring dinner up—"

"Whoa, hold on. If I hide out in the office, the Nix will probably need to change her plans."

"That's a chance we'll have to take."

"But the longer it takes her, the longer I'll be here."

He paused. "I'll call you down for dinner. But say as little as possible. I'll steer conversation in another direction. After dinner, we'll . . . we'll watch the video they picked out." He nodded. "Yes, that's perfect. You won't need to talk."

"Hey, just because I can't fool you doesn't mean I can't pull off a damned good Paige impersonation."

He looked at me.

"Er, a pretty good one," I said.

He kept looking at me.

"I'll keep my mouth shut."

A car door slammed. Savannah called something. I hesitated, but Lucas uncast the glamour spell, then opened the back door and shoved me inside.

I spent the first thirty minutes in Paige's office browsing through the stuff on her computer. I wasn't being nosy. I had nothing better to do. Okay, maybe I was being nosy . . . just a little. After a half hour, though, Lucas popped in to check on me and asked me, very politely, not to mess with Paige's stuff, shutting down her e-mail and other windows, and leaving open only two—solitaire and some file that looked like programming stuff. If Savannah or the Nix came by accidentally, I could switch from the game to the work, and at least look busy. Not that I could actually do anything with the programming code. Lucas had locked it into a read-only file. Geez, you'd think the guy didn't trust me or something.

That lack of trust kind of stung. Okay, not kind of. It *did* sting, almost as much as the distrust I'd gotten from Paige when I'd looked after her in the ghost world. Did I blame them for not trusting me? No. I'd earned it, if not by doing anything to them personally, at least through my reputation. And I guess if you count that broken arm I gave Lucas when he tried to take my grimoires, I had done something to them personally. But, still, I would have thought rescuing them from the ghost world would have counted for something. Maybe it did. If not for that, I suspected I'd be sitting in this chair, not with a game of solitaire thoughtfully set up for me, but tied down and awaiting an exorcist.

So I played solitaire and tried very, very hard not to hear my daughter's voice downstairs, not to think about her down there, finally within reach—physically within reach, that I could go down there and hug her and tell her— But I wasn't thinking about that.

Forty minutes passed, and the back door banged shut downstairs. I looked out the rear window, but no one stepped outside. I tugged open the window and listened. After a moment, I caught two voices: Lucas and Jaime.

I strained to hear what they were saying.

". . . really a beautiful bike," Jaime said. "And you restored it yourself. That is so amazing."

Lucas answered as easily as if he really was talking to Jaime. It didn't take long to realize the Nix had initiated the trip outside. Was she going to kill him in the lean-to? But how did that set up Savannah? And what about me? Maybe we weren't the only ones "going with the flow." Maybe with me—Paige—locked away in the office, the Nix was taking advantage of our separation, and striking at Lucas first. I had to get down there—

The phone rang.

I froze, halfway across the room. *Okay, Lucas, I'm sure you can hear the phone. This is the perfect excuse to come back inside—*

The phone stopped ringing. Good. Now—

"Paige!" Savannah screamed.

Shit! Now what? No, wait, Lucas told her to leave me—Paige—alone, so she'll take a message and—

Footsteps banged up the steps. I didn't move. Couldn't move.

The door swung open, and there stood my daughter. My beautiful fifteen-year-old daughter. Standing there. Looking right at me. At me—not glancing at a spot just to the left of her mother's invisible ghost—but actually at me, seeing me—

"The phone," she said, waggling it in front of my nose. "What are you? Deaf? Geez."

I willed my hand up. She lifted the phone over her head, out of my reach, a mischievous grin darting across her face. Then she handed it to me, mouthed, "Shorty," sailed across the room, and plunked herself down on the other chair.

I stared at her for a moment, then wrenched my gaze away and lifted the phone to my ear.

"Paige Winterbourne."

"Oh, thank God you're home," a woman's voice said. "Liza didn't know what to do and I said, 'Let me call Paige. She'll figure something out.'"

"Uh-huh. Well, I'm awfully busy right now. Could I call you—"

"Oh, it'll just take a second. It's about the EMRAW."

"Em . . . ?"

"The Elliott Memorial Run and Walk?" The woman

laughed. "Guess all your charity events must run together after a while."

"Uh, right."

"Bottles or cups?"

"Huh?"

"The water. We need to have water for the participants. If we bought jugs and poured it into cups, we'd save a lot of money. But it might make us look cheap."

"Cheap . . ."

"Right. So should we go with individual bottles instead?"

For a second, I could only sit there, a "what the hell?" expression on my face.

"Paige?"

"Oh, hell, buy Evian. It's only charitable donations you're spending, right?"

Silence buzzed down the line. I rolled my eyes.

"Cups, obviously," I said. "It's a charity event. If they expect bottled water, they can damned well go jog at the country club instead."

More silence, then a shaky, "Right. I, uh, thought that's what you'd choose, but—"

"Then why call?"

I hung up. Unbelievable. Donating time to charity is all very fine and noble, but how the hell could Paige find the patience for crap like that? She's running around trying to save the world from the forces of evil, and has to deal with idiots who think "what kind of water should we serve?" is a life-or-death dilemma. You ask me, that crossed the line from goodness to martyrdom.

"Lucas was right. You are in a strange mood," Savannah said, still twisting the chair back and forth. "Lucas said I can't bug you 'cause you're busy. But I didn't interrupt you. The phone did. As long as you're interrupted, though, there's no harm in talking to you, right?"

I thought of Lucas, downstairs, alone with the Nix. "Uh, can we—"

"It's about Trevor," she said. "He's acting— I don't *get* him, you know. I think he wants to be with me—but then he acts all—" She groaned and stopped spinning the chair. "He's being weird again."

"And you—you want my advice?"

"Duh, no. I just want to know what you think. I mean, sure, if you want to give me advice, I can't stop you. You always do anyway. But it's not like I have to take it."

I stood there, speechless. My daughter wanted my advice about a boy. How many times had I imagined this conversation, imagined what I'd say, what words of wisdom I could impart—or, considering my romantic track record, what warnings I could give.

Jaime's laugh floated through the open window.

"Shit!" I said.

Savannah looked at me, one brow going up.

"Uh, Lucas," I said. "I needed to tell him— Is he downstairs?"

"Nah, outside. Jaime wanted to see his bike. Like she hasn't seen it before."

"I need to— Hold that thought. About the boy. I'll be right back."

I bolted from the room, then heard Savannah following and checked my pace, settling for a quick march down the steps and to the back door. I threw it open. Jaime turned, and for a split second something very un-Jaime-like passed behind her eyes, a mental snarl of pique.

"Ah, Paige," Lucas said. "Perfect timing. We need to discuss dinner."

"Already?" Jaime said, forcing a laugh. "I thought maybe Lucas could take me for a ride—"

"Aren't we having roast chicken?" Savannah said, slipping out behind me.

"We were," Lucas said. "But Paige has been so busy with that site crash that she hasn't had time to start it, so we'll need an alternate plan."

"Well, you guys figure that out, then," Savannah said. "Jaime and I need to talk."

Jaime looked at her, frowning.

"You know," Savannah said. "About that thing."

"What thing is that?" I asked.

"Curry," Lucas said.

I frowned. "They need to talk about curry?"

"No, for dinner. We'll pick up Indian. You like Indian food, don't you, Jaime?"

She smiled. "Love it."

"Why don't Paige and I go pick that up now, and we'll have an early dinner."

Savannah plucked at Jaime's sleeve and nodded toward the house. As they went inside, I watched, still standing there as the door closed. So much for a mother-daughter boy chat. Maybe later.

I turned to Lucas. "Jaime doesn't like Indian food, does she? The real Jaime, I mean."

"Hates it."

"Ah, so you didn't quite believe me. You could have said so, you know, and we'd have thought up an easier way to test her . . . one that doesn't require us leaving them alone while we go pick up dinner."

He shook his head. "We're not going to pick up dinner.

The Indian query was simply a convenient opportunity to verify that the Nix is indeed still inhabiting Jaime's body. I was quite sure of it when she lured me out here, but 'quite sure' is hardly sufficient, considering what we're planning to do."

He handed me Paige's helmet, and took his own off the shelf.

"I thought you said—" I began.

"We must at least appear to leave. That will also provide us with the opportunity to sneak back and find out what Savannah meant—what she and Jaime needed to discuss."

48

LUCAS PARKED THE MOTORCYCLE AT A TINY COM-
munity vegetable garden half a block away. We left our
helmets locked to the bike, then hurried back to the
house.

"Blur spell?" I asked as we drew close. "Or can you do
that one yet?"

"I believe you'll find my spell-casting much improved
since our last meeting. Being bested by a witch casting
sorcerer magic is bound to have a rousing impact on any
sorcerer. I finally mastered the blur spell last year."

"How about Paige? 'Cause I'm restricted to her level of
magic here. My Aspicio powers aren't working worth a
damn."

"Paige is reasonably adept at it as well. Anything I
know, she knows . . ." A quarter-smile. "Or she is doing
her best to learn."

"How about the cover spell? If you can't do it, I can
cover you—"

"Paige isn't the only one driven to expand her reper-
toire. I can cast most witch magic she knows, including
the cover spell and binding spell, though she continues
to be more proficient at the latter. I believe I've hit the
racial-crossover wall with that one."

"Well, you're the first sorcerer I've met who can do it at all, so you're well ahead of the game."

We paused behind the neighbor's fence. Lucas stood on tiptoe to peer over it. I tried . . . then realized I didn't have a hope in hell of succeeding. Not at this height.

"There," Lucas said. "I saw a movement in the living room. They're in there, or just inside the dining room on the other side."

"Hey, speaking of the dining room, did you know you have a resident residual?"

He frowned down at me.

"Er, never mind. I'll explain later."

We used our blur spells to get to the living room window, then replaced it with a cover spell. Sorcerer blur spells, as the name suggests, only blur your form. They don't make you invisible. Witch cover spells make you invisible, but only if you're standing still. Put the two together, and you have a decent stealth package.

Although the weather was still nippy, most of the windows in the house were cracked open. When we stood beside the living room side window, we could hear voices, but no words. After a moment of closed-eye concentration, I picked up Savannah's conversation.

". . . but if it's dangerous—" she said.

Jaime laughed. "And since when has that bothered you?"

"It *has* to bother me. With my power, I can't just go casting spells any way I want. I need to know exactly what I'm doing and what can happen or—"

Jaime laughed again, the sound taking on a harsh tone of mocking. "God, you sound like Paige. I never thought I'd see the day. Your mother would flip."

I gritted my teeth. *No, baby, I wouldn't flip. Paige is right. You* do *need to be careful. You need—*

"Sure, Paige tells me to be careful," Savannah said. "But it doesn't mean I listen."

"Look, Savannah, either you want to summon your mom or you don't."

My heart thudded.

"Of course I do," Savannah said.

"Well, then, you have to be willing to assume the risks. Like you said, you have the power. This ritual wouldn't work with anyone else. But you can do it. I'm sure you can."

A hand touched my arm. I looked up to see Lucas, who'd broken his cover spell. He jerked his chin toward the sidewalk. I broke my spell and pointed at the house, gesturing that I wanted to hear more.

"Heard enough," he mouthed.

I hesitated, then cast the blur spell and darted across the lawn and behind the neighbor's fence.

"So that's how she'll do it," I said. "She'll make Savannah think she knows a way to contact me. And when we—you and Paige, I mean—wind up dead, she'll say it was because of the spell, that Savannah screwed up."

Lucas nodded and motioned for us to talk as we returned to the motorcycle.

"But how is she going to kill us while Savannah's performing the ritual?" I said. "Necros can't kill anyone—not with magic, at least."

"I suspect the plan is to kill us ahead of time," Lucas said. "Probably individually. That may have been part of her ruse with the bike. Find a way to kill me, hide the motorcycle, and claim I went off on an errand."

"Then kill me—Paige—and, after the ritual, find us dead. Leaving Savannah to think that in her eagerness to contact me, she killed you two. God, when I get hold of that demi-demon bitch—"

"Careful. We have to take this slowly. Play at her pace." He glanced at me. "Is that going to be a problem?"

"Not if it means I finally *will* get hold of her."

As safe as we assumed Savannah was with the Nix, neither of us wanted to test that theory more than necessary, so we skipped the take-out run, and instead decided to tell Savannah and Jaime that the wait had been too long and we were opting for pizza—delivered—instead.

Lucas would do the explaining, leaving me to retreat to Paige's office once again. Then, when he had the chance, he'd get Savannah away from Jamie, and with any luck, Jaime would take advantage of the opportunity to strike at me.

Up in Paige's room, I did a quick drawer search. Took me a few minutes, but I found what I wanted: a length of strong ribbon. I used it to tie back Paige's long, thick curls, adjusting the knot so it would pull free with only a tug. Lucas and I had decided on suffocation as the safest way to "almost" kill Jaime's body. While I had every intention of putting my bare hands around her throat and looking into that demi-demon's eyes as I throttled the life from her, I needed a backup tool. The ribbon would do.

Twenty minutes later, a loud *thump* sounded outside, followed by a shout from Savannah. I bolted from my chair and flew to the window. Another *thump,* coming from behind the house. Savannah groaned and yelled something. I opened the window farther, pried off the screen, and leaned out. Savannah and Lucas were at the far end of the driveway, playing basketball.

As I watched them, I thought of Kristof. I'd dreamed of boy-talk with Savannah. Is this what he dreamed of? Is this what I'd taken away from him? The thought pinged another, and I remembered what he'd said before I'd transmigrated into Paige's body. That he'd stay close. My head shot up so fast I hit the windowsill and yelped. I imagined him laughing, and a shiver ran through me. I turned slowly.

"You're here, aren't you?" I said.

I scanned the room, and strained to listen, to see some sign of Kristof. It was one thing having a ghost around when you didn't know it. But if you knew it, and if you tried hard enough, surely you should be able to pick up some sign. But I couldn't.

"Savannah's outside," I said. "Playing basketball with Lucas."

Nothing. Not even a twinge of awareness that told me he was there.

"Basketball was never your thing, was it?" I said with a smile. "Mine neither. But she's good at it. And she likes it. That's what counts."

The silence swallowed my voice. I shivered, and the quaver went right down into my gut. What if something went wrong, and I couldn't get back? Was this what it would be like, stuck here, talking to myself, wondering whether he was still listening? At least on the other side, I could see this world. From here, the separation was absolute.

Savannah yelled something outside, and I jerked up. If Savannah and Lucas were outside, that meant I was alone in here with the Nix. And if she was making no effort to come and get me, I had to give her a push.

"Sorry, Kris, but we gotta run." I grinned. "Time to try getting myself killed."

* * *

I found the Nix in the living room, sitting on a chair—my chair—and staring into space. At first I thought maybe she saw the crying woman residual. She wasn't looking toward the dining room, though. She was staring straight ahead, eyes as blank as a mannequin's.

"There you are," I said, walking into the living room.

"No!" the Nix leapt to her feet, lip curling in a snarl. "Get out!"

I feigned a wide-eyed back-step. "Jaime? Uh, are you okay?"

Her eyes flicked to mine and she frowned, as if just noticing me.

"What?" she snapped. Then she blinked fast. "Oh, Paige. Sorry."

"Ghost bothering you?" I asked.

Another quick blink, startled. Then a sharp head shake that morphed into a nod and a wry smile. "Yeah. You know how it is. They never leave us alone. So is your work done?"

"Pretty much. I just popped down to see whether we had anything in the freezer for dessert. I should be able to dig up a pie."

"Sounds good."

"If Lucas or Savannah comes in, just tell them I'm downstairs. In the basement. I may be a while—that freezer's packed with stuff."

She nodded, then sat back down, gaze going blank, as if she'd already forgotten I was there. I headed for the basement steps. When I reached the back-door landing, I looked outside. Lucas caught the movement and glanced over. I motioned that I was going into the basement. He nodded, then distracted Savannah before she saw me, and they resumed playing.

"Heading downstairs now," I murmured under my breath. "Into the dark basement. All alone."

For a second, I thought I heard Kristof's chuckle, but the sound turned into the thumping of a dribbled basketball against the driveway.

Once downstairs, I had to look around for the freezer. I knew there was one here somewhere, and I was pretty sure there'd be a pie in it. Not a store-bought one, but something homemade, probably from berries picked by hand. I don't know how Paige found the time. I never did. Of course, I'd never tried to, either.

I finally located the freezer. Sure enough, it was just as full as I'd imagined. There was a whole stack of pies, so I moved some bread on top to hide them, then busied myself pretending to hunt. Upstairs, all was silent.

"Come on, come on," I muttered. "One secluded victim, head conveniently stuck in a freezer. What are you waiting for? Until I've cleared enough room to stash my body?"

The words had barely left my mouth when footsteps sounded overhead.

"About time. Now hurry it up before I get frostbite."

The footsteps crossed the kitchen, then descended to the landing, and paused there, as the Nix presumably reassured herself that Savannah and Lucas were busy outside. I shuffled two boxes of cookies. Chocolate-chip cookies. Were those made with Ruth's recipe? Mmmm. It'd been twenty years since I had those. Maybe I could slip a couple—

The Nix's footsteps stopped.

"I know there's a pie in here somewhere," I muttered.

Paige wasn't the talks-to-herself type, but the freezer was around the corner, meaning the Nix might have some trouble finding me. Yet at least a minute passed, and nothing happened. Would I hear her footsteps? On a concrete floor? *What are you, stupid?* I backed out of the freezer fast, before I did an Abby Borden and caught a hatchet to the head.

Still facing the freezer, I strained my eyes as far as I could to the side. The bare bulb cast my shadow across the floor, along with the shadow of the freezer and stacked washer-dryer combo. But no Jaime-shaped one. For thirty seconds, I stood there, neck cricked slightly off-kilter, watching the floor for a fresh shadow. Finally, I gave up, quietly lowered the freezer door, and slid along the wall to the doorway. Aspicio powers would come in real handy right about now. Damn, I was spoiled.

From the left of the doorway, I could see the bottom of the stairs. No sign of the Nix. I cast a blur spell, then quickly leaned out for a peek, and jerked back. Unless she was hiding in the cold cellar—with the door closed—she wasn't down here. I'd definitely heard her on the steps. Had I heard her descend all the way? No, because I'd been distracted by cookies. There's a defense for the books.

I was pretty sure I'd heard her continue past the back-door landing. What was it Lucas had said? Considering what we were dealing with, "quite sure" wasn't good enough. So "pretty sure" really didn't cut it. I should have been more careful. She could have headed back up while I was ogling a box of frozen baked goods.

"No!"

I jumped, nearly stumbling into the open doorway and blowing my cover.

"I didn't ask— No! This is mine!"

It was the Nix, that same un-Jaime-like snarl I'd heard upstairs. The voice came from the enclosed stairway. Who was she talking to? Not Lucas or Savannah, that was for sure—not in that tone.

A hackle-raising growl reverberated down the stairs. Then a *thud-thud-thud* as the Nix marched, heavy-footed, back up. The screen door squealed open. I hurried from my hiding place to the foot of the stairs.

"Jaime? Is that you?"

She kept walking, letting the door swing shut behind her. I galloped up the stairs and out to the yard. By the time I got there, she was at the edge of the driveway. Lucas stopped mid-throw, and the ball rolled from his hand. Savannah dove to catch it, chortling at his fumble. Then she saw us and stopped.

"Jaime!" I called, jogging after her.

She ignored me.

"What's with her?" Savannah whispered.

Lucas shushed her and said something under his breath, distracting her attention from Jaime. I caught up to the Nix, and touched her arm, but she flung me off and growled something about needing some air. When I turned, Lucas caught my eye and motioned for me to leave her be.

"Time to order that pizza, I believe," he said as he scooped up the ball. "What does everyone feel like? I think Hawaiian might be a nice change. We haven't had that in a while."

"Duh," Savannah said, snatching the ball from him. "We don't have it because I hate pineapple."

"Really?" he said. "I do believe I saw you put pineapple on your banana split last night."

"That's because banana splits are sweet, and pineapple is sweet. Pizza is not sweet. You don't mix sweet stuff and nonsweet stuff. It's gross."

"But you always put plum sauce on chicken strips, and that is definitely mixing sweets and nonsweets, so your logic, it would appear, is faulty, and—"

"Oh, stop being a goof." She whipped the ball at him. "I'll order the pizza and get what I like."

She marched off into the house, hair flipping behind her, thoughts of Jaime long gone.

"Nice save," I said when she'd left. "You're really good with her."

He only nodded and returned the ball to its place at the foot of the hoop. I often wondered what it was like for Lucas, this package deal. If he'd wanted Paige, he had to take Savannah, too. How many twenty-five-year-olds would have gone for that? Not just accepted the inconvenience of having a kid around, but embraced the whole foster-father role? Well, okay, I've known a few twenty-something guys who wouldn't mind having a teen girl as a ward, but there was never any question of that with Lucas. Right from day one, he'd been exactly what Savannah needed—a combination big brother and father figure who balanced her ideological conflicts with Paige. I wanted to thank him for that. I really did. But I couldn't think of any way to do it that wouldn't embarrass him . . . and probably me, too.

"I think it's a ghost," I said when Lucas returned.

"Hmmm?"

"What's happening with the Nix. She was acting pretty freaky inside, staring into space, then snapping at herself. If I have Paige's abilities, then she must have Jaime's, meaning she's probably seeing a ghost. When I mentioned that, I startled her—maybe she didn't realize that's what was happening."

He nodded. "It could be. It could also be Jaime herself."

"Trying to get back in, you mean."

Another nod, then a pause before he glanced over at me. "Does Paige know?" He cleared his throat, tamping down the note of anxiety. "That is to say, you were able to explain this to her, weren't you? What you did?"

"Uh, no. I couldn't, or believe me, I would have."

"So she doesn't know what's going on." He adjusted his glasses, then glanced over at me again. "Is there some way to tell her? To check on her?"

"She's okay, Lucas. I swear she is. And I'll get out of here as soon as I can."

A slow nod. "We should get inside. It doesn't take long for pizza to arrive, and I doubt Savannah is planning to pay for it."

"I hope she ordered mushrooms. Pizza isn't pizza without mushrooms." I shook my head. "This is getting more absurd by the second, isn't it?"

"Playing basketball and arguing over pizza while we wait for an evil demi-demon to get around to trying to kill us?" A tiny smile. "Absurd? Not at all. Though I do wish she'd get on with it. Savannah rented *Pirates of the Caribbean,* and Paige really wanted to see that."

"She's welcome to it. I've had my fill of pirates for a while."

He arched a brow.

"You don't want to know. As for the Nix, I'm starting to think we might need to give her a push. Especially if she *is* preoccupied dealing with ghosts or Jaime's spirit. Maybe— Whoops, here she comes."

The Nix strode around the house, without so much as a glance our way.

"Jaime!" I called. "We've ordered pizza. It should be here—"

"Not hungry," she snapped. "I'll be upstairs unpacking."

Lucas and I waited until she was gone, then exchanged a look.

"I believe a firm push is in order," he said.

"Before or after the pizza?"

"After. While I trust that we will be able to resolve this situation satisfactorily, in the unlikely event that things do go awry, I believe I am entitled to a last meal, even if it is pizza without pineapple."

"You want cookies?" I said. "I saw cookies downstairs."

"Chocolate chip?"

"Sure looked like it."

"Paige has been hiding them on me, has she? Bring some up, then. Savannah knows how to bake them."

The Nix spent dinner in Savannah's room, ostensibly unpacking. As we ate, I tried to resume the boy-talk conversation with Savannah, and earned myself a look of such horror that I spun around, expecting to see Jaime behind me with a hatchet. Seems that engaging in boy-talk while boys—or men—are present just isn't done, at least not if you're fifteen. Lucas seemed more than willing to join in, but after a murderous glare from Savannah, I changed the subject.

After dinner, I helped Lucas load the dishwasher and, with the aid of privacy spells, we discussed our next move. We decided to give the Nix one last chance. Lucas would help Savannah with her math homework while I retreated to Paige's office.

Once the cleanup was done, I thumped upstairs loud enough for the Nix to hear me. Then, for good measure, I called down from the top of the stairs, telling Lucas to hold my calls for the next hour.

Thirty minutes later footsteps sounded in the hall.

"Ready, Trsiel?" I whispered. "You'd better be right where you said you were going to be, 'cause this demi-demon is going down."

I reached up to Paige's hair and fingered the ribbon. As much as I longed to use my hands for this job, the situation seemed to call for something different. I slid from my chair, grabbed the second one, and pushed it behind the door. Then I climbed up on it, adding the extra elevation I needed. Life is so much easier when you're tall.

Balancing on the chair, I tugged out the ribbon. Then I wound it around my hands and waited. The doorknob turned. I crouched, ribbon at the ready.

The door opened, and Lucas walked in.

49

"DO YOU REALLY THINK THAT WOULD HAVE WORKED?" he asked, looking from the ribbon to me.

"With a binding spell, it would have," I said as I hopped down. "Let me guess. Our Nix is showing no signs of impending murderous rage."

"She came down to ask me to take a look at Paige's car."

"Huh?"

"She said it was making a noise when she drove it this afternoon."

I slumped into the chair. "I don't believe this."

"She insisted on giving me a demonstration, even when Savannah 'reminded' her that I know nothing about repairing automobiles, that my mechanical expertise is limited to motorcycles."

"Oh? Oh. I get it. She wants you outside. Away from me, and away from Savannah."

"Precisely. Either she is uncomfortable taking on you with me in the house, or she wants to begin with me, preferably outside, where"—he waved at the window—"it is fast growing dark."

"Ah-ha. Maybe we're making progress after all. But if you go outside, I'm going with you, which is going to cause a problem if I'm the target—"

A scream ripped through the house.

"Oh, my God," I said. "Savannah!"

As I jumped from the chair, Lucas raced across the room, toward the window.

"They're in the living room," he said as he yanked open the window. "Take the stairs. I'll come in the front door. Whoever is first, distract. Whoever is second, attack from the rear."

I was in the hall as his last words floated out to me, muffled as he climbed through the window. I hit the top of the steps running so fast I nearly flew down them face-first.

Another shriek. Then, "You little bitch!"

A blur raced around the corner from the living room and plowed into me as I galloped down the last few steps.

"Get down!" Savannah hissed, pushing me down on the stairs.

"Sav—"

She clamped a hand over my mouth and, holding me down, cast a cover spell over both of us. The Nix strode into the doorway, knife in hand. Blood poured from her nose. She swiped a hand across it.

"Where'd you go, bitch?" She looked from side to side. "Come out, come out, wherever you are."

She smiled, voice taking on a high-pitched singsong that I knew didn't come from the Nix. A ghost had indeed crashed the Nix's party—but it wasn't Jaime.

The woman turned and strode into the living room. I moved, breaking the spell. Still pinning me to the stairs, Savannah cast a privacy spell.

"It's not Jaime," she whispered. "She's possessed, some kind of ghost got into her. We were sitting there talking, and all of a sudden she—"

As the footsteps returned, Savannah cast another cover spell. She held me down. Protecting me. I knew it was Paige she was really protecting, but still, the thought of my little girl taking charge like this, escaping from a killer, protecting *me* . . . Kris was right. Savannah didn't need my help anymore. She hadn't needed it for a long time.

The woman walked into the hall, and took another look around, snuffling blood.

"Can't hide, sweetie-pie," she said. "Cheri knows all your tricks. Yes, indeed. All the tricks. No one escapes from her."

Cheri MacKenzie. Shit! So that's what happened. The parasitic Nix was getting a taste of her own medicine, having her body invaded by a past partner. Ironic, and I'm sure I'd appreciate it a whole lot more if it didn't complicate matters so much. Was the Nix still in there? What if I risked Jaime's life and found no one inside except Cheri MacKenzie?

MacKenzie took one last look up and down the hall, then strode into the living room. Savannah broke the cover spell. As she did, I noticed blood seeping through her sleeve. I grabbed her arm and tried to push up the sleeve.

"It's nothing, Paige," she said, pulling away. "Where's Lucas?"

The front doorknob turned. Seeing it, Savannah started to leap up.

"We have to warn—" she began.

I tugged her down. "He knows. Let him come in and distract her, then we'll attack from behind."

The door slid open a few inches. But there was no one there. I was about to move when I realized Lucas was hidden under a cover spell. I pointed to the living room and motioned for him to go in, then I cast a cover spell over Savannah and me.

Lucas broke his cover spell and banged the door open. MacKenzie bolted from the living room, saw Lucas, and stopped in the middle of the hall, her back to us.

"Where is she?" Lucas said, striding into the hall.

"Your wife or your pretty young ward?" Cheri purred. "Which one interests you more?"

"Where are they?" Lucas's gaze flew to the knife in Cheri's hand. "If you've hurt them—"

"You'll do what? Tell me I'm a very naughty girl and send me to bed? Then come up and climb in with me? Bet you've thought of doing that with her, haven't you? Your naughty ward?"

I don't know who looked more disgusted, Lucas or Savannah. I motioned for Savannah to approach from the left while I slid across the hall to the other side.

"I'll make you a deal," Cheri said, sliding over to Lucas. "Help me catch her, and I'll let you have her. How old is she, fifteen, sixteen? And still a virgin. I can tell. Would you like—"

Lucas coldcocked her.

"So much for distract and attack," I muttered.

As MacKenzie flew back from the blow, I grabbed her and slammed her into the wall. Or that was what I intended to do. But I was in Paige's unathletic body, and Jaime was four or five inches taller. So the slam became more of a shove, and MacKenzie bounced off the wall and rebounded my way, knife raised. Lucas knocked me out of her path.

I hit the floor and cast a binding spell. MacKenzie stabbed Lucas in the thigh. I cast again.

"Binding doesn't work!" Savannah said as she raced toward them. "I already tried. Use something else!"

I cast a shock bolt and flung my hand at MacKenzie. Nothing happened. Shit! Paige must not know it. *What does she know? Think, think . . . Fireball!*

I cast the spell just as Lucas threw MacKenzie into the wall. The ball hit the empty space between them, and nearly singed Lucas's face. He shot me a "be careful" look, grabbed MacKenzie by the right elbow, and squeezed hard enough to make her yelp . . . and drop the knife. As MacKenzie dove for the knife, Savannah cast a sorcerer pull-spell, and yanked it out of the way. I ran forward and kicked it into the dining room. Paige's body might not be equipped for lightning-fast roundhouse kicks, but it could manage that.

"Oh, Lord, why hast thou forsaken me?"

We all turned to MacKenzie . . . or what had been MacKenzie. She stood in the middle of the hall, arms raised to the ceiling, tears streaming down her face.

"Have I not served you well, Lord?" she cried. "Did I not do it all for you? Your faithful servant on earth? And for that you punish me?"

"What the hell?" Savannah muttered.

"She's changed," I said. "It's someone else."

The newcomer turned on me, red-rimmed eyes blazing. "It was you, wasn't it? You betrayed me."

She dove at me. Lucas kicked her legs out from under her and she crumpled to the floor. As I ran for her, Lucas started to cast a spell, and I stopped short, before I got in the line of fire.

Jaime—or whoever was in Jaime—looked up at Lucas, and her eyes filled with genuine terror.

"D-don't hurt me," she whimpered. "I'm sorry. I'm so

sorry. I didn't mean to do it. It was all her fault. Victoria's. Please don't hurt me anymore."

Lucas hesitated. I started to cast a spell, but he stepped in front of the woman on the floor, who'd begun to sob.

"Wait," he said. "This isn't your Nix."

"And it's not an innocent bystander, either. It's one of her partners. That hurt she's talking about—it ain't from heaven."

He hesitated, then started to step away. The woman leapt up. I lifted my hands in a knock-back spell, and Lucas wheeled to grab her, but she lunged out of our paths and raced into the dining room, heading for the knife. Savannah was closest. She turned and ran after the woman.

"No!" I shouted.

As Lucas ran for the dining room, I cast a knock-back spell, aiming it at Savannah, to knock her away from the woman. But Savannah moved too fast, and the spell missed her by a good six inches, hitting Lucas instead and sending him flying across the room. The woman grabbed Savannah from behind. Savannah let out an oath and twisted. Then her eyes went wide as the woman pressed the knifepoint to the base of her skull. Lucas and I both stopped.

"What a pretty child," the woman crooned. She reached up to stroke Savannah's hair.

"Let her go, Suzanne," I said.

Simmons turned toward me, frowning. "You know me? How strange. Is this pretty child yours?"

She looked me—Paige—up and down, then glanced at Lucas. "No, she's much too old to be yours. A niece perhaps?"

Simmons paused, eyes rolling back in her head. Then

she smiled. "Oh, how interesting. So this child belongs to *her,* the one who tricked me."

She traced the knifepoint around to Savannah's throat. A paper-thin trail of blood welled up on Savannah's neck.

I snarled and started to lunge at her, but a motion from Lucas stopped me. Behind Simmons's back, he shook his head. He was right, of course. I was a dozen feet away. She could slit my daughter's throat before I got to her.

"Oh, I will enjoy this," Simmons said, eyes glimmering with the same hunger I'd seen in the visions and in the cemetery. "Now, where to begin . . . ?"

Lucas motioned again, signaling an idea. I gave the barest nod. Lucas counted down on his fingers as his lips moved in a cast.

Three, two, one.

He launched a fireball, hitting Simmons in the back of the head. The moment she stumbled forward, I slammed Savannah with a knock-back spell, throwing her backward, out of Simmons's grip. Lucas grabbed Savannah and shoved her behind him, then went after the knife.

I raced across the room and snatched Simmons's arm as she spun back toward Lucas and Savannah. I yanked, and kicked at her feet, and she went down. While I fought to hold Simmons, Lucas said something to Savannah. They both cast binding spells. Simmons's arm lashed out at me. Her hand bounced off my shoulder. She growled and kicked, but could barely move her legs.

"It's working," I called to them. "Well enough, at least."

I pinned Simmons easily. As my hands went to her throat, Simmons's eyes blazed. Then her gaze went dull, empty. I squeezed, and her eyes closed. I hesitated. Shit! What if the binding spell killed her? It obviously wasn't working the way it should. Maybe—

Jaime's body leapt up, nearly throwing me off. I held on tight and put my full weight on her. I looked back into her eyes, and knew Simmons was gone.

"Welcome back," I said. "You're a little late, though."

The Nix's lips curled and she bucked beneath me. I squeezed harder. Out of the corner of my eye I saw Lucas jump to his feet.

"Keep binding her!" I said. "It's still working. Start a fresh cast."

They did. It didn't bind the Nix, but it kept her demonic strength in check. I bent over her, looking into her bulging eyes as I continued to squeeze her neck.

"Wanna count down with me?" I said. "I figure you have about thirty seconds left."

"Paige!" Savannah yelled. "Stop it! That's still Jaime. You can't kill her."

I tightened my grip. "Lucas, take her out of here. Please."

Savannah had broken her cast, but the Nix had almost stopped struggling, eyelids flagging as she faded from consciousness.

"Paige! No!"

Savannah grabbed my shoulder to wrench me off Jaime's body. I looked up into her eyes.

"It's not Paige, baby," I said. "It's me."

She blinked. "M-Mom?"

And here was my long-dreamed reunion. At last, looking into my daughter's eyes and having her looking back, knowing it was me . . . and I had my hands wrapped around the throat of her friend, choking the life from her.

"You have to go, baby," I whispered. "Please. I know what I'm doing. Lucas will explain. I'll take care of Jaime. I promise."

She just stared at me, eyes wide. "Mom?"

I tore my gaze away from hers and looked at Lucas, standing behind her. He nodded and put his hands on her shoulders.

"I'll be right outside," Lucas murmured to me. "Call me when you need to bring her back."

He whispered something to Savannah, and she let him lead her from the room. I could feel her stunned gaze on my back until they turned the corner. Then I looked down at the Nix and squeezed. When her body went limp, I held her down and waited for Trsiel to do his job.

Would I know when Trsiel had captured the Nix's spirit? How? I looked down at Jaime's face. Her lips had turned blue and her eyes were glassy, pupils dilated. Shit! I needed to start CPR soon. But if I started it too soon, she might resuscitate before Trsiel had the Nix.

"Lucas!"

By the time he got here, Trsiel was bound to have the Nix. Then he could start CPR and maybe, just maybe, the Fates would give me a few moments with my daughter before they whisked me back.

The back door clicked. Jaime's body began to pulse with a dull glow. As Lucas's running steps tapped up the rear steps, that glow began to separate from Jaime's body, just as it had in the community center.

The Nix's spirit condensed, taking on the features of her true form. Lucas rounded the corner, limping from his wounded leg. I held up a hand.

"Just give it a sec. It's almost over. Is Savannah—?"

"Outside," he said, dropping beside Jaime. He checked her pulse, then turned to me. "She's fading. I need to start—"

"Wait. Just a few more seconds." I cast a quick look around. "Damn it, Trsiel. Where are you?"

"So that's the Nix?" Lucas said, one hand still monitoring Jaime's pulse, the other gesturing at the Nix's spirit.

I started to nod, then stopped. "You can see her? Oh, shit! We shouldn't be able to see her. She should be on the other side. That means Trsiel can't—"

"Eve! We're losing—"

His lips parted in a silent oath, and his head whipped down to Jaime's and started CPR. The Nix's spirit writhed and twisted. For a second, I saw her face clearly in the fog. I grabbed at her, but my hands went right through her form. She threw back her head and laughed. Then, with one last twist, she tore herself free, shot up to the ceiling, and disappeared.

"Goddamn it!"

I drove my fist into the wall. Then I squeezed my eyes shut and took a deep breath. Okay, so it hadn't worked. The kids were still safe. As for the Nix, I'd catch her again, this time in the ghost world, where she couldn't escape so easily.

I knelt beside Jaime.

"Is she okay?" I asked. "What can I do?"

He pulled back and began chest compressions. "We lost her for a second, but I think she's coming back. Can you take over the—?"

"Lucas?"

Savannah's voice drifted out from the back of the house. Her footsteps clomped across the kitchen floor.

"Mom?"

"In here, baby. Come—"

A bone-chilling scream cut me short. I sprang to my feet and raced for the kitchen.

50

THE KITCHEN WAS EMPTY.

"She must still be outside," I said as I jogged to the back door. "Go back to Jaime. Make sure she's okay."

"If you need me—" Lucas began.

"I'll call."

I ran out the back door. Though the sun had fallen, the floodlights from the neighbor's yard lit the lawn to near-daylight, and I only needed a single sweep to know Savannah wasn't there. As I turned toward the drive, I glimpsed rheumy eyes glaring through the side fence. Lucas and Paige had erected a privacy fence around their yard, but there was just enough space between the slats for a determined neighbor to peer through.

"You!" I said, wheeling.

The old man wobbled back. I strode to the fence.

"Did you see a—Savannah, my ward—did you see her out here?"

"Watch your tone, girl," he snapped, coming back to the fence. "You—"

"Did you see her?"

"Ran off on you, didn't she? I may be old, but I'm not deaf. I heard them arguing out here, her and your husband. They can whisper all they want, but I know arguing when I hear it."

"Good for you. But Lucas went back inside and then—"

"Then the girl went back inside and someone screamed. I heard that. Don't think I didn't."

I gritted my teeth and wished those slits in the fence were a little wider, just wide enough to get my hand through and grab the old bugger by the throat.

"You saw her go back inside? And then she came out again?"

"Nope. Probably ran out the front door. You kids can't control that girl. And now she's run off, hasn't she? Good riddance, I say."

I flicked a knock-back spell at him. He hit the ground with a yelp.

"Hope you broke a hip," I mumbled as I ran back toward the house.

I threw open the door to the lean-to and crossed the darkened shed, gaze fixed on the still-open back door. Something fell on my back. I went down, slamming face-first into the concrete floor. Knees jabbed into my back and fingers dug into my shoulders.

I tried to flip over, but the hands went to my neck and squeezed so hard I barely had time to register pain before everything went dark.

I came to on my back. Savannah stared down at me, face twisted in hate and rage. For a second, my gut went ice-cold. She thought I'd killed Jaime, maybe even Paige. Then I looked into her eyes, and knew my daughter wasn't in there.

The Nix leaned down, her hands still locked around my throat.

"How does it feel, witch? I could snap your neck right now. Could have done it the moment I grabbed you. But this is more poetic, don't you think? Kill you the same way you tried to kill me."

I squirmed, but her demonic strength pinned me to the cold floor.

"I suppose I should thank you. Had I known I could leap bodies, I wouldn't have wasted my time in that silly necromancer." She closed her eyes and shivered. "This is a body truly worthy of a demon. So young and so powerful."

I opened my mouth to cast, but could only gasp.

"Now it'll be no trouble pinning the blame on your daughter, when it really is her hands choking the life from her guardian."

Her grip tightened and the world dipped into blackness. I fought to stay conscious, writhing beneath her, trying to get an arm or leg free.

"Why do you struggle?" she said. "You aren't going to die. You already did. You'll just return to where you were. It's the little witch who will suffer for your failure. Her and her husband, killed by their dear—"

The Nix jerked back, her grip loosening. She looked up over my head.

"Wait your turn, sorcerer," she snarled.

I tilted my head back to see Lucas pull a shovel from the wall.

"Get off her," he said.

The Nix's eyes went wide. "Lucas? What are you—?"

"I know you aren't Savannah," he said, voice level. "Now get off her."

As he pulled the shovel back, I wriggled out from

under the Nix. She didn't even seem to notice, just smiled and got to her feet. Lucas swung back the shovel.

"Do you really think you can do that?" she asked. "What if you kill her? Hit just the right spot, and down she goes, never to get up again."

Lucas hesitated. I opened my mouth to tell him to do it, to hit her on the shoulder or the torso, just knock her down, but my bruised throat wouldn't let out anything more than a gasp. Lucas dropped the shovel and raised his hands to cast. The Nix charged.

I pushed to my feet, gasping for breath. The Nix grabbed Lucas by the arm and whipped him against the wall. His head struck a beam. She threw his limp body aside and turned on me.

I cast the anti-demon spell. Even as the words left my lips, panic shot through me. Did Paige know this spell? What else—

The Nix went rigid. Her limbs convulsed and she toppled back to the floor. I dove for her, but she kicked me away, stumbled to her feet, and staggered through the back door, into the house. Her footfalls stumbled down the stairs. Perfect. There was no escape route from the windowless basement. She'd have to come back this way. That anti-demon spell had almost drained Paige's reserve, and I was still gasping for air. I needed a moment. I looked down at Lucas. *He* needed me to take a moment.

I knelt beside Lucas and felt his pulse. Still strong. I cast a couple of healing spells in succession. It zapped the rest of Paige's spell-casting power, but I knew it was what she'd want me to do. After another quick check of his pulse and breathing, I leaned back on my heels and struggled to catch my breath.

The Nix was in Savannah. To stop her, I'd need to do what Lucas hadn't been able to do—attack my daughter.

I pushed to my feet and ran into the house.

I touched down on the last step and paused there, scanning the dark basement. To my left was the freezer and cold cellar. To my right, the laundry room. Behind me would be two more rooms—

A roar. I looked up to see Savannah running at me from the workshop. As she charged, she swung a hammer back over her head. And I did nothing. I couldn't. I knew this wasn't Savannah and yet that's who I saw—my child running at me, hammer raised, face contorted with hate.

At the last second, I sprang from the step. The hammer smashed into my shoulder blade. Bone cracked. Paige's bone, not mine. I tried not to think of that, that every blow I took, every injury I allowed, she would suffer afterward. Before the Nix said that, I hadn't considered the implications of borrowing this body, but now, as I danced out of the reach of that flying hammer, it was all I *could* think about.

I cast a fireball, but the Nix brushed it off. What did she care about burns and scars and broken bones? It wasn't her body. Only lethal spells could stop her, and that was one step I'd never take, no matter how bad things got. While she'd been in Jaime's body, there had always been that option, however much I would have regretted it. But now, as we faced off, I saw how powerless I really was in this struggle. So long as she was in my daughter's body, I wouldn't do anything that might seriously harm her. And so long as I was in Paige's body, I wouldn't take any risk that might seriously harm *her*.

The Nix lunged, hammer raised. I spun to the side but, still unaccustomed to this body, I stumbled as I came out of the spin. The hammer hit me again in the shoulder, in the same spot. I howled and crumpled. As I fell, I grabbed for the hammer with my other hand. I managed to snag the head. The Nix swung the hammer and my feet flew out from under me, but I hung on, and the handle slid from her grip.

As I hit the floor, I rolled, ignoring the lightning bolt of pain that shot through my shoulder. I leapt to my feet, still holding the hammer. The Nix rushed at me. I flipped the hammer around and swung. My first instinct was to aim at her upper torso, but at the last second, seeing my daughter's face, I couldn't do it. I swung low. With the sudden change in direction, and the one-handed swing, the blow only glanced off her hip. She grabbed the hammer, threw it aside, and slammed me down to the floor.

In that second, as I went down, I knew there was only one way to save Paige and Savannah.

"I'm sorry, Kris," I whispered as I hit the floor.

The Nix pinned me. Her hands went around my throat. I closed my eyes and sent up two silent words.

"I'm ready."

The room flashed, filling with a bolt of light so bright it blinded me. The light flared again. This time the bolt hit me, filling me with a white-hot heat.

I reached up with my good arm, grabbed the Nix's forearm, and wrenched it from my throat. Her eyes widened. She looked into mine, blinked in surprise, then curled back her lip.

"You think that will help you, *angel*?" she said.

"I sure as hell hope so," I said as I pushed myself up. "It cost me more than I could afford to pay."

She pinned me again. We struggled. I could feel the new strength coursing through me, but it wasn't enough. My shoulder still pulsed with pain, and I could barely move that arm. The best I could do was hold her off. After a few minutes of tussling for the upper hand, I managed to get on top of her. Before I could reach for her throat, she grabbed both my arms and held them fast. Then she looked into my eyes and smiled.

"You can still do it," she said. "All you need to do is kill me. You must have a lethal spell locked in that little brain somewhere. Go ahead. Try it."

Oh, I had a spell, all right. But not the kind she was hoping I'd use. As the last words of the anti-demon spell left my lips, I tensed, ready to rip my hands from her grasp the moment the shock wave hit her.

Nothing happened.

I tried again, tongue tripping over the words. But it was too late. Paige didn't know the anti-demon spell well enough to cast it reliably, and now I'd wasted her power on a miscast.

I'd sacrificed my afterlife to become an angel, and I still couldn't save them. I was going to fail . . . and lose everything.

"Something wrong?" the Nix said, laughing.

She pushed up on my forearms and my body started to lift off hers. I struggled to stay on top, but the cast had sapped more than spell-power. She flipped me off her. When I tried to roll out of the way, she grabbed me and threw me onto my back. Then she pounced, landing on my chest so hard the air flew from my lungs. Her face came down to mine. I started a binding spell, a desperate last-ditch attempt to—

"Wait!"

The voice was distant, almost inaudible. A woman's voice, coming from somewhere inside me.

"Try this," it whispered.

Words flew into my head. The start of an incantation. I didn't have time to think. I opened my mouth and said the words, repeating them as they came. Greek. Something to do with wind. A witch spell.

The Nix gasped. Her head flew back, eyes widening in shock. She whipped her head forward, lips twisting in a snarl. Her hands started for my throat, then stopped as her mouth opened and closed, gasping for breath. Her eyes met mine. I saw my daughter's eyes, bulging, her lips turning blue. And I couldn't do it. I stopped casting.

"No!" the voice whispered. "Keep going."

I hesitated. I was going to kill my daughter. My daughter! No, I couldn't do this. I couldn't take the chance. What if—

"Close your eyes and cast. It'll be okay."

I gritted my teeth and forced my eyes closed. Then I restarted the cast. I could hear the Nix gasping. My daughter's voice gasping. My daughter struggling to breathe, dying. I dug my nails into my palms and kept casting, every fiber in me tensed, waiting for that final breath.

Savannah collapsed onto me. She'd stopped breathing. I flipped her over, mouth going down to hers.

Then I saw the spirit-glow pulsing around her. The Nix. I had to stop her first. No! I had to save my daughter. I stopped, frozen, staring at Savannah and the yellowish aura leeching from her body.

Stop the Nix and you save Savannah.

I tore my gaze from my daughter and pushed to my feet. I put out my hands. My lips moved automatically in another unfamiliar incantation and the sword appeared. Hands trembling, I forced my fingers around the hilt. Then I stepped back, looked down at Savannah one last time, and swung the sword at the Nix.

I saw it connect. Saw it slice into her. Saw her throw back her head in a howl of rage. Footsteps raced down the steps. I looked up to see Lucas running down. I opened my mouth to call to him. Then everything went dark.

51

"SAVANNAH!"

I jerked up my head to see the middle Fate standing at her wheel.

"Where's—?" I began, rushing forward.

She held up a hand and I stopped as abruptly as if I'd hit a wall. With a wave of that hand, a circle of light appeared before me. In it I saw Savannah, sitting up, rubbing the back of her head, Lucas and Paige crouched beside her. The Fate motioned again, and the scene disappeared.

"Sh-she's okay," I said.

"She's fine."

"And the Nix. Did it work? Did I catch—"

"You did. She's back where she belongs."

I stood there a moment, struggling to take it in. When I did, I remembered the price I'd paid for this victory.

"I'm an angel now, aren't I?" I whispered.

She nodded.

"And you can't undo that, can you?"

A slow, sad shake of her head.

I shook off the terror and grief settling into my gut, pulled myself up straight, and looked her in the eye. "I owed you a favor, but I went way beyond repaying that. I gave up everything I had in this world to repay it. You said I have to leave this dimension, that I can't stay with Kristof, but I don't understand—"

"You will," she said softly. "Everything will change for you now, Eve. An angel can't stay here. It's not an arbitrary rule. It's a necessity. You are an angel now, so you must live in their world."

"Then I will, too," said a voice behind me.

I turned to see Kristof there. I stepped toward him, but hit a barrier. I wheeled back on the Fate.

"So this is it? I can't even go near him? Goddamn it, I don't deserve this! Maybe I did some awful things in my life, but I do *not* deserve this."

"This is not a punishment, Eve."

"Well, it sure as hell feels like one."

Kristof cleared his throat. "You said she can't stay here. That's fine. I'll go with her."

The elderly Fate appeared. "You will, will you? You'd have no place there, Kristof, no more than she'd have here."

He crossed his arms. "She made her sacrifice, now I'm making mine."

"Very noble, but the answer is no. We need you here."

"For what? To play ghost lawyer? There are thousands of—"

"Don't question us, Kristof. We have our reasons, and our plans. And your place is here." She turned to me. "And your place is there, with the angels. But there is a way . . ." The old Fate's lips curved a fraction, in something almost like a smile. "There's always a way."

Kristof stepped forward. Before either of us could ask, she moved to the edge of the dais. Then, with a lift of her fingers, she levitated to the floor. One stride and she was beside me. I blinked. She was so tiny, not even reaching my shoulder. She laid a hand on my arm. Her bright eyes looked up into mine.

"You said this feels like a punishment. Do you really think we'd be so cruel, Eve? Yes, we wanted you to join our angels, but when you refused, we accepted that. What you did down there, the sacrifice you made . . . I won't say I underestimated you, because I've always known what you were capable of"—a sly smile—"with the right prompting. But this sacrifice none of us expected. When you made it, we decided we'd do all we could to make it easier on you."

"So I get to stay—"

"In the ghost world? No. That, I'm afraid, is impossible." She returned to the dais, but stayed in front of the wheel. "If there's one thing you clearly understand, Eve, it's the nature of a bargain. You give and you take, in even proportion. That's what we can offer."

The child Fate appeared. "Do you know the story of Persephone and Demeter?"

"A Greek myth to explain the seasons, I think," I said.

"That's right. Hades, Lord of the Underworld, wanted Persephone for his bride, so he stole her away. Her mother beseeched the gods for help, and they made a deal with Hades, that Persephone would spend summers on earth and winters in the underworld. How does that sound?" Her pretty face scrunched up. "Well, not exactly that, but something like it."

Before we could answer, her middle sister took over.

"You now have a job to do, Eve, and we expect you to

do it. You also have another life to lead, and we want you to do that. Half the year you will be with the angels, and half you will live here, with Kristof, as a ghost."

I looked at Kristof. He smiled.

"We'll take it."

Epilogue

THE BIBLE TELLS US THAT GOD CREATED THE EARTH IN a week. I don't know much about religious history, but I do remember that one. As for whether it's true, I'll leave that to the scholars. All I know is that a lot can happen in a week. You can go from being a ghost pining for your daughter to a heavenly bounty-hunter on the trail of a demi-demon killer. And you can go from reluctant crusader to full-time angel, locking yourself into an eternal contract as a protector of justice. And other times, the transition isn't so obvious, but in its own way, just as life-altering.

It had been a week since I brought in the Nix. I was still in the ghost world—the Fates had given me one more month here, as I prepared for my passage to the angel world. I still didn't know what to expect. I'd already sat through two days of orientation crap, but most of it had consisted of a list of rules too long for anyone without a full-blooded angel's perfect memory . . . or, at least, that was the excuse I'd use when I started breaking them.

At the end of the week, the Fates gave Trsiel and me our first assignment. Nothing tough—just a routine rousting of some haunters, but with definite possibilities for fun. Before I embarked on that, though, there was something I had to do.

Kristof accompanied me as far as Lucas and Paige's backyard. I stood in that yard for a while, looking up at the house, remembering what it had smelled like, what it had felt like to be there, really there, committing it all to memory. Then, slowly, I released Kris's hand and headed for the back door.

When I stepped inside, Lucas and Paige were in the kitchen, Lucas's back against the counter, a dish towel over his shoulder, Paige leaning against him, holding his hands, face raised to his as they talked in murmurs.

"Hey, guys," I said softly. "Just came by to say thanks. I know you can't hear me, but I wanted to say it anyway. Thanks for everything. You're doing a great job with her. An amazing job."

Lucas chuckled at something Paige said, and brushed a curl off her cheek.

The back door banged open.

"Anybody home?" a voice shouted, loud enough to shake the rafters.

I turned to see a young man with light-brown hair, broad shoulders, and a broader grin. A familiar face, at least in this house.

"Adam!" Paige disengaged from Lucas and turned as Adam caught her up in a hug, being careful not to jar her injured shoulder. "This is a surprise. I didn't expect you until Monday."

"The real surprise is yet to come." Adam winked over her head at Lucas. "So are we ready for Monday's meeting? Jaime's coming, isn't she? Recovered from her ordeal?"

As they talked, I slipped to the doorway.

"Bye, guys," I whispered. "I wish you all the best. You deserve it."

I found Savannah in her room, dressed in jeans and a bra, talking on the phone as she surveyed a bed covered in shirts.

". . . taking Paige away for the weekend," she said. "Romantic getaway, big surprise and all that." She paused, then snorted. "Yeah, I wish. I can't stay overnight by myself until I'm eighteen. Can you believe that? So they called in Adam."

She lifted two shirts and held them up, one after the other, peering at her reflection in the mirror, then tossing both on the floor with a lip-twist of disgust.

"Yeah, yeah, he's cute, but he's even older than Paige." Pause. "Twenty-six." She pulled a face. "That's sick! No way."

She grabbed a T-shirt from the bed, mumbled "Hold on," then pulled it over her head. It was at least two sizes too small. She looked in the mirror, checking it out from all angles, then gave a nod of satisfaction and reached for her hairbrush with one hand and the phone with the other.

"I have to go, baby," I said as she brushed her hair, still chattering to her friend. "I won't be coming around like I used to, and I just wanted to tell you that. You know it doesn't mean anything's changed. You're still the best damned thing I ever did. But you've got your life, and now, finally, maybe I have mine."

A double-knock at the door.

"What?" Savannah yelled.

"Everyone decent?" Adam called. "I'm coming in."

As Savannah swiped on lip gloss, Adam jangled the door handle. She flew across the room and threw it open.

"What the hell are you doing?" she said. "This is my room. You can't just barge in here."

He rolled his eyes. "Oh, I was just getting you going." He strolled in and looked around. "See you haven't cleaned it since the last time I was here."

"Hey, this is my room! Get out!"

He turned to do just that, and she grabbed him by the arm.

"Don't I even get a hello?" she said. "God, you're so rude."

I shook my head and smiled as they bantered.

"Poor baby," I said. "It's just not going away, is it?" I skirted past them to the door. "I have to leave, but I'll be back to check on you now and then." I hesitated, then stepped closer to Savannah, and leaned over to kiss her cheek. "I know you'll be okay, baby. You don't need me to make sure of that."

I turned to the hall. Savannah sputtered something at Adam, and he laughed. I walked to the top of the stairs, and hesitated. One more look. Just one more—

I squared my shoulders, and walked down the stairs, through the kitchen, and out into the yard, where Kristof was waiting.

About the Author

Kelley Armstrong lives in Ontario with her family. Visit her Web site at www.kelleyarmstrong.com.

Be sure not to miss

BROKEN

the next exhilarating novel from

Kelley Armstrong

This time, everyone's favorite werewolf,

Elena Michaels, returns—

in an edge-of-your-seat thriller

that is sure to delight!

Coming from Seal Books in May 2006

Here's a special preview:

BROKEN

On Sale May 2006

I LOPED ALONG THE PATH, MUZZLE SKIMMING OVER THE ground. The earth was thick with the scent of my prey— a deliberate move, weaving and circling, permeating this patch of forest with his smell, hoping to throw me off the trail. Did he really think it would be that easy? If so, he'd underestimated me—a mistake he'd soon regret.

I untangled the web of trails, and latched on to the most recent. As his scent separated from the others, I picked up speed, the ground whooshing past beneath me. Ahead, the trail opened into a clearing. I pitched forward, straining for the open run. Before I hit the edge of the clearing, I dug in my claws and skidded to a graceless stop.

I stood there, heart tripping, adrenaline roaring, urging me to keep running, find him, take him down. I closed my eyes and shuddered. Too eager. Keep that up and I'd run straight into a trap. After a moment, the adrenaline rush ebbed and I started forward, cautious now, ears straining, muzzle up, sniffing as I walked.

It was my eyes that saved me this time. That and the sun, peeking from fast-moving clouds. One break in the cloud cover and I caught the glint of gold through the trees. He was upwind, crouched to the left of the path's end, waiting for me to come barreling out.

I retraced my last few steps by walking backward. Some things easily accomplished on two legs are much more difficult to coordinate with four. Once I'd gone as far as I could, I craned to look over my shoulder. The trees closed in on me from either side. Not enough room to guarantee a silent about-face.

I took a careful step off the path. The undergrowth was soft and moist with spring rain. I prodded at it, but it stayed silent. Hunkering down to stay below branch level, I started forward. I looped around and slunk up behind him. Once close enough to see through the trees, I peered out. He was crouched there, beside the entrance to the woods, as still as a statue, only the twitch of his tail betraying his impatience.

I found the clearest line of fire, hunched down, then sprang. I hit him square on the back and sunk my teeth into the ruff around his neck. He yelped and reared up, trying to throw me free, but I held on, tasting blood as my teeth sank in for a better hold. With a snarl, he bucked and I toppled over his head. But I didn't let go, and he crashed down with me.

Fangs slashed at my foreleg, but I jerked it out of the way in time. My claws caught the side of his muzzle and he grunted, pulling back fast. He started to rise, then rolled on top of me. The sudden move caught me by surprise and, as the air whooshed from my lungs, I let go of his ruff. I pitched out of his reach, then jumped to my feet and turned around, ready to stave off attack. Instead, I caught only the flash of a gold tail as he dove back into the forest.

With a growl, I tore after him. I caught up just inside the forest and vaulted onto his back. We went down together, rolling and snarling and biting. Then teeth clamped around the bottom of my muzzle. As I struggled, he forced my head back, exposing my throat. I kicked at his underbelly. He snorted as my claws made contact, but didn't let go. He pushed me onto my back and pinned me. Then he released my muzzle and looked down at me, indecision flickering in his eyes. His head shot down to my throat, and I wriggled frantically, trying to pull out of the way, but he only buried his nose in the ruff around my neck and inhaled deeply. Then he shuddered, legs vibrating against my sides. A moment's hesitation. Then a soft growl, and he twisted off me and dove into the woods again.

I scrambled to my feet and set off in pursuit. This time, he had too much of a head start, and I could only get close enough to see his hindquarters bounding ahead, teasing me. He flicked his tail up. Mocking me, damn him. I surged foward, getting close enough to hear the pound of his heartbeat. Then he veered and crashed into the forest, off the trail. I chortled to myself. Now I had him. Cutting a fresh path would slow him down just enough to let me—

A brace of ptarmigan flew up, almost under my feet, and I skidded to a halt, nearly flipping over backward in my surprise. As the panicked birds took to the sky, I got my bearing again, looked around . . . and found myself alone. Tricked. Damn him. And damn me for falling for it.

I found his trail and loped after him. Before I'd gone a hundred feet, a soft gurgling moan rippled through the silence. I stopped, ears going up. A grunt, then panting. He was Changing. Did he think that would save him? Not likely.

I dove into the nearest thicket and began my own Change. It came fast, spurred by a healthy double shot of adrenaline and frustration. When I finished, he was still in his thicket.

I crept around to the other side, pulled back a handful

of leaves and peered through. He was done, but recovering, crouched on all fours, panting as he caught his breath. By the rules of fair play, I should have given him time to recuperate. But I wasn't in the mood for rules.

I sprang onto his back. Before he could react, my arm went around his neck, forearm jammed against his windpipe.

I leaned over his shoulder. "Did you think you could escape that easily?"

His lips formed an oath, but no sound came out. His shoulders slumped, as if defeated. Like I was stupid enough to buy that. I pretended to relax my grip. Sure enough, the second I did, he reared up. I threw myself backward. The added momentum jarred him off balance and we both went down. As we fell, I twisted and landed beside him. Before he could recover, I was on top of him, my forearm against his throat. His hands slid up my sides, snuck around and cupped my breasts.

"Uh-uh," I growled, pressing against his windpipe. "No distractions."

He sighed and let his hands slide away. I eased back. As soon as I did, he vaulted up, toppling me over. A second later, I was flat on my back with him on top of me. He pinned me as securely as he had in wolf-form. Then he lifted up, belly and groin pressing into mine. He slid his hands back to my breasts and grinned down at me, daring me to do something about it now.

I glared up at him. Then I shot forward and sank my teeth into his shoulder. He jerked away and I started to scramble up, but he caught me and we rolled over, nipping and growling, the bites now interspersed with rough kisses and rougher gropes. Finally, I got the upper position. I pinned him, hands on his shoulders, knees on his thighs. He struggled, but couldn't throw me off.

"Caught?" I said.

He gave one last squirm, then nodded. "Caught."

"Good."

I slid my knees from his thighs and slipped over him. He tried to thrust up to meet me, but I pushed down with my hips, keeping him still. I moved into position. When I felt the tip of him brush me, I stopped and wriggled against him, teasing myself. He groaned and tried to grab my hips, but I pinned his shoulders harder. Then I closed my eyes and plunged down onto him.

He struggled under me, trying to thrust, to grab, to control, but I kept him pinned. After a moment, he gave up and arched against the ground, fingers clenching handfuls of grass, jaw tensing, eyes closing to slits, but staying open, always open, always watching. The first wave of climax hit. I let him go then, but he stayed where he was, leaving me in control. Dimly, I heard him growl as he came and by the time I finished and leaned over him, he was laying back, eyes half-lidded, a lazy grin tweaking the corners of his mouth.

"You know," he said. "I'm almost going to be sorry when we do get you pregnant."

I laughed. "I thought *you* liked doing the chasing."

"I'm *accustomed* to doing the chasing. Spent ten years doing it." His grin broke through. "Nothing wrong with it, but being chased isn't so bad either."

I lowered my mouth to his, then caught a whiff of blood and pulled back. Blood trickled from his shoulder.

"Whoops," I said, licking my fingers and wiping it off. "Got a bit carried away. Sorry about that."

"Didn't hear me complaining." He brushed his fingertips across a fang-size hole under my jaws. "Seems I gave as good as I got anyway." He yawned and stretched, hands going around me and resting on my rear. "Just add them to the collection."

I ran my hand over his chest, fingers tracing across half-healed scabs and long-healed scars. Most of them were the dots of too-hard bites or the paper-thin scratches of misaimed claws. The residue of friendly fire. I had them too, tiny marks that wouldn't be noticed from more than a foot away, nothing to draw stares when I wore halter tops and shorts. I had few true battle scars. Clay had more, and as my hands moved over them, my brain ticked off the stories behind each. There wasn't one I didn't know, not a scar I couldn't find with my eyes closed, not a mark I couldn't explain.

He closed his eyes as my fingers moved down his chest. I looked up at his face, a rare chance to look at him without him knowing I was looking. I don't know why that still matters. It shouldn't. He knows how I feel about him. I want to have a child with him—it doesn't get any clearer than that, not for me. But after ten years of pushing him away, trying to pretend I didn't still love him, wasn't still crazy-in-love with him, I'm still cautious in some small ways. Maybe I always will be.

I shifted to look down at him. Gold eyelashes rested against his cheeks. His skin already showed the first beige tint of a tan. Now and then, when he was poring over a book, I caught the ghost of a line forming over the bridge of his nose, the first sign of an impending wrinkle. Not surprising, considering he turned forty-two this year. Werewolves age slowly, though, and Clay could still easily pass for a decade younger. Yet the wrinkle reminded me that we were getting older. I'd passed thirty-five this year, right around the time I'd finally decided that he was right, and I—we—were ready for a child. The two events were, I'm sure, not unconnected.

And now that I'd given myself permission to do something I'd been longing to do all my life, it wasn't happening. I told myself there was no rush. Five months of trying to get pregnant was nothing. I was as healthy and fit as a twenty-year-old. When the time came, it would come, and I had to stop worrying about it. Easy to say; near-impossible to do. I've spent a lifetime perfecting the art of fretting, and I'm not about to abandon my craft now.

My stomach growled. Clay's hand slid across it, smiling, eyes still closed.

"That's what happens when you chase me instead of dinner," he said.

"I'll remember that next time."

He opened one eye. "On second thought, forget it. Chase me and I'll feed you afterward. Anything you want."

"Ice cream."

He laughed and opened the other eye. "I thought that was *after* you get pregnant."

"I'm practicing."

"Ice cream it is, then. Do we have any?"

I slid off him. "The Creamery opened last week. Two-for-one banana splits all month."

"One for you and one for—"

I snorted.

He grinned. "Okay, two for you, two for me."

He pushed to his feet and looked around.

"Clothing southwest," I said. "Near the pond."

"Are you sure?"

"Let's hope so."

I stepped from the forest into the backyard. As the clouds swept past again, shafts of sunlight slid over the house. The freshly painted trim gleamed dark green, the color matching the tendrils of ivy that struggled to maintain a hold on the stone walls. The gardens below were equally green, evergreens and bushes interspersed with the occasional clump of tulips from a fall gardening spree a few years ago, the tulips ending at the patio wall, which was as far as I'd gotten before getting distracted and leaving the bag of bulbs to rot in the rain. That was our typical approach to gardening: every now and then we'd buy a plant or two, maybe even get it in the ground, but most times we were content just to sit back and see what came up naturally.

The casual air suited the house and the slightly overgrown yard that blended into the fields and forests beyond. A wild sanctuary, the air smelling of last night's fire and new grass and distant manure, the silence broken only by the twitter of birds, the chirp of cicadas . . . and the regular crack of gunfire.

As the next shot rang out, I pressed my hands to my ears and made a face. Clay motioned for us to circle back along the woods and come up on the opposite side. When we drew alongside the shed, I could make out a figure on the stone patio, his back to us. Tall, lean and dark-haired, that hair curling over his collar, as sporadically clipped as the lawn. He lifted the gun. Clay grinned, handed me his shoes, then broke into a silent lope, heading around the stone wall.

I kept walking, but slower, having a good idea what he was up to. By the time I neared the wall, he was already vaulting over it. He caught my gaze, and lifted his finger to his lips. As if I needed the warning. He crept up behind the gunman, paused, making sure he hadn't been heard, then crouched and sprang.

Jeremy sidestepped without even turning around. Clay hit the wall and yelped.

Jeremy shook his head. "Serves you right. You're lucky I didn't shoot you."

"Live dangerously, that's my motto."

"It'll be your epitaph, too."

Jeremy Danvers, our Pack Alpha and owner of Stonehaven, where Clay and I lived, and would doubtless continue to live for the rest of our lives. Part of that was because Clay was Jeremy's bodyguard, and had to say close, but mostly it was because he'd never consider leaving. Clay had been no more than five or six when he'd been bitten, and when other kids were heading off to kindergarten, he'd been living as a child werewolf in the Louisiana bayou. Jeremy had rescued him, brought him to Stonehaven, and raised him, and this was where Clay would stay, bound to his Alpha. Now it was my home too, had been really since the day Clay bit me, nearly fifteen years ago. I'll never ask Clay to leave, and he's grateful for that, but it's no sacrifice on my part. I'm happy here, with my family. Besides, without Jeremy to mediate, Clay and I would have killed each other years ago.

Jeremy watched as Clay bounded over to me. He slanted a look my way. "Good run, I take it?"

"Apparently so."

I handed Clay his shoes. Jeremy's gaze slid down to Clay's bare feet. He sighed.

"I'll find the socks next time," Clay said. "And look, Elena found that shirt she lost."

I held up a sweater I'd "misplaced" a few months ago. Jeremy's nose wrinkled as the smell wafted his way.

"Toss it out," he said.

"It's a little funky," I said. "But I'm sure a good washing, maybe some bleach . . ."

"In the garbage. The outside garbage. Please."

"We're going into town for ice cream," Clay said. "Wanna come?"

Jeremy shook his head. "You two go on. But I wouldn't mind you picking up a few steaks at the butcher. I thought we'd have a barbecue. And since Clay seems so energetic, maybe I can persuade him to cart out the lawn furniture and we'll eat outside tonight."

"Let's do that now," I said, swinging toward the shed. "Build up an appetite for those banana splits."

Clay caught my arm. "No lifting, remember?"

"That's *after* I get pregnant."

"But you could be pregnant already, right? We have to be careful."

I looked over at Jeremy, but he busied himself unloading his revolvers. I was reasonably sure you couldn't damage a fetus the size of a pea by lifting a lounge chair or two, especially not when werewolf strength made it the equivalent of picking up a plate, but if Jeremy wasn't going to back me up on this, I wouldn't argue with Clay. I was sure we'd have plenty of things to argue about if—no, *when*—I did get pregnant.

When it came to my health, Clay wasn't the only one overreacting. In the last six months, Jeremy had read just about every book ever written on pregnancy, and erred so far on the side of caution that, between the two of them, I'm surprised I was allowed to get up in the morning. The truth was that, no matter how many books Jeremy read, he couldn't be sure they applied to me at all. Female werewolves were very rare. For one to bear a child, even to a human father, was the thing of legend. Two werewolves reproducing? There was no record of it ever having happened. Maybe that's because it couldn't happen. Maybe all of our planning and dreaming—

"Come on," Clay said. "You can grab the lanterns. Race you there."

I looked at him and I knew he'd seen that look in my eyes, the dark shadow of panic that seemed to come over me several times a day now.

"No," Jeremy said. "You go. I need to talk to Elena."

As Clay headed for the shed, I wandered over to Jeremy and reached for the newly-emptied revolver on the wall. He slid it out of my hand's path and put it into its case.

I sighed. "It wasn't loaded."

"I'm not taking any chances."

I sighed again and leaned against the wall. Jeremy glanced over at Clay, who was moving away at one tenth his earlier speed. When Jeremy asked how I was feeling, Clay picked up his pace, curiosity fading. I said I was fine, then he asked, "Have you been taking the new vitamins?"

I gave him a look. He lifted a finger, then darted his gaze in Clay's direction, telling me to play along.

"Yes, I've been taking the new vitamins and, no, they don't seem to be upsetting my stomach like the last concoction. Next time, though, as long as you're mixing up a batch, think maybe you could add in some cherry flavor? Maybe mold them into little animals for me? Bunnies would be good. I like bunnies."

Clay's chuckle floated back to us, and he quickened his pace to a fast walk. Jeremy glanced over his shoulder, estimating werewolf hearing distance, then lowered his voice.

"Paige called while you were out," he said.

Clay stopped and wheeled. Jeremy grimaced.

"You tried," I murmered. "Does she want me to call her back?"

"No, actually she was just relaying a message. Someone's been trying to reach you. Xavier Reese."

"Reese?" Clay said, striding back now. "The guy from the compound?"

"That's the only Xavier I know."

"What the hell does he want?"

I had my suspicions "Did he leave a number with Paige?"

"You're not going to call him back, are you?" Clay said. "After what he—"

"He saved my life."

"Yeah? Well, if it hadn't been for him, your life wouldn't have needed saving. And I'm sure you didn't need rescuing anyway. You'd have been fine. The only reason he jumped in there to 'save' you was so he could hold a marker over you—" He stopped, jaw setting. "That better not be why he's calling."

I took the paper from Jeremy's hand. "I'll know in a few minutes."

"Hey, Elena!" the voice crackled across a weak cellular line. "Remember me?"

"Uh-huh."

I settled onto the sofa and pulled my legs up under me. Clay sat on the other end, leaning my way, making no effort to look like he wasn't eavesdropping. I didn't care. If I did, I wouldn't have let him in the room in the first place.

"Uh-huh?" Xavier said. "That's all I get after three years? We spent a harrowing week together, locked in an underground prison, fighting for survival—"

"I was fighting for survival. You were drawing a paycheck."

"Hey now, in my own way, I was just as much of a prisoner as you."

I snorted. "A prisoner of your own greed."

"Trapped by my shortcomings. It's tragic really."

"Know what'd be even more tragic? If you teleported into the middle of a wall and got trapped by your shortcomings there. Does that ever happen?"

"My momma taught me to always look where I'm going."

"Damn."

"Ouch. What did I ever do to you—er, better not answer that."

I glanced over at Clay, who motioned for me to hang up.

"What do you want, Xavier? I was just about to head out for ice cream."

"And that's more important than talking to me? No, wait, don't answer that either. Since you're obviously not going to play nice, I'll cut to the point. You owe me a favor."

"No, you said I owed you. I never agreed. As I recall, you offered the trade in return for giving me two pieces of advice about the compound, but you hightailed it out of there yourself before telling me the second."

"It was dogs. They had trained bloodhounds and attack dogs."

"Really? Oh, right, that's what attacked me and nearly ripped my throat out. Left a nice scar on my shoulder, too. Thanks for the warning."

"Okay, so you only owe me half a favor. And you could argue that one, too. I'm really only using that as an opener for a fresh deal. The beginning of what I hope will be a long and mutually profitable relationship. I'm a useful guy, Elena. I could really help you out."

"Uh-huh. So who's chasing you?"

"No one. Let me finish. Last year I started thinking

about this. That I should get in touch with you and renew our acquaintance."

"Uh-huh. And who was chasing you *then*?"

"A Cabal, but that's not the point."

"I'm not a bodyguard for hire, Xavier."

"And that isn't what I have in mind. This particular proposal has zero violence potential. It involves another of your . . . specific skills. In return, I can tell you where you'll find that rogue wolf you've been hunting."

I glanced over at Clay. "What rogue—?"

"David Hargrave. Killed three women in Tennessee. Your Pack has been hunting for him for a couple of months now."

"Who told you—"

"Contacts, Elena. I'm a regular Rolodex of supernatural contacts. Point is, I know where Hargrave is hiding out. That got me thinking. If I gave you that information, you might be willing to do a little something for me in return."

"So I do this 'little something' for you, and you give me an address, and I show up to find Hargrave cleared out a week ago . . ."

"Uh-uh. If you agree to the deal, I tell you where to find Hargrave right away. Not only that, but I wait until you have him, and then you do the favor for me. Everything's on the up and up with this one. I don't con anyone who can rip out my liver with her bare hands."

"What's your end, then? What do you want?"

"It . . . takes some explaining. Come to Buffalo tomorrow and I'll tell you."

"Buffalo? Too far. Meet me halfway, in Rochester."

"Buffalo *is* halfway. I'm in Toronto. Your hometown, if I remember the compound records. Hey, maybe you can recommend a good sushi—"

"What are you doing in Toronto?"

"That's were the, uh, service would take place. Should make it easier for you, right? Operating on familiar ground? Anyway, I'm here setting it up, so I'll meet you halfway, in Buffalo, tomorrow. Got a place all picked out. Nice and public. A daytime meeting. Absolutely nothing for you to worry about . . . so there's no need to bring the boyfriend."

"Uh-huh."

"I like all my limbs where they are."

I rolled my eyes. Clay mouthed something, but I waved him off and took down the time and address from Xavier.